Praise for *Battle of Lion Rock*

From the very first page, *Battle of Lion Rock* is sharp, gripping, and captivating. A pulse-quickening, soul-searching, epic journey walks a tightrope from the edge of this world into stunningly terrifying realms. Such a thrilling and thought-provoking adventure draws you deeper into the world of Beacon Hill, leaving you gasping for breath until the end.

JOHN TELLEGEN, executive producer and writer on the DreamWorks Dragons franchise

Praise for *Secrets of the Highlands*

As with *Hunt for Eden's Star*, this next installment in the Beacon Hill series promises a continuation of characters quickly becoming fast favorites for my bookshelf! The intoxicating story takes me places I didn't expect to go with intense adventure, supernatural allegory, and characters that resonate with a warrior's soul. This sweeping series will enthrall readers of all ages and give you a serious book hangover. Get ready!

JAIME JO WRIGHT, author of bestseller *Night Falls on Predicament Avenue* and *Specters in the Glass House*, winner of the Christy Award and Daphne du Maurier Award

The Beacon Hill series just keeps getting better! *Secrets of the Highlands* is a sequel worth the wait.

JESS CORBAN, author of *A Gentle Tyranny*

T0243339

Praise for *Hunt for Eden's Star*

Fast-paced action and a rich setting boost the beginning of a promising paranormal saga.

KIRKUS REVIEWS

A blistering, high-stakes, fast-paced supernatural thriller that's impossible to put down.

RYAN STECK, author of *Out for Blood*

An original and riveting great read from start to finish, *Hunt for Eden's Star* is a prime action/adventure fantasy from an author with a complete mastery of the genre.

JOHN BURROUGHS' BOOKSHELF, *Midwest Book Review*

An imaginative, immersive story with strong characters worth rooting for. I honestly couldn't put it down!

JESS CORBAN, author of *A Gentle Tyranny*

BATTLE OF LION ROCK

D. J. WILLIAMS

wander™
An imprint of
Tyndale House
Publishers

Visit Tyndale online at tyndale.com.

Visit the author online at djwilliamsbooks.com.

Tyndale and Tyndale's quill logo are registered trademarks of Tyndale House Ministries. *Wander* and the Wander logo are trademarks of Tyndale House Ministries. Wander is an imprint of Tyndale House Publishers, Carol Stream, Illinois.

Battle of Lion Rock

Designed by Eva M. Winters

Published in association with Pape Commons: a gathering of voices, www.papecommons.com.

For manufacturing information regarding this product, please call 1-855-277-9400.

For information about special discounts for bulk purchases, please contact Tyndale House Publishers at csresponse@tyndale.com, or call 1-855-277-9400.

Library of Congress Cataloging-in-Publication Data

A catalog record for this book is available from the Library of Congress.

ISBN 978-1-4964-6276-3

Printed in the United States of America

30	29	28	27	26	25	24
7	6	5	4	3	2	1

Defend the light.

MISCHIEVOUS ESCAPE OF THE NINE DRAGONS

Once upon a century, a young woman with a striking stare strolled through tilled fields on the outskirts of a village near a riverbank. She walked beneath wooden towers and entered a town square alive with traveling merchants offering goods for coins or trade. Villagers bargained, milled about, and lost themselves in the only tavern for miles. She nudged through the crowd with her sights on a carriage parked outside a wooden chapel.

The pounding in her chest intensified as she neared the rear of the carriage, her gaze shifting all around to be certain no one else was watching. She approached with caution, casually reaching beneath the burlap covering the carriage's cargo. From underneath she grabbed two silver bars and hid them inside her coat. Heat flushed her cheeks as she hurried across a muddied road while Rhoxen saddled destrier horses, then watched as each surrounded the carriage and escorted its treasure from the village.

With fiery hair draped over her shoulders, she slipped inside a sweltering shack. A burly, scraggly-bearded man with charcoaled hands slammed an iron hammer against raw metal. *Clang. Clang. Clang.* She stood awestruck by the blacksmith's lair, which was filled with iron horseshoes, picks, shovels, axes, spears, swords, shields, and armor. An orangish glow emanated from a cauldron nearby, and she inhaled a pungent odor. She eyed the blacksmith closely as sweat dripped from his round nose while he shaped soft metal into one of the finest Rhoxen swords she had ever seen.

"I woke before sunrise," his gravelly voice mumbled. "Still, you forge in the shadows."

The blacksmith's beady eyes turned their attention toward the young woman, and she sensed his uneasiness with her presence. She waited until he carried the newly crafted weapon with iron tongs into another room, leaving her alone. A second cauldron was empty yet searing from a flame underneath. She retrieved the silver bars and dropped them into the cauldron. For a moment she watched silver melt slowly until metallic liquid swirled.

Skilled beyond her years, she fueled the forge with charcoal and set the anvil and tongs aside. She had never thought of herself as a blacksmith, but loss fueled her desire to one day become the greatest bladesmith ever known. Flames flickered and silver glistened in the cauldron within the dimness of the shack. Her imagination swarmed with the weapon she dreamed of crafting—one to bring peace to a land threatened by witches, sorcerers, Nephilim, and Merikh.

Night curtained daylight as she worked diligently, stirring the liquified silver to remove all impurities as it percolated and bubbled. She grabbed the tongs and tilted the cauldron enough to pour the silver onto the forge. Silver oozed smoothly from the cauldron and began to harden. She hammered forcefully, sharpened edges, and worked across the anvil masterfully to form an exquisite long blade. Using the tongs, she carried the silver blade and plunged it into a deep bucket of water. Steam wafted in the air, sweeping and swirling mysteriously around her as she prayed.

With eyes opened, she stepped over to the blazing furnace and slid the blade inside. She reached out her hands with palms glowing softly. Crimson fire flared, then dissolved into an icy-blue flame wrapping around the beautiful sword—sealing and protecting its purity from a fallen world.

With the sword in the furnace, she reached for an intricately crafted hilt she had left on a workbench the time before. Her fingers touched the engraved dragons wrapped around the handle, and then she placed the hilt at the very edge of the icy-blue flame. Immediately, the razor-sharp sword and hilt became one. Her palms glowed brighter as she grabbed the hilt and removed the sword from the furnace. With both hands she gripped the sword and swung it back and forth, noticing a gleam of silver in the darkness. She touched the blade with her palms, and its blank canvas of pure silver morphed into engraved etchings of fire-breathing dragons.

Alone in the blacksmith's shack, she sensed Elyon's presence and dropped to her knees in reverence. The flames beneath the cauldrons and inside the furnace vanished, yet the silver sword shone brightly. She snatched a burlap sack from the floor and wrapped it around the sword, then rushed out the door. She couldn't stop herself from knocking down a young man who was passing by the shack. He stumbled and fell into the mud with a great splash, surprised and angered. However, when their eyes lingered on each other, the greatest love story of all time began.

1

A tidal wave of tarred water peaked over Tsim Sha Tsui as screams echoed across the promenade. Unable to see the chaos above, Jack watched chunks of concrete plunge into dark waters of the harbor. In a matter of seconds, the Windstrikers left all three tunnels to Hong Kong Island destroyed. He braced himself on a concrete platform barely wide enough to stand on and only inches above water level.

"Your own father wants you dead," Will seethed. "No one is left to save you, Jack."

"I'm not the one who needs saving." Soulweaver hummed and vibrated in his grasp. "But I'm done running, so you've got one last chance."

"We both know you are the weakest one."

The fire-breathing dragons etched into forged metal of Dragon Soul resurrected into a two-headed beast. At the sharpest point of the blade, the beast's fangs dripped with onyx fire. *Reminds me of Asiklua—except even more wrathy.* A vile shriek shivered down Jack's spine as Soulweaver spun rapidly between his fingers.

"I have killed Elders," Will taunted. "Only one remains. She's next after you."

With his jaw clenched, Jack gritted his teeth hard, knowing Will was talking about Xui Li. He recognized the rage burning in Will's eyes as he harnessed his own fury. Bursts of white lava spit from the heartwood of Soulweaver, surprising him with an astonishing intensity. Will charged and swung Dragon Soul side to side. Jack lunged forward, the power of the rod emanating pure magnificence.

Centuries after the First Great War and the Battle of Everest, Dragon Soul struck with a vengeance against the Rod of Elyon. *Soulweaver.* Black fire exploded against white lava, sending Jack and Will sliding backward in opposite directions. Jack stopped himself on the platform, inches from the water's edge. He stared in amazement at the spinning heartwood, still in one piece. Wide-eyed, he felt a surge of adrenaline rush through him as he turned from defender to raider.

Jack stabbed Soulweaver toward Will, who dodged his attack with a skillful slash of the sword across his ribs. Jack doubled over and lost his grip of Soulweaver, sending the rod skidding across the platform before teetering near the blackened water. Will shoved Jack onto his knees as the two-headed beast's fangs dripped from Dragon Soul before vanishing. With the blade's razored point against his chest, Jack glared defiantly into Will's soulless eyes. He felt the point of the sword press even harder, but it never pierced the tailored hoodie he wore.

"Addison will never be free again." With his bare hands, Jack grabbed the blade and squeezed, attempting to shift the sword away. Blood dripped from his fingers down his forearms beneath his hoodie sleeves as pain ripped through him. "Whatever he's done," he groaned, "it's not too late for you to turn back."

"You think your barmy father used me to get Dragon Soul because of my gifts?" Will forced the blade harder against Jack's chest as his eyes narrowed. "You are nothing without Eden's Star, and you are no one once the compass belongs to me."

"Michael Chung is the one who killed your mom," Jack blurted. "Not me."

Will's eyes flared, then his gaze narrowed. "You're a liar."

Pain seared from the gashes on his bloodied hands. "He killed Rachel too."

"Everyone has suffered because of you . . ." Will pushed the point of the blade harder against Jack's chest, seemingly unfazed by the revelation about his mum or Rachel. "Doesn't matter if it was Chung who pulled the trigger—you're the one who loaded the gun, Jack."

Fighter jets screamed across the harbor, nearly skimming the surface. Will spun around as the Windstrikers sliced through the military aircraft. A fiery inferno exploded, and titanium shrapnel plunged into the harbor. With his head on a swivel, Will turned back and unleashed a pulse of violet lightforce. Pain erupted through Jack's bones as he struggled to defend himself. Another pulse sent him rolling across the platform, gasping for air.

Dazed, Jack balled his bloodied fingers into fists as he crawled onto his knees and readied for another onslaught. Will reached out with his lightforce, then twisted his hand clockwise. Jack's body arched as he cried out in pain, his spine on the verge of splitting in half. As the energy grew stronger, there was no doubt—Eden's Star was being ripped from his body.

He eyed Soulweaver, within arm's reach. *Eden's Star is gonna be torn from my chest—or he's gonna cut it out. Either way, we'll all be dead.* Another burst of lightforce slammed against him, leaving him barely conscious. In the fog of his mind, he kept his sights on the rod as he was left sprawled on the platform. Blood flowed from the gashes on his hands. He tasted bitterness on his lips. With his arm outstretched, his fingers barely wrapped around Soulweaver.

Elyon, I need you now.

Jack mustered up one last ounce of strength and pulled himself to his feet while holding Soulweaver in front of him. Will's eyes narrowed as if realizing the sword and lightforce had not finished Jack off. The Windstrikers whipped overhead as the tarred tidal wave crested, then plunged with deadly force onto the promenade. An eerie silence washed over Victoria Harbour and Tsim Sha Tsui. No more screaming or shouting. He locked eyes with Will a split second before dark water gushed over from the promenade above, sweeping him off the platform into the harbor.

Violet lightforce punched beneath the depths, narrowly missing him as he frantically dove deeper. He barely dodged one of the Windstrikers as the dretium war fan bolted past, hunting for its prey. In the pitch blackness, a searing heat spread across his chest, and he struggled to hold his breath. Without oxygen, his muscles seized and his heart slowed.

One beat at a time.

2

Shortly after midnight an outboard motor whined from a fishing boat drifting downriver. Fishermen on board gazed toward shore while bright lights scattered in the distance amid the Amazon. The serene evening left them at ease as they headed deeper into the rainforest—unaware of the body floating twenty yards away.

Facedown, Jack blinked, but his vision blurred. Frantic, he breathed in deep and swallowed river water. His arms and legs flailed as he choked, disoriented, until he lifted his head and inhaled the humid and sticky night. A strong current pulled him farther from shore before he realized he wasn't in Victoria Harbour anymore. He fought against the current, hands stinging from the cuts left by Dragon Soul. With each stroke, uncertainty swirled in his mind, leaving him exhausted and confused by the time he reached land.

He stumbled up the muddy bank and dropped to his knees, letting his backpack slip off his shoulders and splash into the mud. With bloodied hands he unzipped the backpack and snatched a T-shirt, then ripped it into strips to wrap around both hands. Relieved he was still in one piece, he remembered Professor Burwick's warning: *"A wound caused by Dragon Soul is not of this world."*

Don't tell me if Eden's Star doesn't kill me, Dragon Soul will.

The night was tropical, yet his body shivered. He ran his fingers over the seams of his tailored hoodie, awestruck that Dragon Soul had failed to pierce through. *Salomeh and Emma knew all along. Whatever this hoodie is made out of protected me and Eden's Star. Will tagged me with the pointed blade, but he couldn't slice me in half.* He grabbed at his chest, knowing a few more seconds and the vision that had haunted him would have come true. Eden's Star was still inside of him, and as long as his heart beat he needed to keep it that way.

Victoria Harbour flashed in his mind, the tidal wave plunging onto the promenade. *Elyon, how can you allow the innocent to die?* Another flash struck. Amina appeared in the corridor of Crozier Hospital in total despair. Tears of his own welled up and spilled onto his cheeks. He wiped them away with his sleeve, unable to stop the dam from breaking. He wanted to curse at the top of his lungs, but instead he pounded his fists into the mud until he was breathless. His chest hammered to the beat of a tribal drum, leaving him unable to grasp the loss—*Tim*—another person he loved stolen by the Merikh.

It should've been me.

On instinct he reached for his forearm and stopped cold. "I left Soulweaver behind."

Whoosh . . . whoosh . . . whoosh . . .

His boots sank deeper into the mud as he scrambled to his feet. A shadow rippled across the surface of the river, headed straight toward him. *Great, I'm gonna be attacked by a mythical beast from another realm—who I'm sure is far more lethal than the Nephilim king, Asiklua, or the fanged dragon hidden in Dragon Soul.* His jaw dropped when he realized what the shadow was. Soulweaver appeared from the river and slithered up the shore—glowing with a soft white light. Without hesitation, Jack snatched the rod, and a surge of energy tingled his fingers as the heartwood vibrated.

"For a minute, I thought I'd lost Soulweaver—well, I did lose it." The Rod of Elyon curled and slipped beneath his hoodie before wrapping perfectly around his forearm. Jack eyed his surroundings to be sure no one was watching, then shifted his attention toward the river. "Where's Eden's Star brought me now?" he whispered.

His mind shifted to Rachel, wondering how she dealt with her uncertainty. *She was way stronger than me. I wish I could turn back the clock and tell her that much.* When Rachel had left for Sitio Veterans, he figured he'd see her in a matter of months. He never imagined she'd be murdered, or that the visions haunting his nightmares would offer a glimpse of her lifeless body. He convinced himself that once he knew who killed her, vengeance would right the injustice. Guilt washed over him, knowing he desired to end Michael Chung's life more than he wanted to ask for Elyon's mercy upon his enemy.

Professor Burwick's voice rang in his ears again. *"Jack, whatever it was that took her life was beyond this world."* Her words left him feeling even more alone than on his worst day.

Jack wiped the mud and blood from his hands onto his jeans and tried to shake the dread from his bones. *Not even Soulweaver has been able to end the nightmares.* He reached into his pocket, retrieved the burner cell, and tried to power it on—but the screen remained blank. Frustrated, he tossed the phone into the river, then slipped the backpack over his shoulders.

"Eden's Star brought me here, so let's find out who's gonna try to kill me next."

Avenida Joaquim Nabuco was a short distance from the river, and in the early morning hours traffic on the street was sparse. Several semitrucks rolled past, spewing diesel exhaust as they slowed near the gates of a shipping port. Jack walked casually beneath electrical poles and power lines crisscrossing overhead until he approached the port entrance.

A sign read, *Porto Manaus do Amazonas.*

McDougall once lectured for an entire week on the ancient Amazon rainforest and the issues of sustainability that affected the rest of the planet. Jack barely remembered any of the lectures, but he did remember the capital of the Brazilian state of Amazonas.

"Manaus," he said under his breath. "Whoa . . . I just swam with piranhas."

Dense humidity hung heavy as Jack crossed the road in front of the port entrance and picked up the pace down the sidewalk. *No way I'm getting on another cargo ship. Definitely not in the Amazon. With my luck I'll be swallowed alive by an anaconda.* He entered a brick warehouse with stone floors. Dozens of stalls were stacked with fresh fish. Peacock bass. Arowana red tail. Catfish. *Oh no— not more catfish.* An elderly man stacked crates as if he were in his youth. A piece of paper slipped from one of the crates and dropped to the slimy floor.

When the elderly man turned his back, Jack snatched the paper and stepped away. He glanced at the packing slip and did a double take when he saw the date. *Eden's Star jumped me two months ahead. What does that mean for Emma, Amina, Eliška, Vince, and everyone else? Where am I supposed to go now?* He stuffed the slip into his pocket and walked through the fish market until he reached the opposite exit. On the street, he wondered how he was going to get back to Beacon Hill. Darkness had lifted, and daybreak welcomed the sun. Deep in thought, Jack barely noticed as he ducked inside Cyber Abrego—an internet café.

Even in the early morning, the space was packed with locals playing online games or messaging business clients in faraway countries. Jack kept his gaze fixed on the floor, attempting not to attract attention. Out of the corner of his eye he noticed a door. He slipped between the computer stations and locked himself inside a dingy bathroom. While the tailored hoodie was dry, the rest of his clothes were damp. In the cramped space he changed out of his clothes, then stared in the mirror. His gaze shifted from his bloodstained bandaged hands to the scars on his arms, the crude scarring on his chest, and then to the tailored hoodie.

Whatever that's made of, I better keep it on until this is over.

Jack grabbed a fresh pair of jeans and a T-shirt from his waterproof backpack and gingerly pulled them on, then slipped back into the hoodie and zipped it up once again. He stuffed the wet clothes inside his backpack and unzipped the arm pocket stitched into the hoodie. With great care, he removed the slim wooden box and flipped open the tiny latch. He removed the map of the Highlands, carefully unrolling the worn parchment with his dirty fingers to reveal the object inside. For a moment he gazed at the intricately carved ivory figurine depicting a woman wrapped in serpents.

"Who are you?" Jack whispered. "And why was Rachel hiding you?"

A knock startled him, and he quickly slipped the map and figurine back into the slim wooden box and slid the box into the zippered pocket on his sleeve. He swung the door open and eyed the young woman closely, recognizing she was at the front desk when he entered.

"How much for a computer?" Jack retrieved his wallet. "Thirty minutes, maybe less."

She pointed over her shoulder. *"Vinte dólares."*

"Um . . ." Jack pulled a few bills from his wallet. "I'm not sure . . ."

The woman snatched his wallet and counted out twenty dollars, then handed him a piece of paper with a password scribbled on it. *She's got catlike reflexes.* Jack sheepishly smiled as he shuffled across the room and found an open station. He slumped onto a chair and stared at the screen before entering the password.

A browser launched, and his fingers hovered over the keyboard. He listened for Elyon's voice amid those around him, unable to ignore his disappointment at the silence. He'd been gone for months, and now he faced a choice—one that would either put others in danger or bring them hope. His fingers pecked at the keys as he entered a web address and logged in to Messagezilla: @TheKeepers. His hands shook as he typed the words and clicked send.

I'm alive.

3

Amina hurried down a corridor in the Main Hall, nudging her way between Cherub refugees who had arrived through the House of Luminescence. Professor McDougall gathered the newest group in an orderly fashion, marked their names on a tablet, then assigned each one to Nightingale, Rowell, Upsdell, or Crozier. Amina had watched McDougall perform the same routine for weeks, documenting not only their names but the gateways they were coming from. Rumors spread throughout Beacon Hill from Cherub recounting the devious acts of the Merikh, but none involved any sightings of Jack.

Professor Windsor waved a CT wand over each refugee and noted on her tablet those with specific medical needs. Amina spent most of her afternoons alongside other healers restoring health to those who were injured. Her gifts were growing, but every day she wished she had been strong enough to save Timothy. Windsor nodded as she passed, both sharing an unspoken grief over the loss. Amina followed a group from Vietnam before breaking away and heading for Nightingale. She needed to deliver a message, one that left her barely able to contain her excitement.

A regiment of lightforcers patrolled the grounds, guarding against any further attacks. However, HKPF and Merikh remained beyond the walls and the surrounding streets near Beacon Hill. Weeks earlier, HKPF helicopters stopped hovering after a close encounter with a few warning blasts from a group of lightforcers. Headmaster Fargher's proclamation of the school's reopening was short-lived, as the blockade encircled the district. Amina passed two classes in session on the grassy quad—one taught by Salomeh Gashkori. A class of benders followed Salomeh's instructions, shifting concrete rubble to finish rebuilding Nightingale House.

Amina had not seen Professor Burwick since the tunnels to Hong Kong Island were destroyed. So it was no surprise when Fargher had announced Salomeh as Head of House for Rowell. It was fitting for Salomeh to lead Rowell since she was a legend whose abilities were known far and wide among the highest Cherub. After spending time with Salomeh, Amina remained in awe of this woman she admired who mentored and inspired her to grow stronger in her gifts.

"Humility is not for the weak but for the strong who embrace Elyon's power."

Faizan taught the second class that Amina could see, where healers were seated in a close circle. Anyone who passed would notice this class was less outwardly impressive, but Amina knew firsthand that healers were the most inwardly powerful. *If only I was brave enough to grow in my gifts sooner, maybe I could have saved him.* She mourned her loss and silently questioned Elyon with brutal honesty. Her faith had been rocked the moment Timothy took his last breath, and in the months since then her path back to Elyon had been a struggle.

"'Pray for peace in brokenness.'" Amina quoted the Eternal, her voice barely above a whisper. "'Embrace healing in the light, and his promises shall illuminate your soul.'"

On the second floor of Nightingale, Amina paused outside a door—a room once occupied by Jack, Will, Vince, and Tim. A strong odor of fresh paint filled her nostrils as she slipped inside. The bunk beds had been restored. Leather seats faced one another, a bit more worn, torn, and weathered. Even though the room was put back similar to the way it had been, it had never felt more empty—except for Emma, who was seated in one of the chairs with her eyes closed.

Amina held out her cell phone. "You need to see this."

When Emma opened her eyes, Amina handed over the cell phone and waited patiently while Emma stared hard at the screen—a heaviness lifted slightly.

I'm alive.

"When was this sent?" Emma asked.

"Less than ten minutes ago," Amina answered. "I was using the Zakhar to search through Nightingale's archives and this appeared." She slumped into a chair across from Emma, imagining she was seated in Tim's spot. "No other messages have been sent from TheKeepers account—and only a few of us know the password."

"Might be a trap," Emma suggested. "The Merikh have no limits."

"Months have passed, and now this arrives. We have to respond."

"Can you track where the message originated?"

"We need someone more techy." Amina shook her head. "Timothy could have—"

Emma tapped on an icon in the Messagezilla account, and a video window appeared. Amina leaned forward with her elbows digging into her thighs. On the fourth chime, the call connected, and Eliška's face filled the screen. Amina recognized the courtyard in Quarry Bay in the background and noticed Eliška's gaunt cheeks.

"Power was off yesterday, so I was not able to call you," Eliška began. "Streets are growing more dangerous, especially after dark. Admiralty is off-limits, even to the faction. Most of us have remained within the surrounding blocks, only venturing out far enough to rescue the Cherub who have contacted us. We searched Aberdeen and Stanley, but there are those who refuse to leave because they are afraid of the Merikh."

"Airport remains shut down too." Amina treaded carefully, knowing Emma and Eliška shared disagreements in recent days. "PRC have issued an ordinance to prevent Hong Kongers from leaving by other means, including expats."

"Our supplies are running low, but our spirits remain strong." Eliška's gaze hardened. "Many in the faction believe the highest Cherub have abandoned our alliance."

"I will speak with Bau," Emma replied. "Remain patient, Eliška."

"The clock is counting backward, Emma. Patience will not defeat the Merikh."

"We are on the same side, you two," Amina reminded them.

"Best not to use Messagezilla for now," Emma added. "Account might be hacked."

Eliška glanced away from the screen, then back. "We have been working on the origin."

"You knew already?" Amina's brows raised. "Since when do you have the password?"

"I gave it to her," Emma admitted. "She is one of the Keepers."

"I have been monitoring the account," Eliška explained. "Like you both have been."

"If you are able to determine . . ." Emma's voice trailed off.

Eliška looked away a second time and nodded. "Manaus, Brazil."

For a moment the room fell silent as Amina's gaze shifted between them. *Which one of them will go? Both will want to, of course.* "Merikh *and* Cherub are hunting, so there is a possibility this is not what it seems. But we have to respond, right?"

"We are only able to pinpoint the city," Eliška answered. "I will—"

Before Eliška finished, the video cut out. Emma tried to connect again, but there was no answer. Amina eyed her closely, knowing she was not going to wait.

"You are right." Emma nodded slowly. "We should reply."

Amina grabbed the cell phone and swiped across the screen. "What should we say?"

"Elyon will never leave us nor forsake us."

Amina typed the words. "Sent."

A few minutes passed as they watched the screen in silence. Amina knew the moment Jack had left Beacon Hill—she was the last one to see him. In the following days, she had noticed a shift in Emma, who'd avoided both the faction and Cherub as much as possible. It seemed each dealt with grief in their own way.

They both jumped when a reply pinged.

Above or beneath the ground.

Emma grew glossy-eyed. "I said those words the day we buried the Testimony."

"Jack is alive." Amina exhaled as she squeezed Emma's hand. "You have to go to him."

4

MANAUS, BRAZIL

From across the street, Jack watched the entrance to Cyber Abrego from an outdoor table at Café Haus—a local bakery in the heart of the city. Locals arrived for a morning hit of caffeine and sugar while another hour passed. He'd taken a risk sending the message, and when he read the response, his adrenaline spiked. *Tim, you were right all along about Messagezilla. A total lifeline.* A wave of guilt washed over him as he glanced down at the bangle around his wrist given to him by Emma. *In raging seas and surging tides, Elyon draws close to all who call upon eternity's glory.* His mind flashed to the clock towers at Beacon Hill and Star Ferry, imagining them both counting backward.

How much longer before Eden's Star kills me? Will I die before

I can honor Rachel's promise and save everyone? There's no way to stop time.

While the locals went about their normal routine, Jack battled a rush of emotions. Sorrow. Rage. Disappointment. Shame. He'd failed to live up to who Rachel believed he could be—and people had died because of his failures. He finished off his *pingado*— steamed milk with a splash of coffee served in a glass cup. An uneasiness prickled beneath his skin. He snatched a copy of the *Rio Daily* from an empty table next to him and read the lead story.

Hong Kong's Uncertain Future Threatens Global Turbulence

Months after the chief executive's speech echoed around the world, sources on the ground have confirmed Hong Kongers remain in a tailspin. Her resignation days after the Hong Kong Stock Exchange crashed, known in the weeks since as Black Monday, has created an unstable government as mounting pressure from global leaders remains at a tipping point. Since the unexplained events surrounding the Shek Pik Prison break on Lantau Island, eyewitness accounts once posted on social have been removed, and all account holders within the boundaries of Hong Kong have remained blocked. No one has been able to verify the authenticity of the videos downloaded before the blackout, which documented what appears to be supernatural events. The People's Republic of China continues to argue these videos are nothing more than misinformation fabricated by the West in an attempt to spread panic. Social media companies have confirmed removal of the posts disputed by the PRC but have not issued any further comment in recent weeks.

The UN Council confirmed yesterday that over twenty countries have offered assistance to Hong Kong. Still, the PRC refuses to admit the events occurred, even though flights arriving to and departing from Hong Kong remain restricted. Per our sources on the ground, three underwater tunnels connected to Hong Kong Island have been destroyed; power outages are occurring across the city, leaving millions without electricity; and cell service remains shut down. Elite and powerful Hong Kongers are desperate to leave; however, the PRC has responded with strict curfews, citywide lockdowns, and threats to freeze citizens' assets if attempts are made to leave the country through illegal routes.

Global leaders have requested access on the ground to confirm their citizens who reside in Hong Kong are safe. Satellite surveillance of PRC military within the borders of Hong Kong have leaked through US government officials, yet remain unverified. If these images are authentic, they will serve as further proof that what is occurring within the borders of Hong Kong is an unprecedented act by the PRC and threatens to leave the rest of the world reeling from severe economic turbulence. World leaders and intelligence circles are struggling to determine fact from misinformation and propaganda, leaving Hong Kongers isolated from the free world.

After the rescue at Shek Pik Prison, there was no doubt the world was suspicious of a cover-up. In response, the PRC pushed back with containment over transparency, which was not a surprise to anyone—including Jack. *Will is going to destroy everything and everyone to find the artifacts. Elyon, how do I save him and stop him at the same time? It seems impossible.* He listened for a response while he searched for answers on his own. Disappointment turned to frustration, knowing Elyon remained silent in his moment of need.

A twinge shot down his spine as a group of teens dressed in all black rounded the corner and walked briskly down the sidewalk. His heart pounded as he watched them duck inside the internet café. He reached down and grabbed his backpack, ready to disappear. But he was curious. *Merikh or Cherub? They're much younger than Chung's assassin squad.* Jack slouched lower in his seat and pulled his hood over his head. Less than a minute passed before the teens were back on the sidewalk, glancing up and down the street.

For a second he stopped breathing when Will appeared and strolled toward them. His hair was buzzed close to the skull and his shoulders seemed broader. *He's never looked stronger—or meaner. How did they find me? No way he could've known I'd be here—unless someone gave him the password to TheKeepers.* Panic struck, and he tried to remain steady. He reached for Soulweaver, then hesitated. Will and his crew had a clear advantage.

A voice whispered, "Jack."

Butterflies swarmed his stomach, battling against the effects of Eden's Star. His heart skipped a beat as he fought the urge to spin around. When he mustered up the nerve to glance over his shoulder, no one was there. *I'm going crazy.* Will and his gang moved methodically toward the corner, standing out from the locals, who stared at them curiously. *Stay here and I'm toast, literally.* He kept his eyes fixed on them as he slipped his backpack over his shoulder and casually walked away.

As soon as he rounded a corner, he stopped cold. Emma stood only a few feet away, long jet-black hair draped over her shoulders. Cool slates of blackwork sleeved both arms—pieces of her story he'd yet to discover. She gazed at him with her disarming amber eyes, as she had done many times before. She was peace, and he was a storm. *Better hope she's not miffed for leaving her behind—Jack, you're an idiot.* A lump lodged in his throat as he stepped closer and wrapped his arms around her waist.

"I'm sorry," he whispered.

Emma replied in a hushed voice. "We made a promise."

"Won't happen again." Jack breathed a bit easier. "I hoped you'd be the one to find me."

"I am not the only one searching." She kissed him softly on the cheek, then pushed back gently. "We are outnumbered."

"Never stopped us before." Jack's cheeks flushed as he caught himself staring. "After I left Beacon Hill, Will nearly ended me at Victoria Harbour."

"He has grown stronger—much stronger." Emma grabbed his hand, and their fingers interlaced. "Best we leave the fight for another day."

Jack never thought Emma would back down from the Merikh, but he sensed something had changed since he'd been gone. He knew better than to argue as they headed farther away from Cyber Abrego and Café Haus. With his senses heightened, they reached Avenida Brasil—a long stretch of road lined with traffic—and picked up the pace.

"How did you know where to find me?" Jack asked.

"After you left, the connection between us was lost—until a few hours ago. I feared you were dead, but then Amina received the message and our connection returned. I sensed your presence stronger than ever before. When I traveled through the gateway to Manaus, Elyon's voice led me straight to you."

"I guess that's more than gauging my emotions."

Emma's lips curled at the corners. "Much more, Jack."

In the western district of Manaus, their trek led along Avenida Brasil to Compensa. Jack pushed his body harder as he hurried to keep up with Emma. He dodged traffic as they crossed the streets and ducked between tin-roof shanties, which reminded him of Sitio Veterans. Poverty shared striking similarities across every culture.

Even though his cuts were painful, Jack squeezed Emma's hand. "I can't believe you're here."

"You cannot break our promise again."

"I won't make that mistake a third time," Jack replied. "Boys are idiots most of the time."

"Amina told me you were in Crozier Hospital when—"

"I couldn't stand there and do nothing." Jack gritted his teeth and tugged on his hoodie. "You and Salomeh knew this is made of armor strong enough to protect against Dragon Soul."

"Woven from dretium," Emma explained. "Remember, a metal formed by Elyon."

Jack admired the hoodie as they continued at a quick pace. "Whoa . . ."

"You will not find dretium in the world of today. It was passed down from one Cherub tribe to the next over thousands of years. We were each measured for our own hoodie on Karābu, including Rachel."

24

"There was a moment I thought I was a goner, but it worked against Will and Dragon Soul." Jack paused. "Emma, I wanted to end him, but he's a better fighter than I am. Next thing I know, I'm floating in the Amazon."

Emma nodded toward his chest. "Is Eden's Star still inside?"

"Will tried to rip it from my bones, but I think it's what brought me here. No flare-ups since I arrived, but we can give it a try if we need to."

"First we will travel through a gateway."

"Where are we going?"

"Sanctum of Serenity."

5

JACK'S BOOTS SLOSHED THROUGH thick mud as he followed Emma across wooden planks connecting shanties along the river's edge. Surrounded on both sides, they ducked through the doorway of a shanty perched on stilts over the water.

"I believed if I found Rachel's killer, there'd be peace." A familiar weight pressed down on his shoulders. The floor beneath his boots sagged as he glanced around the room, which was stacked with wooden crates, and inhaled a strong stench of dried fish. "All I wanted was to get justice in her name, so her death wouldn't be forgotten. But none of it has made a difference."

"As long as we keep fighting," Emma replied, "love and light will conquer the Merikh."

"I even thought I could save Will, and if I did, then this nightmare would be over."

"We must believe good is left in him, Jack."

"You have more faith than me." He exhaled and relaxed a bit. "You should've seen Addison when I told him it was Michael Chung who killed Rachel. He was blindsided, and I don't think it was an act." He shook his head slowly. "Emma, there's no way to end the Merikh but payback."

"Revenge clouds the heart," she warned. "Vengeance belongs in the hands of Elyon."

"I haven't been much of a Protector—far from who everyone expected me to be."

"Salomeh has brought balance between the Cherub and faction for now." Emma retrieved silver coins from her pocket and handed one over. "I told her about your message, and she was adamant about going to the Sanctum of Serenity—regardless of whether I found you."

"I still can't tell if she likes me," Jack admitted. "What's the Sanctum of Serenity?"

Emma stepped toward the doorway and cautiously poked her head around the corner, then replied over her shoulder. "A spiritual place where the Elders gathered long ago."

The hair on Jack's arms raised. "What does she want from there?"

"A prophecy rejected by the highest Cherub." Emma kept her gaze fixed beyond the shanty. "Salomeh's instructions are to bring the original writings to Beacon Hill."

"You mean the prophecy about you being the rightful Cherub leader?"

"Bau has been anointed, so one would believe the prophecy is fulfilled. But if there are questions from Salomeh and others, then whatever is within the prophecy must be about someone else." Emma hesitated. "Professor Burwick stepped down as faction leader—Eliška took her place."

"So you think the prophecy is about Eliška?" Jack waited for an answer, but when Emma remained silent, he continued. "Another edge to a thousand-piece puzzle that shifts every time we think we're filling in the center." He was suddenly curious to know what was written in the prophecy, but there was a choice to make. "We need to keep searching for the artifacts before we run out of time and Will gets his hands on one that's even more dangerous."

"We go to the sanctum, then search for the artifacts." Emma dropped a silver coin to the floor. "Elyon will give us the time we need to stop the Merikh from destroying the world."

Jack mirrored Emma and let the coin fall from his palm. "Until the end."

Gateways had swallowed him beneath the dirt before, left him trudging across sand dunes near Mount Hareh, opened the gates to Sakkhela, and allowed him entrance to other realms. Entrance was granted with an offering—silver given to the chosen, embossed with illustrations depicting light, skies, seas, trees, sun, moon, birds, creatures of the ocean, and humanity. He expected nothing less as the coins rolled across the rotted floor—only this time, nothing happened. A few more seconds passed before he reached down and retrieved the coins.

"Um . . ." Jack held them out in his palm. "Maybe these ones are defective."

Emma's gaze hardened. "The gateway is blocked."

"What do you mean, *blocked*?"

"You know gateways are opened with an offering. However, to restrict entrance requires someone with the rare ability to jump a gateway." Emma returned to the doorway and poked her head out-side for a second time. "Someone with this gift can enter through a gateway without an offering, then block others from passing through."

"You think it's Will." Jack stepped alongside. "Are there other gateways in Manaus?"

"Salomeh advised only this one—the others are not as reliable."

"The Sanctum of Serenity might have to wait." Jack stepped toward the middle of the shanty and held his hand out. Emma turned and approached until they faced each other. Their fin-gers interlaced as naturally as before. "We've got Soulweaver and Slybourne's shield—and Will has the Windstrikers. Four artifacts remain, that's all that matters."

Emma's brows raised. "You are certain he found the Wind-strikers?"

"I've seen them up close—too close—and they live up to the hype." Jack squeezed her hand, grateful he wasn't alone. "Those deadly fans nearly sliced me in half. Emma, how could the Cherub not know how powerful Will is?"

"When I arrived on Karābu Island, I was only with the others—Rachel, Areum, and Bau." Emma paused. "We did not know the great Elder trained anyone before us."

"A secret the headmaster kept from all of us too," Jack replied under his breath. "Ready?"

As Emma nodded, Jack slowed his breathing. He was aware that Emma sensed every emotion riffling through him as he settled his spirit. A moment of peace washed over him, and a warmth spread across his chest. With each breath, a welcome heat grew more intense. Eden's Star was alive as he locked eyes with Emma and the rest of the world faded.

In a blink, the shanty and the Amazon vanished. When Jack opened his eyes, he stood within a thick forest along a mountainous region. He led the way as they hiked toward the edge of a cliff and stood amid the trees. Boats below drifted and circled near the center of the lake. *Eden's Star brought us straight to where we need to be. Maybe I'm learning to surrender more.* He unzipped his backpack and retrieved a pair of binoculars, then peered through the lenses to get a better look at the Cherubs' hidden treasure chest.

"Lake Brienz," he said in a lowered voice. "One of the artifacts is down there."

"Where your father is imprisoned in the Dungeon of Savages?"

"The one and only—where you check in but you don't check out."

"How do we get inside?"

"Fang Xue took me to the center of the lake, then created a water tornado." Jack handed Emma the binoculars. "The entrance is at the bottom, and it goes deeper into the vault."

"Fairly basic for a bender."

"Then after dark, it's game on."

6

Starlight twinkled across endless skies as moonlight reflected off glassy waters. With their backpacks slung over their shoulders, Jack and Emma crouched in the brush near the rocky shore and waited. From Victoria Harbour to Manaus to Lake Brienz, a struggle to keep track of the day and time whipped his mind into a whirlwind.

"Why doesn't Eden's Star lead us straight to the artifacts?" Jack asked.

"On Karābu we were taught that the compass reveals precise locations when the Protector is fully surrendered in heart, soul, and spirit. Rachel was the strongest, which is why she was the first of us to search for Eden's Star." Emma retrieved her cell phone while Jack peered over her shoulder and watched her fire off a text to Amina: Found. "There is a reason why she chose you—she knew you wouldn't stop until it was done. That is a rare gift, Jack."

"But I don't have supernatural gifts," Jack protested. "Lightforcer, bender, healer."

"The first time you used Eden's Star, you did not know where the compass would take you, but you were willing to sacrifice yourself." Emma's gaze shifted as she inched forward, still camouflaged by the trees. "If the compass had not brought us to Karachi, we never would have met Faizan or been guided deeper into the Highlands."

"If your gifts weren't restored in Sakkhela, we probably wouldn't have found Charis." He was grateful Emma was healed, but surrendering himself to Elyon fully was too great an ask. *I need Elyon's voice to guide me, so how can I fully surrender if all I hear is silence?* "Eden's Star brought me to you in Aberdeen and Lantau Island because I trusted where it needed me to go. Now the compass has brought us to the edge, *again*."

"Greater surrender in deeper faith leads to the truth and peace we all seek."

I'm not ready to trade revenge for peace, not when it comes to Addison and the Merikh. And right now, Will is on that list too. He could've saved Emma—and he chose to end Tim's life. He won't stop until his gifts end us all. There's no peace until he's stopped and the Merikh are destroyed.

For a brief moment, he nearly promised Emma he would try to surrender more, but he stopped short. He wasn't losing his faith, but there was a piece he kept in the shadows—a piercing of his soul from the City of Gods that remained an open wound. He wanted to settle the score before asking forgiveness, which he knew was against the Eternal even though he'd yet to dive into all the pages. Rachel and Tim deserved nothing less than revenge.

Still, the Cherub guarded the treasures beneath the surface taken from the Exodus Mines, and the Dungeon of Savages imprisoned Addison and whoever else threatened the Seven Tribes.

"Definitely not the right time to ask, but . . ." Jack paused. "Do you remember anything after you were taken from Mount Hareh and before Fortress Hill?"

"I barely remember you and Vince," Emma admitted. "I did not know about Will."

"Headmaster Fargher told me it was Rachel who introduced Will to Peter Leung. She must've known about Will's gifts when you trained on Karābu. Why would she keep it a secret?"

Emma exhaled. "We may never know the answer."

"She trusted the Elder, until she didn't." Jack stared across the lake as flashes struck from the cliffside in the Valley of Grace. *At least I'm not rappelling to my death—but I might be about to drown.* "None of this is getting any easier."

"Doubt exists in faith's absence." Emma's lips pursed as she remained crouched. "You have come a long way in a short time— not horrible for an outlier."

"Not far enough," he sighed. "Don't let me drown, please."

In the darkness, Emma and Jack stepped out from the tree line and knelt at the edge of the lake. Emma reached beneath the surface, where her lightforce was barely visible in the rippling water. A funnel began to circle, growing wider and deeper. It was far less dramatic than Fang Xue's demonstration, but Jack was still awestruck by the ease with which Emma's gifts flowed.

"I jumped into the hole last time," Jack explained. "Not sure how this one works."

"Think of it as a slide to the bottom," Emma replied. "I'll be right behind you."

Jack shrugged his shoulders and mumbled, "What could go wrong?"

He crawled on his stomach into the water and was immediately sucked beneath the surface. A strong current pulled him headfirst toward the bottom. He didn't have a chance to glance behind as the tunnel narrowed, winding as if searching for the brass vault door. Drenched to his bones, he was shocked once he realized he could breathe within the tunnel without inhaling gallons of water. Near the bottom, the funnel shifted again before locking in on the vault door. His momentum was slowed by a force wrapping around his body until he slid gently onto the bottom of the lake. Emma landed beside him. Jack was first on his feet as he stood over the brass door.

"No time to waste," Emma said. "Keep moving."

With the lake peaceful above the surface yet alive beneath, Jack reached down and turned the iron wheel. He opened the vault and descended a ladder into the depths of a Cherub secret. Emma followed and sealed the vault door behind them. A bluish glow illuminated a cavernous space where relics and gold remained piled high. His body shivered beneath his drenched clothes, the cuts on his hands stinging as he pointed toward a second door.

A chill shot down his spine. "Dungeon of Savages."

7

WITH HIS BACKPACK STRAPPED to his shoulders, Jack strolled between mounds of ornate treasure tossed in piles seemingly without regard for the significance of Cherub folklore. The bluish glow illuminated the cavern and reflected off gold, silver, diamonds, sapphires, emeralds, rubies, and jade. A stillness swept over Jack as he imagined ages past displaying relics within Slybourne Castle in Sakkhela.

"This is only a fraction from the Exodus Mines." Jack stood awestruck, then headed deeper into the underwater cavern. A warmth spread through his body. With each step, Eden's Star drew him closer to what remained hidden. "One of the artifacts is definitely down here."

Emma walked alongside and followed his lead. "Allow the compass to guide you."

Rock walls surrounded Ryder Slybourne and Florence Upsdell's bounty. Jack touched the jagged edges of the wall as heat emanated from his fingertips. The basement tunnel within Beacon Hill flashed in his mind and a searing fever washed over him. His cheeks flushed as he steadied himself, harnessing his adrenaline while Eden's Star compelled him onward. The pounding in his chest intensified when his palm flattened against the wall and the power of the compass spread beyond.

"Guardians life." Jack stared intently, hoping the words might unlock what remained hidden on the other side of the Dungeon of Savages. Seconds passed, yet the stone remained steadfast—until a glint caught his attention. Beneath his fingers, the rock flickered. Curious, he removed his palm and stared in disbelief as his handprint transformed solid rock into translucent quartz. "I'll never get used to Elyon's power—and I never want to take it for granted."

"Our journey has brought us into the depths for a purpose."

Jack squinted at the quartz, attempting to see within. He stepped back when Emma offered her lightforce against the unknown. "Eden's Star is microwaving my insides."

When Emma grabbed his arm and squeezed, he sensed the compass ease and the wounds on his hands heal a bit more. She reached out and the wall rumbled. Then she slowly pulled her hand back and the translucent quartz shifted as if a drawer slid open. A slight breeze flowed from an opening as Jack snatched the quartz and pulled it free. He stared cautiously at the stone, leaned in, and peered through the hole, then inhaled an earthy, mossy aroma. No matter how much he squinted, the pitch-blackness revealed nothing more than an abyss.

"Can you move a few more so we can get a better look?" Jack asked.

Emma waved her hand, and more stones shifted before dropping to the ground. A larger hole opened as water seeped beneath their boots. At first it was a trickle, but as the seconds passed the water spread quickly across the cavern.

"I hear something." Emma stepped toward the opening. "Sounds like—"

Stones erupted overhead like cannonballs slamming around them. Debris shot outward before crashing into the mounds of treasure. A waterfall gushed from above, splashing with intense force as relics ricocheted and pinged in all directions. Another wave burst through the opening and whisked Jack off his feet, a swirling current pulling him away.

He lost sight of Emma as Soulweaver slithered down his forearm and extended in his grasp. At the mercy of the strong current, he gripped the heartwood tight and tried to grab hold of anything to stop his momentum. He coughed up a mouthful, then dove beneath the surface.

I'm not drowning in this place—not today.

With Soulweaver pointed toward the bottom, Jack swam with all his strength. Heartwood hummed and vibrated in his grasp while Eden's Star raged within his soul. The water shifted, creating a tunnel similar to the one that brought them to the depths of Lake Brienz. Encircled, he reached the bottom and stabbed Soulweaver into the stone floor. A tornado whipped around him until he stood on solid ground, gasping for air.

He pushed the fear aside and moved with purpose toward an opening, like the night he and Emma led the captives to freedom on Shelter Island. There was no time to marvel at the miraculous power of the rod or compass—he trusted Soulweaver to protect him. The cavern was on the verge of being fully submerged. He searched for Emma as treasures drifted past on both sides. A thundering rumble was followed by the water dividing, leaving Emma standing before him, drenched to her bones.

"I guess you don't need Soulweaver," Jack called out. "We created quite a mess."

"Elyon offers strength," Emma replied, "in the exact moment we need it."

"Let's get out of here before we're fish stuck in an aquarium."

Emma parted the waters until they reached the opening. Jack slipped through first, then Emma unleashed her gifts and lifted the rubble before lodging the stones to seal the entrance. In the darkness, her lightforce offered enough brightness to follow a narrow passageway. Silence lingered and a chill shivered through the air as they headed deeper beneath the earth. Jack led the way with Soulweaver firmly in his grasp. Emma remained at his side, her lightforce guiding their footsteps.

Strange, normally she's the one who's a step ahead. Maybe she's letting me give it a shot—or maybe she's trusting me more. We nearly drowned back there—and we're not even talking about it? That's how far we've gone into the craziness of trying to save the world. Elyon, how much more of this can we take?

The passageway descended until they stood at the edge of a pool.

"Are we in another realm?" Jack asked.

Emma stepped closer to the edge. "We have not traveled through a gateway."

"Right . . . no offering." Jack paused. "Do you think the Dungeon of Savages will flood?"

"I do not know." Emma nodded toward him. "Eden's Star?"

Jack reached for his chest. "Still frying me like bacon."

"Then we are in the right place." Emma glanced around. "Elyon, give us eyes to see."

"We're searching for an ant named George in the Amazon jungle." Jack's dark humor fell flat as he swallowed hard and tried to settle his spirit. He stepped beside Emma and dipped Soulweaver into the pool. "Elyon has not brought us this far to leave us, right?"

A ripple in the water drifted away from shore as Emma cast her lightforce across the surface. Darkness lifted as a white glow hovered over the stillness. Jack watched the ripple widen until an illusion appeared. *Whoa . . . that's not an illusion, Jack.* He couldn't believe what he was seeing—a battered longship drifted toward them. Its tattered sail flapped loosely. Its rotted planks were riveted together, and a deer head with broad antlers protruded from the bow. *Looks more like an oversized canoe than a battleship.* Jack and Emma waited until the vessel stopped directly in front of them.

"In the Eternal, one of the Seven Tribes was known as the Rhoxen," Emma said. "After the Fall and the tribes dispersed across the earth, the Rhoxen were considered by many of the Cherub as outcasts. Sir Ryder Slybourne was raised in this tribe before he fought against the Merikh during the First Great War. Not much was written about him as a child; however, the legend of his bravery returned Rhoxen to the circle of the Seven Tribes and the highest Cherub."

Jack gestured at the longship. "Why would Eden's Star bring us to this?"

"Perhaps we should climb aboard and find out."

He sighed heavily. "I was afraid you'd say that."

8

THE CENTURIES-OLD LONGSHIP drifted into blackness. Near the bow, Jack stood beside Emma as fatigue washed over him. A thundering rush rang in his ears, reminding him of the journey with Areum through Maranat Falls to the City of Gods. The searing heat rushing through him eased a bit, yet remained strong enough to reassure him the compass still guided them.

Rotting planks creaked and the hull groaned as the longship meandered through darkened waters. An eerie silence lingered between each breath as Jack kept his gaze ahead.

So many unanswered questions, and so much guilt weighing me down—like a boulder falling from the peak of Lion Rock and landing squarely on my shoulders. If I believe Emma, trusting Elyon completely is the only way to keep fighting. With her beside me, and Elyon's presence in my soul, maybe it's possible to conquer the darkness. Maybe then Eden's Star will take us straight to where we need to go instead of only getting us close. I don't know if I can do it, but I've got to keep trying no matter what's on the other side.

"You said the Rhoxen were outcasts of the Cherub," Jack noted. "Crozier might've been a descendant—Crozier House's symbol is a deer, so it makes sense, right?"

"He fought alongside Nightingale during the Battle of Hong Kong," Emma replied. "And we know Nightingale was not exactly fond of the Cherub."

"Nightingale trusted Crozier to protect the key before . . ." Jack hesitated as he eyed shifting shadows while the longship navigated on its own. "I'll bet the girl I saw in the tunnel when I used the Zakhar was either Xui Li or Dabria, long before they were Elders."

"One day we will ask them ourselves." Emma retrieved two silver coins and handed one over. "We must be prepared to give an offering."

Jack nodded ahead. "Maybe you should use your lightforce."

"Best we allow Eden's Star to reveal where it wants us to go." Emma slipped her backpack off her shoulders and dug inside before removing a paper bag. "Hungry?"

"You've been holding back." Even beneath Lake Brienz, the aroma of barbecued pork filled his nostrils. *"Char siu bao."*

Emma stepped back from the bow and sat down cross-legged. She handed one of the pork buns to Jack, who slumped down beside her. For a moment he bit into the cold bun and chewed slowly, relishing the sweet flavors of Hong Kong he'd grown to love. *I wonder how long we'll be on this ride? Doesn't matter. We're still breathing, and we're not starving. Faith of a mustard seed, Jack. With* a quick glance toward Emma, he remembered she could sense his emotions—but she couldn't read his mind.

"We nearly drowned back there," he said between bites as he squeezed the coin in his palm. He thought of Slybourne's treasure submerged in the flooded cavern and Addison guarded beyond the iron doors. "Do you think we destroyed the Dungeon of Savages?"

"Much of what is happening is out of our control." Emma checked her cell phone. "No signal this far down, but I do not believe we are in a different realm—at least not yet."

"We're just a thousand feet beneath the surface," Jack mused as he flipped the coin between his fingers. "Feels like another realm."

"Eden's Star guided us to the Rhoxen longship for a reason." Emma paused. "For us to find the artifacts, we must choose light over dark—even when we do not understand what our next steps might be. If the Dungeon of Savages is no more, then that is a sacrifice worth making. I am sorry, Jack. Your father is not the one we need to save."

"He made his choice a long time ago, and he's taken far too many lives." Jack's grip tightened on the coin as he finished off his pork bun. "Have you always been this calm? It's like nothing fazes you—ever."

"I am not without fear," Emma answered. "But fear without hope is a cancer."

"When all of this began, I was afraid of my own shadow. Not so much anymore, even though Eden's Star is . . ." He stopped short of finishing his thought, knowing Emma already knew what he was going to say. "In Kati Pahari, when you were competing in kabaddi against Vince and I was stuck on the sidelines, Faizan told me he was more of a defender in the game—and I surprised myself when I said I was definitely a raider."

"You are more courageous than you believe, Jack. Four artifacts are left to find, and we will find them together." Emma scooted over and leaned her head against his shoulder as he closed his eyes. She whispered, "No matter who stands against us."

The longship continued to drift at a snail's pace, occasionally leaning to one side or the other as if navigating an unseen maze.

One second I'm weighed down with guilt, struggling to find the faith to keep going. Another tick of the clock and I'm not as afraid as when this started. I guess that's what the faith of a mustard seed is about—and being with Emma gives me the courage of a raider even when we're outmatched.

Jack dozed off several times while Emma's cheek rested heavily on his shoulder. He wrapped his arm around her and pulled her in close, listening to the gentleness of the wake drifting away from the longship. He reached for Emma's cell phone on her lap, even though he knew there was no signal.

For the first time he noticed the lock screen was a snapshot of Tim blowing out a single birthday candle at the hostel in Karachi as they all gathered around. He never knew she'd snapped a photo, as he'd been in a spiraling daze at that point. For a long time he stared at the faces of his best friends—Tim, Vince, Amina, *and* Emma.

When this is over, she will be the one.

9

THE CLIFFS OF MOHER, IRELAND

A brisk wind whipped through a cluster of trees and sliced across blades of lush grass along sheer cliffs looming over the North Atlantic. Between the trees and pink yarrows, a shadow appeared from thin air and moved briskly beneath grayish skies before slipping unannounced inside Moher Castle.

Will Fargher pressed his palm against an engraved dragon etched into solid emerald jade. A door slid open, and he stepped into a circular stone room. A single beam of light shone down, and a red laser scanned his retina. The first time he walked the halls of the castle, Addison had used Charlotte Taylor's corpse to threaten the most lethal Merikh to pledge their loyalty. Hidden behind a mask, Will had watched her lifeless body burned to ash, knowing he was the one who speared Dragon Soul to end her reign.

I've killed two of the Elders—unmatched by any other.

With his ability to jump gateways, he returned to Moher often, choosing to leave the treasures taken from the Exodus Mines locked safely in Kreidler. *One day I will return to the mines and take the rest for myself.* Since Addison's capture the Merikh had waged war among themselves, grasping for greater power—evil feasting on its own flesh. Will smirked, as power in the Merikh didn't matter to him in the least, not unless it brought him closer to finding Jack.

"Michael Chung is the one who killed your mom. Not me."

"Jack will say anything to protect his own lies." Will raged against betrayal attacking from more than one direction. "No matter what, Jack is still responsible for bringing death to my family. He will never find all the artifacts, and he will fail to protect the Cherub—I swear to it."

Stone statues dating back to the Qin Dynasty lined a corridor along the inner chamber. Will was within reach of evening the score from Sakkhela, and in Manaus he thought he'd find Jack—but it was another dead end. He glanced around a room where a gigantic table was left shattered across the floor. A folding cot, a portable satellite router, and a mobile transfusion device were in one corner beside a glass-doored refrigerator. Behind the glass were vials of blood, the last of what was taken from Shek Pik Prison before the Cherub breakout.

Not much left—only one vial of the Bennetts'. Jack, you can't hide forever.

Before leaving the room, Will grabbed a tablet from the cot and headed down another corridor, stopping beside a light fixture. A quick glance over his shoulder and he pulled the fixture down. Stone slid aside and disappeared into the wall. Will punched in a code on a keypad, unlocking a large safe, and stepped inside.

When the door sealed shut, he slipped the scabbard off his shoulder and hung Dragon Soul on a wall beside the Windstrikers. From a shelf he grabbed the drawings he'd found inside the backpack left in the bushes at Fortress Hill, then continued through the safe and descended deeper within the castle. At the bottom of a flight of stairs he entered a dungeon. His pace slowed as he approached his only captive.

"Elders are forbidden to lie," Will said, stone-cold. "He was not in Manaus."

"I have told you the truth." Xui Li's weakened voice was barely above a whisper. She lifted her head, her unsettling gaze peering through matted graying hair. Her bony finger pointed in his direction. "Merikh and Cherub fear you, and will come for you."

"Let them come," Will seethed. "I am more powerful than any of the chosen."

"Perhaps that is true—or perhaps not." Xui Li paused. "Jack is not alone."

Will clenched his jaw, realizing what was left unsaid. "Emma . . ."

"The sands of time are running out for you to turn from the darkness to the light."

Will tapped on the tablet screen and held it against the iron bars so Xui Li could see. Rage flowed through him as he swiped through the headlines and photographs from around the globe. A 7.0 earthquake rattled Guatemala. Volcanic eruptions poured fiery lava through Mexico City. Tornadoes ripped across the coast of California, destroying towns and neighborhoods. Aleppo had erupted into violence, leaving citizens hiding in fear. Global leaders escalated grave concern over the PRC blocking access to Hong Kong. Unprecedented disasters, without explanation for why they all happened within days of each other.

Addison's words rang in Will's ears. *"The key to hunting Cherub is to expose their love for one another. Cherub turned my wife and child into fanatics and freaks."*

Impatient and frustrated, Will watched Xui Li closely, angered that she remained unrattled. He turned off the tablet and held up the drawings, fully aware crates of melted gold were being shipped to the PRC to ensure that his unrestricted access to Tai Tam continued.

"Tell me which one of these drawings will lead me to the nether realm."

"Loneliness blinds when grief consumes," Xui Li replied solemnly.

"You know nothing about me," Will argued. "But I'm betting there's a gateway in Tai Tam."

"I cannot tell you which of the drawings will lead you there."

"But you're not denying what I've said."

"I have never crossed over into the realm where the darkest artifact remains." Xui Li paused. "Loss has brought suffering to the innocent—and blinded you to the dangers of your actions."

"All of this will stop once you tell me where to find the gateway—*and* Jack."

"You cannot see that you are loved, despite the terror you are inflicting."

"Love doesn't protect anyone from suffering," Will rebuked. "Love is a weakness that leaves the innocent as the prey. You are aware Dragon Soul takes life from the Elders—and you are the last one. My patience is running out. Either you tell me what I need to know, or you will find yourself at the mercy of the sword."

"A truth you know better than anyone." Xui Li's gaze hardened. "A price will be paid."

"You are right about that," Will snapped. "And he won't see it coming."

10

Jack blinked as he startled awake after dozing off for what he thought was only a few minutes. He was still surrounded by pitch-blackness. Seconds passed until he noticed Emma wasn't leaning against him any longer and the longship was rocking gently in one spot. He touched the palms of his hands and realized the pain from his wounds had subsided.

"Emma," he whispered. "Where are you?"

"Near the front," she replied in a hushed tone. "We stopped moving."

Jack stood and followed the direction of her voice. Adrenaline boiled and scorched his weary muscles and aching bones. Eden's Star brought fire into his soul, so he knew they were still on the chase. He shook off his tiredness and tried to keep his wits about him.

"How long has it been like this?" Jack asked.

"Five minutes—maybe less." A faint glow emanated from Emma's palm, providing enough light to see her in the shadows. "Should we give an offering?"

"What've we got to lose?" Jack trusted Emma more than anyone else. It was hardly a stretch as she was the most gifted Cherub he'd seen. "Let's give it a shot and see what happens."

Emma held the silver coin in her glowing palm, then tossed it overboard. Jack heard the coin plunk into the water, so he stepped over and did the same. He expected the longship to sink or spin into a vortex, something to indicate the offering had granted them access to a gateway. But his mind flashed to the shanty in Manaus, where the coins clinked off the floor and the gateway remained blocked. He remembered Emma's words: *"Gateways are opened with an offering. However, to restrict entrance requires someone with the rare ability to jump a gateway. Someone with this gift can enter through a gateway without an offering, then block others from passing through."* A chill shivered his bones as he guessed they'd been blocked again, which meant there was a strong chance they were still being hunted by Will and the Merikh.

"The offering worked." Emma pointed upward. "We are no longer beneath Lake Brienz."

In disbelief, Jack stared at a cluster of stars in a darkened sky while the longship lurched forward at a quicker pace. "Here we go again, down another rabbit hole."

"Still no signal." Emma held her phone toward Jack. "Best we keep ourselves on guard."

Jack eyed the phone, then turned his gaze toward the starry skies. Darkness faded and twilight spread all around them, revealing a river winding through a thick forest beneath rugged white-capped mountain peaks. Gaps of blue skies closed between grayish clouds as waterfalls gushed over cliffs. A torrential downpour rolled in swiftly, sweeping across the mysterious realm.

In the sudden deluge Jack pulled his hood over his head, allowing his fingers to brush across his tailored dretium hoodie. He grabbed hold of the side of the longship and braced himself as a strong current pulled them hard toward rushing white water.

"Forget being afraid of heights!" Jack grabbed hold of Emma. "We've got killer rapids."

The longship dipped and crashed into the white water, leaving the aged vessel groaning as pieces of the deer head snapped from the bow. Jack and Emma ducked as shards flew within inches of them. Just then, a high-pitched whistle echoed high above—a familiar call. Jack spun around and peered up as a majestic pure-white eagle with colossal wings flew above the tree line, headed toward the mountains.

"No way." Dumbstruck, he pointed skyward. "Sahil?"

"We need to get to shore," Emma replied urgently. "And follow the pentaloon."

Jack stumbled toward the stern and grabbed an oar on the right side. He pulled with all his might, attempting to turn the longship toward the forest.

Too bad Emma's gift isn't flight. Wait a minute—she's not using any of her gifts. I mean, she moved a freighter but she can't move this blasted boat to shore?

Again, the longship lurched and crashed into even stronger rapids. Jack was knocked off his feet as Emma tumbled toward him. Both were tossed back as boulders jutting from the riverbed shredded the aged wooden planks. Large splinters exploded from the hull and water gushed through the opening, swiftly swallowing the ancient Rhoxen warship. Jack was tossed overboard and lost sight of Emma. He tried to keep his head above the surface as more sharp pieces scratched against his hoodie.

On instinct, he reached for his sleeve and panic struck. *Soulweaver is gone—again.* Bewildered, he swam with all his strength as his eyes darted around for Emma and the closest shore. With desperate strokes and kicks, he cleared the edge of the rapids and planted his boots on the riverbed. He trudged ashore, out of breath, but he didn't drop to his knees. Instead he turned his attention to the river and searched for any sign of Emma or the rod. He wanted to believe Soulweaver would slither toward him and wrap around his arm as it had done before, but he doubted it.

"Jack!" Emma shouted. "Help!"

Without a second thought he raced down the shoreline, splashing into the water and grabbing Emma before she was swallowed by the roaring rapids. He wrapped his arms around her waist and pulled her ashore, fully aware she hadn't used her gifts since they'd traveled through the gateway. On the muddy banks, he cradled Emma in his arms and carried her up to the dense forest, unnerved by what he remembered about the other realms.

I've never seen Emma this way—but I have seen Areum.

A shrill whistle echoed off the mountains, causing his heart to race.

"Emma . . ." Jack gazed at her pale face as he laid her down. "Take it slow."

"My lightforce is gone," she mumbled. "And my other gifts too."

"Areum was weakened when we entered the City of Gods." Jack turned his attention toward the river, still wondering if Soulweaver would reappear. Hope faded to dismay. "Now Soulweaver is gone too." He paced near the shore until he noticed what was in the distance beyond the rapids—Rhoxen longships. Uncertainty swirled as he stepped back out of sight. "We shouldn't be here, Emma."

11

WITHIN THE TORRENTIAL DOWNPOUR, pentaloons soared across gunmetal skies, narrowly clearing the tree crowns. *How many more are like Sahil?* Jack stood stupefied until instinct forced him to move. Through the thick forest he raced alongside Emma, who'd caught her breath and was leaping over giant roots and ducking beneath overgrown branches. The harder he pumped his arms and legs, the quicker his muscles fired—stronger than in the weeks and months before.

A blaring horn echoed across the valley, sending his adrenaline surging. The forest whipped past as he tried to keep his sights on the majestic eagles swooping across the skies. Eden's Star raged into an inferno, urging him to push his body even harder. Out of the corner of his eye, he caught sight of others moving swiftly between the trees. Glints of light reflected off armor, shields, and silver blades that looked similar to Dragon Soul. *If those are Rhoxen, then the gateway took us back in time*—Doctor Who *style? Mind officially blown. We can't get stuck in history, or else we'll never know the future.* Shrieks pierced the air, and the ground rumbled beneath his boots.

Emma shouted toward him. "Do not look back."

Fear riffled through his veins at the urgency in her voice even while he resisted the temptation to glance over his shoulder. *I do not want to know what's behind us.* His muscles burned with every stride, and he knew he couldn't keep up this relentless pace much longer. The bone-chilling shrieks sent tingles down his spine as he caught up to Emma at the edge of a clearing. He bent over and tried to stop himself from collapsing.

"I can't believe"—he gasped for breath—"we're chasing pentaloons."

Emma grabbed Jack's shoulder and ducked down. "We are not the only ones."

Streaks of darkness chased the pentaloons across the sky, striking several, who crashed in an open field. Jack's anger boiled at the sight of crimson spreading across the pentaloons' pure-white, velvety feathers. From the edge of the forest, the Rhoxen appeared and moved purposefully in formation toward the pentaloons, surrounding the creatures with wall shields etched with fire-breathing dragons.

"Slybourne's crest," Jack said under his breath. The darkness in the sky morphed into skeletal winged charcoal beasts with dark beady eyes. *The legion.* He counted more than a dozen hovering in midair, each armed with a long spear in its bony grasp. Jack's gaze shifted to the white-capped mountains and a peak higher than all others. "Eden's Star took us to the Battle of Everest."

The fallen angels of the legion were not the disfigured and

tormented beast he'd witnessed the first time he'd seen Asiklua. Rather, they were demons thirsting for pentaloon blood and destruction of the Cherub. *Elyon, you could have stopped death and destruction ages ago, but you didn't. Why?* Jack's eyes darted around, searching for a way to use Eden's Star to rescue them.

"We cannot interfere." Emma grabbed his arm. "History will be undone."

"Maybe Eden's Star and the gateway brought us here to stop all this from happening."

"The compass is a guiding light, not a weapon of war."

"If we save the Rhoxen and the pentaloons *and* protect Slybourne, the Merikh will be toast."

"We must find the artifact and leave before we are discovered." Emma kept her head on a swivel. "Change the past and we risk destroying the future, Jack."

"The legion, Asiklua, Nephilim, and the Merikh will kill and torture the Cherub." Jack's jaw clenched and his fingers balled into fists. "We can stop the Age of Trepidation."

"But if we fail—if we die—the future is lost." Emma hesitated. "We can only follow Elyon's destiny for us and no one else. A narrow path is never one with many choices."

"Turn back"—Jack nodded ahead—"or charge forward."

The betrayers of light attacked the Rhoxen with a dark vengeance, spearing against the wall shields. Jack's head spun around at the sound of a thundering gallop bursting from the forest—horsemen charging into the fray led by a bloodied, silver-haired, armor-clad rider. He wielded a sword that erupted with a two-headed fire-breathing dragon. Lightforcers riding in tandem unleashed colorful lightforces against the legion as the aged sword master swung Dragon Soul with righteous precision.

Awestruck, Jack kept his eyes glued to the rider, knowing he was staring at a Cherub legend: Sir Ryder Slybourne. The two-headed dragon attacked the legion until all that remained of the demons was scattered ash across the open field. Slybourne climbed off a grand gray destrier horse with long silky hair as the Rhoxen stepped away from their dead brothers and sisters in arms and the maimed pentaloons. The Cherub's greatest warrior approached the Rhoxen as he slipped Dragon Soul into the scabbard strapped to his shoulder. Another group of riders dismounted, placing their hands on the bloodied creatures and the lost Rhoxen souls.

"Lightforcers, healers, *and* Slybourne," Jack whispered. "Epic."

Ryder Slybourne paced back and forth between the pentaloons, the fallen warriors, and an army of Rhoxen who gathered in the field. Healers remained on their knees, their voices calling out to the heavens. Jack held his breath, willing the pentaloons and the warriors to return to health. He glanced over at Emma, who remained eerily quiet. A moment later, one of the pentaloons rose and stood among the armored men and women who were shoulder to shoulder. Though bloodied, the great white eagle flapped its wings and lifted into the air, calling out with a high-pitched whistle.

A lump lodged in Jack's throat as another pentaloon rolled from the dirt onto its sharp claws, and then one of the wounded Rhoxen stood and stumbled forward. For a moment Jack expected all of them to be brought back to life, but as the healers stepped back, he realized there were those who were gone from the earth never to return. Slybourne knelt, placed his hands on the dead, and bowed his head.

Elyon, welcome them into your presence.

Elyon's response was crystal clear: *There is a time to be born and a time to die. All will pass through like a shadow into my eternal presence.*

A moment lingered as Elyon's words sank deeper into Jack's soul. He knew Emma sensed his grief over the heart-wrenching loss, even though the Eternal's promises remained unchanged. He held his breath as Slybourne stood and turned his gaze in their direction. Seconds passed, but neither he nor Emma moved an inch from their crouched position in the tall grass.

Jack was aware the clock was ticking, but he was convinced he was where he was supposed to be, and he wasn't turning back. Right or wrong, he was going to try to save Slybourne and the Cherub from their fate on Everest.

"You are the last of the Seven Tribes to gather." Slybourne walked in front of the Rhoxen warriors and mounted his gray destrier. The horse danced from one hoof to the next. "March to the great stone wall, and together we will prepare for battle to retrieve the Rhoxen Stone."

Jack leaned in close to Emma. "What's the Rhoxen Stone?"

She shook her head and squeezed his shoulder. "Is Eden's Star leading us, or is it you?"

"We have to go to Everest, Emma."

12

RELENTLESS RAINS ESCALATED the gloominess in the air as Ryder Slybourne galloped toward the Himalayas, along with a company of lightforcers and healers riding in a pack surrounding the great warrior. The Rhoxen army, thousands strong, marched through muddied fields, leaving a smaller band behind to bury the dead.

Jack remained hidden in the long grass, struck by a looming heaviness. Seconds ticked like hours while Emma remained gone—yet it had only been a matter of minutes. A rustling in the bushes sent him facedown until he realized it was Emma crabwalking toward him. He breathed a bit easier until he noticed dinged armor and bloodstained clothes in her grasp.

"I'm not even going to ask where you found those." He

grabbed the clothes, gingerly slipping them over his hoodie and backpack. A foul odor attacked his nostrils, causing him to swallow the vomit in his mouth. "Just when this couldn't get any worse—or any grosser."

"Rattle your dags." Emma smirked at his blank stare. "Hurry up, Jack."

"Right." He struggled to put the armor on. "Ready to roll."

Emma reached down and scooped up a handful of mud, then slapped it against his face and rubbed muck all over his cheeks down to his neck. He reacted by scooping up his own pile of sludgy earth and gently smearing it over Emma's soft skin, noticing her lips curl. Both slipped on scabbards containing blades of those who were already gone.

"What I wouldn't give for a hot shower," Jack mused darkly. "And a Spitfire Jolt."

"We have never looked better," Emma chuckled.

"This is insane—but we're exactly where Eden's Star wants us to be."

With the last of the Rhoxen army emerging from the forest headed toward Everest, Jack and Emma snuck quietly through the brush before slipping in with the rear guard. He glanced around at battle-weary men and women with heads down and boots trudging through the mud.

"If we are forced to defend ourselves"—Emma kept her gaze fixed straight ahead and leaned in close—"remember, Elyon's power flows through hips, shoulders, and every strike."

"Soulweaver would make this a bit easier." Jack paused. "What about your gifts?"

"I have faith that when we are beyond this realm, my gifts will return."

"Areum started dying as soon as she entered the City of Gods." Jack shouldered the weight of her memory. "What if the same happens to you, Emma?"

Her gaze softened. "Faith of a mustard seed."

"You're one of the chosen," Jack retorted. "Of course that's what you'd say."

"A promise written in the Eternal remains forever true—no matter our circumstance."

For a long while they marched with their gazes fixed on the footsteps left in the mud, attempting to blend in with an army from centuries past. *Stay a ghost, Jack.* Beyond the thick forest, the landscape opened to flatlands beneath the Himalayas and Everest's peak. Tens of thousands of soldiers were gathered at the base of the mountain range, where a great stone wall extended as far as the eye could see.

I've seen this wall before—in my visions and the drawings.

Awestruck, Jack glanced at flags stuck into the mud embroidered with an emerald tree, chestnut deer, bronze lion, turquoise ship, violet temple, silver serpent, and crimson wolf. *Seven Tribes of Cherub.* His gaze shifted to the warriors who represented the lineage of each tribe, and a lump lodged in his throat. He knew where he was in history and what was about to happen to all who stood around him.

Horsemen held the reins of destriers as hooves danced near a massive iron door fifty feet tall. *Reminds me of the lightforcers at Beacon Hill, only old-school. What is the wall guarding on Everest?* Emma nudged him as the Rhoxen joined tens of thousands of Cherub from all Seven Tribes ready for battle. At first he wasn't sure what she was staring at, until he noticed a rippling in the air near the bouldered wall. *A force field.* Beyond the great stone wall spread a snowcapped mountain range filled with steep inclines, deep valleys, and glacial crevasses beneath the magnificent beauty of Everest.

"It's about to get real." Jack's heartbeat quickened and his adrenaline flowed as a regiment of lightforcers stood on the front lines, each with their colorful lightforce glowing. "Eden's Star brought us here to one of the artifacts—the Rhoxen Stone." A chill shot down his spine as a thundering echoed across the flatlands and the ground beneath his boots rumbled. Heavy cavalry appeared on the horizon racing at full speed with pentaloons flying overhead. "Emma, we can't leave them to die on Everest, not when we can warn them."

Emma grabbed his arm tight. "Jack, we must not interfere."

"Maybe if we changed history, Rachel and the others would never have to die."

"There is no way to know for certain. We might return to a present that is much darker."

Ryder Slybourne raised Dragon Soul as the cavalry slowed and surrounded the Rhoxen and other warriors of the Seven Tribes. On the front lines, the warriors stood shoulder to shoulder armed with swords, spears, bows, arrows, and shields. Slybourne rode back and forth as the warriors raised their weapons, clanging them against their shields.

"Elyon brought us to this day—this hour," Slybourne called out. "We are brothers and sisters who stand united against our enemy. Darkness has taken far too many in this war—but that changes on the mountain. On this day, the Rhoxen Stone will restore light to our world."

Slybourne turned and pointed Dragon Soul toward the great stone wall as the warriors erupted in a bone-chilling roar. Far away on the mountain, a shrieking response pierced Jack's ears. He recognized the noise of the legion. Fear riffled through him, yet he was ready to fight. From the point of Dragon Soul, the two-headed dragon appeared to be glowing in ebony. Slybourne swung the sword, and the dragon flew across the flatlands before assaulting the iron door. The warriors around Jack thumped their spears into the mud, leaving him retrieving his sword from the scabbard and gripping the handcrafted weapon as if his life depended on it.

"This is definitely not the Sword and Fan," he mumbled. "When it begins . . ."

Emma retrieved her sword and shot Jack a quick glance. "Stay together."

13

CHERUB WARRIORS READIED THEMSELVES with eyes of fire and ice. As the iron door burst open, a typhoon whipped and rushed down the mountain, sweeping over the great stone wall. Jack stabbed the Rhoxen sword into the earth and braced himself, desperate to stay on his feet and not be swept away from Emma. He stared ahead and caught sight of Ryder Slybourne riding bravely through the entrance, lightforcers and healers on horseback racing after him.

Under a bone-chilling downpour, the armies of the Seven Tribes marched thousands strong through the gates of the great stone wall toward Everest. Jack noticed the mud beneath his boots turn to ice as others around him slipped and stumbled, yet he kept moving forward. *This is not the Zakhar—this is real.* A deafening

roar shook him to his core. His eyes darted around as he anticipated the attack, knowing the worst was yet to come.

From the direction of the mountain, winged demons appeared
out of thin air, arriving from another realm. One was darker and
grander than the rest with Soulweaver in its grasp. *Asiklua and
more of the legion.* Slybourne and his warriors from Sakkhela rode
straight toward the legion with Dragon Soul leading the way.

Demons whisked across the skies as lightforcers released their
powers. Warriors pulled bows and launched thousands of arrows
as the legion attacked. Pentaloons soared over the flatlands, snatch-
ing the fallen Cherub and flying them away from the battlefield.

Emma shoved Jack out of the way as a demon landed near them,
dripping ebony lava from its jaws and claws. Jack rolled over as black
fire struck within inches. Emma moved swiftly, plunged the sword
into the demon, and the beast vaporized. *Whoa . . . Rhoxen swords are
made of dretium, not breilium.* Jack scrambled to his feet and swung
his sword, striking legion who appeared out of nowhere. With the
words from Nightingale's diary ringing in his ears, he stood shoulder
to shoulder with Emma alongside warriors from long ago.

*"Heroes wage war for freedom, yet warriors alone choose death in
battle. . . . Generations to come will never know of the true courage of
these men and women."*

Jack shouted to Emma, "Slybourne!"

In the deathly chaos, Jack and Emma fought with force and flow
through the battlefield as legion closed in on all sides of the Cherub
armies. Assassins wielding razor-sharp katanas attacked from the
flatlands—those who resembled the statues he'd witnessed coming
to life within the Temple of the Nephilim. Slybourne rode valiantly as
Dragon Soul clashed with Soulweaver, shaking the core of the earth.

With lightforcers and benders unleashing powers against

the legion on Everest, the snow-packed mountain shifted before Jack's eyes. His stare narrowed until he caught sight of wild two-legged beasts with snarling fangs and shaggy white fur flanking Slybourne and his warriors. He'd never actually seen Nephilim up close before—the Nephilim king inside the temple in the City of Gods had been cloaked in the darkness. *Jack, keep your mind on staying alive.* One stood tall and growled with an earsplitting roar, erupting a massive avalanche.

Jagged boulders dislodged and tumbled down Everest, camouflaged by a great white cloud. Deep crevasses widened as Jack and Emma stood directly in the path of destruction. With the ice beneath splitting, something squeezed Jack's shoulder and lifted him off the snow. He glanced up and realized a pentaloon soared over him, gripping Emma in its other claw. His mind flashed to Sakkhela when Sahil flew to the edge of the atmosphere to restore Emma's gifts and rescued them from Slybourne Castle. In seconds the avalanche crashed down ruthlessly, smothering thousands of Cherub warriors.

At this high altitude, Jack's lungs burned as he gasped for breath. His attention shifted toward the Nephilim king below, who raised a Goliath paw holding a gemstone that radiated a brilliant turquoise across the Himalayas. Without warning, the pentaloon nose-dived, leaving Jack flailing as they careened toward a steep incline on Everest. The pentaloon slammed into the jagged rocks at full speed, releasing its clawed grip. In a free fall down the icy mountain at breakneck speed, Jack tumbled and rolled countless times before his body stopped.

Dazed, he slowly picked himself up and listened to a hauntingly eerie silence. He shook off the stars twinkling before his eyes and took in his surroundings: a ridge of the mountain overlooking the valley beneath. He was stunned when he realized the avalanche was frozen in midair. Cherub warriors and Merikh assassins were paralyzed, thousands more swallowed by the snowslide. Jack's gaze shifted toward Slybourne and his warriors, who were statues imprisoned midfight—even the double-headed dragon of Dragon Soul was transfixed.

Legion swarmed the Cherub warriors, who were frozen in time, then streaked across the Himalayas with unearthly shrieks. A hole opened in the sky, and the legion disappeared into another realm, leaving the gateway exposed. Asiklua glided toward Slybourne with Soulweaver spitting ebony fire.

"Elyon," Jack whispered, "give me the courage to die."

Jack darted across the icy mountain as Eden's Star blazed within, a brilliant white glow emanating from beneath his tailored hoodie and Rhoxen armor. A scorching heat fueled his muscles as he closed in on Asiklua. He slid on his knees, gripping the Rhoxen sword with both hands, and swung with all his might. Asiklua spun around with Soulweaver in his grasp. A percussive force slammed against Jack before he reached the legion commander. He flew backward, the wind knocked out of him. Drops of crimson pierced the stark-white snow as he rolled onto his knees, coughing and struggling to catch his breath.

"Come on!" he shouted. "Is that all you've got?"

Jack used the point of the Rhoxen sword to lift himself to his feet. His hands shook as he steadied himself for another burst of supernatural punishment. Asiklua's beady eyes stared soullessly, then the fallen angel turned and struck Slybourne with Soulweaver, shattering the great Cherub warrior into a million pieces. Dragon Soul dropped to the snow and vanished.

"No!" Jack yelled from deep within, his voice reverberating off Everest.

A rumbling intensified from behind as Jack kept his stare fixed on Asiklua, knowing he wasn't going to survive. As he harnessed an inferno, he knew Asiklua was drawn to the light bursting from his chest—and then he realized the brilliant turquoise glow had vanished. He glanced over his shoulder and shivered at the Nephilim and their king charging with a relentless fury. Seconds later, pentaloons whipped past the mountainside, knocking the Nephilim and their king over the cliff. Left in the snow radiating brilliantly amid the bloodshed of battle was the Rhoxen Stone.

You can't win, Jack. History is where it belongs.

Pentaloons landed in front of Jack, protecting Eden's Star from Asiklua. Jack inched back as the legion commander attacked the pentaloons with Soulweaver, leaving Jack scrambling before he snatched the Rhoxen Stone. Out of the corner of his eye, he caught sight of Emma sliding down the mountain. He slipped the Rhoxen Stone into his pocket and dove forward, grabbing Emma's arm before she flew off the cliff. He dared not look back as the high-pitched whistle from the pentaloons ceased and the shrieking call of the legion commander pierced his ears.

"Emma!" Jack shouted. "Run!"

Jack and Emma raced across a snow-covered ledge as Asiklua wielded Soulweaver without mercy. Dark forces spewing from the rod destroyed the mountainside, nearly pulverizing them to dust. A crevasse cracked open too wide for them to hurdle. Jack grabbed Emma's hand tight and fell into the hole, sliding down icy walls before slamming into the bottom of the crevasse. He glanced up as Asiklua flew overhead, knowing there was only one escape.

"Settle your spirit and surrender," he whispered to himself.

Emma gripped his hand tight, and in a blink they were gone.

14

PATAGONIA, CHILE

Jack and Emma plunged into a remote glacial lake with alluring jade depths. Seconds passed before Jack poked his head above the glassy surface. Emma appeared a moment later, and both breathed in the peacefulness away from the unspeakable death and destruction on Everest.

We're both alive and in one piece. Unbelievable.

He caught his breath as he treaded water and eyed the vibrant marble-walled caves circling the lake. Beneath clear blue skies, they reached the shore and dropped their backpacks, then slumped against the rocks.

"Are we in another realm?" Jack asked, adrenaline subsiding.

Emma shook her head. "I do not know for certain."

"We didn't stop Slybourne or the Cherub from being slaughtered."

"Eden's Star guided us to the Battle of Everest to find the Rhoxen Stone." Emma's brows furrowed. "There is still a chance our actions have changed history."

"Pentaloons took the Nephilim king and his beastly entourage over the edge, even though the one we were riding crash-landed." Jack reached into his pocket, retrieved the turquoise gemstone, and held it up as light reflected off its purity. He never noticed whether Emma froze in time before he slipped it back into his pocket. "Maybe there wasn't an Age of Trepidation or a Second Great War, which means the Mercy Covenant might never have existed, the gates of the wall guarding Everest are still closed, and the world isn't on the verge of a total meltdown."

"Asiklua controlled the Rod of Elyon on Everest, and we know the rod was corrupted in his possession in Nanimi. While it is possible we have altered history, there is no doubt not all has been saved. We need to know whether we have stopped what Cherub have feared since Slybourne's defeat—a second Age of Trepidation."

Jack flinched at a strange sensation. Dumbstruck, he pulled up his sleeve and stared at Soulweaver wrapped perfectly around his forearm. "The war isn't over yet, Emma."

A white glow emanated from her palm. "We are back in our world."

He exhaled long and hard, relieved Soulweaver remained within his grasp, then leaned his head back and gazed toward the sky. "Such a mind bender—but I'm grateful."

"Never imagined I would witness the Battle of Everest." Emma grabbed her backpack and stood, then stepped behind a cluster of marbled stone. She tossed the Rhoxen armor and her wet clothes

BATTLE OF LION ROCK

aside as Jack followed her lead and slipped behind a few stones on the opposite side. "We should honor Salomeh's request and travel to the Sanctum of Serenity to find the prophecy."

"Ancient Cherub writings might help us know whether we're history changers."

Emma nodded. "We must be certain before returning to Beacon Hill."

"The Rhoxen Stone stopped time, and Dragon Soul vanished." Jack's mind flashed to Slybourne frozen in his bloodied armor, wielding the ancient sword against Asiklua. *He never had a chance once the Nephilim king used the stone.* "A gateway opened for the legion?"

"And we know the legion ended up beyond the Highlands in the nether realm."

"I'm not sure Eden's Star will take us to the sanctum, Emma." In dry clothes, Jack stepped out into the open and wrapped the turquoise gemstone in a Nightingale T-shirt. He stuffed the artifact deep inside the backpack and zipped it closed. "Maybe the compass will guide us back to the nether realm so we can destroy the legion and recover whatever artifact is being guarded there."

"If there is an artifact still there . . ." Emma tucked her clothes into a side pocket of her backpack. "Jack, we should find a gateway to the sanctum and locate the writings, then search for the nether realm. Salomeh was quite insistent the prophecy be found and returned, as it is of the utmost importance to the Cherub. With the prophecy, she might be able to help us understand where to find the nether realm too."

"Out of all the places we could've ended up, Eden's Star brought us here."

Jack hoped for the compass to ignite, knowing they were missing the reason it brought them to the caves. *I got nothing.* He watched as

Emma climbed the rocky hillside to the top, hoping she might have better news. She turned back toward him and shrugged.

"One road leading in both directions, but I do not see any town or village." Emma jumped down and yanked several branches from small shrubs growing between the rocks. "It will be dark soon, so we should rest." She stacked the branches on top of each other, then used her lightforce to ignite a fire. "We will spend a night under the stars and trust Elyon to watch over us."

"When it gets dark, we should take turns sleeping," Jack suggested. "No telling who or what might show up in this place."

"Before I left to search for you, Amina made certain I was prepared." Emma reached into another zippered pocket of her backpack and retrieved several wrapped packages. "Now, we cannot eat it all at once."

Jack's mouth watered as he inhaled familiar aromas. Inside the first package was a row of crunchy rice rolls with roasted sesame seeds glazed in syrup. Beside the rice rolls were several pineapple buns lightly fried and golden brown. She reached into her pack again and pulled out a package of *bak kwa*—pork jerky dried in soy sauce, five-spice powder, and fish sauce. Lastly, she set two cartons of Vitasoy in front of them.

"Compared to catfish and rice," Jack mused, "this is like a feast."

"Elyon, we thank you for watching over us this day," Emma prayed. "And we believe you will walk with us in the days ahead. Bless this dinna and give us your strength."

Jack dug into a pineapple bun, which was one of his favorites. He stabbed a pointed straw into the Vitasoy carton and sipped slowly, wanting to savor every ounce. With each bite, he stared at the dancing fire and wondered whether they'd both make it to the end.

We fought in the Battle of Everest—at least for a moment in time.

15

Daylight dissolved as the sun disappeared over the horizon. Jack wrapped his hoodie over Emma's shoulders as she leaned against him. After their makeshift dinner, they had strolled around the lake and climbed rocks to get a better look around. Emma was right—one desolate road without any sign of civilization. Both were comfortable with silence, which was the opposite of his nights in Nightingale, sneaking out to the Shack with Will, Vince, and Tim. He buried another shovelful of guilt deeper in his soul where no one else was allowed—not even Elyon. The night grew a few degrees chillier as he listened to Emma breathe, convinced he was falling harder than ever before.

She gauges my emotions, so she's gotta know, right? Now is not the time to bare my soul. If I make it through this alive, then I'll tell her—but not until then.

A full moon glowed amid millions of stars scattered across the sky, seemingly endless within a vast universe. Jack tossed more branches onto the fire and gazed out across the lake.

Elyon, have mercy on those I love and keep them safe. Give me the strength to protect Eden's Star and to find the artifacts before it's too late. I'm afraid to ask for forgiveness because there is still a score to settle, but I want to surrender—it's just hard to let go of the past.

Bushes rustled, startling him but not waking Emma. He hesitated until curiosity won and he slipped away, leaving Emma resting against the side of a rock. With the fire crackling, Jack took cautious steps before stopping cold. Light reflected off dark eyes staring back at him—a lamb stood within a cluster of bushes.

"What is a lamb doing out here alone?" he mumbled. "Looks harmless."

In a blink, the lamb headed into the bushes, and the rustling started again. Jack clenched his fists and cautiously stepped through the bushes until he reached a clearing. The lamb stopped and turned its head toward him, as if making sure he was still following. Beneath the surface of the lake, a jade glow drifted through the water before entering a cave. Jack was unsure what to do next, his attention divided between the lamb and the lake.

When he returned his gaze to the lamb, the animal was gone. He climbed down the rocks and stood at the opening of the cave, then glanced back to where he'd left Emma asleep. *Smart thing to do would be to wake her up, but first I'll take a quick look.* He followed the jade glow that illuminated the pool inside. Along a stone edge, he inched his way farther inside the cave and found himself surrounded by purple, pink, and gray swirling marble walls.

Jack stood at the edge of the pool within the cave, his mind flashing to the Cave of Prophets. He jumped when Soulweaver slithered down his forearm and extended into a full rod in his grasp. *That was unexpected. Am I supposed to dip the rod into the water? Elyon, help me understand.* While he gripped Soulweaver, the rod pulled him deeper into the cave. He let go of the rod, and Soulweaver stood on its own, glowing a stark white. *It's hovering by itself. Am I dreaming, or is this the real deal?* His heart pounded harder as he reached out and touched the rod.

A surge of energy exploded from Soulweaver with a blinding light. Jack covered his eyes with his forearm and waited until the light dimmed. Out of the corner of his eye, he caught sight of a ghost darting between tin shanties. *Rachel.* He raced after her as she ducked down an alley, but when he called out her name, his voice was muted.

Desperation washed over him as he reached out to grab Rachel's shoulder from behind. She spun around with a glare and unleashed a violet lightforce. Jack ducked as the lightforce streaked past and exploded in a raging inferno. Stunned, he realized he was standing between Rachel and Michael Chung. *Neither know I'm here. So am I having a vision, or is this Soulweaver doing something else I've never seen it do before?* A chill shot down his spine as his gaze turned toward the river flowing with trash in Sitio Veterans.

Jack stepped back and watched the power of Rachel's lightforce weakening Chung's fiery defense. He remembered his vision of Rachel dying on the banks of the river, but this was playing out differently than he expected. Rachel moved forward with powerful lightforce pulses. *She's about to take him down, but that doesn't make sense.* Rachel closed in on Chung with a relentless attack, leaving him on his knees unable to defend himself. She stood over him as Jack held his breath, begging her to take his life.

"Repent from your wicked ways," Rachel said, matter-of-fact, "and pray for forgiveness."

"You are one of the chosen," Chung replied. "But you are far from the strongest."

Jack spun around and searched the night for whoever lingered in the darkness. His eyes narrowed, desperate to identify a face, as a shadow stepped into the dim light. *Nothing I can do to stop this—the past is history.* He watched the shadow approach with a raised hand and tried to warn Rachel, but his voice was still powerless. No visible lightforce appeared, but Rachel was pulled off her feet and lifted into the air with her back arched. With the swipe of a hand, the shadow's powers struck Rachel, and a bloodcurdling scream pierced Jack's ears. She dropped to the banks of the river, motionless. After all he'd been through—and the vengeance he kept hidden in the deepest part of his soul—his rage burned more intensely than ever. Chung approached Rachel's lifeless body and fired one final shot.

Jack charged toward Chung and the shadow, but when he blinked he found himself back inside the cave where Soulweaver stood straight on its own and glowed vibrantly. His hands shook as he grabbed the rod and allowed it to wrap back around his forearm.

In the stillness of the cave, his breathing quickened, on the verge of hyperventilating. He braced himself against the wall as flashes from the vision struck in rapid succession—including the face of the shadow.

Beneath the serenity of the night, Jack returned to the campfire and slumped against a rock. For a long time he watched Emma's chest rise and fall. Betrayal burned beneath his skin—and disgust at what he'd witnessed in his vision. His fingers balled into fists as he struggled to control himself. Professor Burwick had warned him that Rachel's death was not what it seemed.

A bullet didn't kill her—Emma did?

16

A RESTLESS NIGHT ENDED with Jack stomping out the fire. Hours earlier he had snuck back to the campfire and remained seated across from Emma with arms wrapped around his knees until daybreak. Troubling thoughts and scenarios of betrayal riffled through his mind. He wanted to confront Emma, but he questioned whether the vision could be trusted.

Soulweaver took me to that night in Sitio, but my visions have been wrong before. Why would Emma kill Rachel? She's the most powerful of all Cherub, and both were chosen to protect the light. Doesn't make any sense. C'mon, Jack—you trust Emma, and you're falling in love with her, so how could the vision be right? Keep yourself together until you know for sure. He took a deep breath. *Elyon, show me what's true.*

"Awful quiet," Emma said. "You seem a bit distracted?"

"I'm fine," he answered. "Just want to get going and not waste time."

"Seems the reason Eden's Star brought us here was to rest." Emma slipped her backpack over her shoulder. "Sanctum of Serenity or keep hunting for the next artifact?"

"You're right—Sanctum of Serenity." Jack grabbed his backpack and climbed the rocks. "We need to know whether we've changed history for the better or made all of this worse."

For the first mile, Jack took the lead and kept a brisk pace. Emma walked alongside and reached out her hand. At first he pretended he didn't notice, but he couldn't allow the awkwardness to linger. Once their fingers intertwined, he knew she sensed his uneasiness. He ignored her curious stare and kept his sights ahead. In the distance, a dirty white cloud seemed to hover over the road. As they approached, Jack realized it wasn't a cloud but a flock of bleating sheep.

"Not something you'd see at Beacon Hill." Jack searched for the lamb who'd led him to the cave. *Impossible to pick one—they all look the same.* "Too many to go around."

"Sheepherders should be nearby," Emma noted. "Maybe they will help us."

A bright-yellow pickup barreled down the road in their direction, kicking up dirt in its wake. Jack and Emma waited as the truck slowed and stopped. An elderly man with a scraggly beard and worn overalls climbed out of the truck and limped toward them. His smile framed several missing teeth, and a surprised expression spread across his weathered face.

The man scooted through the sheep around the truck, then greeted them. *"Buenos días."*

"Do you speak English?" Jack asked.

"*Poquito.*" The farmer glanced curiously at Emma. "Very far from Puerto Natales."

"We've been here since yesterday at the caves, but we lost our ride." Jack knew he was skirting the truth, but explaining how they'd ended up there would leave the farmer hightailing. "We have money if you take us to Puerto Natales."

Several others appeared on the road alongside the flock. *Sheepherders.* The farmer called out to them in Spanish, and they surrounded the flock to move them along. Jack and Emma waited as the sheep bleated and nudged one another until all were across the road. He couldn't help but wonder if the lamb was among them.

The farmer motioned for Jack and Emma to follow. "We go to Puerto."

Jack leaned in close to Emma and asked, "Where is Puerto?"

"Puerto Natales is a capital city in southern Chile."

"How could you possibly know that?"

"On Karābu Island, Peter tested all of us on the world's major cities—and many that are lesser known—where we could travel through the gateways that still exist."

"Of course," Jack blurted with a heavy dose of sarcasm. "Makes total sense."

"My friends," the farmer interrupted. "We go now."

An hour and a half along a dirt road then down a one-lane highway, the yellow truck arrived in Puerto Natales, the capital of Natales and Última Esperanza in the southernmost part of Chile. *Once again, Emma is one hundred percent right. She knows more than she's shared with me, which means she might be keeping her own secrets too.* Jack eyed the vehicles as the farmer cut down one street after another, finally pulling over at a gated property on San Martin Road.

In the neighborhood were gated homes guarded with jagged pieces of glass cemented into the tops of the walls. *Reminds me of the homes in Kowloon Tong.* The farmer climbed out of the truck and punched an intercom button. He spoke in Spanish to whoever answered. A moment passed before the gate opened and an elderly European woman greeted them. She exchanged words with the farmer, who waved cordially at Jack and Emma before leaving in his bright-yellow truck.

"My name is Eleanore." She motioned them inside. "Quickly, please."

Jack and Emma followed her through the entrance and waited as she locked the gate. He studied her pointed nose, straight ginger hair, and tie-dyed dress. She led them across a small grassy yard into a simply furnished home. Jack and Emma removed their boots before entering.

"We didn't get a chance to thank—" Jack began.

"Andres said you were lost near the Marble Caves. Quite strange for tourists to stay overnight at the caves without a guide or transport."

"Not exactly our best plan," Emma admitted. "You have not asked us our names."

Eleanore's warm demeanor faded. "I know who you are, dear."

17

JACK AND EMMA WAITED IN a quaint living room while Eleanore excused herself. While the room was homey with dark tiled floors and pale-orange walls, something seemed to be missing. Jack eyed the oil paintings of landscapes on the walls, realizing there were no photos anywhere.

He set his backpack down and inhaled a sweet aroma. "How can she know who we are?"

"Possible she has seen our faces on social," Emma admitted. "Before the PRC was able to block access for the whole world to know we are fugitives."

"Andres didn't make any calls on the way, so she couldn't have known we were coming."

"And yet she is not surprised we are here."

Eleanore stepped into the living room carrying a tray of blueberry muffins and mugs filled with steaming tea. *She must've really known we were coming to have fresh-baked muffins. I'm not complaining, just confused.* She placed the tray on the coffee table and sat on the edge of a wood-framed sofa with her eyes fixed on them.

"Your encounter with Andres was not an accident," she said. "I sent him to find you."

"How did you know we'd be near the caves?" Jack asked, point-blank.

"It was only a matter of time before Eden's Star brought you."

"That doesn't answer the question," Emma pressed. "Eleanore . . ."

Jack's eyes narrowed as he caught a flicker in the woman's gaze, one that was familiar. While an awkward silence lingered, he picked up a plate and a blueberry muffin, having learned from their adventure that the next meal was never guaranteed. While the snacks Emma had brought were delicacies the night before, he bit into the fresh muffin and his taste buds came alive. A twinge tingled down his spine as he watched the way Eleanore held her mug and sipped her tea.

"My childhood was not easy. My father abused my two sisters and me for years. I try to block out the memories, but sometimes there's nothing I can do to prevent them from resurfacing."

"Do you know Professor Burwick?" Jack asked, thinking the story sounded familiar.

Eleanore's lips curled. "Harley is my younger sister."

"Still doesn't explain how you knew we were at the caves."

"Harley surrendered herself to Elyon long before I or our other sister. She has fought bravely and paid a steep price for her sacrifice." Eleanore paused as her gaze shifted between them. Again, she

BATTLE OF LION ROCK

sipped the piping hot tea carefully, then continued. "My family was not raised to believe in Elyon or the Cherub way. We were never granted the supernatural gifts of lightforcers, benders, or healers. When one has experienced severe trauma, one's gifts are either buried or heightened. Harley has used her gifts as a leader to build and strengthen the faction. However, I am unlike Harley and the rest of my family. You see, I am a vision seeker—a gift forbidden by the Cherub."

"I have never heard of such a gift," Emma interrupted.

"Gifts besides the Cherub trinity—lightforcers, benders, and healers—are granted to some of those who believe in Elyon."

Jack leaned forward and dug his elbows into his thighs. "Tell us how your gift works."

"Vision seekers possess the ability to enter the minds of others to experience their deepest thoughts, vivid memories, and visions. Seekers who are strong enough are able to influence those visions beyond what was intended—whether it be rays of light or shades of darkness."

"You are talking about a mind reader?" Emma asked, skeptical.

"Much more than a parlor trick, dear."

"The vision I had last night triggered where we were, so you knew where to find us?" Jack ignored Emma's quizzical stare. "Can you tell me whether it was real?"

"Visions are not always truth, but sometimes they are glimpses of past and future realities." Eleanore's gaze softened as she set her mug down on the coffee table. "There was a time when my faith was clouded and I was lured by the Merikh—a shameful decision I have regretted for many years." She exhaled long and hard, clearly struggling with the words. "Addison and I were quite close during that time. He convinced me to use my gifts to influence Gabriella in order to bring them closer together. Against the Elders' and highest Cherubs' wishes, she fell in love with him, and he believed it would grant him greater power. His gifts were remarkable as the keeper of Dragon Soul and as a lightforcer. However, I witnessed the darkness within him, but I was too afraid to confess what I had done."

Jack hesitated, guessing what was next. "Is Addison a vision seeker too?"

"Charlotte and Peter conducted experiments from ancient writings found in the chambers of Sakkhela in order to extract my gifts—some against my will. Neither of them knew of Addison's ability as a vision seeker. While my gifts weakened, Addison's grew stronger until he reached a depraved state of mind, wanting to control the thoughts of others. During those years, Cherub were coming for him, and Gabriella was chosen to stop him. He was strong enough to invade Gabriella's mind before she was able to protect you and Rachel."

"Does he know where we are now?" Emma asked. "Is he able to invade our minds too?"

"If he remains imprisoned in the Dungeon of Savages, he is not able to."

Jack shot Emma a quick look, then turned back to Eleanore. "What if he gets out?"

18

Stickiness suffocated a misty morning across the mountains of Tai Tam Country Park. On Mount Butler Road, a minivan screeched to a halt and a side door slid open. Eliška climbed out and headed discreetly between the Jardine Terrace apartment buildings as the driver pulled away at a high speed. Behind the apartment complex she reached Country Trail and began a steady jog along a dirt path. Her arms and legs pumped rhythmically, and her gaunt cheeks and braided hair remained taut.

Looking from side to side, she crossed the terrain without a misstep amid a dense landscape of Taiwan acacias and slash pines. Sweat seeped down her neck and spine as her relentless pace continued for several miles until she reached Reservoir Road. Her breathing remained controlled as she moved swiftly between the acacias. She ducked low behind the bushes and kept her sights on the road.

From her pocket, Eliška retrieved foldable binoculars and peered through the magnified lenses. Tucked away within Tai Tam Country Park was a cluster of high-rise apartments. She pointed the binoculars toward a checkpoint leading to the heavily guarded apartment district. Even from a distance, she recognized the Merikh in all black and the Hong Kong Police Force in their standard uniform checking vehicles and verifying IDs of drivers and passengers.

Eliška checked her watch and counted the seconds. A ParkNShop delivery truck rounded a corner on Reservoir Road and slowed slightly. She emerged from the bushes and darted toward the truck, grabbing hold and hopping on to the back bumper. With no time to waste, she slapped the back of the truck twice, and the driver sped up as she climbed onto the roof.

Facedown, she inched forward until she was in the center of the roof. With her body pressed against the metal, she held her breath and waited once the truck rolled to a stop. She heard voices below and sensed people circling around the vehicle. Another moment passed before the security gate lifted and she exhaled a sigh of relief.

The truck parked at the entrance to the ParkNShop grocery store. Eliška slipped off the roof and landed on the sidewalk. She stared inside at the store shelves stocked with fruit, canned goods, fresh meat, and cases of water. She never made eye contact with the driver as she walked in the opposite direction.

With the water shortage causing chaos across most of Hong Kong, she was struck by a large, pristine grassy area and an enormous crystal clear pool. Hong Kongers played tennis on half a dozen premiere courts while others entered Parkview Teahouse— exactly as Professor Burwick described. Eliška kept walking until she approached the Whistling Arrow—once a local travel agency, now the only way for the rich and powerful to arrange international transport away from Hong Kong. Of course, they had to pay a steep price to the Merikh.

Eliška sat on a bench offering a clear view of the open area within the block of apartments that surrounded them. Months had passed since the underwater tunnels collapsed, leaving millions of Hong Kongers struggling to find basic necessities. Starvation and death were a reality for many these days. Eliška eyed her surroundings, sickened by what she witnessed. *All the comforts of life at one's fingertips. Why? Because the rich gladly paid the price, no matter the cost to anyone else.* Burwick had warned her about Tai Tam, but seeing the exclusive district with her own eyes struck a match of righteous anger at the Merikh and PRC's stronghold on Hong Kong.

Ren Lai slipped onto the bench beside her with his gaze fixed straight ahead. "Believe it or not, there are quite a few Cherub in this district, desperate to get out of Hong Kong before it burns down."

"Professor Burwick is convinced you have information that will help all of us, but I am not certain whatever you might offer will make a difference."

"I must be daft trusting you lot." Ren sighed. "I tried to help Jack, and look how that turned out. He poked the dragon, then disappeared. You know the Cherub were supposed to help me and my cousin disappear before Addison or the Merikh found us. Now my cousin is dead, and I've spent my last dollar bribing my way into Tai Tam."

"I have brought the money." Eliška eyed their surroundings, searching for anyone who might be paying attention to them. "In the past, promises were made to many of us, but you have my word. First you need to tell me what you know."

"Since I was young, my father worked for the Merikh until he was convicted of stealing a few hundred million from his clients. Greedy old geezer. He believed his loyalty meant he was untouchable." Ren paused. "After you and Vince marched through the streets like you'd won the World Cup, my cousin was found dead in an alley in Wan Chai. I could not trust the Cherub, so I went to see my father in what's left of Shek Pik Prison. By the way, you lot did a number on that place too. He told me to go to Tai Tam because he knew the Merikh were beginning to smuggle people out of the country. But the thing is, he told me the only way through was a gateway."

"There is a gateway in Tai Tam?" Eliška asked in a lowered voice.

"Listen, I need the money before I say anything more."

Eliška retrieved an envelope from her pocket and slipped it over. "What else?"

"Rumors." Ren hesitated. "Some Cherub say an Elder was kept here, but no proof."

"How were you able to get past the gates?"

"When I left Shek Pik, I emptied the safe at the Shack and headed straight here before the prison turned into ground zero. I bribed an HKPF officer, paid for a flat, and have been waiting for months. Now there is nothing left, and I am ready to disappear."

"You will have enough to leave and start a new life."

Ren slid the envelope into his pocket and retrieved a steel magnetic card. "As promised—you can go in and out of Tai Tam without a problem."

"Do you know where the gateway is?"

"Parkview block 15."

William Fargher appeared out of thin air about thirty yards away, causing a moment of panic as everyone stood stunned. His broad shoulders and buzzed skull were unmistakable. Eliška's heart pounded as she watched him walk across the grassy area and disappear inside Parkview block 15. When she turned her attention back toward Ren, he was gone. She kept her wits as she calmly stood and walked toward ParkNShop, unsettled by how Will had suddenly appeared without traveling through a gateway. She reached the delivery truck, slipped behind the wheel, and shifted into gear.

At the checkpoint she handed over the steel card and waited. Within minutes she was waved through and drove down the mountain along Causeway Road. Her mind replayed the moment when Will had appeared as she passed through multiple checkpoints. The fake ID given to her by Ren worked perfectly. She turned down King's Road to Hoi Chak Street, and within twenty minutes she arrived at Quarry Bay. She pulled the truck into an underground parking lot and tossed the keys to several faction who were waiting alongside Professor Burwick. Immediately, they unloaded boxes of supplies from the rear of the truck.

"Stealing a ParkNShop truck was not part of the plan," Burwick mused.

"Tai Tam is a Merikh fortress, and also a refuge for Cherub who are fleeing."

"Ones with deep enough pockets and not enough faith, I suppose. What did he tell you?"

"Rumors of a Cherub Elder being held there, and possibly a gateway."

"We have heard nothing about a Cherub Elder, and there are other gateways in Hong Kong. Why would one in Tai Tam be so important?" Burwick's brows furrowed. "We were paying for more than rumors, Eliška. Seems his information was not worth the steep price."

"Will Fargher appeared out of thin air while I met with Ren in Tai Tam." Eliška's gaze hardened as she held up the steel card. "And I am going back to kill him."

19

Jack and Emma recounted what had occurred beneath Lake Brienz, from the hidden passageway within the vault to the ancient Rhoxen longship to a gateway back in time to the Battle of Everest, revealed by Eden's Star. Eleanore listened studiously, but Jack stopped short of explaining how he'd snatched the Rhoxen Stone. He reinforced Slybourne's bravery, the unity of the seven Cherub tribes, and the courage of the pentaloons who saved them from the Nephilim king, Asiklua, and the legion.

"You are saying a gateway took you to the Battle of Everest," Eleanore stated pointedly. "Quite strange considering gateways connect to other realms, but never back in history."

Jack guessed she was right, remembering the first time he used the Zakhar and found himself in the trenches alongside Sir James Nightingale and Sir Alfred Crozier. But that experience wasn't tied to a gateway; it was a vision. And the second time with the Zakhar—when he saw the Elders fracture—was a memory pulled from Eden's Star, not a gateway.

"Could Eden's Star have taken us back in time?" Jack glanced at Emma, then continued when Eleanore remained silent. "Maybe we were brought to Everest to stop Slybourne and the Seven Tribes from being killed, but we were too late."

"Eden's Star brought us to the caves," Emma added. "But we do not know why."

"A skeleton is unearthed," Eleanore observed solemnly. "Flesh and bone will be reborn."

"Skeleton?" Jack asked, confused. "What do you mean?"

"Harley will arrive soon. Best we wait until she is present." Eleanore pulled herself up from the sofa and stacked empty plates and mugs on the tray. "You two are a bit ripe. Perhaps a shower and fresh clothes?"

"Beaut bonza." Emma grabbed her backpack and stood. "Lead the way, Eleanore."

"Words I have not heard in many years," she mused. "Jack, kick up your feet and relax."

While Emma and Eleanore left the room, Jack ran his fingers over his forearm to be sure Soulweaver was still there. He couldn't explain why the rod vanished when they traveled through the gateway or how it returned once they reached the caves. Emma appeared briefly between the living room and a hallway. She mouthed the words *Are you okay?* He nodded in response, even though it was far from the truth.

Eleanore returned and sat across from him. "You seem a bit troubled."

"I'm not sure whether to trust my visions." Jack weighed his words carefully. "As a vision seeker, Addison was strong enough to invade my mom's mind—and she was an Elder. I can't help but wonder if he's alive, then maybe he's been invading mine too."

"You are questioning whether he can alter your visions." Eleanore glanced over her shoulder, then leaned forward. "Visions are difficult to interpret unless there is a foundation of truth. I envisioned what you experienced last night, and clearly there are unanswered questions."

Jack leaned forward as well. "I trust Emma more than anyone."

"Your loyalty is admirable—but is it weak enough to accept the truth?" Eleanore eyed him closely, leaving him even more uncomfortable. "If Addison invaded your mind, then it is possible he altered what you witnessed."

"But he'd have to be free from the Dungeon of Savages."

Eleanore nodded. "Darkness is powerless within the dungeon."

"That's a relief, actually. If the vault flooded, then he either drowned or escaped. I don't know how he would've done it, but if he found a way out, then it's likely he's the one altering my visions—which means he wants me to believe Emma murdered Rachel. Sounds like a lot of ifs, to be sure. But if that's all true, then there's no doubt in my mind that my vision was messed with." Jack leaned back and glanced up at the ceiling. "Emma, Rachel, and Areum were as close as sisters."

"Confusion is an enemy of truth." Eleanore paused. "Harley will be shocked to hear about the dungeon being underwater—and the thought of those within surviving somehow to be free.

Jack, if your father has not altered your vision and died inside the dungeon, then there is a possibility your vision is rooted in truth."

Is she saying Emma murdered Rachel or that my vision was altered? If confusion is the enemy of truth, clarity is the ally. But I'm not going to stop trusting Emma, not until she gives me a reason. One vision isn't going to separate us.

Footsteps and voices echoing in the hallway startled him. Salomeh Gashkori and Professor Burwick entered the living room as if they'd been in the house the entire time. Burwick limped toward Eleanore, then the two sisters embraced warmly and wiped tears from their cheeks.

"Never quite understood why the gateway is in your bedroom closet, Eleanore." Salomeh eyed Jack from head to toe, then shifted her gaze toward his crudely wrapped hands. "Are you and Emma okay?"

"We're fine," he replied, realizing he'd forgotten to toss the bandages. "To be honest, I'm not totally sure what's going on."

"Happens to us all," Burwick noted, with a bit of dark humor. "Frankly, this is the last place we hoped you would end up, but we are grateful both of you are alive and well."

"How is Eliška?" He turned toward Salomeh. "And everyone at Beacon Hill?"

"Eliška is leading the faction," Burwick answered. "Her sights remain on the Merikh."

"We continue to receive Cherub through the House of Luminescence," Salomeh added. "Lightforcers, benders, and healers are growing under Bau's leadership."

Jack's muscles twitched at Bau Hu's name, but he mentally applauded Eliška.

"I'll put on a fresh pot of tea," Eleanore said. "Salomeh, coffee with plenty of sugar?"

"Perfect," she answered. "We will not be staying long."

Eleanore disappeared into the kitchen while Burwick slumped into a chair. Salomeh remained standing with her arms crossed, which left Jack feeling as if he were about to be scolded or punished with detention. He was relieved when Emma entered wearing sweats, draping her damp hair over her shoulders. She found a spot next to Jack and squeezed his thigh. He couldn't help but feel reassured as he noticed her tatted sleeves. She was already a warrior of the Cherub, while he was still trying to figure it all out.

One day when this is over, I'll ask her to share the stories about each tattoo.

"How much has Eleanore told you about Addison?" Burwick asked.

"Enough to know she was part of bringing my parents together," Jack answered. "Along with his ability to control Dragon Soul, toss dark bursts of death, and he's a vision seeker too."

"Eden's Star led us to the Battle of Everest," Emma chimed in. "But we were unable to stop the defeat of Slybourne and the Cherub. Have we altered history?"

"Impossible to know for certain," Burwick admitted. "However, the vault beneath Lake Brienz was flooded, and Cherub remain tight-lipped regarding the Dungeon of Savages."

"Harley, you know as well as I do," Salomeh chimed in, "Fang Xue will not disclose."

"Which means Addison could be free," Emma interrupted. "We made a mistake."

"Eden's Star brought you to Everest . . ." Salomeh turned her attention to Jack. "So, did you find one of the artifacts or not?"

"The Rhoxen Stone," he answered cautiously. "Ryder Slybourne and the seven Cherub tribes were on Everest when the Nephilim king stopped time in the middle of the battle. Asiklua used Soulweaver to kill Slybourne, Dragon Soul vanished in the snow, and the legion slaughtered Cherub and pentaloons."

"We brought the stone back," Emma confessed. "We believe it is one of the artifacts."

Burwick exchanged a quizzical stare with Salomeh. "You are the wisest one."

"Jack refuses to reveal Eden's Star," Salomeh replied. "And continues to disobey the Eternal."

"Remember Slybourne's shield," Emma rebuked. "We trusted you with much, Salomeh."

"Emma, it's okay." Too tired to push back, Jack grabbed his backpack and dug deep inside to retrieve the Nightingale T-shirt. He placed the shirt on the coffee table and unwrapped it carefully. The turquoise gemstone radiated as brilliantly as it had done on Everest, capturing everyone's attention. "We marched with the Rhoxen and fought alongside them."

At the same time, Eleanore rounded the corner with a tray filled with tea, coffee, and more muffins. Her eyes caught sight of the gemstone, and she dropped the tray.

On reflex, Jack picked up the stone. Everyone and everything froze. Tea, coffee, and muffins spilled in midair yet hovered in defiance of gravity. He stood up and grabbed each mug, scooping the liquid back into them one at a time. Then he grabbed several muffins, walked over to Burwick and Salomeh, and placed one in each of their hands. Casually, he took the tray from Eleanore and placed it on the coffee table. Only then did he set the Rhoxen Stone down.

In disbelief, Burwick and Salomeh stared at the muffins in their hands. Eleanore looked around, wondering where the tea, coffee, and muffins had disappeared to, while Emma stared at the tray on the coffee table undisturbed. Jack grinned sheepishly as everyone realized what he had done.

"A legend lost in the history books," Burwick said in disbelief. "A gift given by Elyon to protect the Rhoxen in the world of man."

"Yet powerless in another realm," Salomeh added, "and against the evil that lurks in those realms."

"Now we know it's one of the artifacts," Jack interrupted. "The question is, why are we here in Eleanore's house?"

Tears welled up in Eleanore's eyes. "You both have protected me long enough."

Burwick set the muffin down and exhaled long. "Eleanore is more than a vision seeker."

"She is a gateway creator," Salomeh finished. "One of the best I have ever seen."

"The Merikh's ability to travel through gateways has not always been possible."

"I am the one who defied the commands of Elyon," Eleanore confessed. "And corrupted the gateways so Merikh could travel through them with a blood sacrifice."

"Eleanore, you are not the same person you were then," Salomeh reassured.

"She is the only one who can create a gateway to the nether realm," Burwick admitted.

"Why didn't you tell us this before?" Jack asked, angered. "That's where we need to go."

"A gateway to the nether realm requires an ability to embrace darkness," Eleanore explained. "Addison seduced me to believe what remained hidden in the nether realm would protect all others from the wickedness of the Merikh. He was charismatic and quite convincing. Gabriella believed he was sincere too—after all, the Elders trusted him with Dragon Soul."

"Your father and mother traveled through a gateway to the nether realm," Burwick picked up where Eleanore left off. "When they returned, both were on the verge of death—but they brought with them one of the artifacts."

"Which Addison stole," Salomeh chimed in. "Only he knows where it is hidden."

"The most dangerous artifact was left behind," Eleanore interrupted. "Unspoken."

"'I have seen a beast swallowed by darkness,'" Jack recited, "'slumbering amidst wild waves of the sea and wandering stars in the skies. Light must never be brought into this realm.'"

Burwick shook her head. "We cannot help you enter the nether realm."

"Eden's Star brought us here"—Jack stared at Eleanore—"to create or find a gateway."

"Emma, your powers may not protect either of you," Salomeh warned.

"Without any of the Cherub gifts," Burwick said pointedly to Jack, "you will surely die."

"I'm dying already, Professor."

20

"WHAT ARE YOU TWO KEEPING TO YOURSELVES?"

"Doesn't matter." Jack avoided answering Professor Burwick's stern question. "Point is, we're running out of time. I've got Eden's Star, Soulweaver, the Rhoxen Stone, and Emma—I'd say there's no better opportunity to go beyond the Highlands."

Jack grabbed his backpack and removed the slim wooden box from his hoodie. He unrolled the parchment and set the carved figurine of a woman wrapped in serpents aside, displaying a map of the Highlands in front of them. "Salomeh has seen this already, and now you'll see it too." He flipped the parchment over to reveal scripted ink, and the invisible line revealed itself—the same words he'd recited moments earlier. "Rachel kept this hidden since we were young. I don't know where she got it or what she planned to do with it. What I do know is my mom traveled to the nether realm for a reason, and I'll bet Rachel wasn't far behind once she started searching for Eden's Star. I'm not stopping, no matter what's beyond."

Burwick and Eleanore stared at the scripted message until it vanished. Jack knew he was taking a risk showing it to them, but he needed them to understand there was no turning back.

"Salomeh, when were you going to tell me?" Burwick kept her gaze fixed on the figurine and map. "Our alliance relies on full disclosure."

"Full disclosure, Jack trusted me with Slybourne's shield," Salomeh admitted with a touch of sarcasm. "No one fully understands the evil which lies beyond our knowledge of the Cherub ways and the artifacts which are commanded by Elyon to remain hidden. Before we go any further, we need to study the ancient writings kept by the Elders within the Sanctum of Serenity."

"Will is going to use Dragon Soul and the Windstrikers to charge his way into the nether realm," Jack argued. "He's not reading ancient writings, weighing the risks, or reminiscing about the past. He's keeping Xui Li alive for one reason—to find a gateway that leads him there. She won't stay that way if he gets what he wants. I know him better than anyone—being first is all that matters to him."

"We do not know whether Xui Li is still alive after Shek Pik," Salomeh pointed out. "However, she did believe there was once a gateway to the nether realm hidden in Sakkhela."

"Which is one of the reasons she came to you for help," Emma surmised.

Burwick nodded. "She was searching for another way."

"As promised, Eleanore's transgressions were kept between us."
Salomeh's gaze shifted between Burwick and Eleanore. "Gabriella's
words are a warning to us all—one we cannot ignore. We must
know for certain whether the prophecy is true. Clarity determines
our path."

"Gabriella and Addison refused to show me the artifact they
found." All eyes turned toward Eleanore, who cleared her throat.
"But I remember seeing the figurine in their possession."

"My mom traveled to the nether realm," Jack debated. "That's
where I'm going."

"What artifact did she find with Addison?" Burwick asked.
"What was left behind?"

"I have told you before, I do not know." Eleanore's hands shook
and her lips quivered. "I swear, Harley."

Jack turned his frustration toward Eleanore. "Can you create
another gateway?"

"My soul no longer lives in darkness." She glanced between
Burwick and Salomeh, as if searching for a way out of the inter-
rogation. "I will not create a gateway unless the world is on the
verge of its last breath."

"You are asking her to betray Elyon," Emma said to Jack. "We
will find another way."

"This is the way," Jack protested. "But everyone is too afraid
to do it."

He pushed himself off the sofa and stormed out of the house
to the walled front yard. With the curtains opened, he knew they
were watching him from inside. He paced back and forth, attempting to decide what to do. He ripped the bandages from his hands
and tossed the cloth onto the grass. Emma stepped outside and
stood behind him as he spun around.

"We don't need to listen to them," he blurted. "We've made it this far on our own."

Emma held up her hand. "Take a moment and breathe, Jack."

"Don't gauge my emotions—too much is at stake to worry about my feelings."

"Everyone here realizes what we are facing." Emma took a step closer. "We need to consider their wisdom—they have been in this fight longer than either of us."

"What else is in the prophecy? You're the chosen one, and I'm the Protector. Period."

"The prophecy remains hotly debated between Cherub and faction. Salomeh is questioning who is the rightful Cherub leader. It is possible I am not the one, or Bau either."

"I could save us all a lot of time—Bau is not the one." Jack wanted to unleash a curse-driven tirade, but in his weakness he tried to trust Elyon. "Emma, it won't matter who the leader is if the Merikh and Will get to the nether realm first and find the artifact. And now we're pretty certain Addison is loose and messing with my mind, so there's no doubt what he'll be after."

"Protecting everyone requires trust." Emma hesitated. "We should go to the Sanctum of Serenity and bring the writings to Salomeh—and leave the Rhoxen Stone with Burwick."

"Cherub and faction would have one artifact each." Jack weighed the situation, unsure of whether either would hold up their end. "Eliška needs to know what we're doing."

"Fang Xue and the highest Cherub will not look kindly on such an act."

"Burwick and Salomeh have to agree to the same promise they've kept for Eleanore." Jack calmed down a bit, even though his frustration itched beneath his skin. "Okay, let's do it."

When they entered the house, he noticed how all three were still staring at the map, figurine, and the Rhoxen Stone. He picked up the figurine and carefully rolled up the map, then slipped it into his hoodie pocket. With all eyes fixed on him, he grabbed the Rhoxen Stone and wrapped it in the Nightingale shirt.

"Sorry . . ." he mumbled. "We'll go to the Sanctum of Serenity."

"Thank you, Jack." Salomeh's stare remained steadfast. "What about the Rhoxen Stone?"

"The professor will protect the stone, in the same way you are protecting the shield."

"Sounds fair," Burwick agreed. "Discretion between us is critical—to protect Jack."

Emma nodded. "Eliška needs to know where you will keep the stone."

"Never imagined the two of you would get on so well."

"We are doing what is necessary to win this war." Emma reached into her pocket and retrieved several silver coins. "She will need these if she is hunting Merikh."

Burwick reached out and took the coins. "You have my word."

"Our strange alliance continues," Salomeh chimed in. "We will meet at Dragon's Back."

"Jack . . . Emma . . ." Burwick said sincerely. "I would appreciate—"

"'Forgiveness is for all who seek,'" Emma recited from the Eternal. "'None higher than another.'"

Tears welled up in Eleanore's eyes. "I am truly sorry for what I have done."

21

Rooftop access offered a clear view of the surrounding neighborhood on San Martin Road. Each residence was protected by glass shards embedded in the tops of colorful concrete walls. Jack breathed in the morning air and exhaled a heaviness, which lingered from earlier. He'd slipped out of the living room and found an unlocked door on the second floor that led to the roof. Memories from nights lounging with Will, Vince, and Tim on Nightingale's rooftop struck—buried since he dropped a white rose on Rachel's muddied grave in Sitio Veterans.

Eleanore's a gateway creator who figured out how the Merikh could travel with blood sacrifices—and she created a gateway to the nether realm. Definitely more than a vision seeker. After all these years she's still carrying the weight. Is she really forgiven? he questioned Elyon.

A response resonated in his spirit. *All have fallen short, every last one. Yet all who seek forgiveness find redemption. One must choose in a matter of the heart.*

At that moment, Professor Burwick emerged onto the rooftop. Jack weighed his words before speaking to her. "To find redemption means asking Elyon's forgiveness." It was hard to accept that his past could be wiped clean. "I understand surrendering my heart is more important than anything else—but what if I'm not totally ready? I can't let go until I make it right. So, does that mean there's no redemption for me?"

"Matters of the heart are greater than troubles of the mind," Burwick replied. "Sometimes, redemption requires us to forgive ourselves and others, no matter how far we have fallen."

Jack wanted to fulfill Rachel's promise more than anything. He wanted to protect those who were being hunted by the Merikh, and even after all Will had done, there was a part of him that wanted to save his best friend—as crazy as that sounded. Still, vengeance remained rooted against Addison—and Eleanore wasn't without blame. *Who am I to judge anyone? I've failed more than most, but Elyon has chosen me in my weakness. I don't know how to let go of wanting to even the score for all who have suffered, especially those who lost their lives because of me.* A wave of guilt crashed over him as he thought of how he was responsible for flooding the Dungeon of Savages and possibly freeing the evil imprisoned within. No denying there was blood on his hands from the deaths of others.

"If Addison is free," Jack mumbled, "it's because of me."

Burwick leaned slightly to one side. "Difficult decisions all around."

Jack turned toward Burwick with his hands dug into his pockets. "Why didn't you tell me about Eleanore and my parents?"

"We share a common purpose to protect those we love." Burwick grew quiet for a moment. "I am sorry you have been unfairly caught between sins of the past and the present."

He broke eye contact, suddenly uncomfortable. "Mom didn't realize who he'd become."

"Love has a way of blinding us to the shortfalls of others." Burwick limped a bit closer. "But she realized soon enough she should leave the box with Rachel." She noticed his brows raise. "Natalie told me about the night she went with you to Sham Shui Po."

"I've wondered why Rachel never returned to get it," Jack said solemnly. "Professor, do you think we'll find the rest of the artifacts before Will and the Merikh?"

"We are in a race against time, no doubt." Burwick held up the Rhoxen Stone wrapped in the Nightingale shirt as her gaze hardened. "And we will fight with what we've been given."

He mustered up the nerve to ask, "How bad is it in Hong Kong?"

"Millions are trapped in a powder keg—one strike of a match and the city will explode." Burwick eyed him closely, and he sensed she wanted to say more. "Eliška is leading the faction like a ballerina balancing with one toe on a pointed knife. She has seen Will in Tai Tam, and there are rumors a gateway exists within the district. Eliška plans to bring justice for the faction and Cherub."

"Will's powers are brutal." Jack nodded at the covered turquoise gemstone, wondering where a gateway in Tai Tam might lead. *Keep your sights on the nether realm, Jack.* "She'll need every advantage against him, so she should use the Rhoxen Stone."

"Thank you for trusting me, Jack—and Eliška, of course."

"I had another vision." Jack hesitated, determining how much to share. "I was in Sitio Veterans on the night Rachel was murdered. Chung was chasing her through the shantytown, but she had the upper hand and brought him to his knees. She was way more powerful, and she offered him a chance." He swallowed hard, rage surging beneath his skin. "A shadow appeared with no visible lightforce. With a swipe of a hand Rachel fell to the ground—she was already dead before Chung shot her near the river."

Burwick's gaze narrowed. "Perhaps Rachel was killed by a dark force from beyond."

"Professor, the shadow was Emma—but I don't believe it's true."

"Visions require perspective rooted in truth, and at times interpretation."

"Maybe Addison is messing with my mind, or maybe—"

"Vision seekers are rare." Burwick's shoulders slouched. "Your father was one of the strongest Eleanore had ever encountered."

"Are you sure you don't have supernatural gifts like your sister?"

"You and I have that in common. No supernatural fireworks, only stubborn determination."

"Has Eleanore ever told you where the gateway she created to the nether realm is?"

"Never." Burwick exhaled heavily. "Back then, she was young and under his spell."

A piece of Jack wanted to debate the professor, to question Eleanore's betrayal. But he knew better than to peer through a narrow lens. *She created the gateway, but Mom and Addison wanted to travel to the nether realm. All three made a choice—and I won't know whether it was the right one until I go there myself.* Voices snapped him out of his thoughts as Salomeh and Emma stepped onto the rooftop.

"Harley," Salomeh called out. "Headmaster Fargher needs me at Beacon Hill."

"You are my ride," Burwick mused. "Eleanore will not be pleased with a short visit."

Emma chimed in, "Amina is quite insistent."

"Refugees from Myanmar are ill," Salomeh clarified. "Requires an experienced healer."

"Better get the chief healer back to school." Burwick turned her attention toward Jack. "You know where to find the faction when you need us."

Jack stared at Burwick as she crossed the rooftop with her slight limp. He waited until she joined Salomeh near the stairwell before he blurted, "Professor . . ."

Burwick turned and faced him. "Yes, Jack."

"I would've done the same."

22

CURLED UP ON A BED EXHAUSTED, Jack fell into a deep sleep. No visions, only pitch-blackness. Ninety minutes later he blinked, and for a few seconds he thought he was back in the hostel in Karachi. During those weeks hiding from the Merikh and Cherub, his body was beyond broken and his faith was shattered. He rolled off the bed and stretched his aching muscles, grateful his body and his spirit were stronger.

Some days I feel closer to Elyon than others. Hope this is one of those days.

The door cracked open, and Emma poked her head in. "Ready to leave?"

"I've never been ready for any of this," he mused darkly. "But that hasn't stopped us."

"Gateways are never an end point, only a passage between. We must travel through more than one gateway beyond this place."

"Where does the gateway in the house lead?"

"Dragon's Back and Sanctuary of Prayer."

"Gateways go to more than one place?"

"Not all, but some." Emma opened the door wide. "Eleanore is waiting to take us."

Jack followed Emma down the hallway into the living room and grabbed their backpacks. Both followed Eleanore into the front yard, where the gate was already open. He slipped into the back seat of a four-door sedan and stayed quiet while Emma climbed into the front passenger side. Eleanore glanced in the rearview before turning the ignition. The whining engine cut through an awkward silence. Once the sedan rolled onto the street, the gate automatically closed behind them.

What am I supposed to say to Eleanore? You're the reason why my family is shattered? That's not fair, Jack. She could say the same about you.

A few miles from San Martin Road the sedan pulled over outside of Masay Pizza. Eleanore kept her gaze ahead while Emma climbed out and Jack did the same. No goodbyes. Jack inhaled a fragrant aroma as they entered the restaurant. Mozzarella. *Napoletana.* Ticino style. Fresh-baked pizzas were spread out in a packed dining area where locals enjoyed a midafternoon lunch.

"Wasn't expecting a gateway to the Sanctum of Serenity in a raucous pizza joint," he said under his breath. "Seems random, and less Cheruby highbrow."

"Eleanore created this one for herself." Emma cut between tables toward an open kitchen where brick ovens fired at nine hundred degrees. No one paid them any attention as Emma stopped in front of a walk-in freezer. "Salomeh and Professor Burwick warned of blocked gateways."

Jack's brows raised. "Same problem we experienced in Manaus."

"I suppose Eleanore created the gateway in case she needed to disappear from the Merikh who searched for access to the nether realm." Emma unlatched a metal door and entered a subzero space. "Will is hunting for answers, and most likely he is still searching for you."

"He's after Eden's Star." Jack glanced over his shoulder, then entered. "Will doesn't care about me—or you. Not anymore."

Emma's lips curled as she retrieved silver coins and handed one over. Surrounded by frozen fish, rib eye, sausage, ham, dough, and veggies, Jack didn't hesitate to drop his coin on the floor. *Any mention of Will is still a sore subject. Doesn't she see? He'll never be the same. None of us will, actually.* Ice formed quickly on the walls and crept rapidly across the concrete floor. Jack grabbed Emma's hand and squeezed to reassure her they were on the same side. His bones shivered as the temperature plummeted, leaving him unsure of how the gateway was going to pull them through. Ice crept up his legs and covered his waist, then his chest. Condensation dripped from the ceiling. He gasped as the ice shattered into pieces.

In the blink of an eye, grayish clouds loomed over windswept moors and rolling hills. A century-old castle and quaint village stretched across the countryside—which reminded him of Sakkhela. Nearby, a vintage Mini drove along a one-lane road. *We're definitely still in this world, unless Slybourne beat Alec Issigonis and John Sheppard. I'd take Sahil any day over a Mini.* A brisk walk through a lush green valley brought them to weathered brick homes, cobblestoned streets, and an English oak–framed church in the village center.

BATTLE OF LION ROCK

"Professor Burwick and Eleanore grew up in this village with their sister and parents." Emma turned the knob, and the door creaked open. "Her gateway to escape was a passage to return home."

Inside, wooden pews were lined in perfect rows and cobwebbed windows cast a dull light across the dusty floor. At the front of the sanctuary was a simple podium.

"Doesn't look like anyone's been here in a while," Jack noted.

"Salomeh told me that a few years ago the church closed after the Burwicks' parents passed—their mum died only three months after their father. I met them once at the Sanctuary of Prayer with Mum and Dad. I did not know who they were at the time since they are older."

Jack eyed the empty chapel, knowing a fight waited beyond. "Burwick is a believer, but she's not a blind follower of Fang Xue or the highest Cherub. From what I've seen, the Cherub are hiding as many secrets as the Merikh—which makes it impossible to know who to trust."

"We are only halfway." Emma grabbed hold of the podium. "The Elders created this gateway to be unique. No coins this time. Only those with gifts gain access."

Jack's heart pounded faster. "Emma, I don't have any Cherub gifts."

"My gifts are strong enough." Emma's eyes turned bone white and her palms radiated, leaving Jack's adrenaline surging. "Hold fast, Jack."

He grabbed hold of the podium as the lightforce intensified, his body levitating along with Emma's. Amid blinding flashes, the village chapel evaporated, transporting them to the base of a rocky mountain in a barren desert. A scorching heat rushed over him and triggered instantaneous dehydration, leaving his throat bone dry. He gazed up and realized a tiered monastery was camouflaged as an extension of the desert. A fortress hidden in plain sight with glassless windows, jagged walls, and an air of history lost.

"Sanctum of Serenity." Emma exhaled reverently. "Built by the Elders of old during a century of peace, nearly destroyed in the Age of Trepidation, and where the highest Cherub penned the Mercy Covenant by the power of Elyon to bring an end to the Second Great War."

"Definitely isn't Charis, though." He stared intently at the ancient monastery, devoid of lush beauty, and a twinge of uneasiness tingled down his spine. "Hopefully we're not about to start the Third Great War."

Emma pointed upward. "Salomeh told me where to search."

"Let's get out of this sauna before we're roasted like Peking duck."

Halfway up the rocky clay hillside was an entrance to the Sanctum of Serenity that led to a tight passageway deeper into the heart of the mountain. Ancient writings were scripted on the walls, none of which Jack understood. Emma used her lightforce to illuminate the route ahead, showing an open square where stairs were formed into the stone on all sides—each leading to a different passage.

"Which one do we take?" Jack asked.

Voices echoed within the monastery. Jack and Emma ducked behind clay statues of a pentaloon with wings widespread and a timber wolf in mid-howl. Crouched low, Jack held his breath as someone appeared at the top of one of the staircases—someone he recognized.

Bau.

23

JACK'S HEARTBEAT QUICKENED once he realized others were inside the Sanctum of Serenity. He watched Bau step back from the edge of the stairs out of sight. Soulweaver slipped from his forearm but remained shortened in his grasp. When Bau reappeared, their eyes locked for a few seconds. The night in the alley on Hong Kong Island when he stood face-to-face with Bau seemed like an eternity ago. Back then, he was convinced Bau was an enemy, but now Bau was the anointed Cherub leader. It seemed he had traveled alone to the sanctum through another gateway.

Bau is still a muppet.

A voice interrupted the words ringing in his ears as he fought the urge to leave. His grip on Soulweaver tightened, knowing Bau was on his guard for a reason. *Emma and Bau are the last of the chosen, and neither is confronting whoever else is in the sanctum.* A chill shot down his spine as Will and armed Merikh entered the chamber from another passageway. Broad-shouldered and dressed in rich dark violet, Will forced a bound Chinese woman to the ground.

"Stop playing games!" Will seethed as he stood over her bony body. "Elders are forbidden to lie, but all you have done for months is spew riddles."

She's still alive—and this is our only shot.

"I have brought you to what you seek within the sanctum." Xui Li's sunken face had aged, yet her dark-brown eyes peered at her captor with a youthful intensity. "You hold the answers—you need only open your eyes to the truth."

"My patience is over." Will slipped Dragon Soul from the scabbard and pointed the blade against her neck. "Only one weapon is powerful enough to silence an Elder."

"You have stolen far more lives." Xui Li paused. "I am not afraid to die."

"Two Elders and counting," Will taunted. "And you will be the last."

"He's going to kill her," Jack whispered to Emma. "We have to stop him."

Emma squeezed his shoulder, but her gaze remained fixed on Will. Jack knew she was gauging more than one person's emotions, but if Will snapped, then it was game on. *Four Elders are dead— Charlotte, Peter, Mom, and . . . Dabria.* His gaze shifted between Emma, Bau, and Will—determined he wasn't going to allow Xui Li to suffer the same fate.

"You do not know the dangers you have invited into your soul." Xui Li's gaze hardened, defiant. "Without Addison to guide you, you are uncertain how to protect your power. If you turn back to Elyon, then I can help you find your way."

"The Dungeon of Savages is destroyed," Will rebuked. "Addison is dead."

"Great evil remains a danger in this world and the other realms," Xui Li warned. "I have brought you to the prophecy; now it is up to you whether you choose to accept its meaning."

"Words written centuries ago are no longer relevant." Will lifted the blade away from her neck as black flames wrapped around it. He held up a scrolled parchment as if he were raising the Battle of Bashers, Bowlers, and Boundaries trophy. "I will ask one last time—where is the gateway to the nether realm?"

"The prophecy and the Eternal are unwavering. I will never reveal the gateway to a realm where the wickedest of darkness remains chained."

Will's fiery glare flared as he raised Dragon Soul. "Enough!"

If I'm going to save Xui Li, then I've got to do it now. Move, Jack.

Soulweaver extended in his grasp as he lunged forward with the rod humming and spinning. Bau stepped out from his hiding place with palms glowing a brilliant auburn and leapt from the top stair, landing beside Jack while unleashing bursts of lightforce against the assassins. Streaks of white light punched several Merikh in the chest as gunfire erupted. Soulweaver deflected each bullet as Jack charged forward. Emma moved quickly across the chamber—her lightforce and bender powers were relentless as Merikh flew through the air.

Within a matter of seconds, Merikh assassins were down. Will grabbed Xui Li and pulled her close, using the Elder as a shield. The black flames surrounding Dragon Soul morphed into a two-headed dragon. Jack had seen the beast before, and he recognized the empty stare in Will's eyes. Bau and Emma took a few steps forward, both lightforces radiant. Jack stopped Soulweaver from spinning and pointed the rod at Will.

"Let her go," he demanded. "Three against one, and this time no one is running."

Will ignored him and smirked wryly at Bau. "I'll bet you'd like the sword back."

"You stole what never belonged to you," Bau replied, stone-cold. "Jack is right."

Will gripped Dragon Soul tight and kept Xui Li in front. "I control the beast."

"Spilled blood is not the answer." Emma lowered her hands. "Please . . ."

"In the end"—Will's gaze shifted between them—"no one will be spared."

"Release the Elder and surrender," Bau ordered. "Judgment stands before you."

Jack noticed the corner of Will's lips curl, knowing surrender wasn't in his nature. Soulweaver hummed as energy flowed through the rod into his fingers and rushed like the roaring rapids that destroyed the Rhoxen longship. *We can't let him disappear—we may never get another chance.* Xui Li lifted her head and nodded ever so slightly. *Control the rod, Jack. And don't kill the Elder.* A quick stab of the rod and energy rippled through the air before knocking Xui Li and Will backward. It wasn't enough to put them on their backs, but it created a slight separation. Emma reacted with a swipe of her hand, sending Xui Li gliding across the floor in the opposite direction.

Will stood wide-eyed as ebony smoke poured out from the scrolled parchment, engulfing the two-headed dragon flowing from Dragon Soul. Ear-piercing shrieks shuddered the chamber as pitch-blackness blinded everyone. Jack spun around in the dark, sensing silhouettes whipping past. *Legion.* He stabbed the point of

Soulweaver into the floor and a white light exploded, leaving him tumbling across the room. A ringing in his ears intensified and his vision blurred, everything around him moving in slow motion. As quickly as the darkness lifted, the chamber returned to peace and calm. He scrambled to his feet, realizing Emma and Bau were a few steps ahead—all three racing toward Xui Li, who was motionless.

"Is she alive?" Jack blurted, trying to catch his breath.

Emma reached down and grabbed the Elder's wrist, then looked up. "Yes."

"Who is she?" Bau asked point-blank.

"Xui Li—one of the Elders."

Relieved, tears welled up in Jack's eyes on the verge of spilling over. He turned away for a moment to gather himself. His heart overflowed with gratefulness, but he wasn't going to show any sign of weakness in front of Bau. Seconds passed as Xui Li remained unconscious.

"Did he jump another gateway?" Jack asked.

"I do not think so." Bau shook his head. "Another presence entered the chamber."

Emma remained by Xui Li's side. "Bau is right—evil was in the sanctum."

"We should leave." Bau knelt and slipped his arms beneath Xui Li's frail body. "She will need Professor Windsor and the healers."

"Did you know Emma is a healer?" Jack asked.

"She never mentioned it to me." Bau shook his head. "A gateway back is upstairs."

"Best we return to Beacon Hill," Emma agreed. "Too dangerous to stabilize her here."

Jack and Emma followed Bau as he carried Xui Li up the stairs and down a long corridor. Emma reached in her pocket and counted out three silver coins. Jack noticed there were not many left in her palm before she slipped the coins back in her pocket.

How many more gateways before the offerings run out?

"What were you doing here?" Jack asked Bau.

"Fang Xue sent me to retrieve the prophecy," he replied. "And you?"

"Salomeh asked me to do the same." Emma glanced up at him. "Quick thinking, Jack."

"I carry a big stick." He held up Soulweaver, a bit too proud. "Power of the rod, I guess."

"You two have been gone for months," Bau interrupted. "How many have you found?"

"We've got Soulweaver—sorry, the Rod of Elyon—and two others." Jack knew he was playing coy, but he still didn't trust Bau. "Will has the Windstrikers, so there are three left. We believe one of the artifacts is in the nether realm."

"The Eternal is clear: the artifacts are not to be used as weapons, and the nether realm is off-limits to all." Bau stopped at the end of the corridor and entered an empty room. "Emma, you failed to return the artifacts to the Cherub. You have Jack—an outlier—swinging the Rod of Elyon around as if he were the prophet Kaeso. How can I trust you?"

"Salomeh and Fang Xue both wanted the prophecy," Jack interrupted. "Why?"

"After the Dungeon of Savages flooded, Fang Xue sent me to the sanctum to retrieve the ancient writings." Bau hesitated. "Vault and dungeon are totally destroyed."

"Is Addison really dead?" Emma asked.

"He is missing—but he is not the only one."

24

A myriad of colors emanated from within the House of Luminescence—a spectrum of Elyon's creation. Vaulted wood beams were partially covered by thick vines that crept down the walls. Everything seemed to be thicker, stronger, and fuller. Jack breathed easier as he stepped over the vines and walked across copper-colored stone.

"I'll take Xui Li to Windsor," Bau said as he nudged past. "Then we need to talk."

Jack stopped in front of the Mercy Covenant. Eight candles were set on a wooden table covered with an indigo velvet cloth. *I've got so many questions to ask Xui Li about what is going on. And I'm definitely asking about Eliška.* He gazed at the scripted writing, seven emblems of the Cherub, and the Merikh's crimson dragon. *Crazy to think we were just in the Sanctum of Serenity where the covenant was written. Not much serenity, though. How were the legion able to cross over into this world? Where did Will disappear to now? What will he do with the prophecy?* He read the words and wondered whether such a covenant would ever exist again.

Foedus Misericordiae obligat Septem Tribum Cherub et Merikh.

"The Covenant of Mercy binds the Seven Tribes of Cherub and the Merikh." Emma translated the Latin script easily. "All who swear an oath to Elyon, the Lord of heaven, Creator of Eden's Star, Ruler of the earth and other realms, must abide by the Mercy Covenant. They must pass no judgment against the Merikh's free will on earth as long as no Cherub is killed by Merikh, allowing light and darkness to exist in enmity without death or wrath of Elyon."

"Areum once told me the conflict between my parents left many fearing a war between light and dark." Jack's shoulders slouched as he crossed his arms. "She said I was chosen to honor a covenant which has kept peace between enemies for years. But I can't help but wonder if that's possible now."

"You are the Protector of Eden's Star," Emma pointed out. "And Soulweaver."

"How do I honor a broken covenant?" Jack weighed his own question as he read the covenant again. "Pass no judgment . . . as long as no Cherub is killed."

Emma wrapped her arm around his waist. "We are still in the fight, Jack."

"Broken or not, I'm going to honor the covenant." He turned from the Mercy Covenant and shuffled toward the oak door. "And use every artifact we find to do it."

Jack and Emma climbed the basement stairs of the Main Hall without fanfare. Teenagers of all nationalities passed them in the corridor, none of whom he recognized. He noticed classrooms packed with bunk beds, and the trophy case covered in cobwebs and dust. No one seemed to care about trophies anymore.

"I shouldn't be surprised," he mused, "that you and Amina both know Latin."

"Barely." Emma smiled. "She is much more proficient."

"I'm barely able to speak English, let alone another language." Jack and Emma reached the second floor and passed Rowell Library. "What else do you think is in the prophecy?"

"Hopefully we will find answers when Xui Li wakes."

"We don't know how long that will be, Emma."

Babies crying and wailing disturbed the patient wing of Crozier Hospital. Jack remembered the last time when dozens of injured Cherub and captives rescued from Shek Pik Prison occupied the rows of beds. He wasn't prepared for a drastically different scene. Mothers with newborns. Bau waved them through, and they followed him down a hallway into a white-walled room filled with state-of-the-art equipment.

Professor Windsor glanced up and peered over her frames. "Either of you injured?"

"Still in one piece," Jack answered. "How about Xui Li?"

"She has suffered severe internal trauma." Windsor used a syringe to inject Xui Li's forearm. "I don't suppose you three will explain why that is so."

"She is one of the Elders," Emma replied. "We rescued her from the Merikh."

"Healers will be here shortly." Windsor nodded at Jack. "I want to run some tests."

"Please let the others know we have returned," Emma said to Bau. "Thank you."

Jack waited quietly until Bau was gone. "Professor—"

"Do as she asks," Emma said sternly. "We need to know for certain."

"Frankly, I am surprised you are still breathing," Windsor added. "Next door."

Jack shuffled his feet between Windsor and Emma, knowing any attempt to avoid a full body scan was out of the question. All three entered an empty exam room, and Windsor closed the door. She grabbed a tablet from a metal counter and swiped across the screen.

"Shirt off—please." Windsor looked over at Jack. "No need to be shy."

Jack reluctantly unzipped his hoodie, then removed his shirt. He didn't need to look in a mirror to see the crude scars on his arms and chest, partially healed cuts on his hands, or the bruises covering his body. Emma stood in a corner and watched him closely as he sat on the edge of a gurney. His cheeks flushed the longer he waited for Windsor to begin.

"The night you brought Tim from Aberdeen, you were in a rough state." Windsor eyed his wounds, and her gaze grew somber. "Seems you have not fared much better since."

"You wanted to run more tests back then," he mumbled.

"Wounds from Dragon Soul are considered a death sentence." Windsor's gaze narrowed. "Truth be told, I was certain your chances of surviving were no better than Tim's."

"I wish it had been me." Jack swallowed hard. "He deserved a better friend."

"Death cannot separate the bond of true friendships, especially those who honor one another." Windsor grabbed a CT wand and Jack noticed her shaking hands before she steadied them. "Breathe in and out, and hold as still as possible."

He froze on the gurney and tried to slow his racing heartbeat. Windsor studied the tablet screen as she methodically guided the CT wand over his upper body. She set the CT wand down and her brows furrowed as she stared intently at the results. He sensed she knew his secret, but recognizing the concern in her gaze left him wrestling with an inevitable truth.

"Results of your physical exam last year were normal." Windsor turned the tablet around and showed him a hologram of internal organs. She tapped on the screen and the hologram revealed a pulsing white glow covering his organs and flowing through his ventricular system. "Every organ is affected, venous system impacted, and cerebral ventricular system infiltrated. In plain English, your entire body is being taken over by this abnormality. However, I cannot provide a medical explanation." Windsor peered over her frames at Emma, then fixed her gaze on him. "I suppose you two know about the severity already."

"How long do I have left?" Jack asked.

"The sands of time are escaping through your fingers."

25

ON THE SECOND FLOOR of the Main Hall, the exam room offered a bird's-eye view of the northern side of the grounds. Beyond the stone walls, barricades monitored by HKPF and Merikh remained on the road leading to Beacon Hill. Even after months had passed, a stalemate continued to keep Cherub refugees confined and Merikh from attacking the school.

"If you want to talk . . ." Emma began.

"I won't lie, I'm afraid to die—but I made a promise." With his back to Emma, Jack pulled his shirt over his shoulders and slipped into his hoodie to cover his scarred arms—and Soulweaver. Through the window he watched teenage lightforcers and benders on the cricket field being taught by legends of the Cherub— Salomeh Gashkori, Jin Qiaolian, and Aki Katsuo. "An ounce of courage is stronger than an ocean of fear."

Knock. Knock.

Amina opened the door and smiled wide. "You two are a perfect sight."

"Feels good to be back in one piece." Emma sighed. "Where did Bau go off to then?"

"He left to meet with the highest Cherub, but Headmaster Fargher, McDougall, Natalie, and others are meeting in Rowell Library."

Jack caught a boulder in his throat, unable to find the right words. He wanted to beg forgiveness for leaving Amina the night Tim died—and ask her to take him to Elis and Beca Lloyd so he could wrap his arms around them. He wanted to thank her for monitoring Messagezilla and deciphering the message. He wanted to reassure her that Tim's death and the sacrifices she'd made were for a greater purpose. Instead, he stood speechless.

Amina tilted her head as if attempting to read his thoughts. Then she stepped forward and hugged him tight. His mind flashed to the night her earsplitting scream tore through his soul.

"We will see him again one day," she whispered, then stepped back wiping tears from her cheeks. "Your dorm in Nightingale is all fixed up, so you can—"

"I was thinking about another spot—the clock tower."

"Oh . . . okay . . . I will see what I can do."

"Thank you, Amina."

Jack forced a smile as a rush of shame crashed in his depths, where no one else was allowed. He grabbed his backpack and stepped past Amina into the hallway. Maybe it was nostalgia since Nightingale started the original Beacon Hill as a rooftop school. Maybe it was a reminder of the night he walked the planks with Areum in Wan Chai—the night destiny collided with a promise.

Maybe he believed the clock tower was a safe refuge—a place to hide from everyone else. Whatever it was, the clock was counting down.

A few minutes later all three entered Rowell Library and stood near the back. Jack remembered the boarded-up windows and thousands of books on the shelves. But he hadn't anticipated opened crates stacked on one side. *Are these from Nightingale's vault? What did they find inside?* Headmaster Fargher and Professor McDougall taped hand-drawn maps onto whiteboards as a group gathered around, most of whom he didn't recognize.

"We have found more tunnels beneath the barracks." Fargher paced in front of the maps and pointed at each district. "Bau has confirmed the gateways remain unpredictable and dangerous. Traveling through the tunnels allows us to stay clear of the Merikh and HKPF."

"Our network reaches Sai Kung, Sha Tin, Sham Shui Po, Wong Tai Sin, Kwun Tong, and Yau Ma Tei," Natalie interjected as she stepped alongside the whiteboard. "Oliver and Winnie Bennett have established contact from Yau Ma Tei, so Faizan will lead delivery tonight."

"Priority remains to safely distribute food, water, and supplies," McDougall added.

Jack remembered stacks of maps on Fargher's desk in the headmaster's office, and he guessed those were the ones that revealed underground passageways abandoned since the Battle of Hong Kong. *Maybe they found more maps in the crates too.* He leaned over to Amina and asked, "What happened to building an army to fight the Merikh?"

"Bau abandoned the idea weeks ago," Amina replied. "He has been absent quite often."

Jack turned and leaned in close to Emma. "Why didn't you tell me about your parents?"

"Mum and Dad refused to stand by and do nothing," she said in a lowered voice.

"I thought the Cherub were ready to fight," Jack said, confused.

"Will is able to jump gateways without an offering." Emma stepped forward, and all eyes shifted in her direction. "If he gains access through the House of Luminescence, the Merikh will not hesitate to attack from within."

"No attempts have occurred," Fargher reassured. "Lightforcers remain on alert."

"We returned with one of the Elders—Xui Li—who was tortured by the Merikh. Professor Windsor has sedated her, and healers will remain by her side until she wakes. Our hope is once she is conscious she will provide insight into what Will and the Merikh are planning next."

"Will is going to the nether realm, end of story," Jack mumbled. "We have to fight."

Fargher locked eyes on him. "Jack, is there anything you would like to say?"

"Nothing, Headmaster." He was too exhausted to debate. "I'd like to go with Faizan."

26

JACK SLIPPED OUT OF ROWELL LIBRARY as Headmaster Fargher dismissed the group, and Amina joined her parents, Maduka and Oni, who stood near the front. He hurried down the corridor and bounded down a flight of stairs, searching for fresh air as he realized who was missing—Elis and Beca Lloyd—which left his heart shredded once again.

While others milled about the hallways, he cut through the empty auditorium with memories of Fargher's annual welcoming speech echoing off the walls. He snuck out a back exit and inhaled the crisp afternoon, knowing he wasn't ready to talk to Fargher, McDougall, or McNaughton. Not yet, anyway. His boots crunched over dead flowers, patchy grass, and overgrown weeds as his steps led him to the Oasis of Remembrance. He didn't know why but he avoided looking toward Olivia Fargher's memorial.

"Every time I leave this place," he grumbled, "I end up right back where I started."

McNaughton found him alone in the unkempt garden. "You are a sight for sore eyes."

"You've had your hands full with the Cherub." Jack noticed the Glock holstered on her hip. "What happened to building an army to fight the Merikh?"

"Bau and Salomeh disagreed strongly on how best to prepare the lightforcers, benders, and healers. Fargher managed to keep their disagreements private; however, rumors have swirled since Bau chose to stay with Fang Xue and the remaining highest Cherub in Tsim Sha Tsui."

"He was never supposed to be the one—we both know it should be Emma."

"Thanks to Amina and Emma, the underground tunnels across Hong Kong were found, and we have followed the maze beneath the city to reach those in need. Headmaster Fargher has been helpful as he had been searching for months before the attack on Beacon Hill."

"Cherub were rescued from Shek Pik, so why does the school feel like a prison?"

"Beacon Hill remains a refuge, Jack. We are keeping hope alive."

"How much longer will it stay that way?" He crossed his arms. "What have you heard from Eliška and the faction?"

"Burwick handed over the baton to her shortly after you disappeared—but you will need to get me up to speed on what *exactly* has happened." McNaughton paused. "Communication with the faction is limited, especially since Fang Xue confirmed the government is monitoring cell and social activity across the city, which means the Merikh are too."

"Emma and Amina stayed connected with Eliška through Messagezilla," he admitted. "All three are the reason why I was found—and why I'm back."

"Merikh are using the MTR to travel across Kowloon and the New Territories. The train is the only way to reach Hong Kong Island."

"I forgot about the MTR tunnel." Jack's jaw dropped. "So, there is a way off the island."

"Impossible unless Cherub gain control of the trains, which will ignite a severe backlash." McNaughton hesitated. "Were you able to find more of the artifacts?"

"You know we found Soulweaver and Slybourne's shield." Jack weighed his words. "Emma found me in Manaus, and Eden's Star took us to Lake Brienz." He noticed her brows raised. "Long story short, we ended up traveling through a gateway to another realm, where we found the Rhoxen Stone given to one of the Cherub tribes." He trusted McNaughton as much as anyone, so he kept going. "Merikh found one of the artifacts too—the Windstrikers. I nearly got sliced in half like a bagel when I faced off with Will at Victoria Harbour."

"Four artifacts are in play, which means three are still missing," McNaughton concluded. "Did the Windstrikers destroy the tunnels beneath Victoria Harbour?"

"Everything is kind of a blur, but that's what I think happened," he confessed. "Will stole Dragon Soul from Bau, but the Windstrikers make the sword seem like a butter knife. He was willing to kill me, Natalie. And he won't stop until he's buried us all."

"Do you know what powers the artifacts possess? How can we use them to protect us?"

"I've got a better idea now more than ever. But it's best that remains a secret."

"Understood." McNaughton exhaled. "Are you keeping them in a safe place?"

"We separated them," he reassured. "Once we find them all, we'll return them to where they belong, and hopefully there will be peace. Until then, we have no other choice but to try and find the last three."

"What can I do to help, Jack?"

"You are already doing it." Jack glanced around to be sure they were alone. "To end the Merikh, I'll need to stop Will. He's searching for one of the artifacts, one more dangerous than all the others. I believe it's in a place called the nether realm. Headmaster Fargher kept the truth about Will from everyone to protect his son. If he does it again . . ."

"I will keep a close eye on the headmaster." McNaughton's brows furrowed. "I assume you heard from Bau about Addison and the Dungeon of Savages?"

"No one knows whether he survived." Jack paused. "We snuck into the Cherub vault beneath Lake Brienz and found an inner passageway. Opening the passageway caused the vault to flood, so it's my fault that Addison is either missing or dead—who knows what else the Cherub were guarding in the dungeon."

"Addison is no longer the Merikh leader, so if he returns we will face him together stronger than we have ever been—and the same is true of William Fargher."

Jack recognized the edge in her voice as someone who was in the fight and had been knocked around more than once. "When the headmaster searched through Nightingale's maps, did you ever hear him mention the Exodus Mines?"

"Not that I recall." McNaughton shook her head. "Is there an artifact in the mines?"

"Ryder Slybourne and Florence Upsdell moved their treasure from Sakkhela to the Exodus Mines before the Battle of Everest." He knew he was leaping through history, but the more details that bogged them down, the more explaining was required. Flashes from the night he flew from Manila to Kowloon on Addison's private jet flashed in his mind. "Years ago, Addison was taken to the Exodus Mines by Peter Leung in search of the artifacts. Addison used Dragon Soul to gain entrance, which means it's possible he has returned to the mines since Bau lost Dragon Soul. We aren't ready if Addison and Will have joined forces again."

"If that has occurred, then he could be hiding some of Slybourne's treasure anywhere—and the Merikh might have more than the Windstrikers." McNaughton's gaze hardened. "I will see what I can find out about the Exodus Mines from the headmaster. You should get some rest, Jack. I fear the days ahead will push all of us beyond our limits."

He allowed himself a brief glance around the Oasis of Remembrance, imagining when peacefulness watched over those who had gone before. A simple cross without a headstone caught his attention, sending a chill down his spine.

Eighteen years is not long enough, Tim.

27

THE RUBY-RED 1940 DELAHAYE 135 convertible was parked in Nightingale's vault. Jack stared at the collector automobile, remembering the night Vince and Tim whipped around a corner grinning from ear to ear. Last time he was inside, the vault overflowed with Cherub refugees arriving daily. Sleeping in makeshift areas, washing clothes by hand, rationing cans of food, children running about, and a sense no one was returning aboveground any time soon.

"So much has changed in such a short time," Jack said under his breath.

"We moved everyone into the houses and classrooms," Amina explained. "Most of the supplies are now stored in the barracks."

"Headmaster Fargher took a brave stand against the Merikh,"

Emma pointed out. "All who find refuge here now enjoy the fresh mornings and warm sun."

"Not every morning is sunny," Jack replied. "Days are darker now . . ."

"Tim was bothered," Amina interrupted. "He wanted to solve the mystery of how Nightingale stored all of this and the Delahaye in the vault. Headmaster Fargher told me about an entrance through the painting in Rowell Library, but I was to never enter. You remember?"

"I convinced you to do it," Jack noted. "I think you only did it because of Tim."

"He challenged us to search for another entrance—so, after he was gone, we did."

"We went through hundreds of crates." Emma pointed at a standard crate pushed up against a solid concrete wall, then opened the lid and reached inside. "Until we found this one with a lever hidden at the bottom."

"Our theory is that Nightingale brought relics from his adventures—including the Delahaye—into the vault through this tunnel." A solid wall opened wider than two collector cars side by side as Amina continued solemnly, "Tim is the reason we uncovered the rest of the maze of tunnels."

"You were both responsible for finding the first tunnel in the basement," Jack noted.

"We researched the Battle of Hong Kong through Nightingale's writings, which the headmaster collected along with a stack of hand-drawn maps," Emma clarified. "A maze of tunnels stretches from beneath Beacon Hill across districts in Kowloon, once used to transport ammunitions during the war."

"This particular one also leads to Ma Tau Wai Reservoir, which has been emptied and abandoned for years." Amina stepped inside the tunnel and pulled a lever. Incandescent lamps blinked on and hummed from the ceiling. "One other tunnel crosses this one beneath the school grounds—a shortcut to the barracks—and as you travel deeper through the tunnels, there are others that branch out across Kowloon."

Jack entered and followed them down a passageway, struck by the durability of the reinforced concrete and crudely wired lighting. Hard to imagine they were somewhere beneath the Main Hall; Nightingale, Rowell, Crozier, and Upsdell Houses; Dragon's Den; the cricket pitch; and the rest of the grounds. A hundred yards ahead, stuffed backpacks were piled together.

"How are we going to carry all of those?" Jack asked.

Emma and Amina replied in unison, "Benders."

"Right." Jack was reminded that gifts were for more than battle. "Makes sense."

"Jack, you have returned in one piece." Faizan's voice cut through the air as he climbed down an iron ladder with a group of benders right behind. "Good to see you, my friend."

"Good to see you too." Jack stood awkwardly as the others waited. "We're here to help."

The backpacks levitated and clustered together, controlled by the benders, including Emma. As the backpacks floated down the passageway, Jack stayed back and walked alongside Faizan.

"Salomeh was quite pleased when she returned," Faizan said.

"Finally, we're making progress. A big jump forward since Kati Pahari."

"You are the first outlier to gain her trust." He chuckled. "Miracles are possible."

Jack allowed the words to resonate in his spirit. He thought handing Slybourne's shield over to Salomeh would build a bridge. Instead, it seemed trust was forged when he gave the Rhoxen Stone to Professor Burwick. He didn't understand why, but he was encouraged.

"In Kati Pahari, you threw Tim the best birthday ever." The backpacks floated farther down the passageway. "Thank you, Faizan."

"Elyon created him for a purpose, and his purpose will forever be celebrated." Everyone stopped once they reached a red X painted on the wall, and each snatched backpacks from midair. Faizan turned his attention toward Emma. "Your parents are meeting us in Yau Ma Tei."

A slim opening in the concrete wall camouflaged an entrance to a darkened tunnel. Faizan shouldered several packs, quickening his steps along the train tracks. Jack managed the weight of a backpack bursting at the seams and kept up with the others. One by one, each slipped from the darkness and climbed a short ladder onto a platform in an empty MTR station. He watched as each hurried up the stairs and disappeared. Emma pulled him alongside and they moved in unison, climbing onto the platform and darting up to street level. They shot a quick glance up and down Dundas Street before they were flagged down by Oliver Bennett.

28

Once a bustling district mixed with residential high-rises and retail, Dundas Street and Shanghai Street were hauntingly quiet. Century-old fruit and wet markets were closed. Along the sidewalks, Hong Kongers kept their heads lowered as they passed through barricades monitored by HKPF and PRC military.

Oliver Bennett guided them from Yau Ma Tei Station through side streets deeper into the district. In an alley between apartment buildings, Jack stared across at a boarded-up Yau Ma Tei Theatre along Waterloo Road. A digital billboard above the entrance displayed an unwanted surprise—photos of him and the others, along with a reward of one million Hong Kong dollars for information leading to their capture.

Emma. Eliška. Vince. Me. It was only a matter of time.

"We're officially exposed to the world," Jack whispered. "Why didn't you tell me?"

"I was going to, but we were too busy fighting the Nephilim king and legion," Emma replied. "Not to worry—Hong Kongers in the district know we are helping them, so they will not speak to the PRC or Merikh."

"What about Vince and his parents? Has anyone warned them?"

Amina chimed in with a hushed voice. "The Tobiases are aware of the situation."

"You've spoken to Vince? Are they okay?"

"As much as can be expected," Emma answered. "His parents have extensive resources."

"How are you communicating with them?"

"Eliška and the faction established a connection—we are not certain how, exactly."

"Merikh are searching in the shadows." Oliver exchanged glances with Emma. "We have prioritized three drop-offs due to limited supplies. Kwong Wah Hospital. Tin Hau Temple. Prosperous Garden. All are expecting delivery within the hour."

"Headmaster Fargher gave us the locations," Faizan confirmed. "We are prepared."

"So you are aware of the surveillance cameras."

"I have handpicked each person here—no one else can be identified by the PRC."

"Splendid." Oliver paused. "Emma, Amina, and Jack, come with me."

While Faizan and the others dispersed in smaller groups down Waterloo Road, Oliver led his group in the opposite direction through the alley and ducked into an apartment building. Jack glanced over his shoulder once more at the theatre billboard, and a shudder shivered his spine. *One million HKD would make an owl sing. No way they're keeping everyone in the district quiet.* He entered the building and caught up with the others as they reached the second floor.

"Your mum is excited to see you," Oliver said to Emma. "We miss you terribly."

"I am not the one who volunteered on the front lines," she mused.

"Our mere attempt to keep up with our daughter, I suppose." Oliver grew quiet for a moment. "We are still adjusting to our reality—a bit handcuffed without our gifts. Until this is over, we will attempt to put Band-Aids on an active volcano."

On the fourteenth floor they followed Oliver into a run-down corridor. A door creaked open, and Winnie Bennett poked her head out from an apartment. She didn't wait for them to get any closer as she hurried to embrace Emma, teary eyed.

"How much time do we have?" Winnie asked.

Oliver waved them ahead into the apartment. "No longer than an hour."

The apartment was totally empty, with bare walls and worn floors. Jack dropped the backpack of supplies next to the ones that Emma and Amina set down. He remembered sitting across from Peter Leung in Wan Chai in an empty room with only two folding chairs—before he realized there was more going on than honoring a promise Rachel made before she died.

"Why do I feel like I'm left on the outside?" Jack asked.

"You made it easier, actually," Amina answered, "when you volunteered."

"We have waited quite some time to speak with you," Oliver

added. "After we were rescued from Shek Pik Prison, we hoped there would be an opportunity."

"Better to speak freely here than at Beacon Hill," Emma said. "You shared your concerns about Headmaster Fargher, and we share similar concerns regarding Bau and the highest Cherub."

"Fang Xue anointed him as Cherub leader in secret, and she controls the most influential Cherub," Oliver interjected. "However, she remains more interested in maintaining a truce than achieving a lasting victory against the Merikh."

"Isn't that what the Mercy Covenant was all about?" Jack asked. "But it's been broken."

"A covenant of peace for another age," Winnie answered. "A truce will not bring peace."

"Fang Xue knows about the alliance between Salomeh and Professor Burwick," Oliver added. "We confirmed through friends who are close to the situation. She is aware of their intention to form an army from within Beacon Hill to fight against the Merikh."

"Bau must've told her," Jack blurted. "He hasn't changed."

"Explains why he spends more time away," Amina suggested. "Of course, we told Eliška what we discovered, and she passed our message along to Professor Burwick."

"We were with Burwick and Salomeh—their alliance is solid."

"If Bau will not support them," Emma said, "we cannot fight all sides at once."

"Important to pick your battles," Oliver agreed. "Salomeh is continuing to train lightforcers, benders, and healers at Beacon Hill."

"Eliška questioned whether the Cherub were on their side. I cannot blame her."

"Salomeh, Burwick, and Eliška will stand by us," Jack interjected.

"There is more, Jack." Emma's gaze shifted between her parents. "Mum . . ."

"Peter Leung is the one who called the highest Cherub to gather at the Sanctuary of Prayer," Winnie began. "For many years, disagreements and debates have existed regarding interpretations of the prophecy. Some believe the same as Peter proclaimed publicly—only the gifted are deemed worthy to lead the Cherub. The faction influenced others who determined that a leader born into a lineage of the most courageous—even those considered ungifted—would be the one."

"Eliška is a direct descendant of Ryder Slybourne," Jack said.

"Peter promised to bring the prophecy to this gathering, to allow the highest Cherub to read the original writings for ourselves. The Elders kept the ancient writings in the Sanctum of Serenity; however, most of the highest Cherub did not know which gateway would lead there."

"Fang Xue asked Bau to travel through the gateway to find the prophecy," Emma pointed out. "Salomeh told me about one of the gateways, too, but it was blocked. In a roundabout way, we found the Sanctum of Serenity, but we were too late."

"Remarkable." Oliver exhaled. "You have seen more than your mum and dad."

"We also faced off with Will," Jack added, "and now he has the prophecy."

"Darkness corrupted the prophecy," Emma explained. "He was surrounded by the legion before he vanished. We needed Bau's help to bring Xui Li back to Beacon Hill."

Winnie's brows raised. "The Elder is alive?"

"She remains unconscious," Amina explained, "but is being cared for by Professor Windsor and the healers."

"Quite a combination," Oliver noted. "We never had an opportunity to meet the Elders."

"Besides Jack's mum being one," Emma chimed in, "he also faced Charlotte Taylor, escaped the City of Gods with Xui Li, and even crossed a few bridges with Dabria."

"Remarkable," Winnie said, awestruck. "Elyon has granted you favor, Jack."

"Will the prophecy still come true, or can it be altered?" Amina asked.

"If the prophecy is altered," Winnie answered, "then the Cherub will be at the mercy of those in power instead of those anointed to lead us. Many believe the prophecy is to be fulfilled through a bloodline, which has left division between Cherub and faction. We pray the prophecy will come true, the words and meaning redeemed, so light will shine bright in this world."

"When Xui Li wakes, she will have answers," Jack interrupted. "She will know what we're supposed to do and who we're supposed to trust. And she will help us gain support from the Cherub so Emma will take her rightful place."

"Jack . . ." Emma protested. "You heard what was said about the prophecy."

"The faction is in good hands with Eliška, and the Cherub need the same."

"On the day of the gathering on Mount Hareh," Oliver redirected, "we arrived with many of the highest Cherub and were greeted by old friends. Everyone was so excited, anticipating our opportunity to view the prophecy with our own eyes. We waited for Peter to arrive . . ."

"Innocent blood was spilled in the sanctuary," Winnie said somberly. "A vengeful lightforce."

"An ambush by Addison, Peter, and Will." Jack swallowed hard, ashamed to admit the massacre on Mount Hareh was coerced by his own father. "Was Fang Xue there?"

"She was not present." Oliver shook his head. "We have heard rumors about hearings being held by the highest Cherub at the Rosewood hotel regarding your innocence. Of course, we offered ourselves as witnesses to what occurred on Mount Hareh, but we have not heard a response from anyone."

"If the prophecy has been corrupted," Winnie added, "we are in for an Everest battle."

"Rachel kept a secret of her own," Jack replied. "One you deserve to know."

29

TSIM SHA TSUI

In a shake-up previously unseen by global governments, Hong Kong remained blocked from the rest of the world, and negotiations with world leaders had reached a stalemate. Headlines were filled with natural disasters, escalating feuds between countries on the brink of war, international economic downturns, and increasing civil unrest around the world. The severity of the PRC's unprecedented actions escalated tensions among nations on the global stage.

The Central Government Complex and the Legislative Council Complex located in Admiralty were permanently closed. The chief executive officer resigned shortly after the breakout at Shek Pik Prison, accepting responsibility for a failure to protect the homeland—and behind the curtain a failure to keep the PRC's military across the border in the New Territories. No media were present on the streets. Broadcasts aired strictly to Hong Kongers only. The unexplainable events and the march across Hong Kong Island to Beacon Hill were never mentioned.

Military vehicles and armed soldiers replaced the fleet of Rolls-Royces and wealthy guests who had once dropped tens of thousands at the exclusive Peninsula hotel. Bamboo scaffolding in green netting had been removed once the final rebuild was finished—all while Hong Kongers gradually conformed to a new way of life under the PRC's ironfisted rule.

"Listen to what he is offering before you respond," Fang Xue advised.

Bau Hu nodded as they entered the opulent lobby and were ushered to a private elevator. Armed guards stepped into the elevator alongside them, and they all rode to a secured floor. The doors opened to an office that took up half the floor. Windows offered a panoramic view of Victoria Harbour and The Peak overlooking Hong Kong Island—no sign of a city in chaos.

Max Tsang, chairman of the central military for the PRC and newly appointed chief executive, greeted them with a firm handshake. He motioned for each to find a seat at a conference table. Flatscreens surrounded the table, as if those who were not present might videoconference in at any moment—a front-row seat to the newly appointed leader of the Cherub seated across from a pawn of the PRC. All the screens blinked on, displaying thumbnails of thousands of government IDs.

"We have taken over the entire Merikh syndicate and have accessed an extensive database identifying Cherub across the city, including those who were brought to Shek Pik Prison." Tsang swiped across a tablet on the conference table, and the screens switched to only two photos: Winston and Betty Hu. "Your parents lost their estate in Repulse Bay during the fires, and their assets have been seized. I was surprised to hear they are renting an apartment in Tai Tam. An unfortunate fall from the lifestyle they are accustomed to—quite a shame."

"Much has changed for everyone," Fang Xue said coolly. "Why are we here?"

"Resolution requires compromise." Tsang eyed them closely. "Surrender all refugees and gifted who remain at Beacon Hill. In return, we will allow Cherub to live among us unharmed—once the methods the Merikh use to neutralize the gifted are complete."

"We have contained the gifted as our gesture of good faith. Once our patience runs thin, we will be forced to defend ourselves in more aggressive manners." Fang Xue paused. "You may have taken over the Merikh, but you have not seen our unrestrained abilities to protect our own. You will need our cooperation if we are to prevent those you have kept contained within the grounds of Beacon Hill from rising up against your threats and aggression."

"Do you know how many of the Cherub still possess their gifts?" Tsang tapped on the tablet once more and the thumbnails reappeared on the screens, only this time an *X* was crossed over many of them. "Fang, you have the ability to convince your people of anything if you are motivated to do so."

"I am no longer their leader—we have anointed Bau to lead us."

"The Cherub place their fate in the hands of a boy." Tsang smiled slyly, then tapped on the tablet once more. Photos of Jack, Emma, Eliška, and Vince appeared. "Not only will you bring us the gifted at Beacon Hill and restore order, but you will bring these four high-priority targets as well."

Bau eyed the photos on the flatscreens, then glanced briefly at Fang Xue before he responded. "Allow the Cherub to remain free and we will find a suitable resolution to end the standoff at Beacon Hill. We will also pledge our gifts to protect the city and the regime. Our gifts are more valuable than your fear of losing control."

"What will stop you from defying us in the future?"

"As the Cherub leader, my word is final," Bau replied sternly. "A truce with the Merikh is on the lips of the highest Cherub, and the alliance we are offering is unbreakable."

"An intriguing alternative." Tsang leaned back in his chair. "What about the four?"

"We will bring them to you as a sign of our promise."

"Very well." Tsang pushed the chair back and stood. "I will pass this along."

Bau and Fang Xue waited until Tsang was gone, knowing their every move was being monitored, then rode the elevator down to the lobby. With security escorting them out of The Peninsula, they slipped into the back seat of a waiting SUV and remained quiet as the vehicle turned onto Salisbury before taking a sharp left onto Nathan Road.

"Many of the highest Cherub will disagree," Bau said under his breath.

"Tsang is correct in his assumption of the number of those whose gifts were taken." Fang Xue hesitated. "Compromise will protect us and stop Jack and Emma from shattering the commands in the Eternal—the artifacts must remain hidden or the world will end. We should inform the highest Cherub of your willingness to hunt down Jack, and we must retrieve Eden's Star."

30

After returning from Yau Ma Tei, Jack shuffled across the rooftop and disappeared inside the clock tower. Amina found an extra folding cot and a single-bulb lamp—enough for him to crash. He glanced around the tight space, weighing what he'd heard from the Bennetts, then eyed the hole in the floor. *The Elders failed long before I found Eden's Star when they fought over what to do with the compass.* He slumped onto the flimsy mattress as the clock continued to count backward.

Where will I be when it stops? And what will it mean for everyone else?

The compass flowed through his body, swarming his organs, which had dumbfounded Windsor and left him haunted. Exhaustion wore him down as he slowly dozed off.

"Jack!" Emma's excitement startled him. "Xui Li is awake."

He rolled off the cot, snatched his hoodie containing the slim box, and met Emma halfway down the stairs. A few minutes later they stood outside Xui Li's room in Crozier Hospital. Windsor stepped into the hallway, visibly relieved.

"As soon as she woke, she asked for you," Windsor said in a hushed voice. "She is weak."

"Go ahead," Emma encouraged him. "I will stay with the professor."

Jack entered the room and waited at the foot of the bed. Xui Li pulled herself up and eyed him closely. A slight smile pursed her lips. Jack took in her bony cheeks, strands of graying hair, and the scars on her face and arms that were evidence of what she had endured. He was afraid to imagine what kind of pain was inflicted deeper than the scars—but she was a survivor like Professor Burwick.

"For so long I wondered whether you were dead," Jack said, barely above a whisper.

"Elyon still has a purpose for me." Her intense stare was welcome. "And for you."

"I have so many questions . . . starting with the key that Rachel left with the headmaster."

"During the Battle of Hong Kong, the key was returned by Winston Churchill to the Cherub—in the days when the war was lost."

"Nightingale and Crozier were in the trenches," Jack recounted. "Were you the one in the tunnel who took the key from Crozier before he died?"

"I was a young girl, not yet an Elder. Dabria was also in the tunnel on that day. She was the one who took the key." Xui Li closed her eyes for a moment, as if remembering long ago. "We brought the key to Peter—too young to know what it represented in our history."

"Elders don't age in the same way as the rest of us," Jack chimed in. "How could Peter have known the key would unlock the Temple of the Nephilim?"

"He told us a story about Sir James Nightingale finding his way to Charis, where he discovered the Testimony and the Windstrikers. Peter believed the key was connected to the artifacts in some way, so he urged Nightingale to return the key to the Elders in exchange for victory in the Battle of Hong Kong. Nightingale convinced Churchill, and the key was handed off to Dabria in the underground tunnel. As you know, Nightingale was defeated in the battle because the Elders argued over breaking the commands in the Eternal. Peter is the one who chose to go against the Elders, and he used the Windstrikers as a weapon to help the Allies end the war with Japan. When the Japanese surrendered, the Windstrikers were entrusted to Dabria—a gift from Peter for her bravery—even though she was only a child."

Jack sat on the edge of the bed, slightly lightheaded. "Then what happened?"

"As we grew older, no one recognized the temptation brewing within Peter, who was the oldest among us. Many years later, we learned how long he had been searching for Eden's Star when he found the Testimony hidden in Nightingale's vault with the compass inside."

"Whoa . . ." Jack exhaled. "Nightingale was years ahead of anyone else."

"Peter demanded that Dabria return the Windstrikers." Xui Li's stare intensified. "She refused, and shortly after that he stole

Eden's Star and one of the Cherub maps—and the key disappeared with him. We believed he would return even more powerful, so we entrusted the Windstrikers to Nightingale—who swore to keep the artifact hidden from all Elders."

Jack leaned forward captured by her words, yet suddenly hesitant to speak his own. "Dabria is dead."

"Then I am the only Elder left." Xui Li closed her eyes again. "Darkness surrounds us."

"Will found the Windstrikers in Vigan—and he's killed more than one Elder."

"His powers are strong enough to wield Dragon Soul and the Windstrikers."

"Now he has the prophecy too." Jack grew silent for a moment, riffling through more questions. "When you put me on the *Eastern Dragon*, did you know who I would find?"

"My gifts are no more, but I was hopeful your path would cross with Eliška." Xui Li paused. "After Manila, Salomeh Gashkori brought me to Karachi at my request."

"We've met, but I'm not sure she likes me much. She is definitely fond of Emma."

Xui Li glanced past him toward the hallway. "Emma Bennett."

"You know who she is to the Cherub?"

"Rachel spoke about her and the others. Salomeh filled in the missing pieces." Xui Li cleared her dry throat. "Salomeh is cautious when allowing anyone close, but she told me about the rescue in Victoria Harbour. Once I was certain you were safe, the next steps were clear for me to travel through a gateway to Sakkhela."

"Eliška is more than a survivor," Jack suggested. "Emma is the one who saved us in the harbor, and she's been passed over by the Cherub because she chose to stick by me."

"Many years ago, the Elders debated within the Sanctum of Serenity about the meaning of the prophecy." Xui Li sipped water gingerly from a bottle. "Once Peter stole Eden's Star and the map drawn by one of the Cherub tribes, our attention turned to finding him before he found the artifacts. We were so focused on him, we failed to realize danger remained in our circle."

"Charlotte Taylor," Jack noted. "With a little help from the Zakhar, I saw Nightingale bring the Windstrikers to the Elders at the Sanctuary of Prayer. And I know there was a time when you all trusted Addison with Dragon Soul."

"Our judgment was not without errors." Xui Li shifted uncomfortably in the bed, clearly aching from the torture she had endured. "After Peter disappeared and Addison nearly killed Gabriella, our search led us closer to the City of Gods. We were convinced Peter had traveled there with the help of Eden's Star. I remained with Gabriella as we searched for the right path to enter another realm. When we traveled through Maranat Falls, we discovered we were correct. However, we were too late. Peter narrowly escaped the Pyramid of Stars after battling against the Nephilim king. Your mother had a vision of Eden's Star being left inside the temple. We entered not knowing the price we would pay with what remained of our gifts. We found the key inside the chamber, moments before the Nephilim king attacked and was struck down."

"Mom was killed too—but you survived," Jack said, barely above a whisper. "Peter returned to the Cherub even more powerful. Addison gave back Dragon Soul because he was afraid of breaking the Mercy Covenant—even though it was already broken—and he wanted to keep himself safe from Elyon's wrath."

"I waited in the City of Gods to guard the entrance to the

Temple of the Nephilim." Xui Li nodded slowly. "Many years passed before Rachel arrived, and a sliver of hope returned."

"You're the one who gave Rachel the key," Jack guessed. "She needed it to enter."

"When she found Vigan in the mountains outside of Sitio Veterans, Dabria is the one who showed her the way—and trusted I would recognize the bloodline."

"All the while, Peter kept the facade that the Elders were still together." Jack had waited months to listen to Xui Li shed light on the mystery. "Peter needed the chosen to enter the City of Gods to retrieve Eden's Star because he'd lost his gifts too."

"Rachel was the first one to experience the depravity within the pyramid, which I encountered with your mother. I have told you the strongest of Cherub gifts are taken when one is drawn near the deadliest of sins. Rachel nearly died each time she attempted to retrieve the compass, only to find healing when she returned to Vigan."

"So when she started to believe Peter was keeping secrets from the Cherub, along with who she thought were the Elders, she grew more suspicious." Jack remembered reading Rachel's writings in her notebook, and how she was torn by what she believed was right. "That's why she left the key with Headmaster Fargher—she knew her life was in danger."

"Your presence in the City of Gods resurrected the Nephilim king from a darkness reaching from the nether realm." Xui Li sipped again and sat up a bit straighter, still weary. "Salomeh agreed to allow me to travel through the gateway to Sakkhela to find a way to stop anyone else from reawakening a beast swallowed by darkness in the nether realm."

Jack stepped alongside the bed, shocked by Xui Li's words.

A beast swallowed by darkness—the same words Mom wrote on the back of the parchment inside the box. Jack, you can't bombard her with questions.

"Eden's Star led us deeper into the Highlands, where we found Charis—and the Rod of Elyon."

"Then Elyon has certainly guided your path."

"I barely passed creative writing, so it's impossible for me to describe what we witnessed. Emma and Eliška were there too." Asiklua flashed in his mind, but he didn't want to get sidetracked or ask Xui Li much more. "How did the Merikh catch you in Sakkhela?"

Xui Li clasped her hands and rested them on her lap. "I chose to surrender, Jack."

"You let them catch you." Jack's jaw dropped. "Why did you lead Will to the prophecy?"

"To keep our enemy close." Xui Li's stare hardened. "What you witnessed in the sanctum proves the prophecy was corrupted long before our debates as the Elders began. I do not know for certain, but I believe it occurred during the years when Peter was missing. As you suggested, he returned from the City of Gods without his gifts, yet more powerful in other ways. Dabria told me many stories of those within the highest Cherub who were convinced of his lies. She remained in Vigan as a safe haven as Charlotte emerged with her sights on leading the Merikh."

"How does Eliška fit into the prophecy?"

"The prophecy is open to interpretation depending on who is reading the words. Cherub focus on a promise, seekers are drawn by the quest of an outlier, and the faction root their cause in a descendant of the great warrior Ryder Slybourne. You see, all three of you are connected."

"Eliška *is* a descendant of Slybourne," he affirmed. "So, she is part of the prophecy."

She nodded slowly. "I cannot tell you who will lead the Cherub when this is over."

"Eden's Star took us beyond Charis to the edge of the Highlands," Jack confessed. "We stood in a graveyard of Cherub—one Emma said was never written about in the Eternal. The legion were there, too, on the other side of some kind of force field."

"You reached the nether realm," Xui Li confirmed. "Centuries ago, during the Second Great War, a battle was waged against an adversary more dangerous than Asiklua, the legion, or the Nephilim king. The Elders of old used their gifts to contain evil in the nether realm, centuries before your mother, Dabria, Charlotte, Peter, or I were born. Gabriella believed what was imprisoned in the nether realm was the most dangerous artifact of all—guarded by the darkest of betrayers."

"Eden's Star is inside of me." Jack tapped his chest. "The compass led us there."

"And now the prophecy is summoning another to the nether realm to free the chains that bind the darkness. His soul is blinded to the deathly shadow he is being lured to unleash."

"Where is the gateway to the nether realm?"

"The prophecy is believed to reveal the only known gateway, and one must possess the prophecy in order to go beyond the edge of the Highlands."

"Addison gained your trust once, and he used the Elders to gain entrance to the nether realm." Jack wanted to guard Eleanore's secret, but he needed to say just enough for Xui Li to understand. "He used my mom to travel through a gateway and return with one of the artifacts—which I believe he has hidden somewhere."

"How do you know this to be true?" Xui Li asked.

"When they returned, both were near death." Jack hesitated, anticipating a response, but Xui Li remained quiet. "While they brought one of the artifacts back, they left the most dangerous behind in the nether realm. I'm guessing it's the same artifact you're referring to as a deathly shadow." Jack removed the slim box from his hoodie and handed it over to Xui Li. He waited as she opened the latch and examined the scrolled parchment and ivory figurine. "My mom left a warning with Rachel when we were both young."

"Gabriella never told us about the artifact Addison stole." Xui Li closed her eyes for a moment, then opened them slowly. "She must have brought this back from the nether realm as proof of the danger that lies beyond the Highlands."

"She left a hidden message too." He waited as Xui Li read the words that appeared on the parchment. "What did they leave behind in the nether realm?"

"If you enter the nether realm with Eden's Star, then you will surely die." Xui Li rolled up the parchment with the ivory figurine wrapped inside and handed it back. "Keep your fight in this world, and pray what is in the nether realm remains chained."

31

PROFESSOR WINDSOR INTERRUPTED and insisted Xui Li rest and recover. Ten minutes later, Jack's mind still swirled with all she had revealed, especially revelations about his parents and the nether realm. He knew Eleanore created a gateway, and his parents found and brought an artifact back—but he decided to keep Eleanore's actions from Xui Li. Still, he was troubled by what Addison kept hidden and what it meant for everyone.

Overgrown weeds covered what was once a lush green hillside forming a natural outdoor amphitheater overlooking the Wishing Tree. Sparse leaves on a wide crown of branches were all that was left of that Cherub gift from long ago. Strange to stand in the empty amphitheater where Headmaster Fargher ushered first years toward their destiny.

"She is the last Elder," Jack said. "And she's terrified."

"We should listen to her warning and not enter the nether realm." Emma was seated on an empty row of the amphitheater. "You will be no use to anyone if you are dead."

Jack nearly shot back a response, but he held his tongue. "Xui Li allowed herself to be captured and tortured to stay close to the Merikh to try and stop what's happened."

"She risked everything when she took Will to the Sanctum of Serenity."

"We were too late to rescue her in Shek Pik," he replied. "She didn't know how long they'd keep her alive, so she did what was necessary."

"Will has the prophecy and will do anything to enter the nether realm if he has not found a way already. Without the prophecy in our hands, the nether realm is another dead end—at least for now. We do not know a location for the Exodus Mines, and without Dragon Soul or Bau we cannot gain entrance to Slybourne's treasure to search for another artifact."

"We're running out of options." Jack dug his elbows into his thighs and leaned forward. "Addison has found the Exodus Mines, and from the vision I'm certain he took treasure from there. If he's still alive, he'll need resources, and who knows, he might have more than one artifact in his treasure chest." He racked his brain to think of anyone who might know the answer. "We need to go to Banyan Garden."

"The tunnels do not reach Lai Chi Kok," Emma replied. "Is it worth the risk?"

"It's the only way I know to get the answers we need."

Jack gazed at the Wishing Tree, remembering the day he'd first seen Emma and the night she'd revealed her lightforce in the basement of the Main Hall. In this quiet moment between them, he breathed in all they'd been through and exhaled a hope they'd be together when it was over.

"My parents pulled me aside before we left," Emma admitted. "Both are worried."

"Merikh took their gifts at Shek Pik." Jack clenched his jaw. "It's not right."

"Volunteering in Yau Ma Tei is a way to deal with the change."

"Emma, delivering food and water isn't building an army."

"I need to speak with Bau after we are done in Lai Chi Kok."

"Are you sure he won't hand us over to the Cherub?"

"I am not certain of anything—not anymore."

Jack and Emma headed for the barracks, where shelves were half-filled with canned goods, water, dry foods, blankets, and extra clothes. Emma nodded toward a hole in the floor where the top of a wooden ladder poked out. He climbed down the ladder and waited until Emma joined him. Four tunnels headed in different directions, each illuminated by a dull light. He followed Emma into a tunnel that led to an iron-grated access point to the Argyle Street station.

Hong Kongers waited on the platform, which was not as packed as normal. Jack and Emma stayed in the darkened tunnel until the last second. Jack kept his head on a swivel, fully aware cameras were monitoring those inside the station. He guessed HKPF and PRC military guarded the street-level entrance as he watched several armed soldiers stroll back and forth on the platform.

A silver train screeched down the tracks before slowing to a stop. With the rear of the train inside the tunnel, Jack and Emma climbed aboard. Emma's palm glowed as she grabbed a locked latch, opening the door and slipping inside as the train pulled away. The train lurched left and right through the underground railway, then emerged on a bridge between high-rises. A few more stops and the MTR stopped at Lai Chi Kok Station.

Emma pushed Jack forward as they stepped off amid the other passengers. A brisk walk through the station and up the stairs left them on Cheung Sha Wan Road. Jack led the way through West Kowloon Corridor toward Lai Chi Kok Road until they reached a cluster of seven high-rise towers among the tallest buildings in the city—some with fifty-seven floors.

"Banyan Garden," Emma read a sign over the entrance to an Italian-inspired terra-cotta residential building. "I thought you meant a garden."

"I lost ten grand playing mah-jongg here," he said. "Not my last mistake."

"Who are we here to see, Jack?"

"A Triad commander." Butterflies swarmed his stomach. "Shen Jiahao."

Jack and Emma rode the elevator to the fifty-seventh floor and stepped into a hallway. He noticed the difference between Banyan Garden and the apartments in Yau Ma Tei. *I guess not everyone in Hong Kong is starving.* He knocked on apartment 5710, waited, then knocked again. The door cracked open, and a disheveled and unshaven Shen Jiahao sneered at them. Jack glanced down and noticed a Glock in the Triad's grip. Emma's palm glowed, which caught Shen's attention, and he opened the door a bit wider.

"Jack," Shen hissed. "Hurry before someone sees you."

The apartment was fully furnished with expensive leather sofas, a flatscreen the size of an entire wall, and a table stacked with mah-jongg tiles. Weapons were lined up on a kitchen counter with plenty of ammo. Clearly, Shen was prepared for anyone who might enter his domain.

"Wanted fugitives by the PRC." Shen pointed at Emma. "Merikh or Cherub?"

"Cherub," she replied pointedly. "Jack said you are a Triad commander."

"The Triads have been eaten by a greater tiger." Shen relaxed a bit and set the Glock on the kitchen counter. "PRC have taken over the Merikh, who feasted on the Triads. So, to survive, one becomes a ghost in a concrete jungle."

Jack found it a bit strange that Shen had asked whether Emma was Merikh or Cherub even though he saw her flash her lightforce. "We need your help."

"You dare risk coming to my home," Shen bantered. "And now you ask for my help?"

"Where have the Triads hidden their riches?"

"You ask me a question I cannot answer." Shen's gaze shifted. "Everything has a price."

"I'm searching for where my father has done the same—and I'm guessing he'd pick the most secured location on earth." Jack paused. "He has taken tons of gold from the Cherub—if you help us find it, there will be a reward."

Shen walked over to the window and gazed out on Banyan Garden. "Kreidler in Zurich."

Jack's heartbeat quickened. "Can you get us inside?"

"You have gone from mah-jongg junkie to freedom fighter to thief." Shen hesitated. "Kreidler is the most secure bank in the world—there is one way in, but you will not like it."

"So you will help us?" Emma asked, dubious. "Do not betray us."

"If I refuse, Addison will surely burn this city down."

32

SHEN JIAHAO NUDGED JACK AND EMMA out of the apartment and slammed the door, leaving them standing awkwardly in the hallway. He'd told them what he knew about Kreidler, and nothing more. *He's right. I don't like it one bit.* Of course, Shen expected payment for his assistance and threatened to expose them to the PRC and Merikh if they failed to hold up their end of the bargain. Once again, Jack owed a debt he wasn't sure he could repay. Both hurried to the elevator, knowing all signs pointed to Hong Kong Island.

"We have to find a way to Repulse Bay." Jack punched a button on the wall. "And we should pay a visit to Tai Tam to check whether Will has been seen."

"Star Ferry is not an option, and Merikh are monitoring the MTR stations more closely between Tsim Sha Tsui and Admiralty. No one has been allowed to travel to Hong Kong Island." Emma pressed the button again. "We do not know whether Shen is telling the truth."

"Shen's eye twitches when he's lying. That's how I knew to bet when we played. I watched him close while he was talking, and he was deadpan. Emma, searching Addison's penthouse is a plan B until we find a lead to Will's whereabouts. If Addison left behind a way to gain access to his vault in Kreidler, then maybe we'll be one step closer to finding all the artifacts."

Elevator doors opened and they stepped inside. On the ride down to the lobby, Jack's exhaustion eased as the adrenaline of the chase kicked into another gear. While they were definitely improvising, at least they weren't stuck on the grounds of Beacon Hill.

"If we can't find Will, then we'll have to take a chance on our own in Repulse Bay."

"Even if we make it inside Kreidler, then what?" Emma asked. "We do not know what we are searching for, Jack."

"You're a lightforcer and bender—and I've got Soulweaver and Eden's Star." The elevator doors opened again, and they found themselves inside the lobby. He retrieved a burner cell that Shen gave them before they were kicked out of his apartment and handed it over. "Who can get us onto Hong Kong Island?"

Emma dialed a number and quietly spoke their location into the phone. "Banyan Garden. Lai Chi Kok."

Once she hung up, she removed the SIM card and crushed the phone beneath her boot, leaving it shattered on the tiled floor of the lobby. Jack stepped toward glass doors, peering left and right as double-decker buses, minibuses, and taxis sped past on the street. From inside the lobby, the city looked the same as it had months earlier, but beneath the veil so much had changed.

No question who she called, but what other choice do we have?

Fifteen minutes passed before a delivery van slowed in front of the building. The driver glanced briefly in their direction but never fully stopped. Emma and Jack slipped out from the lobby and headed down the sidewalk beside the moving van. When the side door slid open, both hopped inside, and the driver accelerated down Lai Chi Kok Road.

Tsing Sha Highway merged onto West Kowloon Highway as the driver kept his sights ahead, occasionally glancing in the rearview. Exiting onto Kowloon Park Drive, the van continued toward the Langham hotel before looping around to Ashley Road and parking outside of Mon Kee. *An appropriate name for who's waiting for us.* Jack and Emma climbed out of the van and entered the café while Cherub lingered nearby on the streets.

"Feels like déjà vu," Jack grumbled. "Only this time he's in charge."

The tables were empty except for one booth where Bau was seated. Jack glanced around to be sure they were alone, then slid onto the bench alongside Emma.

"Thank you for helping us at the sanctum," Emma began. "Xui Li is awake."

"She will be useful to the Cherub." Bau eyed Jack with a flare of contempt. "You have the Rod of Elyon, Eden's Star, and I am assuming other artifacts?"

"We have found more than one," Jack confirmed. "Did Emma tell you what we need?"

"The Merikh are no more, at least not in the way we have known. Without a leader, the PRC has already taken over their syndicate and is controlling the Golden Triangle." Bau turned his attention to Emma. "They have made us an offer—a truce. If we reach a compromise, then the war is over and peace will allow the Cherub to live on."

"You were supposed to build an army," Jack blurted. "You abandoned the plan."

"The trial of Detective Ming begins today," Bau stated. "She will be found guilty and will spend the rest of her life in prison because of what you have done. The lives lost since you disobeyed the Eternal rest squarely on your shoulders."

"Seriously?" Jack bantered angrily. "I've lost as much as anyone."

"If we choose to fight, more will die." Bau kept his eyes fixed on Emma. "We are no longer strong enough to defend ourselves, and we will suffer unless we reach a compromise."

"Shek Pik took more than gifts from the highest Cherub. It has taken their courage." Jack pressed another notch harder. "You don't deserve to lead the Cherub—you're a coward."

"A compromise keeps the Cherub and the innocent alive."

"Why would the PRC be willing to offer such a deal?" Emma asked calmly.

"I have met with the chief executive officer and begun negotiations." Bau hesitated. "He demanded to strip all Cherub of their gifts, but I have offered an alternative. I am certain the PRC will understand our gifts are valuable, not a liability. A truce means the Cherub remain free as long as we pledge to protect the city and regime."

"Then you're no different than the Merikh," Jack argued. "Doesn't sound like freedom."

"What about Beacon Hill?" Emma asked. "What will happen to the refugees?"

"We will find a suitable resolution to end the standoff."

"And what about Will? He is far too dangerous to ignore."

"He has taken the prophecy, and his whereabouts remain unknown." Bau's gaze hardened as he kept his focus on Emma, ignoring Jack's contemptuous glare. "You were the one called to lead the

Cherub, but you have chosen another path. I am the anointed and must do what is best to protect the Cherub—and all who believe in Elyon."

"The great Cherub leader"—Jack waved his arms around them—"hiding out in a café."

"Remember who you are, Jack—the Executioner's spawn. You are an outlier, not one of the chosen. You disobeyed the Eternal, and your actions have caused much bloodshed. You unearthed dangers beyond your understanding, and you remain a threat to the Cherub. So do not lecture me about courage or freedom." Bau looked past them for a moment, then turned his gaze toward his hands as a vivid auburn lightforce glowed in his palms. "You are left with only one choice: return the artifacts—including Eden's Star—and surrender."

Soulweaver gradually crawled down Jack's arm beneath his hoodie. Emma's palms glowed stark white as she nudged him out of the booth. She kept her back to him as he cautiously moved toward the glass door. Jack glanced briefly over his shoulder as Emma and Bau stood face-to-face, which gave him a chill.

Emma lowered her hands to her sides, and Bau unleashed a pulsing lightforce. Jack swung Soulweaver, and the rod harnessed the impact of the lightforce. He charged forward as Soulweaver spun between his fingers. Bau fought back with more pulsing blasts. Booths and tables exploded, pulverizing into splinters. Jack stayed aggressive, allowing rage to flow through him, and caught Bau by surprise. With a quick snap the rod struck Bau in the ribs, sending him stumbling backward. Jack swung again and nailed the same spot with precision.

Bau dropped to his knees as the breath was knocked out of him. Flashes of memory struck Jack in rapid succession from the cricket field when he tackled Bau, and the night he was humiliated at the

Sword and Fan. His muscles tensed, ready to stab Soulweaver with a final knockout blow.

"Jack!" Emma yelled. "Stop!"

Still tempted to strike, he stepped back and reluctantly lowered Soulweaver. *Elyon, give me the strength to walk away and not surrender to the temptation.* He followed Emma toward the glass door as Bau scrambled to his feet and unleashed one more pulse. Without looking back, Emma released her own lightforce, which punched Bau hard enough to send him crashing into the one table left standing.

Jack and Emma stepped out onto the sidewalk as the Cherub who lingered across the street stood frozen. *We are about to get ambushed, but Emma doesn't seem worried.* Emma's palms still glowed, only now her eyes radiated a stark white. *If they know what's good for them, they'll let us pass.* The Cherub remained as still as statues, none of them attempting to get any closer.

"Best we not push our luck," she whispered. "We will find a way across the harbor."

"Can we do the funnel like we did in Lake Brienz?"

"Too dangerous to stretch that far, especially since you are not . . ."

"Gifted. You're afraid I'll drown halfway across."

"Not every solution requires the supernatural."

Jack and Emma walked briskly in the opposite direction, and in the distance behind them the Cherub finally moved and rushed inside Mon Kee. Soulweaver wrapped around Jack's forearm and squeezed away the anger within until he breathed a bit easier.

"You could've taken out both of us," he speculated. "Why didn't you stop Bau?"

Emma's brows furrowed. "I swore an oath never to harm a Cherub."

"Well, Bau didn't read the same *chosen* handbook as you."

"Typhoon shelter," she retorted. "That's how we get across."

33

Sweat seeped down Jack's spine beneath his shirt and hoodie as he and Emma strode quickly through Olympian Park on reclaimed land in West Kowloon. Cherub were prepared to place him on the altar, *again*. *I'm learning to trust the path ahead one step at a time—to keep my trust in Elyon beyond all else. Maybe I'll always be an outlier to the Cherub, but there is no doubt in my soul—I'm a follower of Elyon.* They headed toward the Yau Ma Tei Interchange, across from the typhoon shelter. He couldn't help but wonder whether crossing Victoria Harbour to search for Will in Tai Tam or attempting to enter Addison's fortress in Repulse Bay was worth the risk.

"Bau wasn't telling us everything," Jack said. "There's more to the deal."

"'We will find a suitable resolution to end the standoff,'" Emma quoted Bau. "PRC will demand more than Cherub loyalty and gifts to ensure peace—they will want total control."

"Only way that happens is if Cherub are less powerful." Jack weighed his own words, answering a question he was on the verge of asking. "Bau was ready to hand me over, and he tried to stop you from leaving. What if the endgame for the PRC is to use the methods the Merikh created to take Cherub gifts, like they did to those imprisoned in Shek Pik?"

"Especially since they know the procedure works," Emma agreed. "It is a mistake."

"Bau's following in Xui Li's footsteps and won't admit Addison is still dangerous."

"We do not have proof Addison is alive," Emma pointed out. "Only the words of a Triad commander, who was more than eager to toss us out."

"Bau's the Cherub leader, keeper of Dragon Soul, a light-forcer, and Head Boy at Beacon Hill—titles that inflate his ego." Bitterness dripped from each word. "He doesn't realize how fragile peace and freedom will be once the real battle begins."

"He broke the chosen rule," Emma admitted, "and used his lightforce against me."

"You defended yourself." Jack darted across the interchange alongside Emma. "Maybe we should go after Will in Tai Tam first—to stop him from entering the nether realm."

"Impossible to know whether or not he is already gone." Emma continued walking toward the Western Harbour Crossing tunnel restricted by a fluorescent orange blockade. "The prophecy is corrupted and he is being summoned, but he might still be in this world. He also might have entered the nether realm—which means there is nothing we can do to stop him."

"Everyone sees him now as a killer of Elders, Cherub, and the innocent. Hard to believe he was once my best friend." Jack unzipped his hoodie and allowed a muggy breeze to cool his sweaty body. "If he is in Tai Tam, then we have a chance to stop him from crossing over."

Hoi Po Road paralleled Highway 3, which led to the tunnel entrance, and on the opposite side a chain-link fence surrounded the Yau Ma Tei Typhoon Shelter. Jack remembered the night he escaped through the basement tunnel at Beacon Hill, and now months later the hunt left him running on fumes. He was stronger in his faith yet had no clue how to stop a war. Emma approached a uniformed guard at the entrance while he waited near the road. She spoke with the officer, then waved Jack over. He hurried toward the entrance as the officer opened a security gate, allowing them to enter the secured typhoon shelter.

"How'd you make that happen?" Jack whispered.

Emma nodded toward the officer. "Seems the faction have followers everywhere."

"I thought he looked familiar—Quarry Bay." Jack turned his attention toward cameras mounted at the entrance. "Emma, we're being watched."

"Our arrival will never be seen—the faction will make sure of it."

"How did you know to come to the shelter?"

"The faction established an underground network to smuggle out those who are in most need from Hong Kong Island, then through a gateway in Kai Tak. The shelter is a midpoint."

"Do you have a way to reach Eliška?"

"We only communicated through Messagezilla—but the account is now disabled."

"Will accessed TheKeepers," Jack guessed, "which is how he knew about Manaus."

"Amina has not figured out how he knew the password or how long he monitored our messages. We kept our words few so we wouldn't reveal the faction's location."

On the deck of a sampan, a fisherman wrapped up a fishing net. He had weathered skin. Tattered clothes. Bare feet. He eyed them as they approached and stepped off the boat to greet them. Emma retrieved a silver coin and placed it in the man's sandpaper palm. The fisherman stared at the coin for a long moment, then looked up with a toothless smile.

Jack and Emma climbed aboard and settled in beneath a blue tarp covering part of the deck. Both leaned against rubber tires, split so the other half of the tread was used as a buffer against the pier. Emma leaned into Jack, her cheek pressed against his shoulder. While the sampan remained docked, Jack closed his eyes and tried to relax as another hour passed. No matter how hard he tried to slow the world around him, he couldn't keep his mind from racing.

Eden's Star took us back in history to the Battle of Everest. Why? I thought it was to stop Slybourne and Cherub from being defeated. Where would this world be if we changed history? Better? Worse? Well, it can't get much worse. We found the Rhoxen Stone, so was that the reason? And now we have the stone, so what happens if we use its powers?

Questions fired in rapid succession as Jack kept his eyes closed, recalling the Battle of Everest with Emma by his side. He never would've imagined such a moment if he hadn't been there alongside the Cherub warriors and pentaloons. Elyon's voice interrupted his thoughts.

Gifts given to the Seven Tribes of Cherub were meant for them to serve one another and to honor me as their Creator. Yet those artifacts now threaten to destroy and leave this world in a blinding darkness. Man's greed overshadows my grace, and a hunger for greater power starves the wicked from a freedom found in my presence. History is on the verge of repeating the darkest of ages. Walk cautiously, Jack, along a narrow path with what has been entrusted to you—or you will fall.

Jack heard Elyon's voice clearly, and he understood the warning. He didn't want to end up like Addison, but he also wasn't willing to let the sins of his father go unanswered. For a while he repeated Elyon's words to himself until the message was rooted deep in his soul.

Late afternoon faded, and night spread across West Kowloon. Once darkness enveloped the city, the fisherman pulled the line and started the motor. Jack jerked awake, and so did Emma. The sampan backed away and drifted between dozens more docked at the pier. Water slapped against the hull as the vessel headed past the Sky100 Hong Kong Observation Deck toward Victoria Harbour.

As the unlit sampan navigated across the harbor, green-and-white ferries remained docked at Star Ferry beside a cruise ship left empty since the city was cut off from the rest of the world. Peacefulness drifted across the water, while a raging trembling beneath Jack's skin left him on edge. He stared toward the iconic skyline devoid of neon lights and a majestic symphony hall where the arts had been abandoned. Anticipation swelled as the sampan drifted west away from Central. Emma spoke briefly with the fisherman, then stepped alongside. He knew she didn't need to grab his hand to gauge his emotions—the tension was thick.

"Are we going to Repulse Bay or Tai Tam?" Jack asked.

"Wherever you go," Emma said softly, "I will be by your side."

Jack flinched as he heard a voice call out in Cantonese. The fisherman slowed the sampan as a shadow appeared in the dark. Another vessel pulled alongside, packed with a dozen or more women and children. In the midst of Victoria Harbour, Jack and Emma helped them aboard until they stood shoulder to shoulder. Without being prompted, Jack and Emma jumped from the sampan onto the other vessel and watched as the fisherman and his cargo disappeared in the night.

No words were exchanged as the vessel they were on returned to a dock outside of Western Wholesale Food Market a few miles away from Central District on Hong Kong Island. Jack and Emma stepped onto dry land and hurried between delivery trucks outside of a warehouse where workers milled about. Jack grabbed Emma's shoulder and pulled her back between several trucks. He pointed at the gates where PRC military officers were stationed. A ParkNShop delivery truck headed in their direction and flickered the headlights.

"Right on time," Emma said. "C'mon, Jack."

Before he could ask what she meant, the delivery truck stopped beside them. Emma moved first and climbed into the passenger seat. On instinct, Jack piled in beside her and closed the door before glancing toward the driver.

"You're full of surprises." His gaze shifted between Eliška and Emma. "Both of you."

Eliška's smile faded. "So where are we going?"

"Tai Tam."

34

Twenty minutes later, Eliška pulled over on Island Road in Deep Water Bay after leaving Central and traveling through Pok Fu Lam Village and Aberdeen. On the drive from Western Wholesale Food Market, Jack asked the reason for the longer route and Eliška confirmed the roundabout way was to avoid major checkpoints in Central, Admiralty, Wan Chai District, and Happy Valley. He'd never seen the streets of Hong Kong Island so desolate.

"Ren provided a way to get past security in Tai Tam." Eliška flashed a magnetic card. "I have used it several times, and it has worked so far. We have waited for an opportunity to get close to Will and the Merikh, and tonight is our chance."

Jack's brows raised. "Ren and his cousin were supposed to be protected by the Cherub."

"His cousin was killed," Eliška retorted. "Ren does not trust them."

"I can't say I blame him." Jack glanced briefly at Emma. "Is he still in Tai Tam?"

"He was attempting to be smuggled out of the country through a gateway. Many are paying fortunes to escape—Cherub, Hong Kongers, and tourists who have been stuck here since the shutdown. In exchange for access, we provided Ren with enough money to leave."

"Who is providing access to the gateway?" Emma asked. "Cherub or Merikh?"

Eliška shook her head. "I do not know."

"Now gateways are for sale." Jack tried to wrap his head around what Eliška said about Ren, and his heartbeat quickened at the thought of facing Will again. "Are you sure he's there?"

"I have seen Will in Tai Tam only once." Eliška checked her watch and the side mirror. "I do not know for certain whether he will be there tonight, but our window is closing."

"Merikh only access gateways with a blood sacrifice," Emma pointed out.

"Which means Cherub and Hong Kongers are still being killed by the Merikh." Jack gripped the armrest of the van and tried to keep his heart from pounding through his chest. No matter which gateway they traveled through or what street he found himself on in Hong Kong, whenever he mustered up courage it wasn't without an equal dose of fear. "Will is able to jump the gateways, so even if we do find him in Tai Tam it won't be easy to catch him."

"How were you able to pay Ren?" Emma asked.

"Cherub left us behind, but we have allies," Eliška replied

coyly. "Friends of the faction, as well as Beacon Hill. We would not have survived this long without them."

"Burwick was supposed to give you . . ." Jack interrupted.

"The Rhoxen Stone remains with the professor." Eliška sat up a bit straighter behind the wheel as another delivery van passed from the opposite direction. "We tested the stone at Quarry Bay and confirmed the holder of the stone possesses the ability to stop time."

"It's crazy, isn't it?" Jack smiled. "We witnessed the same thing in another realm—during the Battle of Everest."

"Battle of Everest?" Eliška's brows raised. "Did you see Ryder Slybourne?"

"For a moment in time, we fought alongside the Rhoxen." Jack knew what Eliška was asking, but he didn't have the heart to share how Slybourne died. "A fantastical blur."

Every time they'd found an artifact, it seemed answering questions was trial by fire. On Everest everything happened at lightning speed, but there was no doubt he'd moved while the pentaloons, Cherub, and Slybourne were frozen. Legion were gone, and he wasn't sure whether the Nephilim warriors were too. When he tested the Rhoxen Stone at Eleanore's house, everyone and everything froze except for him. He couldn't think about any of the artifacts and ignore the truth within the writings of the prophecy.

Cherub focus on a promise, seekers are drawn by the quest of an outlier, and the faction root their cause in a descendant of the great warrior.

"All three of us are connected to the prophecy." Jack noticed Eliška's eyes flare and knew no further explanation was needed. *She's not surprised.* Emma and Eliška remained quiet, so he continued. "At least we know what the Rhoxen Stone can do, so we need to stay focused on how it can help us. Should we go get it before we head into the Merikh's den?"

"It is a greater risk to have the Rhoxen Stone with all three of us," Eliška pushed back. "Professor Burwick will guard the stone until the right opportunity presents itself."

"So, we risked our lives to find the artifact but we're not going to use it. Good plan."

"Eliška is right, Jack. Best we keep the artifacts separate from one another for now."

"Give me a minute—I'm still getting used to you two being on the same page."

Jack eyed the driver's-side mirror and watched the van that passed pull a U-turn. Eliška rolled her window down as the van slowed alongside. She exchanged words with the other driver, but Jack couldn't hear what was said. As the van accelerated, Eliška shifted into gear and followed at a distance.

"I'm guessing those are faction?" Jack asked.

Eliška nodded. "The most skilled from Quarry Bay."

"Seems like we're going in a little light, don't you think?"

"We have been effective so far." Eliška turned onto Repulse Bay Road, leaving Deep Water Bay behind. "And now we have both of you as well."

A winding mountain road through Tai Tam Country Park was almost deserted. Jack's grip on the armrest tightened as he stared out the passenger window. With a full moon shining bright within a twinkling night, Taiwan acacias and slash pines whipped past as mere shadows.

Eliška broke the silence. "The gateway is in Parkview block 15."

"You have an ID to get through the checkpoint, but what about us?"

Brake lights interrupted Eliška's answer as she slowed the van. Both vehicles switched off their headlights and stopped on the shoulder of Repulse Bay Road. Eliška climbed out, so Jack and Emma did the same. By the time they rounded the rear of the van, a group of armed men and women were gathered. Jack's heart skipped a beat as a wide smile left him stunned.

"What are you doing here?" Jack exhaled in disbelief.

Vince stood with the group, a semiautomatic strapped over his shoulder. "Same as you."

"But you left with your parents . . ." Jack glanced toward Emma. "Did you know?"

"No clue," Emma replied, equally surprised. "Vince, it is good to see you again."

Jack stepped forward and grabbed Vince's wide shoulders. "Still a specimen."

"Sounds like you two have been on quite an adventure." Vince's smile faded as he exchanged looks with Eliška. "Keepers reunion will have to wait."

"Emma and Jack will go with you," Eliška ordered. "And I will meet you there."

"We're about fifteen minutes on foot," Vince replied. "Give us a head start."

While the faction's elite headed into a thick forest, Eliška walked over to the delivery truck and opened the driver's side door. Vince stepped away, leaving Jack and Emma standing between the truck and the forest. Jack watched as Vince leaned down and kissed Eliška on the cheek. *This night is already full of surprises.* Headlights blinked on as the truck pulled onto Repulse Bay Road and headed further up the mountain. Vince waved them toward the forest.

Jack and Emma hurried to catch up with the others as Vince pushed the pace. A jolt of adrenaline riffled through Jack, leaving him ready to fight a dozen Nephilim kings.

"I can't believe you're here," Jack said between breaths. "What about your parents?"

"You rocked their world when you and Natalie disappeared off the yacht." Vince took the lead as Jack did his best to keep up. "We only got as far as Macau before Hong Kong was cut off from the rest of the world. My parents were afraid to head across the China Sea, so we docked in the harbor and waited. Burwick found us there—I don't know how—and asked for their help."

"Your parents are the allies," Jack guessed. "Didn't see that one coming."

"Eliška thought it was better to keep it a secret." Vince paused. "Too risky."

"Tim was right—they're way smarter than us."

"You're preaching to the choir, bro."

35

A cluster of high-rise apartments appeared between acacias and pines. Everyone breathed hard as they reached the edge of the forest. Vince remained focused on a checkpoint in the distance while Emma waited alongside Jack, who was doubled over, attempting to push through a cramp piercing his side. She squeezed his shoulder, and his breathing steadied.

"Are you ready to get him?" Jack asked.

"He's going down for what he's done," Vince replied.

Jack pointed at the semiautomatic in Vince's grasp. "You know how to use that?"

"I've been trained by the best. Turns out, Eliška is quite a sniper." Vince kept his gaze fixed on the checkpoint as he held up his fist. "Once the fireworks start, don't look back."

"Parkview block 15." Jack felt Soulweaver slip down his forearm and extend into its rod form. "Whenever this happens, I know we're heading straight into the insane."

Emma's lips curled at the corners. "No time to run from a fight."

All eyes were fixed on the ParkNShop delivery truck approaching the checkpoint. Merikh surrounded the vehicle and looked beneath the chassis. *Nightingale and Crozier fought in the Battle of Hong Kong, not much older than we are now. This is real, Jack. Life and death.* Another moment passed before the gate was lifted and the truck drove through the checkpoint. Vince motioned ahead, and the faction on the ground moved stealthily at double speed through the night. Jack's grip on Soulweaver tightened as he chased after them in the direction of a chain-link fence with razor wire along the top.

Vince grabbed a bolt cutter strapped to his back and knelt along with the others at the base of the fence. Jack and Emma did the same as the night remained eerily quiet. *What are we waiting for?* Soulweaver hummed in his grasp, and he knew things were about to get exciting. An explosion boomed across Tai Tam, followed by a reddish-orange fireball streaking toward the sky. Vince didn't hesitate as he cut apart the fence and slipped through the opening, then headed between apartment buildings as the others followed him.

The ParkNShop truck was engulfed in a fiery blaze on a pristine lawn near an enormous crystal clear pool. Hong Kongers lounging near the tennis courts darted indoors as Merikh in all black appeared and moved in unison toward the truck with weapons raised. Jack was startled when Eliška stepped out of the shadows and pushed him inside block 15. Vince opened a door to a stairwell and waved everyone through.

In a lowered voice, Eliška said, "Twentieth floor."

Faction peeled off to guard each floor entrance, leaving only Vince, Eliška, Emma, and Jack to reach the twentieth floor. Jack's instincts jackhammered as Vince aimed the barrel of his weapon toward the door. He gripped Soulweaver with both hands while Vince pushed the door open. All four entered an empty space that was the full width of the building. A putrid stench filled his nostrils, sickening him to the core.

Jack walked across bloodstained concrete. "A gateway is definitely in here somewhere."

"Merikh are sacrificing Cherub to enter wherever it leads." Emma retrieved a silver coin and stopped in the middle of the space. "Eliška, do you know any more?"

"We have not spoken to anyone who has traveled through, but we found a Cherub in the grocery store who told us which floor they believed was being used. Turns out they were right." Eliška held out a silver coin of her own. "Secondary mission is to follow the gateway."

"Might be our only chance." Vince took the coin from Eliška. "I'm ready."

"You can't go by yourself," Jack argued. "What about searching for Will?"

"If he's not here, then there's a chance he's somewhere on the other side."

"So what should we do?" Jack asked Emma. "Nether realm or gateway?"

"What is he talking about?" Eliška asked. "Will is in the nether realm?"

"There is a possibility," Emma admitted. "We came back to find out for certain."

"Clock is ticking," Vince said. "Staying or going?"

"Emma and I will go," Jack replied without hesitation. "You two search Tai Tam."

Vince flipped the silver coin in the air, and Jack caught it in one hand while gripping Soulweaver in the other. *I can't believe we're leaving again.* Emma dropped a coin onto the concrete, and he did the same. The solid concrete shifted to slush, spreading into a large puddle. Jack reached out and grabbed Emma's hand—their fingers interlaced naturally. As they stepped into the gateway, gunfire erupted in the stairwell. Vince and Eliška spun around as the door flew open. Bullets ricocheted off the concrete within inches of Jack and Emma as they sank into the floor. In the last few seconds, he didn't have a chance to shout or to stop himself. All he saw was Vince and Eliška moving toward the door returning fire.

36

JACK AND EMMA ROSE FROM the earth within a darkened catacomb until their boots were on solid ground. Millions of embedded skulls created walls on both sides and a ceiling overhead. Emma's lightforce glowed, illuminating their route deeper into a subterranean passageway. Soulweaver slipped from Jack's grasp, slithered beneath his sleeve, and wrapped around his forearm.

"We should go back," Jack said urgently. "Vince and Eliška . . ."

"Both can handle themselves," Emma reassured. "Keep going—follow the gateway."

"Definitely doesn't look like a road to freedom." His boots splashed through the catacomb as a putrid stench assaulted his nostrils—bitterness worse than death. "Whoever escaped wasn't expecting to end up in this place."

Further into the catacomb, a chill loomed and the walls of skulls turned icy. Jack swallowed puke in his throat as the stench grew worse. Eden's Star flared, sending his instincts into overdrive. A loud rumbling groaned in the passageway. When he glanced over his shoulder, a wave of skulls, ice, and rock appeared out of the darkness.

"Emma!" Jack shouted. "Run!"

Lightforce brightened the way ahead, searing and melting the icy walls. Jack and Emma raced through the catacomb to keep ahead of a collision. Skulls and stone crumbled and rolled beneath their boots, leaving them slipping and stumbling. Suddenly, Emma pulled him back from falling off a steep drop and used her bender gift to block the debris from slamming into them. With nowhere else to run, both jumped off a ledge as skulls and stone dropped into an abyss.

A free fall into nothingness lasted several seconds before they found themselves slowing to a stop. Neither slammed into the ground, splashed into a lake, or dug out from the sands near Mount Hareh. Jack's eyes darted around as he attempted to figure out where they were. Finally, his boots seemed firmly planted on a solid mass.

Emma squeezed his hand. "I am here, Jack."

A blinding flash of brilliant light pierced the blackness, erupting into burning buildings across Hong Kong. Jack braced himself, recognizing the vision. A raging inferno spread swiftly as the city crumbled. Beacon Hill appeared, and thousands wailed and screamed outside the flaming gates, piercing his ears and reverberating disturbingly.

"Are you seeing what I'm seeing?" Jack called out.

Flames reflected off her amber eyes as she nodded. "Settle your spirit—we are in the Scourge. Everyone from Tai Tam ended up here."

Fear riffled through him. "What's a Scourge?"

"A domain of suffering and torment. Keep your spirit fixed on Elyon to guide us so we do not surrender to the Scourge and remain lost." Emma's voice was steady, which gave Jack a sense of calmness. "Will may have corrupted and redirected the gateway—to leave those who pass through tormented in the Scourge."

Dark silhouettes whipped around the thousands unable to enter the gates of Beacon Hill. Vile squeals were deafening as the legion swept across a sea of people, leaving them dead.

Vince, Eliška, Amina, Bau, and Faizan. But this isn't the same vision. None of them were dead before. Hold on—this isn't a vision if Emma can see it too. Jack blinked and the deathly scene dissolved. He breathed a bit easier, believing he'd made it through the Scourge's test—but he was wrong.

Beacon Hill dissolved into the shantytown of Sitio Veterans, and he saw the shadow who lifted Rachel into the air before dropping her onto the banks of the river, lifeless. He glanced to his right and locked eyes with Emma, whose confused expression was unnerving.

"Jack . . ." Emma began, teary eyed.

"I know I can't trust my visions—not since Addison started messing with them—but if this isn't a vision, then what is it?" As soon as he spoke the words, the chaos within the Scourge faded and silence hung heavily. He remembered the photo in Areum's apartment: Rachel, Emma, and Areum smiling widely with their arms wrapped around each other's shoulders. *No doubt, they were family.* "Rachel wasn't killed by Chung or a bullet—but it wasn't you who was there that night."

"If I had been, then I would have sacrificed my life to save hers." Emma gathered herself. "Addison is a vision seeker, but I am seeing the same as you within the Scourge."

"Someone or something else killed Rachel." Jack settled the rage boiling beneath his skin. "Until we find out the truth, I'm trying to keep my soul rooted in Elyon."

Emma hugged Jack as the catacomb crumbled around them, leaving them standing in an endless bloodied desert. Dead bodies were piled as far as the eye could see—more than those who wished to escape through Tai Tam. He couldn't find the words to ease the horrific sight, beyond the devastation of the graves in Sakkhela or the ones on the edge of the Highlands.

"The gateway from Tai Tam to freedom is no more," Emma said softly.

Jack's hands balled into fists. "Will allowed them to die."

A figure moved among the dead, a woman with fiery red hair wearing a silver robe. She glanced over her shoulder with a striking stare—blue eyes with a tinge of orange. Another figure walked behind her, appearing as if from nowhere. Jack didn't recognize the woman, but there was no doubt who followed in her footsteps.

Soulweaver vibrated between his fingers as he darted across the sand. His pace quickened, passing the dead forgotten by the world. He readied himself to attack, never looking back to see whether Emma was behind. Will and the woman watched him with a deadpan stare as he lunged, swinging Soulweaver with a righteous vengeance.

"No!" Jack shouted, desperate, as they vanished. Soulweaver stabbed into the sand, causing a tremor strong enough to crack the earth. He dropped to his knees, angered and frustrated. "Elyon, why won't you rain down justice?"

Dejected, he pulled himself to his feet and turned toward Emma. She hadn't moved and she hadn't used her lightforce, which left him puzzled. He glanced around at the deceased, realizing the woman and Will were never real—merely another test and a vision that challenged him whether to believe or surrender to his darkest impulse. He trudged across the sand, and with each step the bodies in the Scourge disappeared.

"What did you see?" Emma called out.

"A woman was leading Will across the Scourge." Jack's brows furrowed, knowing the risks and warnings were woven together. "Millions more will die unless we go to the nether realm." He sensed her reluctance, so he held out his hand until she intertwined her fingers with his—seamlessly. "Emma, we need to convince Eleanore to show us where she has hidden the gateway. There's no other choice now."

37

JACK AND EMMA STEPPED OUT from Parkview block 15, where the delivery truck was a charred, defiant landmark of the faction's revolt. *Elyon, you can't allow anyone else to end up in the Scourge. Have mercy on this world for all who believe, and those who cannot see.* Near the ParkNShop store several more trucks were parked. Jack was relieved when Vince hurried over with his semiautomatic slung over his shoulder.

"You're alive," Jack said in disbelief. "What about Eliška?"

"We've secured the perimeter, but it won't last long." Vince motioned for them to follow him. "You weren't gone long, so what did you find on the other side?"

Jack avoided looking toward the bodies across the courtyard. "The Scourge."

"Sounds devious." Vince waved at Eliška, who was busy loading supplies. "Hustle up."

While the faction who arrived with them kept watch, they hurried over and helped others load trucks to capacity. Canned goods. Paper towels. Toilet paper. Boxed cereals. Dried goods. Fresh fruit. Bottled water, and gallons too. Jack blocked his mind from imagining what happened in Tai Tam while they were in the Scourge. Vince tossed him a box, snapping him out of thinking beyond the moment.

"Gateway is closed," Emma said to Eliška. "No one else is leaving through Tai Tam."

"Merikh will respond to keep control of the district, especially now."

"Will is not returning to Tai Tam anytime soon—he is heading to the nether realm."

A door slammed on one of the trucks and the faction were ready to leave. Vince forced one last box into the truck in front of them and closed the cargo area. Eliška climbed behind the steering wheel while Jack, Emma, and Vince piled into the cab. Trucks ahead pulled away, and armed faction securing the area pulled back and climbed on the running boards.

"I gotta admit," Jack said to Vince, "all of this seems to fit you perfectly."

"Eliška is showing me the ropes, and we're doing all we can to make a difference."

"What're your parents saying about all of this?"

"You are only promised sunlight for today—don't ignore the light."

"Don't ignore the light," Jack repeated. "Sounds like your dad."

"I'm proud to be their son." Vince smirked. "Wait until they see you."

Jack nearly asked about Tai Tam but instead fist-bumped Vince. "Truth."

With the checkpoint opened, trucks barreled through before skidding onto Wong Nai Chung Road. Eliška slowed the truck and hit the brakes hard before following the caravan down the mountain toward Happy Valley.

"Merikh and HKPF will be searching," she said, matter-of-fact. "If there is somewhere else you need to go tonight, this is our opportunity."

"Repulse Bay," Jack replied. "And we need to talk to Burwick."

Eliška wasted no time, punching the accelerator and turning down another road away from the caravan. She grabbed a walkie-talkie off the dashboard and relayed a message. "Deliveries and return to Homeland. Late night run, do not wait up."

"Copy," a crackly voice replied. "Don't wait up."

Jack leaned back in his seat, awestruck by the faction's resolve yet haunted by the Scourge. Vince and Eliška were leading the faction courageously at another level, and he'd never been more inspired by his friends. Months had passed for everyone, but it seemed like only a matter of weeks to him since he was transported to Manaus. Eden's Star was a gift, and he was the Protector. But the compass also skipped time, which left him off balance.

I've traveled into other realms beyond this world, but the world is passing me by on this side.

Late that night, all four were crammed into the cab as Eliška navigated the winding roads with apartment buildings on both sides—all eerily dark. *Why don't the Merikh and HKPF monitor this side of the island?* He wanted to ask the question, but he remained quiet, sensing an uneasiness from the other three. In that moment, Elyon's voice spoke deep within.

Blessed are the promisers of peace, for they will be called Elyon's warriors. The weapons you fight with are not weapons of this world, but divine powers to demolish the demons of old. There is a time for love to rule over hate, yet on this day a time for war is upon you to bring a lasting peace.

Tension was thick, too thick to cut through with words. He decided not to mention what Elyon whispered in his spirit and instead rallied against the weariness seeping into his bones.

The fight is hunting us whether we're ready or not. Elyon, we are your warriors. Unleash your powers through each one of us until it is done.

Fifteen minutes later the truck slowed beneath Violet Hill in Repulse Bay, the southern district known as the most expensive residential area in the world. Streetlights were dark. No other vehicles were on the road. No lights shining from what was left of the luxury apartments and beachfront properties. Repulse Bay was a ghost district. Influence and wealth had abandoned this hideaway once relished and envied by Hong Kongers, expats, politicians, celebrities, and the global elite.

"The Oceanside on Belleview Drive," Jack said. "That's where we need to go."

Eliška followed the route and parked outside a luxury apartment building. "Merikh were here?"

"Addison used this as a hiding place." Jack nodded at Emma. "We'll go inside."

"Make it quick," Vince interjected. "Longer we are out in the open, the worse it will be."

Jack and Emma climbed out of the van and entered the lobby of the Oceanside. The elevator doors were open, but there was no power. *Less talking. More walking.* He headed straight for the stairwell and double-timed the steps from one floor to the next.

"You're right about Eliška and Vince," Jack said over his shoulder. "Both are where they belong."

"We discover who we are when we stand in the fire alongside Elyon." Emma paused. "Some flames force us to grow up quicker than others."

"Let's hope Shen Jiahao isn't sending us on a wild-duck chase."

At the top of the stairwell was a locked door. Emma stepped forward with her hand outstretched. The metal twisted and imploded, then the door burst open to a penthouse apartment. *Her lightforcer and bender powers are growing even stronger, which is a good sign for anyone who stands on our side of the kabaddi line— way more than a fire mood experiment.* Jack stepped over the threshold, expecting to see the space untouched by the destruction found on the streets and throughout the district.

But on the white marbled steps, he stopped and looked down on a ravaged living room. Furniture and artwork were smashed and destroyed. Bulletproof windows were partially shattered. Shards of glass were scattered across the floor. He picked up a painting of a ship floating in a bay, which was shredded.

From one room to the next, the penthouse was in total disarray. Jack entered a bedroom and immediately noticed a deep-burgundy and light-blue striped jersey with the number 8 stitched on the front, left tossed on the bed. "Addison brought Will here."

Jack and Emma entered the hallway, where a glass wall revealed some kind of laboratory, which had been ransacked as well. He kept walking through the apartment until he entered a master bedroom with a study attached. An empty glass-topped desk. No photos of any kind. It looked as if no one had slept in the room in months.

"Shen said every penthouse in Repulse Bay has a safe room," Jack noted. "Most of them are in the master bedroom, as an easier way to hide. Question is, where is it?"

Jack walked around the room searching for an access point. He didn't know Addison well enough to guess what kind of entrance he would've created, but he was certain one existed. While Emma stepped into the study, he checked behind the bed before turning around. He stared at himself in a framed mirror, recognizing how ragged he appeared.

"Emma . . ." He stepped closer to the mirror. "Check this out."

He touched the mirror and ran his fingers around the sides of the frame. Nothing seemed out of the ordinary until he touched a lever. With the flip of a switch, he pulled the mirror from the frame, revealing an entrance into a safe room. He stepped inside the square room equipped with blankets, water, first aid kit, packaged food, flashlights, portable toilet, and gas mask. One wall was lined with weapons, and a crate sat in the corner.

"Are you feeling anything from Eden's Star?" Emma asked.

"Nothing." Jack grabbed the top of the crate and opened the lid. "But this is a treasure."

"When he attacked us in Aberdeen," Emma said, "Addison thought he would return."

Inside the crate, gold and jewels were piled to the brim. Jack reached in and grabbed a brooch, then held it out in the palm of his hand for Emma to see Slybourne's crest.

"He must've brought this from the Exodus Mines." Jack placed the brooch back into the crate. "We should take this with us, Emma. It's part of Eliška's heritage."

"Nothing here that will give us access to Kreidler." Emma tossed the packaged food on the floor, then looked inside the first aid kit. "I am sorry, Jack."

"Would've been too easy," he sighed. "At least we found some of Slybourne's treasure."

38

QUARRY BAY, HONG KONG ISLAND

Shortly before midnight, the delivery truck returned to an underground parking lot beneath the district. Faction were waiting to unload and move supplies into a storage area. Several of the other trucks from Tai Tam had returned from drop-offs across Hong Kong Island, and all were parked one behind the other facing the entrance. Vince and Eliška grabbed the heavy crate from the back of the truck and carried the treasure into a stairwell.

Jack was impressed by how organized the faction operated. While there were similarities to those who were living at Beacon Hill, the faction seemed more prepared and efficient. Not only were they distributing much-needed supplies across Hong Kong Island, but they were actively fighting back against the Merikh at the same time.

Professor Burwick approached with a slight limp. Her cauliflower ears and the scars on her face were visible, but she seemed stronger than when he'd seen her in Puerto Natales.

The ridges on Burwick's forehead deepened. "Come with me, both of you."

He expected to head straight for the rooftop, but instead Burwick stopped on the third floor and entered a hallway. The doors to the apartments were opened wide. Faction milled about from one room to the next. Jack glanced into several, noticing a heavy stock of weapons.

Burwick entered through a door where the wall between two apartments had been knocked down. Eliška stood with her back to them, scribbling on a hand-drawn map of Hong Kong that filled an entire wall. Vince was sorting through the crate, methodically setting each piece of treasure on a long folding table.

"The gateway in Tai Tam took people to the Scourge," Jack said pointedly. "No one has been set free from that place since this began—Cherub or anyone else."

"We hoped the gateway was a way out for many." Burwick's gaze hardened. "Eliška planned on securing Tai Tam for the faction."

Eliška glanced over her shoulder. "Months of planning, for nothing."

"The gateway is closed," Emma replied. "No one else will access it through Tai Tam."

Jack watched Eliška closely as she marked with a Sharpie on the wall. Red X marks labeled certain districts, and green lines displayed the routes between each one. Black circles were the only markings he couldn't decipher.

"What do the circles represent?" Jack asked.

"Checkpoints," Vince replied without looking up. "We have control of half of them."

"Do the Merikh or HKPF know?"

"We have managed to keep it a secret so far." Eliška turned and faced them. "After tonight, they will crack down on access since we failed to secure Tai Tam for ourselves."

"Eliška mentioned you traveled to Repulse Bay," Burwick redirected. "Why?"

"One of the artifacts," Jack replied. "We thought it might be there."

"Addison left a crate in a safe room of his penthouse," Emma explained. "Inside we found a portion of Slybourne's treasure. We do not know whether any of the pieces are significant."

"Most likely he brought it from the Exodus Mines," Jack suggested. "He didn't count on being caught when he attacked in Aberdeen, so it was left behind."

"Eden's Star?" Burwick asked.

"We searched, but I got nothing with the compass." Jack paused. "In the Scourge, we experienced the same vision that I've seen before—the same one Salomeh saw, Professor."

"A city burning," Burwick said under her breath. "Countless dying."

"Only this time the vision was darker—more destruction and death."

"Your vision is growing stronger, which means we are drawing closer to its becoming reality."

"Will was in the Scourge, along with a woman." Eliška and Vince stopped what they were doing and turned their attention toward Jack. "Flaming-red hair, eyes of fire, and she wore a silver robe. One minute they appeared, and the next they were gone."

"The Scourge is a domain of suffering, torment, and punishment." Burwick recited what Emma told Jack. "What you experienced in the Scourge mirrors the spirit realm, when souls pass through to eternity in the presence of Elyon—or remain tormented in the darkness of despair."

"Professor, Will is getting closer to the nether realm, and he's following the woman through the Scourge to get there. We may not find the last three artifacts in time to stop him from bringing what lies beyond the Highlands into this world."

Burwick shuffled across the floor and left the room. Jack glanced between Eliška, Vince, and Emma, wondering if anyone knew what was happening. A moment passed before Burwick returned with a leather-bound book in her grasp. The book appeared similar to the copy of the Eternal she gave him before they left Ine Town.

"Many years ago, I was given a gift from a dear friend—your mother." Goose bumps raised on Jack's arms while Burwick placed the book on the table beside Slybourne's treasure. "Illustrations dating back to the early centuries, a visual depiction of history throughout the ages." Jack, Emma, Eliška, and Vince gathered around as Burwick slowly flipped through the pages. "Gabriella was one of the Elders, and she was also a student of history—curious to learn about great kings, queens, explorers, and warriors." Burwick stopped on a page and stepped back, allowing Jack to lean in closer. "This one was finished shortly before the Battle of Everest, capturing Sir Ryder Slybourne and Florence Upsdell."

Slybourne's fire-breathing dragon crest was prominent on his armor. His dark eyes and weathered features were those of a man who had fought many battles. Beside Slybourne, Florence Upsdell stood regally in an embroidered silver robe with a leather scabbard over her shoulder, revealing only the hilt of a sword. Long, wavy flaming locks. The tinge of orange in her mournful eyes was haunting.

Jack stared intently at every detail while the others remained quiet. He noticed how Slybourne held Dragon Soul vertically, offering a detailed glimpse of the etchings in the sword. His mind flashed to the Battle of Everest, the Nephilim king, Soulweaver, Asiklua, and the Rhoxen Stone. He blinked several times as his gaze shifted back to Florence Upsdell, and he leaned so close he could see the grains in the parchment. She was holding something in her hand, clear enough for him to make it out. Jack took a step back as a chill multiplied his goose bumps by a million.

"I recognize the look in your eyes," Vince said. "What'd you see?"

Jack unzipped the pocket on his shoulder and retrieved the slim wooden box. He opened the box and unrolled the parchment, then placed the ivory figurine onto the page next to the illustration. It was a perfect match. He stepped back so everyone could get a better look.

"Florence Upsdell is the one summoning Will to the nether realm."

A passage from

MISCHIEVOUS ESCAPE OF THE NINE DRAGONS

Florence Upsdell and Ryder Slybourne, saddled to galloping destrier horses, pursued one another through a lush emerald forest. With her fierce red hair whipping, Florence rode like the wind as laughter burst from her lips. A scabbard slung over her shoulder protected the silver sword forged in the blacksmith's lair. Her gaze narrowed as she closed in, nearly knocking Ryder off his horse when she passed between giant oak trees and vine roots jutting from the earth. A clearing appeared ahead and she pulled on the reins, slowing the destrier to a prance.

"Cheater," Ryder chided half-heartedly. "At least you did not fall off this time."

"You taught me well," she mused. "Perhaps I am the master rider now."

"Your horse was faster." Ryder dismounted his destrier. "It was only fair."

"Because I am a woman?" Florence's eyes flared. "Ryder, we are equals."

"Of course." His cheeks flushed. "Forgive my ignorance, *my lady*."

"You are forgiven." She smirked slyly. *"Apprentice."*

Ryder chuckled. "A tongue as deadly as a titanoboa."

Without hesitating, Florence climbed off her destrier and grabbed him with both hands. She pulled him close and kissed him gently, then stepped back with a sheepish grin of pure innocence. From the moment she'd knocked him down in the village months earlier, she had fallen in love like never before. She welcomed the banter between them and ensured her quick wit kept him off balance. But she knew deep in her soul she was willing to sacrifice herself to save his life if needed.

"We are forbidden from going any further," Ryder said.

"Are you afraid of what lies beyond?" Florence smiled. "I am not."

Ryder's brows furrowed. "What are you up to, Florence?"

"I want you to meet an old friend—Kaida."

"You are saying Kaida lives beyond?"

"Quite smart for a Rhoxen."

In the quiet, Florence led the way deeper into the forest. The lush greenery faded to shades of gray. She shivered as their surroundings turned frosty. She knew Ryder was fearless on most days, and she admitted her bravado and love for him pushed her beyond her own nightmares. A bone-chilling shriek startled them, and they ducked behind a fallen oak tree. Huddled together, they stared toward the skies as a great winged beast flew above the tree line in the direction of the village.

"Dragons are protectors of the Rhoxen," Florence whispered. "Not badgers or weasels."

"Never seen one up close." Ryder inched a bit nearer. "How much further?"

"You are closer than you might imagine."

Adrenaline surged as she continued deeper into the unknown, shadowed by Ryder. She stopped suddenly and grabbed his arm, keeping him in the bushes. Dead ahead, a cave camouflaged within a rocky hillside caught her attention. She eyed the cave intently, searching for a sign, while an eerie stillness lingered. A twinge rippled down her spine. She expected Kaida to greet them, but the silence remained deafening.

Florence darted from the bushes toward the cave, stopping cold at the entrance as she stared at shattered eggshells and dark crimson splattered on the rocks. Ryder was on her heels as she struggled to comprehend what had occurred.

"Dragon's blood." She slipped the sword from her scabbard and steadied herself.

"Hold on a minute." Ryder's brows raised. "Best we leave and return to the village."

"We cannot go back until I am certain Kaida is safe."

"Fine." He retrieved his sword and pointed ahead. "I am with you always."

Inside the pitch-black cave, Florence and Ryder moved quietly through a passageway wide enough for a full-grown dragon. She glanced down as her boots sloshed, and then she halted Ryder again. Both stood motionless, unsure of what was ahead. She knelt and stabbed her finger into the dirt, then smelled dragon blood on her skin. Fear riffled through her veins as she fought against the unthinkable.

"Do not be afraid, Ryder."

"What do you mean?"

Florence's palms glowed a dull ocean blue, illuminating the passageway enough for them to see what was directly ahead. Ryder's eyes widened as he stepped back with his sword at the ready. Florence knew she had kept a secret from him far too long.

"Are you a witch?" Ryder blurted. "Or a sorcerer?"

She shook her head. "I am a Cherub."

"I have never seen a Cherub with gifts before."

"And now you are in love with one." Florence's stare hardened, the flecks of orange in her eyes glimmering from the blue glow surrounding them. "There is much to tell you, but it will have to be later."

Florence moved swiftly through the passageway, knowing there was more dragon blood beneath her boots. When she was a child, her father had returned home with a black egg larger than she had ever seen. It was the night of an unexpected birth—when she gazed into the striking eyes of Kaida—before death swept through their home, and by daybreak Florence was left an orphan.

The passage led to a dragon's den and a stunning, beautiful creature sprawled out on the stone. Florence stepped forward as Ryder stared in disbelief at the magnificent dragon before him. She was struck by the devastating wounds on Kaida's scaly skin, unlike any she had seen before.

"These wounds are not from a dragon," she whispered, "or from a weapon of man."

Labored breathing echoed off the stone walls, sending a chill through Florence's body. She gazed into Kaida's piercing eyes, and her soul welled up with tears. A low groan rumbled as Florence caressed Kaida softly, hoping to offer comfort and peace.

"Kaida," she said somberly, "I cannot bring healing."

"Florence . . ." Ryder stood wide-eyed. "This is your friend?"

"She is more than a friend." Florence swallowed hard as Kaida groaned. "She is family."

"Tell me what I can do to help."

Florence hurried down Kaida's enormous body, then knelt alongside her. From beneath the belly of the dragon she retrieved one black egg, then another. Ryder peered over her shoulder as she counted nine dragon eggs. She lined the eggs in a row and rushed back to lock eyes with Kaida. Her hands pressed against the dragon's jaw, and the blue glow spread over the beast's body. Florence leaned in close with tears seeping down her cheeks. She stared into Kaida's steely gaze as the dragon's heartbeat vibrated against her body—slowing one beat at a time.

"Elyon, if it is your will," she said, "I ask for mercy."

Kaida exhaled, and the beating of her heart ceased. Florence stepped back, her palms glowing bright. An earth-toned flame appeared above Kaida and hovered in front of them. Florence held out the silver sword and watched as the flame was drawn closer. She gripped the hilt tight as the flame surged the blade, seeping into the etchings, and vanished.

"From this day," she said solemnly, "the sword will be known as Dragon Soul."

"I cannot believe what I have witnessed," Ryder admitted, "and yet my eyes have seen it."

"We must not tell anyone," Florence warned. "A secret between us to the grave."

"If Kaida was the dragon protecting our village, then what was the beast in the sky?"

39

Jack paced the rooftop, unsettled by the discovery of Florence Upsdell, the ivory figurine, and the realization that she was guiding Will closer to the nether realm. An hour earlier, he'd tried to convince Professor Burwick the way forward was to speak with Eleanore, but the argument had left everyone isolated. He stepped near the chain-link fence surrounding the rooftop and gazed out on the city he loved which once glowed bright in the night—now left with only a fraction of a spark.

My plans are set before you, to guide others toward hope and a future where light illuminates darkness. In my strength you will soar on eagle's wings—you will run and not fall until the fight is done.

Elyon's voice resonated as Jack kept his sights on the city, fighting back a wave of emotions threatening to spill over onto his cheeks. He welcomed the words into his spirit and was reminded once again of what was at stake.

Vince was seated on a mattress, leaning back against a wall in a space on the rooftop far tidier than the Nightingale dorm. Eliška's cot was where it had always been, but there were more weapons lined up nearby—which was a strange sight because the first time he'd seen her aboard the *Eastern Dragon* she seemed so helpless. Emma had found a bed close to Eliška and watched him pace back and forth while remaining silent.

"Eleanore is the only one," he blurted. "No one else knows how to enter."

"Don't get everyone fired up again," Vince warned. "Burwick said she'd give it a shot."

"You know what will happen if you enter the gateway to the nether realm," Eliška said.

"If I go to the nether realm, yes, I might die—which, believe me, is not on my bucket list—but all of you know I'm already dying." Jack walked briskly toward the trio. "This is more than a promise to Rachel or even finding the artifacts. It's about stopping what might end this world."

"We spent months building a network across the districts. Soon we will launch a revolt against the PRC and Merikh to control the checkpoints on Hong Kong Island. We need to remain strategic, Jack."

"You're not the only one sacrificing," Vince pointed out. "We are all fighting."

"But I'm the one with Eden's Star burning a hole inside of me."

"And we're the ones trying to keep you alive—that's the truth."

Jack knew deep down they were right, but the fight wasn't

getting any easier. *Who do I think I am? I'm no hero. I'm no chosen Cherub. I'm an outlier. I'm the one who thinks of the Rod of Elyon as Soulweaver. I'm the Executioner's spawn. I'm an addict and a gambler whose sister died to pay my debt. And I'm the weakest one among us.* Frustrated, he slumped onto a mattress next to Vince and grumbled under his breath.

"Jack, you do not have to save the world alone," Eliška said. "We are by your side."

"You're not getting rid of me this time either," Vince teased. "That's a promise."

"Now your parents know the truth," Jack mused reluctantly. "It's all on you."

"Three artifacts are left," Emma finally chimed in. "One is hidden by Addison, and we have no clue where to find it. The second is possibly in the Exodus Mines or Kreidler—and we have no way to enter either one. The third, we believe, is in the nether realm—an unimaginable choice."

"And Will has a head start, Emma." Jack hoped she was surrendering to the idea of heading straight into the fire. "Every hour we debate, we fall further behind in stopping him."

"Rhoxen Stone." Eliška sat up on the edge of her cot. "That is how we enter Kreidler."

"Not a bad idea, actually," Emma admitted. "Professor Burwick might know a gateway to Zurich."

"If Addison is still alive, he might head to Zurich to retrieve what he has kept hidden there." Eliška's gaze darkened. "He will not allow the PRC or Will to rule the Merikh."

"So we take a gateway to Zurich," Vince reiterated, "and wait for Addison to surface."

"Which still leaves the nether realm," Jack said. "There is no way around it."

"Jack, it is late," Emma replied. "Burwick will let us know in the morning."

"One thing I've learned from keeping up with Eliška and the faction," Vince suggested, "is that you better sleep and eat whenever you get the chance. Rest up, Jack. You're gonna need it."

Jack unzipped his hoodie and tossed it at the foot of the mattress. He eyed Soulweaver wrapped around his forearm, then glanced toward the weapons lined up near Vince and Eliška. *What battles have they fought while we've been gone?* Both seemed to carry themselves with a heavier burden, and an even greater purpose. He slumped onto the mattress and lay back as his muscles ached and his soul remained troubled. In the stillness, he searched his spirit for another ounce of courage.

Silence lingered as each one settled down for the night. Vince shuffled across the rooftop and flipped a switch. The lights beneath the metal overhang shut off. No doubt Jack had experienced moments of freedom and exhilaration along the journey, especially when he sensed Elyon's presence in every stride. But even he admitted that the nether realm was a one-way ticket. With his eyes closed, graves from the edge of the Highlands and the dead abandoned in the Scourge flashed in his mind, unwritten pages beyond the Eternal.

I wonder if Xui Li knows the truth about the nether realm—and if she's willing to tell me.

"In the fiery battles of this world," Emma said softly in the dark, "Elyon promises strength with a righteous hand and courage poured out upon our bravery."

"We will not fear—and we will not be dismayed," Vince continued, "for we are chosen to glorify Elyon and defend the light, in this realm and beyond."

"For us to live is Elyon," Eliška seamlessly picked up where Vince left off, "and to die is a gateway to eternal glory."

"Amidst the darkness unchained through flames and strife"— Jack's mind shifted to reading this line in Rachel's poem for the first time—"lies a hope our souls may be reborn from death to life."

"Elyon, we stand before you as one." Emma finished the warrior's prayer. "Amen."

Jack whispered along with Eliška and Vince, "Amen."

For a while he lay on the thin mattress, anticipating another vision to haunt his dreams. He listened to his heartbeat thumping to a steady rhythm and pictured what Professor Windsor showed him in the exam room. Tears welled up in his eyes, dripping down his cheeks. He gritted his teeth to stop himself from breaking down, then rolled over and curled up in a ball.

I miss Rachel, Areum, and Tim.

40

By late morning, Eliška and Vince crested the summit with Shek O Peninsula in the distance below. Beyond Pottinger Gap, a forested landscape wrapped around urban high-rises where a path diverted from the trail. Another half-mile trek through thick brush and over a water channel brought them to several concrete military shelters overgrown with thick vines and moss.

"He didn't give you any idea what he wants?" Vince asked.

"If he is risking a meeting, it must be important."

"We're keeping Jack and Emma on the down-low, right?"

"Not one word about either. We do not know how long they will stay."

"Jack's determined to find the nether realm." Vince checked his watch. "When he sets his mind to something, he's like a dog with a bone. He will do anything to protect those who are close, and I'd do the same for him."

Eliška smiled slightly. "Seems we share that in common, Vince."

"Listen, you haven't dealt with Bau," Vince replied. "I'm the only one in the bunch who gets along with him, especially since we won the Bashers, Bowlers, and Boundaries."

"With the Tai Tam gateway closed, we need to move the timeline up." Eliška glanced around to be sure no one had followed them. "If Bau lends us access to the Cherub, we have a better chance of securing the checkpoints across Hong Kong Island."

"A big favor to ask of Bau," Vince said in a lowered voice. "It'll take some convincing."

Eliška was first through the doorway of one of the shelters. "Sorry we are late."

"We don't have maps to the gateways." Vince fist-bumped Bau. "Or enough silver coins."

"Rumors spread about your return." Bau smiled slightly. "You two have reached legendary status among the Cherub after freeing those at Shek Pik."

"Who knew a walk through Admiralty would turn us into fugitives?"

"The faction are fortunate to have you on their side."

"Different teams, but the same side—like Beacon Hill."

"The school is no longer what you remember." Bau shifted uncomfortably. "Cherub who continue to arrive and remain on the grounds are refugees—fewer lightforcers, benders, and healers than we hoped. Time is running out before the PRC and Merikh will find a way to enter and target every last one of them." He turned his attention toward Eliška. "Last night the faction were in

Tai Tam and caused quite a commotion. Everyone in the district is afraid of the uproar and blowback from the PRC."

"You are wondering about the gateway," Eliška surmised, "because of your parents."

"Not only my parents, but all Cherub and Hong Kongers who wish to pass through."

"Tai Tam gateway is closed—which is best for everyone."

"The gateway led to the Scourge," Vince added. "Not a place of freedom."

"The Scourge," Bau repeated, thrown a bit more off balance. "You are certain?"

"Your parents are lucky. You have the faction to thank."

"And I suppose Emma and Jack were not involved."

Vince kept his game face on. "Not sure what you mean—"

"How were you able to close the gateway?" Bau pressed. "Neither of you are gifted."

"All you need to know is no other Cherub will be trapped in the Scourge because of the Merikh tricking them into entering the gateway when they're desperate to leave."

"Why are we here, Bau?" Eliška interrupted. "Must be more than Tai Tam."

"PRC offered a truce between Cherub, Merikh, and the government." Bau hesitated. "In light of you lot marching across the city with Cherub gifts on full display, then disappearing off the face of the earth, they want to use the Merikh method to strip Cherub of all gifts."

"The Merikh and PRC will not stop with Cherub gifts. You are smart enough to know that, I hope."

"There is a chance to find a resolution to keep the peace—with a counteroffer."

"You are planning to hand us over to them," Eliška said pointedly. "That is your truce."

Vince charged forward and grabbed Bau by his shoulders, pinning him against the wall. "You've made a big mistake—worse than choosing Upsdell."

Bau's palms glowed a vivid auburn as his lightforce struck Vince, sending him sliding backward across the dirt floor. While Bau knocked Vince off balance, he didn't knock him off his feet. Vince braced himself, ready to charge again as Eliška remained steady.

"I am not as daft as you lot believe." Bau held up his palms and the lightforce vanished. "I offered the PRC an alternative to allow Cherub to keep their gifts, and in return we will protect their interests. And yes, I promised to deliver all four of you to them. What else was I supposed to offer to keep them from raiding every district?"

"Are you betraying us?" Vince asked, angered. "To save yourself?"

"Fang Xue is more than willing to honor this promise to the PRC, but I am not. However, allowing the PRC to believe I am willing to give them what they desire will enable Cherub to retain their gifts for when the real war begins."

Vince's brows furrowed. "They won't wait forever, Bau."

"If there is a truce to be made, it should be between Cherub and faction."

"We are not refugees," Eliška pointed out. "You need us to do what the Cherub cannot."

"An army of Cherub from Beacon Hill will not win against the Merikh." Bau exhaled long and hard. "You are right, Eliška—the faction is needed more than ever."

"I am open to a truce with conditions." Eliška stepped forward. "First, we need your help to take control of the rest of the checkpoints and force Merikh and HKPF from the island. It is the only way for us to be prepared for what is coming. Second, we begin evacuating through other gateways, which you will open for Cherub, faction, and Hong Kongers."

"Isn't there a gateway in one of these buildings," Vince interrupted, "which takes you to the Sanctuary of Prayer?"

"You have spoken with Emma and Jack." Bau shook his head. "An outlier . . ."

"Terms of the truce are clear," Eliška pressed. "And the faction will stand with Cherub."

"I give you my word." Bau held out his hand. "We will find the right gateways."

"One more thing . . ." Eliška shook his hand. "Will is searching for the nether realm."

"Someone is summoning him there," Vince added. "Florence Upsdell."

Bau's jaw dropped. "You mean *the* Florence Upsdell?"

"She is leading him through the Scourge—to the most dangerous artifact of all."

"A truce is a truce," Eliška bantered. "You gave us your word, Bau."

41

Alone on the rooftop, Jack dug his elbows into his thighs and squeezed his eyes shut. A migraine pulsed at the back of his skull and pressed intensely against his pupils. Lightheadedness washed over him as his grip on the metal frame of the cot tightened. His heart pounded in his chest, harnessing a twinge of fear beneath his skin. He controlled his breathing, sinking from the present deeper into another vision.

Shadows brightened within the inner chamber of the Dungeon of Savages. Flaming torches encircled Addison while angelic Cherub warriors in pure golden armor stood guard with silver swords. Addison's dark eyes stared intensely at the Cherub. His scraggly hair and beard were gray with filth, and his blackened hands and crooked fingers hung by his sides.

214

Jack clenched his teeth, and his knuckles turned whiter the harder he gripped the frame. A flash from the last time he'd seen Addison interrupted for a split second. Addison was shouting uncontrollably, his curses muted within the chamber. Unafraid, Jack pressed deeper into the vision, surrendering willingly to experience the unknown.

Elyon, show me what's hidden.

A rumbling shook the inner chamber, and the walls of the vault crumbled when Jack discovered an opening leading to the ancient Rhoxen longship. Within the chamber he stepped closer and counted every second, remembering nearly drowning inside the vault. *Four. Five. Six. Seven.* He remained unseen by angelic warriors and Addison. A rumbling roared beyond the chamber and shook the stone beneath his feet. He glanced over his shoulder expecting a tidal wave to burst through, but the iron doors remained sealed.

Jack's attention was divided between Addison, angelic Cherub guards, and waiting for the flood to sweep through the chamber. Dark shadows whipped among the flames surrounding the invisible force field confining Addison. At first glance, the shadows seemed to be an illusion caused by the flickering fire. But when the angelic Cherub lifted their swords, Jack knew there was more going on than what could be seen. He shuddered as wailing and screams echoed in his ears, guessing those were the prisoners being held on the other side of the inner chamber.

Cherub floated swiftly across the chamber with swords raised. Addison stood unwavering with a dead stare. From the darkness, ebony flames erupted against the angelic warriors, who defended themselves with their wings. Shadows morphed into legion, who swept around Addison with charcoal spears pointed toward the

Cherub. The standoff lasted only seconds. Legion attacked the angelic warriors mercilessly.

Jack wanted Soulweaver to slip from his forearm so he could defend the Cherub, but he was simply a spectator to the past. A shiver shuddered his bones when Addison stepped beyond the circle. *The invisible force field is gone.* Legion surrounded Addison, whipping around his body as the Cherub warriors counter-attacked. Light and dark clashed, but when the Cherub warriors floated away, the legion and Addison had vaporized.

Jack released his grip on the metal frame and exhaled. With his eyes still closed, a few seconds passed before he fully returned to the present. He pushed himself off the mattress and paced the rooftop, gathering his thoughts. *If Addison is alive, the legion took him. But maybe the Cherub killed them all. Either way, the Dungeon of Savages is no more.* Addison had messed with his visions before, so in the quietness of the morning he sifted through what he'd seen and tried to determine whether it was what had occurred.

Guilt lingered, as he knew he was responsible for flooding the vault when he and Emma found the Rhoxen longship and opened a gateway. While the vision didn't reveal the moment the dungeon flooded, so far everyone who knew had confirmed it was so. He mumbled under his breath, "Is it possible the legion entered the chamber when the gateway was open?"

If you live in the past, your future remains dead.

Elyon's voice resonated in his spirit, and he welcomed the wisdom. So much of his struggle dealt with letting go of the past and of unanswered questions that left him guessing whether he was on the right path. He carried the weight of his failures, no matter the miraculous events he'd encountered since Rachel's death. He didn't know how to bury his sins without digging them back up when uncertainty about the future left him questioning everything. But Elyon's words rang true. *Live in the past, and the future remains dead,* he told himself. *I've got nothing left to lose, and the clock is ticking. Doesn't matter how the legion entered the Dungeon of Savages—they were there, and now Addison is gone.* The rooftop door opened, snapping him out of his thoughts.

Emma and Professor Burwick stepped out from the stairwell, and Jack noticed the tension between them. As he walked toward them, he was struck with a sudden urge to know what the secret meeting was about between Eliška, Vince, and Bau.

"I spoke with Eleanore," Burwick said, matter-of-fact. "Of course, she is reluctant."

Emma held up her hand, anticipating his reaction. "Jack, there is a twist."

"Should've known it's not as easy as dropping a coin," he replied. "Listen, the stakes are higher than anything we've faced so far, and there is no other way."

"Eleanore is insistent you be aware of the consequences," Burwick said. "She created the gateway in such a way that only someone who shares the same bloodline as Gabriella and Addison can pass through."

"Well, it's settled then." Jack waved his arms. "I'm their son."

"If you enter the gateway with Eden's Star, then you will die," Emma reminded him.

"So I can enter the gateway because of my DNA, but I'll die because of the compass."

"Eleanore cannot say whether Emma will survive the gateway either," Burwick added. "She created the gateway for your father and mother, but she is fearful the passageway is corrupted."

"One of the artifacts is in the nether realm, and odds are it's the worst one." Jack's shoulders slumped a bit. "But we have to try, or else we might as well surrender now."

Professor Burwick exchanged a disapproving look with Emma. "I cannot—"

"I'm the Protector of Eden's Star," he retorted. "I know what's at stake."

"You are too valuable to the fight to risk a reckless decision."

Jack pulled up his sleeve and revealed his scarred arms. "We're beyond reckless now."

"Wherever the fight leads," Emma interrupted, "I will stand with you."

"Seems like you have both made up your minds," Burwick noted.

"Professor, if there's another way," Jack pressed, "tell us what it is."

"Faction and Cherub are barely surviving," she admitted. "But it will not last."

"Please tell Eleanore we need her help and we're ready to go."

"She has told me where the gateway is hidden," Burwick replied. "I will spare her from the torment of sending you and Emma to the nether realm."

"Where is the gateway?" Emma asked.

"Xui Li has offered to take you." Burwick hesitated, clearly struggling. "It's on Thalren Isle."

42

HONG KONG ISLAND

Along Fenwick Pier Street, a delivery truck slowed without rolling to a full stop. A door slid open along the side of the van, and Jack hopped out with Emma right behind. Both picked up a brisk pace along the nearly empty sidewalk, heading north before reaching Tamar Park, next to the Legislative Council Complex. No doubt street cameras captured them, and within minutes their identities would be confirmed by government surveillance.

"Eliška and Vince will be cross when they return," Emma said.

"Neither would've let us go without them, but they're needed by the faction." Jack kept close to a tree trunk with leaves and branches shading overhead. "Honestly, I wish you'd stay with them instead of risking everything to go with me. You are needed by Cherub *and* faction."

"We made a promise to each other, Jack." Emma eyed the grassy area intently. "Since we left Quarry Bay, I have been thinking about what Professor Burwick said. Only someone who shares the same bloodline can pass through. Eleanore created the gateway based on your parents' DNA—your DNA. Your father's blood might have been transfused into me when my gifts were taken by Charlotte."

Jack's brows raised. "You might've cracked the case, Sherlock."

"But Burwick never mentioned how much is needed to pass through the gateway."

Directly across the park, Xui Li crouched near another tree. She held up her hand to stop them from crossing over, which dropped a boulder into the pit of Jack's stomach. In the distance, sirens wailed and tires screeched. Xui Li stood and moved swiftly along the tree line toward Victoria Harbour. Without questioning, Jack and Emma chased after her on their side of the park.

Armored vehicles rambled in front of the Legislative Council Complex, then left deep tread marks in the grass of Tamar Park. Jack pumped his arms and legs to keep up with Emma, and hearing the vehicles gaining ground, he pushed his muscles even harder. Xui Li reached the end of the park and leapt off the boardwalk into the harbor.

Gunfire erupted as bullets splintered tree trunks and kicked up dirt beneath the grass, inches from piercing Jack's boots and his body. Jack caught up to Emma, and both jumped over the edge at the same time. He plunged deep into the murky yellowish-green water. Bullets pierced the surface and streaked past into the depths. A hand grabbed his arm and pulled him deeper as he struggled to hold his breath. Desperate to keep his wits about him, he realized there were two others beside him. The water was so murky, he couldn't tell which was Emma and which was Xui Li. He dove with them until all three entered a dark hole. Seconds passed before they surfaced in an underwater cave beneath Admiralty.

Jack coughed up a mouthful of water. "Nothing like nearly drowning to wake you up."

"Hopefully they believe we have drowned," Xui Li said. "Did you bring the coins?"

Emma retrieved the silver coins from her pocket. "Not many are left."

"We only need three for the next step," Xui Li explained. "I must ask each of you if you are certain the nether realm is where you wish to go."

"I'm positive," Jack said without hesitation. "Even though I'm pretty sure the City of Gods is an amusement park compared to what we're up against."

"The consequences will be severe if you fail." Xui Li turned her attention fully toward Jack. "With Eden's Star within you, even if you succeed, you risk losing your life."

"We will not fail," Emma replied, resolute. "And I will be with Jack the whole way."

"Professor Burwick said something about Thalren Isle." Jack glanced around the cave. "Is the gateway here instead or what?"

"Two gateways are required." Xui Li's gaze remained steadfast. "We must give an offering to reach Thalren, which is where Eleanore created the gateway to the nether realm."

"Then let's go," he pressed. "I'm not changing my mind."

"Which is why Rachel chose you to fulfill her promise." Xui Li grinned proudly. "I had to ask so when Salomeh and Professor Burwick question me I have an answer. You have earned the right to choose your destinies, and I will take you as far as I can go."

Emma handed each of them a silver coin. Xui Li dropped one into the water and stepped back. Jack and Emma did the same, uncertain of where the passageway would emerge.

I hope we're not diving back in and heading to the surface.

Right before his eyes, the cloudy water turned to solid ice. Xui Li stepped onto the ice and motioned for them to follow. All three stood face-to-face as the ice split into pieces, popping and cracking. Jack gasped for oxygen as they dropped through at the same time. Taking a mouthful of air, he plunged beneath the ice, but strangely his boots landed on soft sand. Once he realized he was underwater, he pushed off the bottom and swam to the surface. His head popped above calm waters, leaving him stunned by the beauty unveiled before him.

43

THALREN ISLE

Out of a turquoise and rich-blue ocean, rocky-edged mountains jutted from a desolate horseshoe-shaped island, camouflaged beneath lush greenery. Eerie bright-red sap dripped down countless dragon's blood trees. In the center of the island, daylight reflected across a serene glassy surface. Jack waded through the pool, rippling water in his wake, then trudged up a white-sand beach. He touched the dretium on his sleeve, surprised his hoodie and the rest of his clothes were bone dry. Xui Li and Emma neared the shore, stepping out with dry clothes too.

"Welcome to Thalren," Xui Li said reverently, "where the Elders of old are remembered."

"Reminds me of Karābu," Jack replied, "except this is even more beautiful."

"Why did Eleanore create the gateway here?" Emma asked.

"Elders are the only ones permitted on Thalren." Xui Li took several steps across the sand as if she were strolling along her own land. "Many years ago, we often escaped to this place for refuge from the battles we waged against darkness. During those days we were united, until . . ."

"Peter stole Eden's Star and began searching for the artifacts," Jack suggested. "Eleanore broke the rules by coming here with my mom and Addison, since neither Eleanore nor Addison are Elders."

"Gabriella loved him so deeply, failing to see darkness in his soul. Jack, she is the one who broke the rules of Thalren by allowing them to enter through the gateway." Xui Li shook her head slowly. "Addison convinced her to enter the nether realm to recover the artifact before Peter found what was hidden. An artifact kept beyond the Highlands since the Siege of Plagues. Eleanore was under his spell, too, so she disobeyed the Eternal *and* Elyon when she created the gateway in Thalren."

"I have never read about the Siege of Plagues in the Eternal," Emma pointed out.

"Not all history is written on the page." Xui Li slumped onto the sand and pulled her knees close to her chest. She waited until Jack and Emma were seated, then continued. "During the Second Great War the Seven Tribes of Cherub battled against an enemy far greater than the Nephilim king, Asiklua, the legion, or Merikh— the Queen of Sakkhela."

"Florence Upsdell," Emma whispered. "The statue in Sakkhela is of the queen."

"After Ryder Slybourne was killed on Everest, Florence turned away from the light." Xui Li paused. "Wickedness deeper than the vilest sins in the City of Gods consumed her soul. She fought with a lethal vengeance and waged a mighty war against Cherub and Merikh."

"'I have seen a beast swallowed by darkness,'" Jack recited, "'slumbering amidst wild waves of the sea and wandering stars in the skies.'"

"Florence Upsdell swore vengeance against all who failed to save her lost love." Xui Li's gaze shifted between them. "Cherub and Merikh were powerless to stop the plagues."

"What kind of plagues?" Emma asked.

"Vast oceans turned to blood, animals on every continent massacred, hailstorms mightier than the worst thunderstorms, locusts swarming the lands, darkness blocking the sun, and curses that killed the firstborns of all Cherub and Merikh. Still, only the Elders of old knew it was the Queen of Sakkhela who unleashed her deadly rage against this world."

"Were you there during the Siege of Plagues?" Jack asked.

"I am old, Jack"—Xui Li smirked slightly—"but I am not that old."

"The Elders wrote about this age somewhere other than the Eternal," Emma guessed.

"You are wise beyond your years. The writings have remained in Thalren."

"Whoa." Jack exhaled hard. "How did the plagues end?"

"Cherub fought against legion and forced the battle to the edge of the Highlands, where no Cherub remained alive." Xui Li's gaze hardened. "Elders fought darkness with darkness, forcing Florence Upsdell into the nether realm, where she remains trapped with the remaining legion."

"Only the Elders of old knew the truth," Emma reiterated. "No Cherub or Merikh."

"The Elders scribed the Mercy Covenant between the Seven Tribes and the Merikh to end the Second Great War." Xui Li paused. "Only the Elders feared Florence Upsdell would one day return—and that her vengeance would be far greater than the plagues."

Jack ran his fingers through his mop of hair, blown away by the story as he eyed the serenity of Thalren Isle. "The Siege of Plagues isn't in the Eternal because of how the Elders won."

"What happens if light is brought into the nether realm?" Emma asked.

"In the ancient writings it is not clear where the Queen of Sakkhela is in the nether realm, or whether she is able to reach beyond," Xui Li answered. "However, once light enters, she may be set free along with the legion and a deathly beast. The gateway will remain opened as long as light shines in the nether realm."

"If she is summoning Will to open a gateway . . ." Emma glanced at Jack. "There is light left in him, and a hope to save his soul before it is too late."

"We know what we witnessed in the Scourge," Jack chimed in. "She's definitely luring him closer to whatever other gateway brings the light. But I thought the gateway here in Thalren was the only way to enter. Now you're telling us there could be others."

"Eleanore created the Thalren gateway; however, another may be hidden in the Scourge."

"Did my mom know about the plagues and the battle at the edge of the Highlands?"

"Gabriella studied the Siege of Plagues while she was in Thalren, then experienced visions which haunted her dreams. She believed Peter entered the City of Gods and lost Eden's Star to the Nephilim king, then traveled to the edge of the Highlands, where

Cherub warriors remained buried since the plagues. Gabriella believed Peter was attempting to enter the nether realm to retrieve the artifact, awaken Florence Upsdell, and unleash the beast."

"But there was no light left in him," Emma bantered. "He deceived the Cherub for years."

"And Mom tried to stop another war of the worlds, but her love for Addison allowed him to go with her once Eleanore created the gateway." Jack swallowed hard. "She didn't realize his true intentions—he used them to satisfy his own craving for greater power."

"When Gabriella returned with Addison and one of the artifacts, neither spoke of what they encountered," Xui Li said. "I asked her about the artifact, but she refused to disclose its identity or its whereabouts."

"And she failed to find Peter," Emma added. "Addison was not the only one seeking control—Peter and Charlotte were both thirsty for greater supremacy."

"We suspected Charlotte was not to be trusted and was closer to following in Peter's downfall. Which is why we met with Nightingale at the Sanctuary of Prayer to exchange Dragon Soul for the Windstrikers. When Charlotte disappeared, we trusted Addison to protect the sword."

"And you traveled with my mom to the City of Gods," Jack finished.

"When we did not return, Dabria hid in Vigan and waited many years—until Rachel arrived."

"Peter ruled the Cherub after you left," Emma said. "Long before we were chosen."

"Elders are not without regret or sin—and I have carried both since those days."

227

"'Emma is the essence of truth—and she is the strongest among us.'" Jack recited Areum's words to him the night he'd first seen Emma use her gifts in the basement of Beacon Hill. "Will she survive if she goes with me through the gateway into the nether realm?"

"I assume Professor Burwick explained how the gateway works," Xui Li replied. "Only someone who shares Addison and Gabriella's bloodline may enter. Beyond the gateway, it is unknown what will happen."

"She is talking about DNA, right?" Emma asked. "Charlotte and Addison took my gifts from me, and the only way we have seen this occur is through a transfusion from those who were imprisoned in Shek Pik. What if Addison's blood was transfused into me?"

"When you were captured, do you know whether it was Charlotte or Addison?"

"Charlotte was the one with all the power at Fortress Hill," Jack said. "Not Addison."

"Then you will need to find another way, or Emma should remain with me."

"I am going with Jack," Emma insisted. "And trusting Elyon to protect us."

"Now this just got real," Jack mumbled to Emma. "One-way ticket to crazy realm."

"A gateway to the nether realm requires one to embrace the darkness," Xui Li warned.

"Emma is the light—but I'm the one tiptoeing in the dark."

"Very well." Xui Li pulled herself to her feet. "Time to prepare you both."

44

ALONG A PATH ON THE SOUTHERN SIDE of the island, a cool breeze welcomed them to the top of the hillside, where canopy tree vines created several natural enclosures. Stone pillars carved with characters and ancient etchings formed a circle rising from the ground. Xui Li headed toward one of the pillars and motioned the others over.

"In Manila, I told you I had visited Dabria but did not tell you that she believed Eliška was being trafficked aboard the *Eastern Dragon*. I did not want to place you in more danger if it was not true." Xui Li removed a blade from her pocket. "Rachel told Dabria about Professor Burwick's request to find her daughter, Darcy, *and* Eliška. Of course, we hoped you might find both."

"We know who Eliška is," Jack said. "She's a descendant of Ryder Slybourne."

"And she is part of the prophecy," Emma added. "Is she the one to lead the Cherub?"

"No one can say for certain, and anyone who says differently is simply guessing," Xui Li answered. "However, I believe strongly all three of you carry a piece of the prophecy."

"I'm sorry about Dabria." Jack stared at the pillars, surprised he understood why Xui Li had kept Eliška a secret. If she hadn't been on the cargo ship, he would have arrived back at Beacon Hill safely—and the traffickers would've dropped off their cargo in the South China Sea. "Dabria watched over Rachel and kept Vigan a safe place. She didn't deserve to die—but I'm afraid she won't be the last if the Cherub agree to a truce with the PRC that seems totally sketchy."

"Death hunts us all—only Elyon promises life beyond this world." Xui Li dug a sharp pointed knife into the stone and skillfully worked the edges. She carved methodically and efficiently. *Areum engraved* pathfinder *and* hunter *into stone on Karābu in memory of Rachel.* Alongside Emma, Jack watched quietly until the Elder finished the characters: 聯合.

"What does it mean?" he asked.

"I chose one word in memory of Dabria," Xui Li replied somberly. "Unity."

"Cherub, faction, and other followers of Elyon need to hear the same message."

"Bau has chosen to prioritize the highest Cherub." Xui Li slipped the blade into her pocket and brushed her fingers over the stone. "Salomeh asked me to help prepare the gifted who remain at Beacon Hill to defend the others when the time comes."

"Where is the gateway on the island?" Emma interjected.

"To enter the nether realm is not as simple as dropping a coin." Xui Li pointed toward another pillar. "Many years ago, Dabria traveled to Thalren to block the gateway from all others after your mother died, and I remained in the City of Gods."

"She was a gateway jumper," Jack surmised. "To stop Peter and Charlotte?"

"With Eleanore's help, another gateway was created—the one we traveled through is now the only way to reach Thalren." Xui Li pointed at letters on the pillar in a language he couldn't read. "Dabria also returned to honor your mother. This is a Tagalog word that means *peace*—that is all Gabriella desired."

Jack's fingers touched the engraved letters, slowly crossing over each one. Emma squeezed his shoulder and stood quietly alongside him. *I wish I could remember more about Mom, but I'll never forget seeing her with Rachel and Areum in full Cherub armor—that was epic in its own way.* Xui Li entered one of the habitats, and Emma followed. Jack waited near the pillar for a moment, staring at the word *peace* and questioning whether it was possible, then disappeared inside the enclosure.

In the center was a firepit dug into the earth, and on one side were stacks of centuries-old books and scrolls unaffected by the elements. Blankets were folded up in a pile and wood was bundled in another corner. Xui Li grabbed one of the scrolls, then knelt and unrolled it flat on the ground. Jack and Emma sat across from her and eyed a blank canvas.

"Gabriella and Addison never spoke of the artifact they brought into this world. However, your mother was certain a more dangerous one remained in the nether realm."

"A beast swallowed by darkness," Jack said.

"She kept the location of the gateway a secret, even from us. Addison and Eleanore are the only others who know, but neither may enter Thalren unless in the presence of an Elder. Dabria made certain the command would not be broken a second time." Xui Li paused. "Jack, do you have the box Rachel kept hidden?"

He unzipped a pocket on his hoodie sleeve, then opened the latch and handed over the rolled parchment with the ivory figurine tucked inside. Xui Li set the parchment on top of the scroll, and black ink spread beyond the map of the Highlands, revealing a broader landscape across the scroll of the nether realm and an illustration of Thalren Isle near one edge.

Even more of the map is revealed—Thalren and the nether realm.

"Each must pass a test to enter the gateway." Xui Li stabbed her index finger against the canvas. "To leave Thalren, your challenge begins here." She rolled up the scroll and handed it over to Jack, then retrieved her blade again. "Hold out your hand, both of you."

Jack and Emma followed her instructions and each extended one hand. Xui Li grabbed their hands and turned them face up, then cut a small incision in their palms. Jack's body tensed as blood seeped across his skin, similar to the crimson spreading across Emma's palm. He followed his instincts and grabbed Emma's hand—blood on blood. A lightforce emerged from beneath their grasp, a majestic violet flame spiraling into a mini tornado as it wrapped around their hands.

Fire mood experiment just turned supernova.

When Jack let go, Emma's lightforce evaporated and her healing powers sealed the incisions without scars. He gazed into her eyes, knowing they were more connected than ever.

"Whether you were infused with Addison's blood no longer matters," Xui Li said to Emma. "The Reynolds blood now flows through your veins."

"Take us to the spot on the island," Jack said to Xui Li. "Let's get the test started."

45

DARK CLOUDS GATHERED in the skies as waves thundered against the rocks. Winds howled and roared as Jack, Emma, and Xui Li raced across the island amid thick brush. *She still moves quick for an Elder—no way she'll ever admit her age.* Branches whipped against clothing and nicked bare skin, but the relentless pace only intensified. They reached a rocky cliffside across the island from the enclosures and above the turquoise pond marking the epicenter.

Jack slouched over, desperate to catch his breath. "What are we supposed to do?"

"Trust one another," Xui Li answered. "Emma . . . an offering, please."

Emma retrieved silver coins and handed several to Xui Li, who wasted no time dropping one onto the ground. No goodbyes. No more words of wisdom. No warning. Xui Li was swallowed by thick bushes and vanished. Jack jumped back as the island shifted strangely. Emma was standing a few feet away when the ground beneath her moved in the opposite direction. He grabbed hold of a tree trunk and held on as segments of land spun rapidly.

"Makes the Mental Disruptor seem like a joyride at Ocean Park," he mumbled.

His grip tightened as the island spun with greater force. Emma whipped past him again, mirroring the same confusion. Beyond her spinning segment, another portion of land spun in the same direction as his. Trees and boulders tumbled down the mountain and splashed into the pond, which was filling up with water from the waves breaking over the rocks.

A two-dimensional dial. Clockwise. Counterclockwise. Why?

With the ground spinning more quickly, he realized the ocean was swallowing up the island. *We'll be underwater in less than a minute. Gotta move, Jack.* He counted the seconds, attempting to time his next step, and then he jumped and rolled across the ground as Emma used her bender powers to stop his forward momentum.

"We're sinking like the *Titanic*." Jack pointed down. "We know how that story ended."

"Get to the top, and do not stop until there is no land left."

Jack and Emma hopped from one spinning portion of the island to the next, a dizzying escape that left them stumbling as more boulders rolled down the mountain. He ducked and dodged until he found himself in the direct line of a large rock tumbling toward him. Emma unleashed her lightforce, exploding the rock and scattering its fragments.

With the summit in sight, Jack darted between swaying trees.

Each segment they crossed swept them in the opposite direction. His stomach was in a vise grip as he imagined what astronauts must feel when tested in a centrifuge. *You're not going to the moon, but you are trying to enter the nether realm—which is way scarier, I'm guessing.* He kept his wits about him as he reached the top of the mountain with Emma on his heels.

She spread her arms wide and the rotating island slowed, clockwise and counterclockwise portions merging together once again. *She never ceases to amaze me—her gifts are greater than any lightforcer, bender, or healer I've seen.* A hundred yards beyond the island, a tidal wave formed and loomed over the summit.

"We're gonna get crushed," Jack said, awestruck. "And I mean pounded."

"Part the waters." Emma pointed toward a spear of rock jutting out from the ocean, separated from Thalren Isle. "You have done it before."

"That was Clear Water Bay, not a massive ocean." Soulweaver slipped down his forearm into his grasp. "Great! Even the Rod of Elyon is pressuring me."

"No time to waste." Emma's arms remained outspread as she slowed the looming tidal wave ever so slightly. "Get cracking, Jack."

With the tidal wave bearing down on Thalren, Jack and Emma slid down the side of the island another fifty feet before stopping themselves at the edge of dry land. He dipped the point of Soulweaver into the water as the rod hummed in his grasp. A tremendous strain pulsed through his muscles as he pushed himself harder to harness the energy of the rod, causing the tidal wave to split and shift directions. Emma used her bender force to help move the divided waves further away from Thalren. Another rogue wave formed, higher and wider than the skyscrapers in Admiralty.

"My bones are about to shatter." Jack grimaced. *Walk by light, not by sight.* Elyon's voice was crystal clear and spoke with great authority. "Emma, do you trust me?"

She kept her sights on the curled wave and massive barrel. "Of course I trust you."

"We're not stopping the next one, so here goes everything." Jack dug his boots deeper into the ground and swung Soulweaver toward the spear of rock jutting from the ocean, as tall as the largest wave. A streak of light shot out from the point of the rod and created an energy-beamed tightrope to the top of the rock. "You go first, then bring me with you."

Holy Cherub, Soulweaver is full of surprises.

Emma kept her arms wide, attempting to slow the tidal wave, which was on the verge of swallowing the island whole. She stepped onto the beam of light, balancing as she walked across a raging ocean. Jack gritted his teeth and tried to keep Soulweaver steady while he locked his eyes on Emma. *If I look at the death wave for too long, I'm gonna end up like Dory, lost at sea.* Emma moved with ease, seemingly unfazed by the danger surrounding them. She reached the top of the rock and turned her attention toward him.

"I trust Emma as much as she trusts me," he whispered. "Probably even more."

As soon as she turned her bender force toward Jack, the tidal wave increased in strength and ferocious power. *Don't look. Don't look. You looked.* His eyes widened as the tidal wave crashed over the summit of the island. He lowered Soulweaver to his side as his boots lifted off the ground and his body grew weightless. Against the rules of this world, he flew across the skies as the ocean swallowed Thalren. Unable to control his muscles, he surrendered to

Emma's powers, and she brought him to the top of the speared rock where he landed gently.

A boundless sea of royal blue surged against the speared rock, no wider than twenty yards. As far as the eye could see, there was nothing but gunmetal clouds and an infinite ocean. Jack stepped back from the edge as Soulweaver shrank and slipped onto his forearm. He was braver when he was with Emma, but as he stared out at the seas he feared they'd missed their one chance.

"We never made it to the gateway," he said. "Now we're stuck on a rock."

Emma stepped across the rock, her gaze fixed downward. She knelt in front of several rocks stacked on top of each other— a makeshift altar. Jack hurried over, curious to see what she'd found. He peered over her shoulder, disappointed there wasn't a neon sign. A few more seconds passed before he realized what she was staring at so intently. A small engraved indentation in one of the rocks, barely noticeable unless one was searching for a clue.

"Jack, open the box." Emma reached out her hand and waited for him. "The figurine."

He snatched the ivory depiction of Florence Upsdell, then handed it over as he knelt alongside. Emma carefully placed the statue into the indentation, and it fit perfectly. A few seconds passed, but nothing happened. Jack was on the verge of a tirade until the speared rock opened beneath their boots and they fell into the darkness.

Across an endless ocean, the seas calmed and Thalren Isle emerged from the depths, returning to a tranquil island where centuries of Elders once found refuge.

46

After midnight, an unmarked minivan rolled into the underground parking lot and idled as a sliding door opened. A dozen Cherub from Beacon Hill, including Amina and Faizan, climbed out and were greeted by Eliška. She eyed each closely, surprised Bau had held up his end of the deal so quickly.

"We took the underground tunnels to Kai Tak," Amina said. "A gateway in Runway Park brought us to another one a few miles from here in the Eastern District."

"Bau requested twelve of the most gifted," Faizan added. "Benders and lightforcers."

"He did not explain much else—or where Jack and Emma have disappeared to either."

238

"Tonight, the start of our liberation begins." Eliška glanced over her shoulder as a door slammed shut. Vince approached in jeans and a T-shirt with a wide grin. Amina gasped and walked briskly toward him, wiping a few tears from her eyes.

"Vincent Tobias, what are you doing here?" She wrapped her arms around him as far as they would go, then stepped back and turned toward Eliška. "You kept him a secret all this time?"

"The Tobiases are allies of the faction, so it is necessary to keep Vince off the radar."

"Not so easy when the Merikh and PRC are searching," Vince mused.

Amina punched him playfully in the arm. "Tim would be so proud."

"He sure loved you, Amina." Vince's smile faded. "We're going to make the Merikh and Will pay for what they've done to everyone. I promise, Tim's courage will never be forgotten."

"Truth." Amina's eyes narrowed. "He will never be forgotten."

"What is our purpose here?" Faizan asked. "Bau said to do whatever you ask."

"Cherub will settle in tonight." Eliška waved one of the faction over. "Take Faizan and the others to the rooftop and make certain they are comfortable." As the faction led the rest of the Cherub into the building, Eliška turned her attention toward Amina. "If you are not too tired . . ."

"Wherever you are going, I'm going too. Beacon Hill is a bit smaller these days, so it is nice to be out and about."

Eliška flashed a red velvet pouch. "Jack and Emma left this with the faction."

"Xui Li returned to Beacon Hill earlier but has not spoken about either of them."

"I'm not thrilled about what those two are doing," Vince replied. "Amina, they're trying to find a way to get into the nether realm."

"Nether realm?" Amina's brows furrowed. "How do they know where to look?"

"Wait until you see what they left behind." Vince nodded toward the pouch. "Definitely will blow your mind. Seriously, makes the Zakhar look like a PlayStation."

"Both of you are going to ignore my questions," Amina stated. "You must have a reason."

"Too much is unknown right now," Eliška offered. "Vince, are we ready?"

"Message is delivered, so everyone is waiting." Vince leaned in close to Amina. "Truth is, I don't think anyone knows what's going on, so best to go with the flow."

"Got it." Amina nodded. "Seems to be how all this works anyway."

A driver behind the wheel turned the van around and stopped. Eliška, Vince, and Amina climbed in an empty cargo area, and Vince pulled the door closed as they all sat on the floor. During the drive from Quarry Bay to The Peak Tram Station, conversations were kept to a minimum. Eliška had waited months for an opportunity to take the fight to the Merikh and PRC, but she needed leverage. She reached into her pocket and wrapped her fingers around the velvet pouch.

In front of an empty fountain outside of The Peak Tram Historical Gallery on Garden Road, the van stopped briefly, allowing all three to jump out and move quickly toward the entrance. Eliška pulled on the door, but it was locked, so she headed around the side of the building. Vince and Amina were on her heels as she stopped in front of a brick wall blocking access to the terminus.

Eliška planted her boot on Vince's palm, and he boosted her over the top. Amina was next, and then Vince got a running start and grabbed hold of the top of the wall as the last one to land near the terminus. Since the curfews were enforced, Hong Kongers now avoided tourist spots, including The Peak. Trams remained shut down, leaving one of Hong Kong's most iconic locations dormant. Vince accessed an electrical panel and flipped a few switches, then entered the tram and powered on the engine.

Amina stepped aboard. "You two seem to know your way around."

"One of the faction in Quarry Bay was a tram driver." Eliška closed the door. "We asked for the Cherub's help, but until earlier today our requests fell on deaf ears."

"You met with Bau," Amina guessed. "That explains him being extra bossy."

In the dark, Vince released the brakes and shifted the tram into gear. Interior and exterior lights on the tram remained off as wheels rolled across the tracks and ascended Mount Austin.

"Nothing else to say about Jack and Emma?" Amina asked.

"Eliška was right when she said neither would stick around long." Vince kept his sights on the tracks ahead. "Not surprised when we got back and they were gone."

"Does not mean we are happy about it, though," Eliška added. "We each have a part to play, so we will focus on playing ours tonight."

The tram continued a slow climb, a steep ascent which left skyscrapers and apartments appearing skewed. A scattering of lights glowed from windows, but most of the buildings on the mountainside remained pitch-black. Halfway up the mountain, Vince applied the brakes and the tram stopped.

"Better go the rest of the way on foot," he explained. "No one will expect a tram here."

A fifteen-minute hike brought them to Barker Road. All three climbed the steps and reached The Peak lookout, which was empty. Eliška led the way onto a deck that offered a panoramic view of Hong Kong Island, Victoria Harbour, Kowloon, and beyond toward the New Territories. On most nights, before the chaos that had erupted across Hong Kong, the city was lit up with white lights and neon signs. Eliška gazed out across the dark skyline, struck by the visual of millions of Hong Kongers under mandatory curfew.

Vince checked his watch. "Less than two minutes."

"Two minutes until what?" Amina asked.

"Until we see how many need to be rescued." Eliška retrieved the velvet pouch. "Jack is trusting one of the artifacts to the faction—the Rhoxen Stone."

"What does the Rhoxen Stone do, exactly?"

"We are hoping it is a spark to become the Merikh's worst nightmare." Eliška motioned Amina closer. "When we use the artifact, I will need your help."

Vince nodded at the velvet pouch. "Eliška's the only one of us who's tested it so far."

"Most of the Merikh are staying either in Tai Tam or Admiralty." Eliška pointed toward Victoria Harbour. "On the southern side the checkpoints are few. Repulse Bay and Aberdeen are abandoned, except for the fishermen. Tai Tam is mostly locals and highest Cherub, who we have been exchanging supplies with since the gateway was closed. We are building loyalty slowly, but we need to know which districts we might be missing."

"Wan Chai is mostly Hong Kongers and faction," Vince

continued. "With the tunnels destroyed, if we control access to the checkpoints in Admiralty, then we will control access to all of the other districts."

"How will we move the Merikh and HKPF away?" Amina asked, a bit confused.

"Fifty seconds," Vince announced.

From their vantage point, seconds seemed to pass like hours. Eliška gripped the pouch, anticipating answers to questions she'd asked herself for months. *How many are waiting for us? Five. Four. Three. Two. One.* At exactly 2:45 a.m., a cluster of orange flares appeared on multiple rooftops of apartment buildings across Central, Admiralty, Wan Chai, and Western District. Vince pointed his cell phone toward the city, snapping photos and capturing video. Another cluster of flares appeared, only these were red.

"Who are they?" Amina asked quietly. "What do the flares mean?"

"Orange represents districts where faction and Cherub are hiding out." Vince paused. "Red signals where the Merikh and HKPF are patrolling in addition to the checkpoints."

"A dozen Cherub lightforcers and benders will not be enough," Eliška said. She opened the velvet pouch and dropped the Rhoxen Stone into her palm. Vince stood frozen with his cell phone in hand. She stepped over to Amina and placed the stone in her hand while still touching the smooth turquoise herself. An eerie silence spread across The Peak. Eliška recognized the dumbstruck gaze from Amina, the same one she'd had when the stone was tested in Quarry Bay.

"The Rhoxen Stone stops time," Eliška explained. "From what Jack and Emma said, and with what I have seen, only if someone touches the stone will they be able to move about in the present."

Amina's brows raised as she stared closely at Vince, who remained a statue. "Remarkable."

"Our plan is to use the stone and the Cherub to rid the island of the Merikh and PRC. If we succeed, we will have a better chance of defending ourselves when the war begins." Eliška stepped closer to the edge as Amina walked alongside, both touching the Rhoxen Stone while they stared out on dozens of flares frozen in the night. "I cannot send the faction or Cherub into these districts without being by their side." She turned toward Amina. "When the time comes, you will be the one to keep us alive."

47

Black SUVs pulled up to the entrance of the Rosewood, a five-star luxury hotel overlooking Victoria Harbour turned into a protected refuge for the highest Cherub known by Merikh and PRC. Like Beacon Hill, the Rosewood remained off-limits since the prison break at Shek Pik. HKPF and Merikh watched the hotel from a distance, as the government was eager for any opportunity to resume control. However, neither was willing to face the lightforcers or benders—no matter their age.

Bau climbed out from one of the SUVs shadowed by lightforcers, and he entered another world. Water and food were in short supply across Kowloon, and the situation on Hong Kong Island was unknown. The Rosewood was for the privileged

Cherub—away from the eyes of Hong Kongers restricted under curfew and fellow believers hiding across Kowloon. Fang Xue had suggested Bau bring his parents to the Rosewood immediately after he was anointed amid the rubble of the Sanctuary of Prayer. He declined, wanting them to leave through the gateway in Tai Tam.

The entourage headed into The Legacy House, a fine-dining Cantonese restaurant popular for dim sum. Bau ignored the stares of those who were enjoying breakfast with a picturesque view of Victoria Harbour. From their vantage point, not much changed in Hong Kong even though everything had shifted forever. Bau's security positioned themselves outside of a private dining room as he entered through double doors.

Fang Xue and others were seated in custom-stitched leather seats around a long table. Metallic butterflies hung overhead, and silver suede carpet partially covered smooth concrete. Pristine silverware and plates were set perfectly in front of them. On one side, floor-to-ceiling windows offered a southerly viewpoint across the harbor toward Wan Chai.

"Good morning, Bau." Fang Xue sipped fresh coffee. "I believe you know everyone."

"Yes." Bau glanced around the table and nodded. "My parents send their regards."

"So you have spoken with them." Fang Xue hesitated. "We received confirmation that the gateway in Tai Tam is closed, but we do not know how it is possible. Witnesses described an attack, most likely the faction. A reckless act which will only lead to panic among the Cherub and increased pressure from the PRC. Strange—we are not aware of any faction who possess the ability to block a gateway."

"Tai Tam was never a path to freedom—it was a gateway to the Scourge."

Everyone around the table exchanged troubled looks, clearly surprised by such a bold and disturbing statement. Fang Xue was first to break the awkward silence that lingered.

"No one has heard anything of the kind. How do you know this to be true?"

"It does not matter how the information reached my ears; it is a fact." Bau dug his elbows into the table and clasped his hands together. "My parents were only days from traveling through the gateway because you were confident it was the safest passageway to escape. How many Cherub have we sent to their deaths?"

"Bau . . ." Fang Xue began.

"We cannot send Cherub through any gateways until we know where they lead." Bau paused, expecting someone to speak up, but the tension remained thick. "I would like my parents to be brought to the Rosewood. I do not care how it is done. And we need to establish communication with the faction immediately."

Fang Xue nodded at one of the men at the table, who excused himself and slipped out of the room. "Faction remain far too unpredictable considering . . . Why the sudden need?"

"I returned to Beacon Hill." Bau noticed the disapproval of those around the table, but he was determined to exercise his authority. "When I traveled to the Sanctum of Serenity to search for the prophecy, I found one of the Elders held captive by William Fargher."

"Which Elder are you speaking of?" Fang Xue asked, surprised.

"Xui Li is the only Elder who has survived." Bau shifted in his seat. "We know she was imprisoned at Shek Pik, then taken the night Cherub were slaughtered by Will and the Merikh. She was unconscious when I brought her to Beacon Hill; however, now she is awake and recovering. Headmaster Fargher will notify me when she is strong enough to speak with me."

"An Elder returning is quite a revelation." Fang Xue leaned forward. "Our priority remains to bring peace to the Cherub before the PRC or Merikh strike again."

"Rescuing the Elder has shifted my perspective." Bau eyed each one closely. "I was wrong to consider a truce with the Merikh and PRC."

"Perhaps we need more time to discuss and decide."

"If we surrender our gifts," Bau retorted, "we surrender our souls."

The door to the dining room opened, and Salomeh Gashkori, Jin Qiaolian, and Aki Katsuo entered to the surprise of those seated around the table—most of all, Fang Xue.

"Sorry we are late," Salomeh announced. "Underground tunnels. MTR stations."

"Good morning, everyone," Aki said cordially. "You have found quite a safe house."

"Fang, wipe that frown from your face," Jin blurted. "We are all one family."

"I am curious why you—" Fang Xue paused. "I was not aware—"

"Salomeh, Aki, and Jin are here at my request," Bau interrupted. "Decisions will include those who represent Beacon Hill. Once communication is established with the faction, we will consider their opinions as well."

"Bau, you are making a mistake," Fang Xue protested. "May I suggest—?"

"My decision is final." Bau motioned for them to find a seat.

"Two gateways are certain—Dragon's Back and the House of Luminescence."

"House of Luminescence leads to more than one place," Salomeh agreed. "Dragon's Back will take those who travel through to either the Sanctuary of Prayer or Puerto Natales, Chile."

"We have spoken with the Cherub at Beacon Hill," Aki added. "None wish to leave."

"Headmaster Fargher has agreed to remain at Beacon Hill and ensure all who wish to escape Hong Kong are able to through the House of Luminescence—if any change their mind."

"Excuse me," Fang Xue cut in. "What are we talking about?"

"An exodus," Jin answered, "to help Cherub and the innocent escape what is coming."

"Which is why you are seated at this table," Bau confirmed. "To strategize a plan."

"And why you wish to communicate with the faction," Fang Xue surmised. "Such an aggressive tactic to move Cherub across the city and beyond will bring repercussions from the PRC and Merikh."

"Fang, take a look in the mirror," Salomeh retorted. "Not all Cherub enjoy such luxury."

"Months have passed while we have struggled to care for those at Beacon Hill," Aki reiterated. "We have established a distribution network in the districts, but that will not last much longer."

"A resolution is under consideration to negotiate a truce with the Merikh and PRC," Fang Xue replied. "There will be costs to many, but we will save the Cherub from certain death."

"Madness." Salomeh exhaled. "Negotiating with our enemy is not the answer."

An argument erupted among everyone at the table, even those who had not yet spoken. Disagreements escalated quickly into yelling and shouting. Bau glared around the room and slammed his fists against the table, rattling polished silverware, handcrafted plates, and leftover food. All eyes turned toward him in shock at the disruption.

"Will has taken the prophecy and is being summoned to the nether realm," Bau said pointedly. "We either choose to surrender or we choose to fight against the darkness."

Salomeh's lips pursed. "Beacon Hill is ready for battle."

48

NETHER REALM

Brutal winds whipped over jet-black sand and across a rough onyx ocean. Jagged basalt columns jutted from beneath the waters toward gunmetal skies. At the base of the sheer cliff was an opening to a cave. Jack and Emma emerged and trudged through the sand, bodies shivering even though their clothes were dry.

"Can we have a do-over?" A piercing chill sliced Jack to the bone as he pulled his hood over his head. "I'd like a warmer realm and food for one hundred, please?"

Emma tugged at her jacket, buttoning it to the top. "Hopefully we will not stay long."

"Anything less than eternity would be appreciated."

Jack shoved his hands into both pockets, searching for one

more degree of warmth. His muscles tensed as he imagined summer afternoons at Beacon Hill with Will, Tim, and Vince, complaining about the unbearable heat and humidity. The wind smacked him in the face, nearly ripping the breath from him and bringing him back to a stark reality.

We're in the nether realm, where Mom and Addison walked years ago.

"Now you know why I was never a Scout." Jack blew on his hands, a feeble attempt to spread heat beneath his skin. "Xui Li should've warned us about entering the Arctic Circle."

Emma pointed ahead beyond the black sands. "This is the way."

"We should search for a sauna." Jack's teeth chattered. "I'd even take a match or a candle right about now."

They left the onyx sands and found themselves at the edge of the Dead Forest. Huddled together, they ducked behind an enormous tree trunk, which was flattened against barren ground. An uncontrollable shiver rattled them both.

Emma wrapped her arms around Jack and pulled him close. Immediately, warmth from her palms spread over him. He knew it was her lightforce, and he welcomed the momentary relief. He could've stayed in her embrace forever—if they weren't in the nether realm.

"Warmer?" Emma asked with a shy grin.

"Whoa . . ." Jack's cheeks flushed. "You may need to do that again."

"Stay focused on the task at hand," she teased. "We have a world to save, remember?"

As far as the eye could see, the Dead Forest spread across the land. Emma slipped the ivory figurine and nether realm map from beneath her jacket. She unfolded the scroll and pointed at squiggly lines on the map.

"The Thalren gateway brought us to . . ." She read the scripted ink. "The Shores of Mericier."

"Double whoa—you grabbed the statue and kept the map in one piece during all that chaos."

"Both were inside the cave when we appeared." Emma's hands trembled slightly as she handed the figurine over to Jack. "Best you keep this in your pocket."

"Right, who knows what else it might open?" He unzipped his sleeve pocket and slipped the figurine inside. "Emma, your hands are shaking. Are you okay?"

"I feel a bit strange, honestly. How about you?"

"One hundred—well, let's say seventy-five and a half percent to be safe."

Emma ran her index finger across the map. "Best route is to follow the Chasseuse River."

"You know, I didn't notice it before . . ." Jack's eyes narrowed. "The handwriting looks just like my mom's writing of the warning on the back of the parchment piece."

"No one else has entered the nether realm since she returned with Addison. Your mom would have been the one to mark the way and name the markers."

He pointed at one of the landmarks. "Mourning Labyrinth?"

"Definitely sounds like a puzzle." Emma rolled up the map and tucked it beneath her jacket. "We will face whatever is there together."

"Even the Mental Disruptor is a catchier name—just saying." His dark humor failed to ease the fact Emma was a bit off, similar to Areum in the City of Gods. "Emma, if you feel like you're struggling, then you need to tell me."

"You should do the same. For now, best we get going." Emma stepped around the tree trunk with her head on a swivel. "Time is not what we expect in this realm. We do not know what we will face ahead, so best we take advantage of the light before the darkness leaves us blind."

"We didn't bring anything with us—no food, water, clothes, supplies."

"Less we carry with us the better," Emma replied. "We have what we need."

"Plan is to get what we came for and hightail it out before dinner."

"Florence Upsdell was banned to this realm and forced to stay."

"We need to be sure she remains and doesn't find a way beyond through a gateway."

"If we find Will in this realm," Emma pressed, "we must save him."

"Only if he wants to be saved."

"I believe there is still light within him, Jack."

"If that's true, then the gateway is already opened."

From one dead tree to another, Jack and Emma kept their sights ahead, behind, and on both sides. Further into the Dead Forest, ducking and darting, Jack imagined life once existing in the harsh climate of the nether realm. *Maybe a forest overflowing with emerald green. An immense, thriving woodland. Sounds so poetic— like something Rachel would've written in her notebook.* He guessed once they reached the Chasseuse River, all they'd find would be a dry riverbed.

"We're walking in the footsteps of my mom and Addison when

they were still in love." Jack weighed his words, accepting that his family was more than partly responsible for the dangers facing those in the present. "Rachel tried to fix what was undone. Now it's left to us."

For a while they moved through the Dead Forest until Emma suddenly grabbed Jack's shoulder and pulled him down. Crouched behind a cluster of trees that had fallen on top of each other, Jack felt his heart pound as a shriek echoed across the land. Ducked low, he stared toward graying skies as a massive fiery-orange owl with sharp talons spread its wings and glided away swiftly.

"What in Elyon's name is that?" Jack whispered.

Emma's palms glowed. "So it begins."

49

JACK AND EMMA STAYED LOW as the orange owl circled the Dead Forest searching for prey. Jack closed his eyes, took a deep breath, and attempted to control the fear raising the hair on his scarred arms. When he opened his eyes and blinked, the owl turned and soared in their direction. Another shriek echoed, stopping him cold. He spun around and peered through a gap in the cluster of decayed trees.

"Emma," he whispered urgently. "There are two of them."

"Stay close to me." Emma's palms glowed brighter. "Be ready."

"Right." He clenched his fist, and Soulweaver slipped down his forearm seamlessly into his grasp, extending into a rod. "Maybe we should make a run for it."

"No time to run." Emma brought her palms together, and a ball of white light emerged and hovered in midair. "I will take the one in front, and you take the one behind."

The two owls shrieked in unison with talons spread wide. Jack braced himself as the monstrous beasts came closer, their wing-spans appearing to stretch. He squeezed Soulweaver, and the rod hummed with authority. At breakneck speed, the owls nose-dived straight for them. Soulweaver spun between Jack's fingers as he forced fear down into the depths of his soul.

"They have definitely seen us," Emma said steadily. "Jack . . ."

"I hear you—just trying not to puke."

Emma stood as her lightforce glowed brighter, and her eyes turned a stark white. She unleashed a great force, striking the owl in front of them squarely. The beast dropped from the sky and hit the ground with a resounding thud, motionless. Jack turned his sights to the owl approaching them from behind. A pulse of energy shot from Soulweaver, narrowly missing the beast. Its talons grabbed hold of his shoulders and swept him off the ground.

With pain searing through his bones, Jack stabbed Soulweaver against the beast's underbelly, and the owl released its taloned grip. Jack dropped to the ground, tumbling over and over. Facedown, he gasped for breath as stars flickered before his eyes. He scrambled to his feet and looked past Emma, who was racing toward him—and he realized the owl she'd struck down was not dead.

With Soulweaver spinning faster than one of Bau's cricket pitches, pulses of energy shot past Emma before striking the owl with deathly force. He didn't stop attacking as he closed in on the beast. Out of the corner of his eye, he saw the second owl swinging around and soaring toward him. He didn't need to look back to know Emma was right behind him as her lightforce flew over his shoulder and hit its target again.

Force and flow.

Wide-eyed, he stood over the owl he'd struck as Soulweaver slowed and swung directly in front of him. He loosened his grip and watched the rod touch the owl's skull. Black flames rose from the owl's feathered body and engulfed the beast. Jack glanced up a split second before the other owl was about to snatch him again. All of a sudden, the owl's trajectory shifted violently, and it hit the ground and rolled across the Dead Forest, slamming into trees and vines. Before Jack or Emma could react, the owl squealed and rolled onto its clawed feet—again. Instead of attacking, the beast rose to the sky and flew in the direction of where they were headed.

"So that was the welcome party." Jack exhaled. "Can't wait to see the main event."

Emma grabbed his arm. "Are you hurt?"

"I'm still in one piece." He tapped his chest. "Dretium hoodies should be mandatory."

"Agreed." Emma nodded ahead. "We have not seen the last of that one."

A shiver rippled down his spine as their surroundings grew a few degrees colder. His gaze darted around, and he held Soulweaver at the ready. Emma mirrored his movements while an eerie silence drifted through the Dead Forest. A vision struck him for only a second: a flash of the legion whipping through the nether realm.

"They're coming," he said. "Emma, we need to run."

Jack and Emma raced through the Dead Forest, pumping their arms and legs with growing effort. Jack's heart pounded, slamming into his ribs as if challenging Eden's Star to lend a hand. He jumped over a dead vine, then ducked under clusters of fallen trees. Emma was quicker, passing him on one side. Another vision struck— legion hovering where he'd been moments earlier. On the verge of collapsing, he pushed himself faster to stay on Emma's heels.

"Emma!" Jack breathed hard. "We can't outrun them!"

The Dead Forest, which had seemed endless when they first arrived on the Shores of Mericier, whipped past in a whirlwind. Emma dug her boots into the earth and slid to a stop. Jack nearly slammed into her, but she used her power to slow him down. Breathless, both stood on the edge of a granite cliff from which a colossal waterfall of onyx tar surged with monumental force. Jack peered over the edge and realized there were dozens more of equal enormity. A massive downpour of tar disappeared into the blackness below.

Wails. Screams. Howls. Screeches.

Jack's ears rang with them all at once. "Legion."

"We cannot fight them all." Emma peered over the edge. "Eden's Star?"

"I don't know where it will take us, or whether we'll be able to get back here."

"Then there is only one choice, Jack."

"No way—that's insane."

"Not as bonkers as being ravaged by fangs of the legion."

"That doesn't sound like a Fabulous Friendly." More vision flashes struck, showing the legion whipping high and low on the hunt across the Dead Forest. They were closing in fast. Jack grabbed Emma's hand and squeezed while Soulweaver slithered up his forearm. "Let's hope it's a soft landing—here goes everything."

Jack and Emma leapt off the cliff, falling rapidly amid the rush of onyx tar before splashing into a deep, inky pool. Beneath the surface, Jack pulled Emma until their heads popped up for a second as the legion reached the cliffs above. A quick breath, and they submerged themselves again. He held his breath and counted, knowing he'd never gone longer than forty-five seconds. Emma squeezed his hand, and he knew she sensed his dread. Desperate for air, he swam to the surface and slowly emerged. He gasped for breath as he eyed his surroundings, relieved the legion were gone. Emma's head popped up beside him, and both swam to shore and slumped onto the hardened ground.

"We've been here five minutes." Jack tried to brush the tar from his clothes, but residue covered his hoodie and jeans. "And we've nearly died a dozen times already."

"That was too close." Emma retrieved the map from a pocket stitched inside her jacket. She unrolled the scroll, pointed at a series of inked lines, then nodded toward the surge rushing over the cliffs. "These must be the Cascades of Tombé."

"No way we can follow the Chasseuse River without being caught now."

Emma's finger ran across the map, stopping on an arch. "We can cross Diable Bridge."

"We don't have a clue how far any of these are from each other." Jack caught himself from descending into an endless rant. "I'm up for a bit more sightseeing in the nether realm."

"Now that's the spirit." Emma smirked. "Maybe we will BASE jump next time."

He replied with a heavy dose of sarcasm, "Oh, can we please."

Time passed as Jack and Emma followed the Cascades of Tombé, hundreds of onyx falls plunging into endless ponds. His shoulders ached, still feeling the talons wrapped around him, but he breathed a bit easier with Emma by his side. Quietness between them brought a sense of peace. *Everyone thought I was going to die if I entered the nether realm. Not gonna lie, I thought I'd be struck dead too. But that hasn't happened . . . yet.* Strangely enough, he was still alive—Elyon must have more for him to do.

50

In the years since Kai Tak Airport was closed, a park was established for Hong Kongers and tourists to enjoy along the Runway Waterfront Promenade. Since the curfews and checkpoints, the park had remained mostly abandoned. Near the water's edge, a Jetstream 41 fixed-wing aircraft was on display. An access door on the jet opened slowly, a gateway hidden in plain sight. Eliška and Amina hopped out onto dry grass, then walked briskly away from the jet toward Kowloon Bay.

Kai Tak was once the most legendary and scary airport landing in the world, with a runway surrounded by water on three sides. Skilled pilots dropped in on final approach above Victoria Harbour and Kowloon City, north of Mong Kok's Bishop Hill. The pilots searched for Checkerboard Hill, a mountainside painted with a large orange-and-white checkerboard.

With Checkerboard Hill in sight, pilots veered hard right at a steep angle so close to high-rise apartments that passengers could peer at laundry drying on bamboo poles and televisions through apartment windows. Pilots relied on their skill—not aircraft instruments—for final approach in a landing known widely as the Kai Tak Heart Attack.

Eliška had studied the history of Kai Tak late at night on the rooftop in Quarry Bay. She found the history intriguing as pilots used their instincts rather than instruments to land their planes. Since she was rescued and brought to Hong Kong, she'd observed how decisions from the Cherub were rooted in interpreting history through rules and regulations. While there was much to learn from history, she admired Burwick for leading the faction by relying on her instincts when it mattered most.

Elyon has given us instincts so we can see what cannot be seen in instruments, rules, and regulations.

Eliška was still determining what kind of leader she wanted to be, but she found inspiration from Jack—who broke every Cherub regulation to get to the truth and save the innocent. He didn't worry about what others thought—he relied on where Elyon was leading him.

He's broken Cherub rules, and he's been far from perfect along his path—but his heart for those he loves is undeniable.

Amina led the way as they turned a corner and passed the Lido before stopping outside of Café Aberdeen. Eliška glanced around, fully aware they were the only ones in the park. She pulled at the door, but it was locked. She knocked twice and waited. Amina stood slightly behind and glanced around as well. They had grown used to watching each other's backs.

The blinds behind the glass door parted slightly; then the dead bolt disengaged and the door cracked open. Both slipped inside the café, dimly lit but bright enough to see who was waiting.

"Good to see you again, Eliška," Salomeh said cordially. "Amina, thank you."

"Why were we not told about the Eastern District gateway?" Eliška asked firmly.

"You have now traveled from the district to Kai Tak. Imagine hundreds, if not thousands, attempting to escape through this gateway. No one would be free."

Eliška's gaze shifted toward a woman standing off to the side. "Why are we here?"

Amina leaned in close and whispered, "Xui Li, the Elder."

"Bau challenged the highest Cherub earlier today," Salomeh explained. "I did not believe he had the courage to lead, but he has disturbed Fang Xue and others with great influence. He asked for our help to prepare those at Beacon Hill to defend the innocent—in battle if necessary. In addition, he requested that direct communication with the faction be established." She glanced at a clock on the wall. "I suppose right about now, Fang is attempting to persuade Bau to change his mind."

"Many of us were hopeful you would one day be found." Xui Li stepped forward, her stare locked in on Eliška. "Professor Burwick was quite distraught when she asked for Rachel's help to find you and Darcy. I have waited a long time to meet you in person, Eliška."

"Were you at this meeting with the Cherub?" Eliška asked, point-blank.

"My presence would have created an even greater firestorm." Xui Li paused. "You do not look surprised about what occurred."

"Communication with Bau has already been established," Amina chimed in. "I brought a dozen lightforcers and benders to the faction last night at his request."

"He knows the Cherub are not unified enough to defend themselves." Eliška hesitated. "While we have remained underground, fighting to rescue Cherub, faction, and the innocent on Hong Kong Island, the *influential* ones in Kowloon enjoy the comforts of the Rosewood."

"I see you know about this already." Salomeh frowned. "A stalemate between Cherub, Merikh, and PRC exists; however, I was surprised to see with my own eyes what you have said. Regardless, Bau acted this morning as if he had not spoken with any of the faction."

"We agreed on a truce," Eliška explained. "One the highest Cherub will not approve."

"Faction will fight alongside the Cherub," Amina added. "Bau agreed to help secure the checkpoints on Hong Kong Island. With the gateway closed in Tai Tam, I think we got his attention, since his parents were attempting to leave."

"We have communicated with those in Tai Tam not to attempt to travel through the gateway any longer." Eliška paused. "No one knows for certain whether the gateway can be opened once again—perhaps by a gateway jumper."

"You are speaking of William Fargher," Xui Li suggested. "His sights are on the nether realm, and if he chooses to jump the gateway back to Tai Tam, then he will not be alone."

"Bau mentioned the Scourge during our meeting." Salomeh grabbed a chair and slumped down. "Eliška, how will you control the checkpoints?"

"Most are on the northern side," she answered. "We have marked where Cherub and faction are hiding across the island. When we are ready, we will launch an attack along with the light-forcers and benders. But we will need more lightforcers to create a large enough force field."

"And what will this accomplish?" Xui Li asked.

"There is a gateway at Dragon's Back," Amina picked up. "If we can get everyone through the gateway, it will take them either to Mount Hareh or . . ."

"Puerto Natales," Salomeh finished. "You plan to use the Rhoxen Stone."

"Cherub use a force field at Beacon Hill, and it has worked to stop Merikh and the PRC from storming the grounds." Amina exchanged a quick glance with Eliška. "To guard an entire island will require hundreds of lightforcers. If the artifact kept in the nether realm is brought against us, we will not win this war. Yes, we plan to use the Rhoxen Stone—only long enough to save those who wish to escape."

"A rescue mission." Salomeh exchanged a troubled look of her own with Xui Li. "Bau spoke of the same when we discussed the House of Luminescence and Dragon's Back gateways. We have offered an escape to all at Beacon Hill, but so far the major-ity wish to stay. Does Bau know the faction has the Rhoxen Stone?"

"We have kept the artifact to ourselves for obvious reasons," Eliška said. "Everyone must be given an opportunity to choose—flight or fight."

"Harley was quite insistent you are a fighter. I would have pic-tured you rallying the faction and the Cherub to battle until the very end. Why have you chosen a rescue mission?"

"PRC offered their own truce to Bau and Fang Xue—Cherub gifts for peace."

"What exactly does that mean?" Xui Li asked directly.

"Cherub would surrender their gifts, stripped away using the Merikh's method." Amina crossed her arms. "I have seen what this method has done to many, including Emma. In exchange, the Cherub would be allowed to live under the PRC's rule and would defend the PRC if required."

"Do you believe Bau has agreed to this offer?" Salomeh pressed.

"Bau has a bloated ego," Amina replied, "but deep down he will not surrender."

"We are relying on Jack and Emma to find an artifact in the nether realm," Eliška interrupted. "If they fail—and I for one am rooting for them to succeed—we will not be able to stop what is coming. We must prepare a rescue effort and brace ourselves for war."

"Do we even know if they made it to the nether realm?" Salomeh asked.

"I brought them to the gateway in Thalren," Xui Li confirmed. "I do not know if they made it through, as their test would not begin until they were alone."

Eliška turned her attention toward Xui Li. "What is the artifact in the nether realm?"

"A question without a definite answer." Xui Li hesitated. "But I am afraid a queen scorned from your bloodline is watching over the most dangerous artifact created by the hands of Elyon."

51

THE ROSEWOOD

Daylight faded as Bau stared across Victoria Harbour from a room on the fifth floor of the Rosewood. A plaid sofa, leather chair, glass coffee table, and fresh sheets on a queen-size bed had been his home base since he returned from Mount Hareh. He'd spent most of the day meeting with the Council, who argued for hours about the right path forward after Salomeh Gashkori, Jin Qiaolian, and Aki Katsuo excused themselves.

By late afternoon, he left the Rosewood with his security to visit Cherub a short distance away in Hung Hom. PRC and Merikh allowed them through the checkpoints, a sign the chief executive was keeping them in his sights while offering an olive branch.

In Hung Hom, Bau spoke with hope and conviction, encouraging those who proclaimed their support of him as their leader.

By the time he returned to his room, he was second-guessing his deal with the faction. Professor Burwick and Eliška were wild cards, and Jack and Emma were just as unpredictable. He tried to bring them in for their safety, and yes, to deliver Jack to the PRC as a sign of good faith. Jack was an outlier, and that would never change—which made him a liability to anyone protecting the Cherub. A restless night was ahead after listening to Fang Xue and the Council attempting to persuade him.

He'd invited Salomeh, Jin, and Aki to the council meeting without warning Fang Xue. After months of listening to her counsel, he wrestled with the reality that the Cherub were no safer than they had been after the Shek Pik Prison break. He'd chosen a different path and now risked losing the support of the highest Cherub.

Night consumed what was left of the day as Bau stepped over to his luggage. He carefully removed a royal-purple Upsdell House jersey with a lime-green stripe from his perfectly folded clothes and held it in his grasp. His mind shifted to winning the Bashers, Bowlers, and Boundaries trophy, wearing Beacon Hill's uniform without the house colors. While he struggled to trust the others, there was no denying he trusted his teammate Vince.

Knock. Knock.

Bau opened the door and was greeted by Fang Xue. He left the door wide open and tossed his Upsdell jersey onto the other clothes packed in his luggage, then waited for her to speak.

"A challenging day," Fang Xue said. "Lively discussions continue downstairs."

"Have we established communication with the faction?"

"Your request has many troubled." Fang Xue paused. "I wish you had spoken to me about bringing the faction and Beacon Hill into our inner circle."

268

"What about my parents? When will they arrive?"

"They have been granted safe passage from Tai Tam by the PRC and should be arriving within a few hours." Fang Xue paused. "Chief Executive Tsang has requested another meeting with us, and I suggest we hear his counteroffer."

"I meant what I said this morning," Bau replied. "My decision is final."

"The faction cannot be trusted to be our savior."

"Aki was right about Beacon Hill and so many other districts." Bau stepped over by the window and gazed out on a scattering of lights but no neon skyline. "We will need their help if we are to evacuate Cherub from Kowloon *and* Hong Kong Island."

"Headmaster Fargher will not open Beacon Hill to the outside." Fang Xue crossed her arms. "And attempting to usher thousands through the gateway in Dragon's Back is too great a risk without controlling Hong Kong Island."

"Which is why we need an alliance with the faction—and open communication."

"What do you know about Professor Burwick's protégé? Do you not see? She is their leader not only because of ancient history but because she is dangerous and unpredictable. She does not possess the gifts of a Cherub and does not follow Elyon's commands in the Eternal."

"I followed your advice and tried to bring Jack and Emma." Bau turned and faced Fang Xue. "While I do not agree with their actions, I will never hand over Emma, Eliška, or Vince to the PRC. Whatever must be done to hold Jack accountable for the Sanctuary of Prayer will be done within the Cherub under my leadership—but only after we have established peace."

"Who told you the gateway in Tai Tam leads to the Scourge?"

"Someone I trust who is outside of the bubble we have created at the Rosewood." Bau eyed her closely, knowing he was on the verge of revealing too much. "A friend who is also helping the faction."

"Considering your disdain for Jack Reynolds, I will assume you are speaking of either Vince Tobias or Emma Bennett. If it is Vince, then clearly the faction is using him too." Fang Xue grabbed the Upsdell jersey and held it up. "You are no longer the Head Boy of Beacon Hill, and you do not owe an alliance to the faction. To be frank, we do not know whether the gateway in Tai Tam leads to where you have been told. Allow me time to confirm if it is true."

"Wheels are in motion," Bau pushed back. "I am asking for your support."

"You are young, Bau, with much to learn." Fang Xue tossed the jersey on the bed. "Decisions either create greater trust or cause revolt among the most loyal."

"I am trying to unite us so we do not end up as slaves."

"Well, the Council wishes to further discuss the offer from the PRC."

"Not all who believe in Elyon enjoy the luxuries of the highest Cherub." Bau picked up the jersey and folded it neatly, then returned it to his luggage. "I spent today looking at myself in the mirror, and I am ashamed of what I have allowed at the Rosewood. Tomorrow I will meet with the Council and challenge them to do what is required to defend our freedom. Those who have found comfort here will no longer be allowed to hide from the fight."

"Take the night to reconsider." Fang Xue headed for the door, then stopped. "Perhaps your parents should join us in the morning."

When Bau didn't answer, Fang Xue opened the door and left.

52

NETHER REALM

Jack and Emma stopped to catch their breath as they neared the end of the Cascades of Tombé. He stretched his muscles after sneaking past hundreds of cascades, ducking and hiding the whole way whenever they heard the faintest sound. At the bottom of the cascades, the ponds of onyx tar dumped into a winding river. For a while they followed a flowing current until they reached an arched lava-rock bridge directly ahead. He knelt and eyed the bridge, which connected the two banks of what he guessed was the Chasseuse River.

"We've made it this far without being eaten," he said in a lowered voice. "Victory."

"Darkness may fall before long," Emma replied. "But we have brought light with us."

"No sign of anyone else in the nether realm, except for legion and vampire owls."

"At least no one we can see." Emma retrieved the map and scanned the landmarks. "If this is the Chasseuse River, then we will need to cross the bridge."

"Diable Bridge." Jack peered over her shoulder. "Definitely sounds like trouble."

"I will go first if you want me to."

"It was my idea to enter the nether realm." Jack grabbed his forearm to be sure Soulweaver was still there. "Can't get any worse than wandering this place for eternity."

Jack and Emma moved quickly along the river, leaving the cascades behind. As they approached the bridge, Jack noticed the arch reflected on the surface of the river, creating the illusion of an endless circle. A memory flashed in his mind from inside the Pyramid of Stars, when he nearly surrendered to his darkest desires. He steadied himself, convinced in the nether realm there wouldn't be a second chance at redemption.

"I'm guessing my mom didn't write directions to the artifact on the back of the map," he mused as they reached the bridge. "Her warning was clear, but now we're here. I'm betting it won't be as simple as crossing over to the other side."

"One step at a time," Emma encouraged. "I will be right behind you."

"Which is the only reason why I'm volunteering to go first—so you can catch me."

He stepped up to the bridge and inhaled deep, harnessing another mustard seed of courage. With his fists clenched, he took one step, expecting the legion to swoop in out of nowhere and ravage his flesh. Frozen, he was relieved he was still breathing. His eyes darted around. *Keep going, Jack. You're a sitting duck waiting for hunting season.* He took another step and then another over the arched bridge. He stopped again and glanced over his shoulder. Emma stood at the edge of the bridge, confusion spread across her face.

"Jack . . ." she called out. "Wait."

Adrenaline spiked as he turned around and walked toward her, until he was pushed backward by an invisible force field. He reached out his hand and felt the energy resisting his palm. *Seriously? There's gotta be a way through, like in Arishiyama.* Emma held her hand up and mirrored him, neither able to feel the other's touch. He stared into her amber eyes, sensing sparks of fear in her gaze.

"I'm okay." Jack smiled half-heartedly. "Maybe when I get to the other side it'll open."

Alone on the bridge, he turned around before he lost his nerve. His muscles fired as he crossed the bridge, one foot in front of the other. He climbed the curved stone until he reached the halfway point. *I can't believe no beast has surfaced to rip me to shreds.* Curious, he glanced over the edge and peered down on the onyx tar as a current flowed beneath. Instead of seeing the bridge and gray skies above, another world reflected back.

In a blink, everything around him shifted and he stood on the banks of the river in Sitio Veterans. He'd been there more than once before—in the real world and his visions. Still, there were unanswered questions and confusion about what really happened when Rachel died. He willed himself to surrender to the world that reflected off the onyx current, a world unfolding again before his eyes.

Rachel emerged from between tin shanties along the banks. Then Jack stood between her and Michael Chung as the vision from the Marble Caves played again. Rachel unleashed a luminous ocean blue lightforce, which left Chung weakened and on his knees. She moved with purpose and confidence, on the verge of striking down the Merikh's most lethal assassin. Jack heard Rachel's voice and Chung's response.

"Repent from your wicked ways, and pray for forgiveness."

"You are one of the chosen, but you are far from the strongest."

Consumed by the clarity of his vision, Jack didn't realize he had climbed onto the edge of the lava-rock bridge. Unable to hear Emma's pleas, he locked his sights on Rachel and Chung—anticipating a shadow to emerge. In the vision he had experienced in the Marble Caves, the shadow showed itself to be Emma. As he'd seen before, the shadow appeared and Rachel was lifted off the muddy banks. On reflex, Jack shouted, but his voice was muted. On Diable Bridge, his boots inched even closer to the edge.

With the swipe of a hand, the shadow's powers struck Rachel without any visible lightforce. A bloodcurdling scream shattered the past and the present. Rachel dropped to her death, and Chung stumbled over to fire one final shot.

A bullet didn't kill her.

Jack charged toward Chung and the shadow at the same time, only in this vision Soulweaver was in his grasp. The Rod of Elyon hummed with a mighty force. Jack swung skillfully, striking the shadow once and narrowly missing Chung. Within a split second, he caught a glimpse of the shadow's face, which left him even more stunned and disturbed than the last time. Tears welled up in his eyes as he stared into the haunting gaze of his mom, Gabriella.

His arms spread wide as he slowly surrendered to darkness and despair on Diable Bridge. In the fogginess of his vision, Sitio Veterans faded and he found himself standing on the grounds of Beacon Hill. He was bewildered and haunted by his mom's sudden appearance—and he desperately wanted to believe it was another manipulation.

Can Addison control my visions in the nether realm?

Jack walked down an empty sidewalk toward the quad, where he found Nightingale, Upsdell, Crozier, and Rowell Houses abandoned. In total silence, he entered the Main Hall and searched for Headmaster Fargher, Natalie, Amina, Professor Windsor, Salomeh, Faizan, or even Professor McDougall. The classrooms were vacant, and a ghostly eeriness drifted through Beacon Hill.

Fear shuddered his bones to the core of his soul as another shadow appeared farther down the corridor and walked toward him. He reached for his forearm, but Soulweaver was gone. With fists clenched, he braced himself for a brawl. The haziness lifted as the appearance of the shadow sharpened. For a few seconds Jack stopped breathing, but he exhaled once his friend smiled.

"You are a sight for sore eyes," Tim said. "I have been waiting for you."

"I don't have a clue what is happening right now. Hold on, am I dead?"

"If you are seeing me, then I am guessing things have not gone as planned."

"Not even close," Jack answered, still awestruck. "Where . . . ? How . . . ? Why . . . ?"

"Only Elyon can answer those questions, mate." Tim motioned for him to follow as they walked through the door of the Main Hall and were instantly transported to the Wishing Tree. "Nightingale. Amina. You. Vince. Even Will. I have no regrets about any of it—except sharing a bit too much with Will, I suppose," Tim said.

"You didn't know what he was up to or who was pulling his strings."

"Truth." Tim paused as the Wishing Tree swayed gently. "The same is true for you."

"All of this is because of me." Jack swallowed hard. "I never should've gone after . . ."

"Rachel was murdered," Tim pushed back. "What else were any of us supposed to do?"

"You never would've died—and I'll carry that with me forever."

"What happened in Aberdeen was not your fault—it was your twisted father, definitely."

"Of course it was my fault. I brought all of you into this mess."

"You do realize the whole world does not revolve around you, right?"

"My choices have brought so much pain." Jack exhaled. "I'm so sorry, Tim."

"Each one of us has a path we are destined to travel, and for sure, you nudged me further than I expected, but I also rediscovered a faith which belonged to my parents—and now belongs to me. I will forever be grateful, Jack. And I'm thankful for all of the fun times, and the times we were out of our minds. You cannot live in the past, or you stop living in the present."

"You were always the smartest one of us." Jack breathed in the serenity of the Wishing Tree. "We miss you so much—and I'm praying one day we'll see you again."

"I am counting on it—tell Amina I love her more than words." Tim wrapped his arm over Jack's shoulders and squeezed hard. "You are not done yet, mate. But the path ahead is about to get insanely harder."

"If that's your final pep talk, then McDougall would definitely give you an F."

"You know we are in an alternate reality when you are the one talking to me about my grades." Tim let go of Jack's shoulder and

276

smiled, which warmed Jack's heart while breaking it for the thousandth time. "No regrets."

Beacon Hill and Tim faded as Emma's voice rang in his ears. "Jack! He is here!"

He opened his eyes and nearly fell off the edge of the bridge. Instinctively, he leaned back and tried to keep his balance. Emma's words hadn't sunk in yet, not until he hopped off the edge and stood on the bridge. On the other side of the force field she was darting back and forth, attempting to find a way through. He saw terror in her eyes for the first time.

Soulweaver slipped into his grasp, and he knew that meant nothing good was on its way. He spun around toward the opposite end of the bridge with the rod in front of him. At first he didn't see anyone until a vindictive figure stepped up from the other side wielding Dragon Soul. Jack tightened his grip on Soulweaver, knowing the stakes had never been higher. He glanced over his shoulder and watched Emma's light-force explode against the force field, but the wall of energy remained strong. She wasn't coming to his rescue, no matter how hard she tried.

Since he'd faced off with Will in Victoria Harbour, there was a piece of him that wanted to finish what was started. Deep within he battled between saving his best friend and stopping his enemy from killing others.

"Nowhere left to run," Will seethed. "You will always be a melt."

"Both of you, stop!" Emma's voice rang out. "You do not want to do this. Please."

Jack didn't look back a second time. "You've already lost, Will."

"And you have hidden from me long enough," Will rebuked with a nasty sneer.

"Oh, I'm not hiding." Jack clenched his jaw, embracing retribution. "I'm a raider."

53

"Jack . . . wait!"

At the edge of Diable Bridge, Emma shouted at the top of her lungs. She realized the force field was keeping her from stepping onto the lava rock. Bewilderment shifted to her training on Karābu Island where she was one of the chosen listening to the instructions of the Elder. She needed to find a solution quickly, and above all else, remain calm. Jack turned and walked toward her before reaching out his hand. She couldn't feel his touch, and a twinge of terror chipped at her determination.

"I'm okay," Jack said. "Maybe when I get to the other side it'll open."

Emma wanted to believe he was right, but she was well aware

traveling through the nether realm was beyond any rules she'd been taught as one of the chosen. She summoned her lightforce and pressed her palms against the invisible wall. Jack turned his back and crossed the bridge until he stopped halfway. She watched him closely, noticing he was staring intently at the onyx tar flowing below. As seconds passed, she feared he might remain a statue for eternity.

"He is having another vision," she whispered. "Jack!"

Emma raced back and forth along the riverbank, unloading a barrage of lightforce while harnessing her powers as a bender. She grew more desperate to find a crack in the force field to slip through. A chill shot down her spine when Jack climbed onto the edge of the bridge, swaying back and forth before spreading his arms wide. She shouted at him even though she was uncertain whether he could hear her voice.

"Elyon, grant me your mighty power." Emma's eyes turned stark white as she unleashed her lightforce against the invisible wall. She stopped cold at the sight of Will approaching the bridge.

"Jack! He is here!"

Raw fear surged through her veins when Jack nearly fell off the bridge, struggling to keep his balance. She moved swiftly along the riverbank with lightforce bursting from her palms, striking against the immovable force field. Jack hopped off the edge and stood in the center of the bridge, leaving Emma even more desperate to charge through. Soulweaver appeared in Jack's grasp, offering her an ounce of hope that the Rod of Elyon would defend him. Her gaze met Jack's for a flash, long enough for her to know he wasn't going to back down.

I will not get to him in time, but I cannot lose him.

"Both of you, stop! You do not want to do this. Please!"

Emma shouted her plea, still unable to know whether either of them heard. Jack pointed Soulweaver in front of him as Will swayed Dragon Soul side to side. From Everest to the nether realm, once again the most powerful weapons were on the verge of clashing in another battle. In the graying skies, a black cloud moved swiftly toward them. Emma was powerless to stop what was coming. Legion swarmed across the Chasseuse River, heading straight for Diable Bridge.

At the same time, Jack charged against Will with Soulweaver spinning in a blazing inferno. A two-headed dragon pushed to the razored edge of Dragon Soul, and a mighty eruption exploded as the weapons clashed. Black and orange flames burst out, engulfing the lava rock and melting sections of the bridge. Jack stayed on the attack with pulses of white energy shooting from Soulweaver like a cannon.

"Legion!" Emma's warnings failed to alter what was unfolding, yet she screamed at the top of her lungs while tears streamed down her cheeks. "Jack, watch out!"

A swarm of silhouettes whipped over the bridge, smothering both Jack and Will. Shrieks and wailing from the pit of the darkest souls shuddered the nether realm. Emma watched helplessly as the legion lifted Jack off the ground with his arms and legs stretched wide. He hovered in the air for a moment before the demons whisked him away across the land.

An eerie silence replaced the fading shrieks as Emma stared hard toward the edge of the bridge. She took one step and walked through, surprised the force field was gone. Amid the unspeakable, she stood on Diable Bridge with her fiery gaze locked on Will's dark eyes. The two-headed beast of Dragon Soul raged while her gaze shifted to the rod left on the bridge. Will's eyes widened as he rushed forward to snatch the rod. She raised her hand, and the rod flew across the bridge into her grasp.

For the first time since Jack found the Rod of Elyon in Charis, Emma felt the power of the heartwood between her fingers. She took another few steps along the arched stone, sensing an unfamiliar rage in her soul. Since she was a child she'd been taught and trained to protect the innocent and search for the good in all things. *"Bring peace where there is chaos."* Peter's voice echoed in her mind as she realized there was more than *surrender* to being a Cherub.

What keeps Jack fighting as an outlier? A righteous anger.

"Will, where have they taken him?" Emma asked boldly. "Tell me right now."

"Not even you can stop what's coming against him." Will swung Dragon Soul side to side as a sly grin twisted his lips. "Emma, you are the one who chose to stay with him."

"You are right." She remembered finding Will in the original headmaster's office, presumably searching through maps stored since Headmaster Nightingale died. "And you are the one who said the past will always remain history, but you have surrendered your future to the Merikh."

"Look around—this is way bigger than the Merikh," he chastised. "Do you know who rules the nether realm? She is more powerful and deadly than any Cherub trinket."

"You have a choice in this moment. Take me to where the legion are headed."

"There is no redemption for the sins committed with Dragon Soul—or the Windstrikers." Will kept the sword at the ready while gripping the dretium war fans, which were secured within a leather sleeve strapped to his leg. "Everyone has abandoned me, even you."

"I entered the nether realm to save you." Emma's lightforce wrapped around the heartwood as the rod hummed with authority. "We have not abandoned you, William."

"When I offered you an escape, you turned your back." Will's gaze hardened. "We could have found a place away from Cherub and Merikh, but you chose Jack over me."

She replied with tears in her eyes. "I am begging you."

"Darkness is all that's left."

Will lunged and sliced the sword at Emma, who ducked and counterattacked with the Rod of Elyon. She was more skilled with the rod than Jack, even without the force emanating from the heartwood. In rapid succession, she landed a strike to Will's ribs and another to his leg. Will stumbled backward as the two-headed dragon defended him. Emma stabbed the rod into the lava stone, and it stood by itself. She held her arms wide as her lightforce glowed in her palms, then she clapped her hands together and her power joined with the Rod of Elyon.

A great wind nearly knocked her off the bridge as her pupils turned bone white and a roaring lion burst from the rod, savagely attacking the dragon. Emma grabbed the rod and moved swiftly forward as Dragon Soul fell onto the lava rock and Will flew through the air before landing flat on his back. She pounced on top of him, allowing her darkest instincts to consume her thoughts. *He will never change. He has killed so many. He deserves to die.* Voices screamed in Emma's mind, willing her to put an end to *the* enemy of the Cherub.

"You were never the chosen one," Will ranted as he stared with dead eyes. "Everything you believe is a lie."

Emma's anger boiled with his lack of remorse as he laughed in her face—leaving her feeling as if she were worth nothing.

Without a second thought, she plunged the Rod of Elyon into his chest, and the lava rock beneath cracked.

She blinked, and it was over. Will was gone. He'd vanished. She realized everything that happened since the moment she stepped onto the bridge had been a hallucination. In disbelief, she ran her fingers through her hair and eyed the bridge and surroundings.

No cracked lava stone. No Dragon Soul. No Rod of Elyon. No William. No Jack. My darkest nightmare revealed itself to me. Elyon, I am strong enough to end his life. I beg you to stand between us if that time comes. I cannot imagine what nightmare consumed Jack before he was taken.

Emma crossed to the other side of Diable Bridge and removed the map from inside her jacket. She studied the names written down by Jack's mum. *Shores of Mericier. Cascades of Tombé.* Her index finger followed the path they traveled. *Chasseuse River. Diable Bridge.* She looked ahead on the map and stopped when she read the next landmark.

Sombre Hedges.

54

After midnight, Bau slipped out of his room and took a stairwell to the ground floor of the Rosewood. Instead of leaving through the lobby, which would have triggered a full security detail, he slipped out an exit on the side of the building near Salisbury Garden. He pulled his hood over his head and kept a brisk walk as he crossed the road on the same block as The Peninsula. For weeks he'd been watched like a hawk, and now he knew for certain it was so Fang Xue could monitor him.

Tonight, the attention of his security, Fang Xue, and the highest Cherub was focused on bringing his parents safely from Tai Tam. Bau knew about the tunnels left abandoned after the Battle of Hong Kong, and he remembered using one beneath Nightingale's

284

vault to bring supplies during the days Beacon Hillers and Cherub refugees were secluded underground.

Bau glanced around at the city he loved, known to Hong Kongers as Nine Dragons. He was angered by what it had become—and the threat the government posed to its future. He reached Nathan Road and picked up the pace as he passed shabu-shabu restaurants, The Alley, Arome Bakery, and Toyo Leather Ware Co. Traffic on Nathan Road was sparse, but there were scattered groups of homeless people huddled together to stay warm.

Once he reached the MTR station, he stopped and watched the Tsim Sha Tsui Mansion from across the street. In the shadows, he waited until the sidewalks and streets were clear. Most who were not Hong Kongers assumed the mansion signified an important place in Hong Kong's history, but in reality it was nothing more than a hostel with a cool name.

Bau climbed the concrete steps and slipped inside, then headed down a hallway leading to the back of the building. He entered a small kitchen where Faizan, Eliška, and Amina waited.

"We have waited for hours," Eliška said. "We were beginning to think you were not coming."

"All eyes are on me at the Rosewood." Bau grabbed a Vitasoy from the fridge. "I left as soon as it was safe."

"We met with Salomeh and Xui Li earlier," Amina explained. "Sounds to us like you are stuck in the middle."

"That is an understatement. Fang Xue will leverage my parents."

"I thought your parents were in Tai Tam," Eliška retorted. "How will they be leveraged?"

"Cherub are bringing them to the Rosewood with free passageway from the PRC." Bau popped the top off the bottle and took a long drag. "Fang Xue is not thrilled about the faction."

"We knew it was a possibility," Amina replied. "Faizan has some news."

"Yes, well . . ." Faizan cleared his throat, as if he were about to speak to a king. "Salomeh and Xui Li returned to Beacon Hill and met with Headmaster Fargher and Natalie most of the afternoon." Faizan paused. "The headmaster called an assembly tonight where Salomeh and Xui Li confirmed that all who remain at Beacon Hill must prepare themselves to fight, or they will need to leave through the House of Luminescence."

"Both kept their word." Bau turned toward Eliška. "What about Hong Kong Island?"

"We will need more lightforcers and benders." Eliška pulled out a tablet and swiped through a series of still photos. "Actually, this was Vince's idea. Orange represents districts that need our help, and red marks the locations where Merikh and PRC patrol beyond the checkpoints, which are marked in black. As you can see, attempting to rescue everyone will be near impossible."

"Faizan, speak with Salomeh and Xui Li," Bau instructed. "Send more lightforcers and benders to the faction through the gateway at Kai Tak."

"Of course," Faizan replied. "I will speak with them tonight."

"Where is Vince? I thought he would be with you."

"He is figuring out a way to mark the districts on the ground," Eliška answered.

"All of us are aware of the risks you are taking," Amina added. "We are grateful."

"I see no other way," Bau replied. "Trust goes both ways, right?"

Eliška leaned forward with her elbows on the table. "What are you asking?"

"I need to know the truth about Emma and Jack."

"We hope they made it into the nether realm, but we do not know for certain."

"Nether realm . . ." Bau shook his head slowly. "How soon can we begin evacuating?"

"We are already coordinating between Beacon Hill," Amina replied, "and the faction."

"Less than a fortnight," Eliška added. "Any longer and we will be too late."

55

Legion streaked across the skies and barren lands, whipping back and forth above the Sombre Hedges. Will soared on trails of the black silhouettes while Jack wrestled against burning restraints around his wrists. Pain ripped through his body as a searing heat raged in his chest. *Eden's Star is awake—which means we're going in the right direction whether I'm ready or not.* On Diable Bridge, he thought he'd gained the upper hand until he was ambushed. When the legion swarmed, he'd lost his grip on Soulweaver, and without the rod there was no way to fight for his freedom.

Behind clenched teeth, he fought through the agony, knowing Emma might still be stuck on the other side of the force field. *Elyon, protect Emma—and give me the strength to guard Eden's Star until the end.* The legion turned sharply, swooping low across the land. His mind flashed to the vision in Sitio Veterans where he'd stared into his mom's eyes. *No way she was the one. I can't trust my visions right now. Rachel wasn't killed by Emma or Mom. But who else was there with Chung?* Suddenly, the legion released its vise grip on him, and he fell from the sky. He never had a chance to brace himself before he slammed into the barren land, tumbling until he stopped facedown.

Dazed, Jack groggily pulled himself onto his knees as Will landed softly in front of him. He stared at Soulweaver in Will's grasp, the Windstrikers holstered on his hip, and Dragon Soul tucked into the scabbard over his shoulder. *He's more powerful than he's ever been. Without Soulweaver, I don't stand a chance.* Jack stayed on his knees, unsure of what was about to happen, and waited for Will to make the next move.

"Get up," Will ordered. "Your nightmare is only beginning, mate."

"You wanted me." Jack pulled himself up and shook off floating stars. "So here I am."

"I am not the only one." Will spun Soulweaver between his fingers. "Tricky stick."

"Tell you what . . ." Jack held up his wrists, which continued to burn beneath his skin. "Let these loose, and I'll show you what Soulweaver can do."

"Soulweaver," Will mocked. "And you surrendered it like a muppet."

"You're afraid of a fair fight against Dragon Soul and the Windstrikers?"

"Wait until you hand over Eden's Star," Will rebuked. "Now that *will* be painful."

Will shoved Jack, who stumbled backward, nearly losing his balance. *I'm not going down again.* Anger fought against the restraints, and deep down, sadness lingered in the pit of his stomach. *Will was my best friend. How did all of this fall apart?*

Will moved behind Jack and struck him across the back with Soulweaver. Again he stumbled but refused to fall. "Walk, Jack."

Thunder rumbled and lightning sparked the atmosphere, but there was no downpour. Jack counted the seconds and realized the lightning was less than a mile away. For a while he walked straight ahead without glancing over his shoulder even though he sensed Will's presence right behind him. *Why did the legion drop us where they did? Why not take me all the way to my death?* He thought about these questions until a theory materialized.

"At the Sanctum of Serenity, the legion took you because you had the prophecy." Jack waited for a response, but when Will remained silent he continued. "Florence Upsdell lured you through the Scourge for the same reason—and because she knew we would come searching for you."

"Rubbish," Will mumbled. "I was summoned to the nether realm to find the artifact."

"How many Cherub died entering the gateway in Tai Tam?"

"Maybe the highest Cherub gave the wrong offering," Will ridiculed. "High-and-mighty do not care about those left behind, only about saving their own skin. Each paid a price of their own, and you will see how deep they have fallen. Jack, you're fighting on the wrong side."

"Florence is confined to the nether realm for a reason," Jack argued. "If she leaves this place—if you help her escape—she will destroy not only Cherub but the world."

"You know, she sensed you and Emma in the Scourge," Will

said flatly. "I followed her into the nether realm because I have chosen my path—a path away from the myths of Elyon." Will stepped in front of Jack and waved the prophecy in his face. "I chose to spare Emma because I promised I'd remember her in the end. You act like you have all the answers, but you don't have a clue."

"What did Florence promise you?" Jack barely reined in his anger. "To resurrect your mom?"

"Shut up!" Will lunged forward and slammed his fist against Jack's jaw. Jack stumbled but refused to go down, gathering his balance and winning a moral victory. *Maybe not so moral and Cherub-like. I'm an outlier—a raider—so what do I expect? Elyon, you have to see this from my side, right?* He gained his balance and glared at Will, who ranted, "All you ever cared about was finding Rachel's killer. You never thought for a second what that meant for the rest of us."

"You were as amped as I was about finding who'd done it," Jack clapped back. "I never thought Addison, Chung, or the Merikh would go after your mom and dad. The headmaster kept massive secrets from me and everyone else to protect you because you were spiraling. The legion protect you because that was the only way to find us. Florence Upsdell doesn't care if you live or die, but I do—we do—because we know you're hurting."

"Now you're telling a porky." Will's gaze hardened. "I'm stronger than all of you."

"You trained on Karābu Island with Peter Leung," Jack pressed. "Who cares if you didn't make the *chosen* cut? What matters is Elyon gave you gifts to fight against the darkness."

"Not one more word," Will warned.

For the next few miles, both walked in silence. Jack's wrists burned intensely. He'd been through pain before, both physical and emotional. He thought of losing Rachel, Areum, and Tim, and then his mind flashed to the weeks hiding in a dark hostel room battling against his demons in Karachi. All the pain, all the heartbreak had created a wall protecting the deepest corners of his soul.

I can handle being in this much pain because I never want to hurt anyone else again. I'm a target on all sides with Eden's Star flowing inside of me. Maybe the world is better off if I'm the only one who suffers until Eden's Star is buried in the soil with me.

"Hold on," Jack blurted. "Legion dropped us off for a reason."

"Keep walking, and stop talking."

"Florence Upsdell lured you here, but you haven't actually spoken to her."

"She led me through the Scourge. So I'd say what you're spewing is fake news."

"You don't know if that was real—she could've been a vision within the Scourge."

"How you found any of the artifacts is beyond me," Will chastised. "No wonder you're an outlier—and a charity case for Emma."

As Jack put one foot in front of the other, inmates on death row flashed in his mind—those who were escorted from their prison cell to their final moment of judgment. The nightmare began when he stood over Rachel's grave in Sitio Veterans, and it had only grown darker the longer he breathed in life. He struggled to accept that he'd failed to keep Rachel's promise and protect those he loved. His head hung low as he stared at his worn, muddy boots kicking up dust. He thought of the artifacts they found and the stolen prophecy in Will's grasp. In that moment when defeat swirled in his mind, Elyon's voice broke through.

I am the vine rooted in soul and spirit. Remain in me, and I will live in you. Depart from my ways, and you will wither and die. You have brought light and darkness into this realm. Hold fast, Jack.

56

DAYLIGHT FADED ACROSS the nether realm, yet total darkness remained elusive. A dim light cast shifting shadows across the Chasseuse River. Boulders jutting out above roaring rapids glistened with onyx tar. In the hours since the legion and Will snatched Jack on Diable Bridge, Emma had followed the river at a relentless pace. Every step left her eyes darting all around in search of the legion or whatever other beasts lurked in this realm. She pushed herself to the brink of collapsing, which left her gasping for air once she stopped to take a quick glance at the map.

With the hourglass draining, Emma continued along the riverbank before climbing up a hillside where boulders blocked a clear way through. She shattered them into crumbled rock and shifted them to the side, revealing an entrance to a monstrous labyrinth which stretched as far as she could see in both directions. She'd seen the maze drawn on the map and knew she would have to find a way to the other side to keep going. With crumbled rock piled behind, she faced twisted and wretched thorns woven tightly together. She unleashed her lightforce and bender gifts against the maze, but the thorns of the labyrinth remained steadfast.

"Mourning Labyrinth," she whispered. "Only way through is to follow the maze."

Emma cautiously stepped through the entrance and headed down a pathway which grew narrower the deeper she headed into the maze. Around a corner, she reached a dead end. A shrill scream pierced her ears, leaving her spinning around ready to defend herself, but no one was there. She quickly retraced her steps in the direction she'd come from moments earlier. Twisted vines shifted within the labyrinth, closing one path while opening another. She followed a new pathway as more screams spread throughout the maze.

"I could be stuck in this forever," she said under her breath, "wasting too much time."

As she searched her way through the labyrinth, her mind flashed to the weeks she'd trained on Karābu Island with the other chosen. She'd learned how to control her gifts and harness a mental strength that forced her to go beyond her limits. *Rachel was the one who pushed us all, and I miss her as much as I miss Areum.* She remembered standing in Areum's apartment after her gifts were taken, staring at the photo of the three of them together—sisters beyond the Cherub.

I doubted my gifts could be restored, but then Sahil flew me and Jack to the heavens. Elyon, you have prepared me as one of the chosen—you have granted me gifts beyond what I deserve—but I cannot lose Jack. Guide my steps. Give me strength. Grant me favor.

A heavy fog drifted through the Mourning Labyrinth the deeper she traveled. She reached another dead end and turned back as the maze shifted again, revealing an alternate pathway. Thick, sharp thorns stabbed at her as she struggled to see what was ahead, leaving her wrestling against more thorny vines attempting to wrap her in a cocoon. She grabbed hold as her lightforce flowed from her fingertips and spread across the needly barbs, splitting them apart. More stabbed at her as she hopped over the dead ones to escape. Screams shuddered the silence as the twisted thorns sealed another pathway.

Emma slowed her breathing, controlling the adrenaline surging through her body. Gashes stung and blood trickled down her fingers, dropping to the ground beneath. She turned down another path and found herself in the center of the labyrinth. Off to the side, she caught sight of beady eyes amid the thorns. Unsure whether she was hallucinating, she blinked, and the eyes disappeared. All the other pathways shifted, closing around the circle. She waited for one to reveal itself, but as the seconds passed, she knew she was trapped.

Why did Gabriella name this place Mourning Labyrinth?

"'Tears fill our eyes when flesh and hearts fail,'" she recited from the Eternal. "'In life and death, sorrow and suffering bring pain into this world and the realms beyond. Anguish and torment haunt our souls until we pass through these realms into eternity.'"

Emma looked around the circle as dozens of eyes—too numerous to count—now stared between thorny vines. She stepped back as vines parted and a monstrosity entered the circle wielding a pointed spear dripping with lava. Half human, half skeleton. A bone-chilling roar ignited gut-wrenching screams from within the labyrinth. Black flames flowed from the creature's spear across the circle, engulfing the vines as Emma dodged out of the way. On the attack, the beast stabbed the spear as Emma rolled across the ground before slamming into the sharp vines. Again the beast roared and the screams resounded all around.

Emma stood with palms glowing, but instead of a ball of energy she formed a lightning rod of her own. She grasped the lightforce with both hands and counterattacked. Lava and light exploded against one another. Emma's eyes turned stark white as she summoned all of her gifts against this beast with deadly skills. Within the circle, the beast moved swiftly and nicked Emma with several blows. Her adrenaline rushed, washing over the stinging pain. Her lightning rod landed several strikes of its own as she fought the monstrosity to a standstill.

As the beast roared again, Emma snapped the lightforce in half and grasped volts of power in each hand. The beast charged like a raging bull, and its spear sailed through the air as Emma leaned back and swung both lightning rods across her body, slicing the spear in half. The beast slammed into her, but she softened the impact with her bender power.

Bloodied, Emma kept her balance and darted toward the vines, planting her foot then launching herself into the air. With a warrior's call, she plunged both lightning rods into the beast. An explosion of lava and blinding light erupted, plowing through the Mourning Labyrinth.

Emma braced herself until the maze grew hauntingly silent. She stared into the lifeless eyes of the half-human, half-skeletal beast, haunted by who it may once have been. The lightforce vanished as the adrenaline subsided and her nerves steadied. She gathered herself and walked through the opening created by the explosion, searching for the eyes that had watched her, until she reached the other side of the maze.

On the edge of a barren field, countless hooded figures blocked her way. She clenched her fists, ready to go another round against the darkness. In unison, all eyes looked up and a deep pain pierced her spirit. Teary eyed, she gazed upon those who had been cast into the nether realm. Words were impossible to describe what she witnessed as a flood of sorrow poured out from the lost ghostly souls.

"Elyon, your light has returned to the nether realm," she prayed. "You are healing those who mourn, those who are suffering, and those who failed to escape the darkness."

Emma stepped forward, and the sea of souls parted. She held up her hands and sensed healing spread across the darkness. Wide-eyed, she watched each figure remove their hood as their dark eyes dissolved into vibrant colors. *Life restored to tortured souls.* Emma kept walking through the masses as the miraculous unfolded. She glanced over her shoulder to see those behind her disappear one by one. In the midst of a tidal wave of healing, Elyon's mercy welcomed souls beyond death into the everlasting.

57

AFTER HOURS WITH WRISTS RESTRAINED by an invisible power, Jack's body was burning on the inside as he eyed legion streaming across the skies headed in the direction he'd come from. He couldn't help but worry about Emma. *If she made it across Diable Bridge, then she's going to face the legion alone. But if she's still on the other side of the force field, she won't reach me in time.* As Will shadowed him, Jack lowered his head and walked toward glowing reddish-orange torches at the entrance to a natural tunnel created by thick hedges.

"How did Florence Upsdell find you?" Jack asked, exhausted. "How did you find her?"

"I never used the gateway in Tai Tam," Will answered coldly. "Not until the prophecy."

"After the legion found you in the Sanctum of Serenity, and you stole it."

"You were there, mate—Bau and Emma too. All of you wanted it, but I snagged it."

"Did you know Florence is a vision seeker who causes others to see what she wants them to see?" Jack was guessing, though he knew this was true about Addison, but he pushed a bit harder to keep Will talking. "Where are we going?"

"In the Scourge she called it Bitterhelm."

Jack weighed his words. "You do know she will kill us both, and that's just a start."

"When she sees I've brought you, I will be welcomed by her side." Will paused. "Addison promised riches and power, but he lied—he's as responsible as you are for killing my mum. Selfishness must run in the Reynolds family."

"Every family has secrets," Jack countered. "Headmaster and you share plenty."

"But my mum was innocent—you and yours are the ones who got her killed."

"You're right—all of this is my fault." The restraints burned hotter as sweat drenched his clothes beneath the dretium hoodie. "I'm sorry, Will—for everything."

"Your words mean nothing to me." Will prodded him forward. "Keep moving."

"Have you heard of the Siege of Plagues?" Jack walked and waited for an answer, any sign he'd be able to convince Will before it was too late. "Florence Upsdell used her powers to send plagues around the world, even killing Cherub and Merikh firstborns."

"Another Cherub fable you are daft enough to believe," Will rebuked.

"Cherub fought against legion to the edge of the Highlands, but she killed them all." Jack entered the tunnel and shuffled his boots beneath hovering flames illuminating the way. "Only the Elders of old were strong enough to force legion and the Queen of Sakkhela into the nether realm."

"You do not understand the destruction unleashed against the world at my hands—there is only one path left, and it is with the queen."

"Whatever she promised you is a lie." Jack hesitated. "Elyon will forgive you for what you've done."

"Soon you will hear the truth, and the truth will bury you."

If you don't see the light soon, the queen will bury all of us.

At the other end of the tunnel, Jack and Will stood at the edge of a sheer cliff where a narrow bridge stretched over a deep ocean to a desolate lava rock. Jack peered down at onyx tar crashing against the rocks, then turned his gaze toward the gunmetal skies, searching for a sign. *"Slumbering amidst wild waves of the sea and wandering stars in the skies."* Torches lined the bridge across to the lava rock, flames of amber, crimson, and ebony.

"Addison and your mum took something from this place." Will poked Jack forward using Soulweaver. "Now the queen wants it back, Jack. I suggest you hand it over without a fight."

With the waves raging beneath, Jack walked across the bridge. A chill shot down his spine once they reached Bitterhelm and were watched closely by legion. Rising out of the ocean, a barbaric volcanic fortress loomed. He'd seen the silhouettes at the edge of the Highlands and faced them in the nether realm, but these demons were not the same. Skeletal and beady-eyed with scarred wings, unholy battle armor, and weapons corrupted from the blood of the innocent, the legion of Bitterhelm were not hunting forgiveness but guarding revenge on a lava rock wrapped in eternal torment.

Jack's spirit grew heavy as he entered through an opening in the lava rock. His chest flared suddenly, a sign the compass was pointing him toward one of the artifacts. *If Will knows Eden's Star is within reach, there's no telling what crazy thing he'll do.* Shadows shifted as blackness enveloped him. He continued deeper into the passageway with Will at his shoulder, and he touched rock walls on both sides to help guide his steps. They entered a chamber, but Jack was the first to walk straight toward an ebony boulder in the center. He ran his hands over smooth onyx, fingers touching a small hole in the stone barely visible to the eye.

"She's buried in Bitterhelm?" Jack asked. "Will, we need to leave this place."

"Nonsense." Will stepped closer. "I'm thinking Eden's Star will do the trick."

"I don't have Eden's Star on me." Jack skirted the truth, as technically the compass was *inside* of him. "Are your gifts strong enough to face the Queen of Sakkhela?"

In a split second, Jack was slammed face-first against the rock, unable to move a muscle. Will searched his pockets and patted him down aggressively. His hand stopped over the top of the zippered pocket on Jack's sleeve, then unzipped it cautiously. Will grabbed the ivory figurine hidden inside, then released his hold on Jack.

"Is this Eden's Star?" Will asked. "Not what I expected."

Jack shook his head. "It's not the compass."

"But it is important enough for you to hide." Will glanced toward the ebony boulder, and his stare locked in on one spot. He stepped toward the boulder and held up the ivory figurine next to the camouflaged hole. "You brought a key and didn't even realize it."

"Will . . ." Jack's wrist restraints loosened and the searing heat cooled. He rubbed his hands together, grateful for the relief, yet knowing he was outmatched. "You don't know what will happen—"

"Nowhere else to run, mate. Only one of us is leaving this place."

Mom kept the key to Bitterhelm hidden—the same key that unlocked the gateway in Thalren. I guess I'll never know how Rachel got her hands on the box, but I understand why she left it lost.

Legion appeared within the chamber, blocking the only clear way out. Will inserted the ivory figurine into the hole. Jack held his breath, bracing himself for the worst. Then the onyx boulder cracked.

58

THE ROSEWOOD

By midmorning, Bau was seated at the head of a table where the Council and Fang Xue were gathered again. While it was the same private room as the day before, now the table was empty of silverware, plates, or delicious cuisine—and blinds were closed, blocking the view across Victoria Harbour.

Since becoming the Cherub leader, Bau spent more time sitting in meetings and shaking hands with those he didn't know than being among the people who were struggling to survive. In a way, he was jealous of Eliška, Amina, and Vince because they were on the ground making a difference without the political maneuvering.

Shortly after the meeting began, Winston and Betty Hu arrived and found seats beside their son. He had been with them earlier for breakfast, relieved they made it safely across the city. His parents recounted the previous weeks they'd spent amid a growing tension in Tai Tam, especially the attack only a few nights earlier. For the first time, Bau realized neither was aware the gateway led to the Scourge.

"I trust each of us have spent time contemplating our lively discussion yesterday." Fang Xue nodded toward Bau. "Requests have been made, and it is up to us to reach a consensus on what is in the best interest of the Cherub. Let us begin with—"

"What was discussed was not a request," Bau interrupted. "It was my final decision."

"Unfortunately, those of us around this circle remain concerned about your intention." Fang Xue glanced toward Winston and Betty. "Your son made several unsettling requests, which leave us questioning whether he is ready to lead us during this challenging time."

"There is nothing unsettling about what I said," Bau argued. "We will lose this war without allies."

"I cannot imagine my son making any decision against the Cherub," Winston added. "We are unaware of your discussions, but allow me to remind you it was you who anointed him to lead. Our family's loyalty to the Cherub has never been questioned."

"Until yesterday, there was no reason, Winston." Fang Xue eyed the others around the table. "Bau's comments and actions are erratic, and unfortunately they expose his naive youth."

"We are grateful for your loyalty to Bau," Betty interjected. "I am certain wherever there is division, a consensus can be reached, even if those decisions require compromise."

"Your son demanded we include those from Beacon Hill— Salomeh Gashkori, Jin Qiaolian, and Aki Katsuo—within this circle. Second, he demanded we establish ongoing communication with the faction, which we can only interpret as an alliance. Third, he refuses to consider a truce offered by the PRC which will enable Cherub to live free."

"Respectfully, the first decision is without controversy," Winston replied. "Salomeh, Jin, and Aki have been highly respected within Cherub circles for decades, and they are clear bridges to the faction who believe in Elyon despite our differences." He cleared his throat and shifted uncomfortably. "Perhaps you are unaware of the risks the faction are taking on Hong Kong Island, which we have witnessed firsthand. In these times, an alliance is a wise decision."

"As for a truce with the PRC," Betty chimed in, "what kind of lasting truce is possible?"

"PRC wants to strip us of our gifts," Bau answered. "At the very least control us."

Winston's brows raised. "Fang, is this true?"

"I am the Cherub leader." Bau glanced between his parents, then eyed each person around the table. "What has been anointed by Elyon cannot be undone."

"Power and influence residing with one individual has harmed Cherub in the past." Fang Xue exhaled. "Merikh actions altered our present and threaten future generations. Gifts already stripped from those who believe—lightforcers, benders, healers—leave us unable to defend ourselves. We must establish a truce or risk suffering greater losses."

"What are you implying?" Winston asked. "You speak as if Bau is a traitor."

"A shift is necessary." Fang Xue waved around the room. "A majority vote will decide."

"Respectfully, you are the one who is trying to control everyone." Bau pushed his chair back and stood. "I respect all at this table, but I am your leader—a vote cannot change that."

Bau stormed out of the room and cut through The Legacy House restaurant. Winston and Betty hurried behind, catching up to him in the lobby. Bau's security detail kept their distance as parents and son stopped near a corner.

"Bau, why did you not tell us about this?" Winston asked.

"I did not want either of you to worry, and I thought you would be through the gateway already."

"We still do not understand why we were brought here," Betty added.

"The gateway in Tai Tam leads to the Scourge," Bau replied. "Countless are lost."

"Oh dear . . ." Betty grew teary eyed. "Fang Xue knows of this?"

"If she did not know before, then all of them know as of yesterday."

"Then your decisions are justified." Winston crossed his arms. "Fang regrets giving up her authority, and she will not hesitate to resume her role if given the opportunity."

"I need you both . . ." Bau paused. "To help me stop that from happening."

"Leave it up to your father and me," Betty answered. "Do what must be done."

"Even if it means going against the highest Cherub?"

"We will stand by you, Son."

59

NETHER REALM

An underground passageway was revealed once the onyx boulder cracked in half. Jack stared into a dark hole as legion stood guard. He glanced over his shoulder at their dead eyes, wondering whether any could be redeemed like Asiklua. *How could we get them all to Charis?* An impossible question with an elusive answer—unless Elyon intervened.

"So I guess we're supposed to just waltz on in," he said.

Will stayed a few steps behind him. "You go first, Jack."

"Of course, you're the one with Dragon Soul, Windstrikers, *and* Soulweaver—a trifecta of deadly weapons—but I'm the one who has to enter this death trap unarmed."

"I won't ask a second time, mate."

With clenched fists, Jack knew attempting to fight his way out of Bitterhelm against Will and the legion was against any odds left in his favor. *If I miraculously escape from Will, I'll be ravaged by legion before I make it across the bridge. What about Eden's Star?* He hoped the compass would guide him, and in that moment a warmth spread across his chest. Even if Eden's Star could whisk him away from the nether realm, he wasn't leaving without Emma.

Surrender to the compass, and I'd risk abandoning love in the darkest of worlds.

Jack breathed in deep and exhaled slowly, knowing the only way forward was to go deeper into the unknown. Peering down, he found rock steps descending into the catacombs. He reached the bottom expecting to find a tomb, but instead he found himself inside another passageway.

In the dim light, he glanced at etchings in the stone which appeared in remarkable detail. A young girl surrounded by dragons and serpents stood gripping a sword nearly as tall as she was. His gaze shifted to the other side, where a broad-shouldered warrior stood beside a beautiful woman, both wearing armor from another age. Before he had a chance to take in the other etchings, Will shoved him hard and he stumbled forward.

Will stayed at his shoulder as he continued while the warmth in his chest grew hotter. *One of the artifacts is definitely down here.* He kept his wits about him as he reached the end of the passageway and entered a white-stone room that appeared to be centuries old.

Charcoal drawings scattered across the walls depicted angels in the Garden, the Testimony carried into war by battle-weary warriors, Elyon's Vine with its massive crown guarded by a rushing waterfall, and a mountain peak pointing toward the blackened ceiling. Crude smudged and frayed illustrations of a lion, temple, tree, deer, serpent, wolf, ship, and dragon stood out from the rest. The drawings struck Jack with a looming familiarity.

Seven Tribes of Cherub and Merikh in the Chamber of Shadowlight.

Bloodied armor, engraved with a depiction of Slybourne's crest of a fire-breathing dragon, lay on the floor. A woman in a bloodstained silver robe knelt beside a throne. Jack's mind flashed to the statue in Slybourne Castle, and he realized he was in the presence of the Queen of Sakkhela—the bladesmith of Dragon Soul.

Jack's legs grew weak, and a child ran across the floor and grasped the woman's robe. Eden's Star erupted in his chest, a sign that one or possibly more of the artifacts were somewhere in the room. He'd nearly forgotten about Will, whose gaze remained fixated on a mystical portrayal of an eerie Chamber of Shadowlight in an age long ago.

Florence Upsdell stood and turned toward them. Jack took in her long, wavy locks the color of flame. The haunting orange in her scornful blue eyes. The leather belt that secured a scabbard at her waist. The hilt of a sword that resembled the styling of Dragon Soul. Beside her was the child, no older than two or three. As the Queen of Sakkhela kept her stare on Jack and Will, she never acknowledged the child's presence.

With a clenched jaw and gritted teeth, Jack fought through the agony of Eden's Star as his hands shook and his legs grew weaker. Will approached the queen and handed over the ivory figurine and the prophecy, then knelt with his head lowered as if surrendering to her will. Jack was captivated by her beauty while fully aware of the destruction left in her wake over generations.

"You have done well," Florence addressed Will. She studied the ivory figurine, then slipped it beneath her robe along with the prophecy. "In your pain there will be vengeance."

"I have done all you have asked," Will said in a lowered voice. "Allowing them to see us in the Scourge brought them to the nether realm, and now I am ready to stand by your side."

"Legion will find the girl and bring her to me. Your loyalty will be rewarded."

"When will my mum return?" Will pressed. "You promised her life for theirs."

"Patience, dear boy." Florence turned her enchanting gaze toward Jack. "An outlier is in my presence, the Protector of Eden's Star—and the bloodline of my enemy."

"You're a vision seeker—and a murderer." Jack fought against an anguish gripping his soul, then grew even more terrified when the child simply vanished. "And I no longer believe your lies."

"Lies are the genesis of revolution." A smirk pursed her lips. "It is why you are here."

Florence raised her hand and Jack's throat closed, his muscles seized, and his bones twisted to the point of snapping. An unbearable pain ripped through his cells as the power of Eden's Star attacked with every heartbeat. With his windpipe blocked, he fell onto his knees, grabbing at his throat as the queen choked the life from him. His ribs and organs felt on the verge of exploding through his skin. Blood rushed to his head, then dripped out his nose, and he struggled to stay conscious. In excruciating pain, he felt his body lift up, and he floated helplessly across the room as the charcoal drawings spread across the white-stone walls until the room was covered in ebony.

Will spun around and stared wide-eyed at Jack hovering with

his spine arched and limbs frozen. In midair, Jack's body hung before the Queen of Sakkhela. His heartbeat quickened rapidly, then skipped from a steady rhythm to sporadic jolts. Florence pressed her hand against his chest, and his body convulsed violently as crimson continued to flow from his nostrils.

When his throat opened slightly, Jack fought for every ounce of oxygen. A fiery inferno consumed him on the inside, and he unshackled a yowling cry when the dretium hoodie ripped apart. Destructive darkness and unrelenting rage sliced through him until Florence pulled her bloodied hand away with the golden emblem of Eden's Star in her palm.

"Oi, you made me a promise." A violet lightforce formed in Will's palms. "You said you would bring her back to life—that was our deal."

"My exact words were that I would unite you with your mother."

Florence tossed Jack aside, and with a lightning swiftness brought Dragon Soul from the scabbard on Will's shoulder to her grasp. She wielded the sword with precision and struck with deadly accuracy. She swung with the skills of a great warrior, yet narrowly missed her attempts to stab Will in the heart as he dodged with equal quickness. But Will never had a chance to release his lightforce before the sword sliced through his femur, severing his leg from the rest of his body. Jack's ears rang with the piercing cries of his friend. Will fell to the ground with blood spilling where his right leg was a split second before.

Amid the sudden chaotic attack, Jack's body was ablaze from the inside out as he gasped for one more breath to stay alive. He never noticed when the wound in his chest cauterized, broader than the crude scars left by Eden's Star when Emma used her lightforce to hide the compass inside him. Will's desperate cries snapped him back from the verge of surrendering to the pain.

Dragon Soul slipped into a second scabbard over Florence's shoulder. She removed the sword on her hip and placed Eden's Star into its pommel, from which the hilt started. The compass and the sword were one. The Windstrikers rose into the air away from Will, then slipped onto the leather belt around Florence's waist.

Legion shrieked, wailed, and screamed from the chamber throughout Bitterhelm, their cries reaching every defiled corner of the nether realm. Facedown, Jack was nearly deafened as his breaths grew narrow. His head turned and his stare locked in on Will's broken body left in a pool of blood. Out of the corner of his eye, he caught sight of Soulweaver slithering across the floor as coldness and emptiness seeped beneath his skin.

You have to fight, Jack.

Crimson was spread across his shredded dretium hoodie. Jack desperately stretched out his bloodied hand, reaching with every ounce of strength. Soulweaver slipped beneath his fingers and a surge of energy flowed from the rod. Florence wielded her sword, snakes slithering on the blade. On his knees, Jack gripped Soulweaver with both hands as one of the snakes from Florence's sword struck out with venomous fangs.

"Soulweaver is weakest against Scarlet Widow," Florence raged. "Outlier."

Jack struggled to pull himself to his feet, coughing and wheezing. His eyes darted between Florence and the legion as he steadied himself. The fear surging through his veins crashed against a righteous anger. Soulweaver spun faster between his fingers until a supernova of light formed into a solid circle. Pure energy flowed through his arms and chest. He lunged with the rod pointed forward, and an energy pulse shot across the catacomb before exploding into the lava rock.

Legion attacked on all sides as Jack battled to defend himself. Soulweaver burst with even greater intensity, deflecting each strike against him. He swung the rod with force and flow, Elyon's mighty power humming through heartwood to strike down legion. With a second wind, he darted across the catacomb and slid on his knees before striking the final legion demon, who vanished into thin air.

Florence attacked him with Scarlet Widow, clashing mightily against the heartwood. Her power was unbreakable until Soulweaver formed an energy wall between them. Jack stared across the catacomb, stunned by the power of the rod while realizing Will was on his side of the force field. Florence glared through the barrier of energy, and then in a blink she was gone.

"No . . . no . . . no . . ."

Jack lowered Soulweaver to his side and the energy faded. He scanned the catacomb, expecting legion from outside to burst into the chamber. An unsettling reality struck when he heard no more screaming or squealing, only silence.

"Florence used Eden's Star—she's free from the nether realm."

60

Jack tore off what remained of his dretium hoodie and hurried over to Will, who was unconscious and bleeding badly. Soulweaver slithered up around his forearm. Lightheaded, he ripped strips off the hoodie and tied a makeshift tourniquet around Will's horrific wound. He glanced over his shoulder and realized the rest of Will's leg was gone from the catacomb. *How can that be? Stay focused, Jack.* With larger pieces of the hoodie, he hurried to wrap the open wound and pull the dretium tight with shaking hands. Will's eyes shot open, arms and legs flailing.

"Listen to me right now." Jack wrestled Will and pinned his arms to the ground. "You will die if you don't let me help you."

"I don't care if I die," Will blurted, defiant. "Not anymore."

"Well, I care, you stubborn mule." Jack reached under Will's arms and lifted him into a seated position. "Only you would taunt the Queen of Sakkhela."

Will groaned as he glared at the bloodied tourniquet. His eyes welled up with tears, and Jack noticed a shift in his demeanor. *No time for kumbaya.* Jack slipped his shoulder under Will's arm and slowly pulled him up. Will screamed in agony, leaving a lump lodged in Jack's throat. His heart broke for his best friend, but there was no time left.

"We're not dying in Bitterhelm." Jack braced himself against Will's body, then grunted as he lifted Will over his shoulder. "I've got you. Hang on."

Though he wasn't bleeding to death, Jack struggled with the aftermath of Eden's Star being ripped from his body. He glanced down at his torn shirt where the cauterized scar was spread across his bare chest, sensing the real damage was beneath the skin. In a daze, he carried Will through the catacombs and reached the underground passageway.

A mustard seed is all you need.

Jack dug deeper than his darkest days, shouldering the weight of his friend and willing himself to keep going. Will's body grew heavier as Jack climbed the steps to the opening in the lava rock, crossed the chamber, and reached the bridge out of Bitterhelm. Legion had vanished, and onyx seas were calm.

"Stay awake," Jack said urgently. "Will, do you hear me?"

When he didn't get a response, panic paralyzed him. He stopped and laid Will down, blood soaking through the makeshift bandages. Will's freckled nose and cheeks were pale and his breathing labored. Jack grabbed his own chest as pain tore through his organs. He tightened the dretium tourniquet, but a pool of crimson formed on the bridge beneath Will's body.

We'll never make it to the gateway. Elyon, we need you now.

"In the days when skies are filled with smoke and fire," he said under his breath. "The end will draw near; our nights will be dire. Amidst the darkness unchained through flames and strife lies a hope our souls may be reborn from death to life."

With tears welling up, Jack grabbed Will's arm and shook him hard, attempting to keep him awake. He didn't know how else to reassure his best friend it was going to be okay—because it wasn't. In that moment, words failed as the fear in Will's eyes silenced him before they closed again.

A sudden tightening in his chest left him doubled over. He fought against his reeling body, failing to keep his balance as he collapsed beside Will. One last time, he reached out for his best friend as he stared up at blurred skies. Even though Eden's Star had been ripped from his body, he sensed the damage left within was causing his organs to shut down and his heartbeat to slow. On the verge of losing consciousness, he wrapped his fingers around Will's arm and squeezed.

"Bring us into your presence—both of us."

Fight, Jack. Fight.

"Jack!"

In the fogginess of his mind, he heard Emma's voice. His eyes opened to a wondrous sight: Emma kneeling between him and Will with her hands extended. His vision sharpened, muscles fired again, and heartbeat steadied. Still groggy, he rolled onto his knees and peered over her shoulder while her hand pressed against Will's chest. Jack eyed the distance beyond the bridge, expecting deathly creatures from the nether realm to show themselves.

A few seconds later, Will's eyes slowly opened.

"Welcome back," Emma said, relieved. "Will . . ."

He mumbled, "You're a better sight than Jack."

"Right." Emma glanced at Jack. "Eden's Star?"

Jack shook his head. "Will, can you jump the gateway?"

"Never tried with one leg before," Will moaned. "I've done it with other people, though."

"Fifty-fifty chance." Jack shot a quick glance at Emma. "Better odds than we're used to."

"Will, we need to go," Emma pressed. "You have lost a lot of blood."

"Get me up," Will groaned. "I'll give it a shot."

Jack and Emma each grabbed an arm and lifted Will to his feet. Still dizzy, Jack shouldered the weight and grimaced as his chest constricted. An onyx waterspout emerged and whipped across the silky ink-like ocean, churning into a funnel. One step after another, all three struggled across the bridge as a rippling in the atmosphere followed the tornado. Before they could reach the other side of the bridge, the tornado enveloped them and whisked them from the nether realm.

61

In the early morning, HKPF and PRC conducted their 24-7 shift switch monitoring the blocks surrounding the school. A handful of close calls occurred in the days after the prison break at Shek Pik when lightforcers faced off with Merikh, only to stand down when ordered by Headmaster Fargher. Months without any encounters left a routine shift change feeling rather mundane.

Jack, Emma, and Will appeared on Sheung Shing Street. Stationed at both ends of the block, HKPF officers guarded the street with their vehicles and barricades, but none noticed three shadows suddenly appear out of thin air. Jack and Emma carried Will, who was barely conscious, into the bushes out of sight until they stopped at a stone wall.

"Guardians life," Jack said in a hushed voice. "Come on."

The tunnel opened and they slipped inside, shouldering Will's weight as the wall sealed behind. The darkened tunnel led them toward the basement. Within seconds, a group from Beacon Hill cautiously peered into the tunnel with lightforces glowing in their palms.

"Who is there?" A voice rang out. "Say your names."

"Emma Bennett," she answered. "Jack Reynolds and William Fargher."

Jack recognized a young girl in the group as Navi before she stepped out of sight, while the others rushed into the tunnel and scooped up Will. Before they reached the basement, Natalie McNaughton appeared with Navi by her side and darted forward to help Jack and Emma.

"Jack . . ." McNaughton stood wide-eyed. "What has happened?"

"All that matters is saving Will." Jack watched her eye his injuries. "Please, Natalie."

McNaughton spun around and ordered, "Wake Windsor and Salomeh."

Several in the group rushed out of the tunnel with Will, heading up the stairs of the Main Hall. McNaughton and Navi stayed on their heels, leaving Jack and Emma alone in the tunnel. Emma placed her hand on Jack's shoulder, and a warmth spread over him. Blood remained on his shirt and jeans, but his cuts and gashes healed before his eyes.

"Tell me about Florence Upsdell," Emma said, "and Eden's Star."

"Will forced me to cross the bridge to Bitterhelm and enter where she was imprisoned. Legion stood guard at the entry and inside the chamber, preventing anyone else from being able to go further." Jack's mind flashed to the moment the lava rock cracked, and regret punched him in the stomach. "We used the ivory figurine as a key, like we did at the gateway in Thalren, then ended up in a catacomb."

"All this time she was being kept in a catacomb?"

"We found her kneeling before a throne, and she looked exactly like she did in the Scourge—except a child was with her for a blink."

"A child?" Emma asked, shocked. "Who is the child?"

"I don't have a clue, and I don't think Will does either. Florence Upsdell had her own sword, similar to Dragon Soul, with venomous snakes instead of a two-headed dragon. She called it Scarlet Widow. My guess is she forged it from dretium and corrupted it somehow."

"What else happened, Jack?"

"One minute the child was there, the next she was gone." Jack paused, ashamed he'd failed to stop the Queen of Sakkhela. "Florence took Eden's Star from inside of me—I have no clue how she did it, though. She placed the compass into the hilt of her sword, and it fit perfectly. Then she took Dragon Soul and the Windstrikers too."

"Salomeh and Professor Burwick were wrong." Emma's gaze softened as she released her grip on his shoulder. "You did not die in the nether realm."

"Soulweaver protected me." Jack shrugged. "At least we still have the rod."

"With Eden's Star, Florence Upsdell will hunt for the other artifacts." Emma hesitated. "We need to speak with Xui Li *and* Eleanore."

"And we need to warn Salomeh, Eliška, and Burwick."

"No one is safe, not even those at Beacon Hill."

"After all this time, I never figured out how to use Eden's Star properly." Jack shook his head, dejected. "I'll bet it won't take the queen long to track the ones we've found."

"And the ones we haven't found too."

Jack and Emma climbed the steps to the main floor, where they were greeted by Professor McDougall, whose striped pajamas hung loosely over his slender shoulders. Jack had not seen McDougall in so long, he was stunned by the professor's slimmed-down appearance.

"If you have returned, trouble is chasing your footsteps." McDougall eyed them closely. "Tell me how horrible it will be this time, Jack."

"Florence Upsdell—bladesmith of Dragon Soul."

"Queen of Sakkhela." McDougall crossed his arms. "Leave it to you to awaken a warrior matched only by her love, Sir Ryder Slybourne. How many more must die before there will be peace?"

Neither Jack nor Emma responded, silenced by a question which haunted all who believed in Elyon—and all those who searched for answers to the chaos in recent months. McDougall turned and headed to the second floor, snapping his flip-flops across the tiles while Jack and Emma walked behind. No other words were spoken as the tension remained thick in the air.

By the time they entered Crozier Hospital, Professor Windsor was moving between rooms with urgency. McNaughton stood in the hallway alongside Salomeh and Xui Li. All three women fixed their gaze toward Jack and Emma. Jack lowered his head and fought the urge to turn around and leave. It was the same urge he'd surrendered to the night he heard Amina's screams, unable to accept Tim's death.

Emma's fingers intertwined with his own. She squeezed gently, encouraging him to take one more step. He followed her lead and walked through the hospital until he stood beside the others outside of an exam room. Inside, Fargher stood in one corner while Professor Windsor and Cherub healers surrounded the headmaster's son, who was sprawled out on a gurney.

"I can't stop the hate inside for what he's done," Jack whispered to Emma. "But we can't lose him—not like this."

Emma squeezed his hand gently. "Forgiveness comes to all who ask."

"He didn't have to bring us back, but he did." Jack glanced briefly toward Headmaster Fargher, knowing devastation hung in the balance. "I guess only time will tell whether he did it to save himself, or if he's really sorry for murdering the innocent."

"Time is a healer too." Emma squeezed his hand firmly. "As long as the clock keeps ticking."

Windsor stepped toward the doorway and leaned close. "Dragon Soul?"

"Yes." *A wound caused by Dragon Soul is not of this world.* "Professor . . ."

Windsor's brows furrowed as she looked past them toward McNaughton, Salomeh, and Xui Li, then eyed Jack and Emma once more before shutting the door.

MISCHIEVOUS ESCAPE OF THE NINE DRAGONS

Across the still waters of the river, a beastly shadow swooped low and unleashed violent bursts of fire across the Rhoxen village. The wooden chapel, tavern, and warehouse erupted into flames as villagers scrambled in chaos. Throughout the centuries, deep within the Eternal, the beast was known as Criberus. It had the wide, scaly wings, fanged jaws, and slitted eyes of a dragon—yet the arms, claws, and legs of a Nephilim. An indescribable and frightful sight to villagers desperate to defend themselves.

Armed Rhoxen, including the blacksmith, rushed across the town square, wielding swords, spears, axes, and shields. Criberus spewed a blazing inferno through the crisp autumn afternoon. Rhoxen gathered quickly, staring into the deathly gaze of a creature formed by Elyon to protect an artifact entrusted to the highest of Cherub among the Seven Tribes. A beast lured and corrupted by Asiklua during the Fall, long before the First Great War.

Two destrier horses galloped across the river with Florence and Ryder in the saddles. Florence raised Dragon Soul, and a two-headed dragon burst in onyx fire from the blade. She charged, unafraid and unrelenting. Criberus attacked the Rhoxen, who shielded the innocent while the two-headed dragon advanced against the beast.

Florence was not only a master bladesmith, but she was quick and lethal with the sword. Rhoxen stood awestruck when her lightforce glowed in the palm of her hand. She gripped the hilt of the sword tight as her lightforce released a lightning bolt of ocean blue, which soared across the town square before wrapping around Criberus. A resounding roar left the villagers as still as stone. Criberus broke free from the powerful lightforce and pounced with an even greater vengeance.

Claws swiped and slashed as Florence defended and attacked with Dragon Soul. Criberus moved swiftly for a large beast, knocking her hard and sending her tumbling to the mud. She rolled over, losing her grip on Dragon Soul, and scrambled to her feet. With the sword out of reach, she faced Criberus with only her lightforce.

Ryder slipped off the saddle of the drestrier in full stride and snatched Dragon Soul. The two-headed dragon at the tip of the blade spewed black fire as he darted straight ahead. He leapt with the silver sword extended, stabbing Criberus deep in the chest. Criberus dropped to the ground, motionless. Ryder pulled the sword back, ready to plunge the blade a second time. A moment passed before he lifted Dragon Soul above his head as the two-headed dragon returned to the etchings in the blade. Rhoxen villagers approached cautiously, then one by one each knelt before him.

Florence gathered herself, surprised by Ryder's bravery and his ability to wield Dragon Soul. When she forged the sword and imparted her lightforce into the blade, she'd believed she would be the only one strong enough to use it. Her lightforce dulled as she approached Ryder, who held out the sword.

"Dragon Soul belongs to you," she said. "You captured Criberus."

"Captured?" Ryder smirked. "The beast looks dead to me."

"Criberus cannot be killed—before nightfall he will awake again."

"We saved the village." Ryder held up the sword. "Dragon Soul is remarkable."

"The Elders of old must be summoned at once." She noticed the villagers eyeing her fearfully, except for the blacksmith. "Criberus must be banned to the nether realm."

Immediately, the blacksmith disappeared among a growing crowd of villagers who inched forward to get a better look at the dragon-Nephilim. Ryder pulled Florence aside.

"Why would Criberus kill Kaida and attack the village?" Ryder asked.

"To find one of the artifacts of the Seven Tribes."

"And you know what one of these artifacts is?"

"The night my father returned with a dragon egg—Kaida—was the last night of his life. Our home was burned to the earth, but a gift was left in the ashes."

"Are you saying your father found one of the artifacts?"

"Perhaps the greatest of all—the reason for my power." She grabbed his hand and squeezed. "When the Elders arrive, I must remain a ghost."

"Florence, you cannot leave me."

"Today your bravery will bring the highest Cherub to the Rhoxen." She took a few steps back toward the crowd. "Tomorrow we stand together, again."

Florence slipped past the villagers and mounted her destrier, then rode like the wind across the river into the forest. She kept her grip on the reins as the destrier raced over lush greenery, jumping thick vines and cutting between trees. Once she reached the dragon's den, she hurried through the passageway until she reached Kaida. Her eyes darted toward where they'd left the row of black eggs, and she stopped cold. All nine were missing. She searched the den and was struck by the loss.

"Kaida," she whispered. "I have failed you."

Florence forced herself to move toward a corner in the den. She knelt in front of a stone wall and pulled one of the stones free. Her brows furrowed as she stared into an empty hole—a hiding place where she kept the iron box. A secret she'd protected until Kaida was born. In the years since, she had trusted the dragon to guard the artifact, never imagining a day would come when her quest meant leaving the village to find and protect it again.

"I will search for the nine dragons—and I will hunt for the artifact."

Florence stood outside of Kaida's camouflaged den, and using the gifts of a bender she moved a large stone across the entrance. She rode the destrier through the forest toward the village, stopping across the river. From the bushes she watched the aftermath of Criberus's attack, haunted by the disappearance of the dragon eggs and the iron box. A while passed before she noticed Ryder and the blacksmith walking alongside a group of robed men and women—the Elders.

The Elders approached Criberus while the villagers watched closely. Ryder gripped Dragon Soul in one hand, which brought a sense of honor to Florence. She knew he was destined to be a great warrior, and she'd crafted a weapon greater than all others. With their hands raised, the Elders circled Criberus, and in a flash they disappeared with the beast.

Florence hid across the river, knowing the secret she lost was a danger to mankind.

62

BEACON HILL

After an hour pacing the hallway of Crozier Hospital, Jack left the main wing and headed for Upsdell Dining Hall. He'd yet to change out of his bloodied and torn clothes, not caring how disheveled he looked to everyone else. Before he left the hospital, he noticed only a few Cherub under medical care. He didn't know whether to take that as a good sign, fearing a day was looming when the beds would not be enough to keep the innocent alive. Jack entered the dining hall to find Emma and McNaughton packing clothes into a backpack.

Emma handed him a fresh shirt. He turned his back and slipped it on quickly to prevent either of them from staring at the scars on his chest and arms. From the moment he found Eden's Star in the

City of Gods, he fought to be the Protector. But when Eden's Star was ripped from his body in Bitterhelm—leaving a scar over what should've been a gaping wound—a piece of him died too.

"I will guide you through the tunnels," McNaughton said. "Nearest gateway to Hong Kong Island is Kai Tak. It is about a thirty-minute trek."

"Natalie cannot reach the faction," Emma explained to Jack. "We must warn them."

"Highest Cherub are holed up at the Rosewood," McNaughton added. "Once I leave you at Kai Tak, I will stop by the hotel to speak with Bau."

"I never meant for anyone to die," Jack said softly. "I'm so sorry."

"As soon as I hear anything about Will, I will call you." McNaughton grew teary eyed when she handed him yet another burner cell. "Text when you reach the faction."

Salomeh and Xui Li entered the dining hall and walked briskly toward them. Jack's stomach twisted into knots at the unthinkable. *I don't know if I'll ever forgive Will, but that doesn't mean I want him to die—not anymore.* His fingers balled into fists as he struggled to hold back his own tears. Emma zipped up the backpack and slipped it over her shoulder.

"Will . . ." Jack began.

"He is still in surgery," Salomeh interrupted. "Another few hours."

"Healers are caring for him too," Xui Li added. "As you know, the wound is from Dragon Soul—but everyone is doing all that is possible."

"I've survived Dragon Soul before," Jack offered. "There is a chance."

"You also had Eden's Star to fight against such wounds," Salomeh reminded him. "Professor Windsor wants to take a look at you—she is quite worried."

"There's not time," Jack retorted. "She needs to focus on Will."

Elyon, you redirected my path because of Rachel. I pray the same is true for Will, whoever it might be that points him in the right direction. Have mercy on him as you had mercy on me. Give him the faith of a mustard seed.

"Tell us what occurred in the nether realm," Xui Li pressed. "It is important."

"We entered through the gateway in Thalren." Jack glanced at Emma, who waited patiently. "Legion and Will were there, and we got split up. I was forced to enter a place named Bitterhelm. Inside, Will and I found Florence Upsdell imprisoned underground, but she wasn't buried. She was kneeling next to a throne wearing a silver robe—and armor with Slybourne's crest was on the floor beside her." He forced himself to hold it together. "Eden's Star was raging inside of me within the catacomb, so I knew there was an artifact close."

"Is it possible for the artifacts to be something other than an object?" Emma asked.

Salomeh crossed her arms. "No one has ever asked the question."

"All that is certain are the artifacts you have found," Xui Li answered.

"She took Dragon Soul, Windstrikers, the prophecy, *and* Eden's Star."

"No doubt she will hunt for the artifacts using the compass," Salomeh said. "If she is able to gather all of them together, then we do not stand a chance."

"She wasn't alone in the catacomb," Jack chimed in. "Legion

stood guard, but she had her own sword called Scarlet Widow—and there was a child."

"Another artifact—a queen, her sword, or her child?" Xui Li's brows furrowed. "The Elder Scrolls speak of a blade sharper than blades touched with Elyon's hands. Most believed the sword to be Dragon Soul, but the blade is man-made with breilium—a sister sword."

"Dragon Soul was crafted by Florence Upsdell, so it's possible she is the one who created the sister sword—and corrupted it when she went insane," Jack surmised.

"Which means it's possible Scarlet Widow is the blade from the Elder Scrolls."

"We need to question Will as soon as he is awake," Salomeh suggested.

"He saved us from the nether realm," Emma said. "He must be shown mercy."

"Answers to these questions will determine our future, as well as his own." Xui Li turned her attention toward Jack. "In the catacomb, what happened to the child?"

"I don't know—she vanished." Jack shook his head. "All we have left of the artifacts are Soulweaver, Slybourne's shield, and the Rhoxen Stone."

"Salomeh, where are you hiding the shield?" Emma asked.

"Patel Custom Tailors," she replied, matter-of-fact. "He is quite resourceful."

"Can it be protected from the legion and Florence?"

"As much as the faction will be able to protect the Rhoxen Stone."

"Speaking of the faction," McNaughton interrupted. "Clock is ticking."

The Upsdell Dining Hall doors swung open, and a group of Cherub entered. Jack eyed each one, recognizing the diversity of all who were represented: every age, race, and gift. More arrived and gathered around. Hundreds of lightforcers, benders, and healers filled the dining hall.

Jack, Emma, and McNaughton slipped through the crowd, leaving the dining hall and heading toward Rowell Library. Jack barely noticed the boarded-up windows. *We used to complain about McDougall's research assignments in this place, and now we're one step away from the world spiraling out of control.* Moments later they entered through the opening in the painting, then raced down the spiral steps and crossed Nightingale's vault toward an entrance to the tunnels.

McNaughton checked her cell phone. "Roughly, two and a half miles."

"Isn't there a golf cart down here? Hold on . . ."

Emma and McNaughton waited as he turned around and darted across the vault, then hopped behind the wheel of the ruby-red 1940 Delahaye 135 convertible. He turned the ignition and the engine rumbled to life.

Jack shifted the Delahaye into gear and the car lunged forward—but then the engine stalled. Emma and McNaughton waited at the tunnel entrance with their arms folded and smirks on their lips. He held up his hand to signify it was all under control.

"How embarrassing," he grumbled. "Slow and easy."

The ignition whined a second time, and Jack shifted into gear before easing off the clutch as he pressed the accelerator. The Delahaye lurched forward again as he gave it more gas, and it rolled across the vault. He was too afraid to fully stop, so he only slowed enough for Emma and McNaughton to jump on board.

"Not a word," he said, "from either of you."

Jack's cheeks flushed as he couldn't deny his lack of driving skills was as clear as his inability to hit a spinner on a cricket pitch. McNaughton called out turns as he cut down one tunnel to the next beneath Kowloon, in the opposite direction of Tai Kok Tsui.

Behind the wheel, he got the hang of the Delahaye and hit the brakes, then the accelerator without downshifting. While the engine's rumble echoed off the tunnel walls, he gripped the wheel and followed McNaughton's instructions. His mind shifted from replaying the conversation with Salomeh and Xui Li to the encounter with Tim in what he could only define as a vision.

Why didn't I tell them about Tim? Maybe because it was only for me.

Beneath the empty streets of Kowloon, the Delahaye raced from Mong Kok to Tsim Sha Tsui. A thirty-minute jaunt was cut down to less than fifteen. Jack slammed on the brakes once McNaughton called out the station, and tires screeched against concrete. He turned the ignition off and glanced at McNaughton and Emma with a sly grin.

"Your first driving lesson," McNaughton mused. "A passing grade."

"Is it safe to leave the Delahaye here?"

"I will drive back to Beacon Hill once I am done with Bau." McNaughton checked her watch again. "Gateway to Hong Kong Island is inside the Jetstream 41 in Kai Tak. Do you know what I am talking about?"

"Yes," Emma replied. "The aircraft on display in the park."

All three climbed out of the vehicle and stood in the tunnel facing each other. After an awkward silence, Jack stepped forward and hugged McNaughton hard.

"Sorry . . ." He stepped back and wiped a tear from his eye. "Okay, let's do this."

63

HONG KONG ISLAND

Jack and Emma stepped out from a fish stall inside Sai Wan Ho Market, which was busy before sunrise with Hong Kongers stocking minimal supplies of fish, meat, and dried foods. With their heads on a swivel, Jack and Emma reached the street outside and headed down Shau Kei Wan Road. Trams, double-deckers, and minibuses passed—but most were empty.

"When you gave Natalie a hug," Emma said, "that was sweet."

"She was the first one to tell me the truth, and now she's family."

"We are all one family, Jack."

"Truth."

On the empty streets of the Eastern District, they were left in the open—targets for the HKPF and PRC. Jack had been to the district a handful of times with Will, Vince, and Tim after sneaking out of Beacon Hill. He guessed the restaurants, themed bars, and coffee shops along the waterfront were permanently closed— the Grand Promenade, Les Saisons, and Lei King Wan. He picked up the pace along Shau Kei Wan, passing landmarks of what the district had once been.

"How long do you think before Florence attacks the city?" Jack asked.

"At least two more artifacts remain missing," Emma replied. "Depends if she searches for those artifacts before Eden's Star brings her here to Hong Kong. But she will be here sooner than we will be ready. Eliška needs to know what we are up against, and we need to choose together the perfect time to use the Rhoxen Stone."

Jack and Emma hurried west and rounded a corner onto Kornhill Road. Residential buildings were stacked along the hillside, covering a past when squatter settlements had lined the same land. They continued in the direction of Cityplaza, Kornhill Plaza, and the business district of Taikoo Place. He couldn't believe the eerie quiet of this city that never slept.

"How do you feel without Eden's Star?" Emma asked.

"Feels strange not being able to use the compass," he admitted. "And it's still painful."

"Professor Windsor wants to do another scan, and I think it is a good idea."

"There's a million ways for me to die before this is over." Jack kept his sights on the sidewalk ahead, knowing if he locked eyes with Emma, she'd realize how much he was struggling on the inside. "No time for tests—we're in the final exam."

Less than a mile from Quarry Bay, Jack glanced over his shoulder and noticed several men and women following them across the street while others shadowed on the same side. He squeezed Emma's hand, a sign they weren't alone. Emma casually peered back, then started walking faster. Jack couldn't help himself from looking back again. With Soulweaver wrapped around his forearm and Emma right beside him, he questioned whether it was better to outrun or face them right on the street. A third look backward and he realized they were closing in.

"Gaining ground," he whispered. "We won't make it to Quarry Bay."

"You take the ones behind us, and I will take the ones across the street."

Jack opened his hand and expected Soulweaver to slither down, but to his surprise the rod remained wrapped around his arm. He flexed his muscles, hoping to jar it loose. Eight men and women were now following on the sidewalks, and another four appeared at the corner in front of them.

"Seriously?" Jack mumbled. "Soulweaver is stuck."

"What do you mean *stuck*?" Emma asked, confused.

"Normally, the rod knows when it's needed and ends up in my hand."

Emma stopped suddenly and spun around. The men behind them froze. Jack tugged at Soulweaver, but the rod didn't budge. He stared ahead as the four men approached cautiously. He should've been freaked out, but he sensed something different was happening than an ambush.

"If they were Merikh, we'd be in a fight already."

Jack waited while the others approached until they were surrounded. Emma's palms glowed, but she didn't raise her hands to wipe them out. Jack second-guessed his original theory when all of the men and women aimed semiautomatic weapons.

BATTLE OF LION ROCK

One of the men asked, "What are you doing on the streets?"

"Let's cut to the chase because we don't have a lot of time," Jack answered, confident he knew what was happening now. "Tell Eliška that Jack and Emma need to see her immediately."

Another of the men relayed the message on a walkie-talkie. A staticky voice responded, which left Jack pumped and a bit relieved.

"Keep watch on the streets," Vince answered. "And send the dynamic duo to the roof."

64

THE ROSEWOOD

Natalie McNaughton met one of Bau's security guards outside of the hotel and was escorted through a side entrance. She followed him through a commercial kitchen into DarkSide, a popular cocktail parlor transformed into a private meeting room. Soft light illuminated deep purple and lavender chairs, turquoise curtains, frosted glass windows, and black-and-white photos capturing the history of Kowloon—past and present. The guard motioned her toward Bau, seated in a corner.

"We need to be brief," Bau said, matter-of-fact. "Eyes are watching in the Rosewood."

"Jack and Emma have returned—along with William Fargher." Natalie eyed him closely. "In the nether realm, Eden's Star was taken from Jack by Florence Upsdell."

"Queen of Sakkhela." Bau exhaled long and hard. "I warned Emma about Jack, but her feelings clouded her judgment. Now we are in even greater danger."

"Legion and the queen have escaped. Jack and Emma believe she will use Eden's Star to hunt for the artifacts." Natalie hesitated as she watched Bau fume beneath the surface. "She took Dragon Soul and one of the artifacts—the Windstrikers—from Will, and it seems she has her own deadly sword, Scarlet Widow."

"Is that another one of the artifacts?"

"No one can say for certain, but Jack believes it might be an artifact."

Bau leaned forward, pressing his elbows into the lacquered table. "How many more have been found?"

"The Rod of Elyon, Slybourne's shield, and the Rhoxen Stone." Natalie glanced over her shoulder as security remained near the door. "Two more artifacts are still unknown."

"Eliška and Vince know about this?"

"I split up with Jack and Emma in the tunnel under the MTR station." She checked her phone, wondering how much longer before he texted. "All of them should be together soon."

"Fang Xue and the Council are questioning my leadership," Bau confessed. "If they choose to go against me, I will not be able to offer much help to Beacon Hill or the faction."

Natalie was reminded that Bau was a teenager, and he carried a heavy weight even though he was gifted and possessed an ego strong enough to lead beyond his age. "You were chosen, Bau."

"Does not seem to matter." Bau paused. "My parents are worried."

"I will admit, Jack's decisions have seemed reckless at times, but there is no doubt his heart is in the right place. When the time comes, he will do what is needed. Now you must do the same."

"Cherub lost more than we will realize in our lifetime. Stolen gifts. Broken spirits. Selfishness will be our downfall, unless we choose to unite."

"You are wise, Bau. Fang Xue would be smart to listen to you."

"How do we stop the legion and the queen when we cannot even find a way to fight against the Merikh and PRC?" He looked past Natalie and nodded toward his security. "Time is short. You must leave. But first I need to send a message to Emma."

Natalie handed over her phone, and Bau typed a quick text before hitting send. She was impressed by his resolve, and her respect for him grew a few notches. Fang Xue and the Council praised him as a leader for the future, but it seemed that they were reluctant to surrender their power and influence.

"Go straight to the people," Natalie urged. "Let them see who you are, Bau."

Natalie turned and followed the security guard back through the commercial kitchen and out the side door of the Rosewood. She tapped on her screen and read the text—PM. HV.—BH.— knowing the leader of the Cherub was still in the game.

On her way to the MTR station on Nathan Road, she remembered the night Detective Susan Ming was arrested in Three Fathoms Cove. For months, Ming had remained in solitary confinement at Lo Wu Correctional Institution in the New Territories. Natalie's thoughts were still consumed with ways to gain Ming's freedom, but so far she had failed to think of anything but another prison break.

Near the steps of the station, Natalie was unable to shake the haunting sense she was being watched. She stopped and glanced around, studying the streets and buildings. For a few seconds she stared at a shadow across the street, but when she blinked the shadow was gone.

Her uneasiness intensified as she took the stairs down to the station and returned to the tunnel where the Delahaye was parked. She climbed behind the wheel, turned the ignition, and made a tight U-turn. As the engine roared, she punched the accelerator and raced through the tunnel toward Nightingale's vault.

65

Jack stepped onto the rooftop and inhaled a sweet aroma, then watched as Vince hovered over an open gas flame with a wok in one hand. Emma huddled with Eliška near the cots Jack had slept on more than a few nights. More cots were lined up beneath the tin-roof section of the rooftop, designated for Cherub lightforcers and benders sent to assist the faction. He wasn't sure where any of them were as he walked toward Vince. Flashes struck him from the night he returned Vince safely to Vince's parents' yacht.

I'm still an outlier, but even more, I'm a follower of Elyon. I'm not sure how to balance between Cherub and faction, but that's who I am. My addictions defined me once, but never again. Rachel left a gift behind—one last chance to point my life toward something greater. She nudged me when she promised Areum that I would follow in her path. I am still the weakest one, but Elyon's presence and the strength of others carries me through the unknown.

"I must be imagining things," Jack called out. "Are you cooking at 3:00 a.m.?"

"Figured you'd be hungry—and the Cherub squad is on a late-night mission to finish marking the districts." Vince tossed egg noodles, yellow onions, bell peppers, shiitake mushrooms, and minced cloves of garlic. He poured in oyster and soy sauce, then finished the mix with rice vinegar and toasted sesame oil. "If you're showing up in the middle of the night, it can't be good."

"We made it to the nether realm," Jack replied. "Long story short, Florence Upsdell has Eden's Star, the Windstrikers, Dragon Soul, and a sword of her own—Scarlet Widow. And she escaped with the legion."

"Which means she's going to use Eden's Star to find the rest of the artifacts." Vince mixed the noodles and sauce a bit more. "Just when I thought we were making a difference."

"We brought Will back from the nether realm—he's at Beacon Hill."

Vince grabbed four bowls and dished up homemade chow mein. "How is he?"

"He was ready to sacrifice me to the Queen of Sakkhela—but he's injured pretty bad." Jack paused, a rush of guilt washing over him for judging. "Your leg was healed in Ine Town, but I don't think the same will be true for Will. I don't know whether time with Headmaster Fargher will bring him all the way back to who we remember."

"Part of me wants to rip him apart." Vince set the four bowls on a table and slipped onto a folding chair. "And the other part feels sorry for him. Do you know what I mean?"

"I thought I'd feel different. Forgiveness isn't an easy choice."

Jack found a seat and grabbed a pair of chopsticks. He dug into his bowl, realizing he wasn't sure how long it had been since his last meal. With the chopsticks between his fingers, he shoveled noodles and veggies into his mouth. Emma and Eliška sauntered over, seemingly more at ease with one another than he'd seen before. Both grabbed a bowl and chopsticks while Vince and Jack eyed them closely.

"You are full of surprises," Emma mused. "As good as my mum's, if not better."

"Beaut bonza," Vince chuckled. "Never thought I'd want to be a chef."

"Maybe you found your true calling," Jack said through a mouthful. "It's delicious."

"In recent weeks, the PRC has restricted internet access and phone lines." Vince shifted the conversation. "Communication with Beacon Hill has been spotty, so we'll need to make sure everyone is on the same wavelength when the fireworks start."

"We have designated areas in Admiralty to gather for evacuation," Eliška said. "Our plans were to begin next week, but what Emma told me changes everything."

"I got the CliffsNotes from Jack," Vince confirmed. "Florence Upsdell and Eden's Star."

"Natalie is meeting with Bau," Jack added. "Dragon's Back still the plan?"

"Actually, Xui Li disclosed an alternate gateway," Eliška replied. "Happy Valley."

"A midpoint between Admiralty and Quarry Bay," Vince explained. "Gives us a better shot at getting them to the gateway without being caught."

"Even with a few dozen lightforcers and benders, it will be difficult—if not impossible."

"When do we begin?" Emma asked.

"We will need a few hours to prepare," Eliška replied, "so after dark."

"Game time," Vince said. "We're players in the battle, and winning is all that matters."

"We each have our role," Emma agreed. "No surrender until all are safe."

The door to the rooftop opened and Amina stepped into the muggy air. She caught sight of the four of them seated around the table and smiled wide. Vince slipped out of his seat and grabbed another bowl, dishing up some chow mein. He handed Amina the bowl and chopsticks as she took his seat at the table.

"All of the areas in the districts are marked," she said softly. "Tim would be proud of us."

Jack's burner cell buzzed: Message delivered. PM. HV.—BH.

"Is Bau aware of the alternate gateway?" Emma asked.

"Natalie must've convinced him to hold the line." Jack pointed the phone screen toward the others so they could read the message. "He wants to meet at Happy Valley. Gives us a chance to see the gateway for ourselves."

"I'll take you straight to it," Vince offered. "I know a few shortcuts."

"We will prepare the lightforcers and benders," Emma interjected. "Eliška?"

"Faction teams and Cherub will be ready before nightfall." Eliška set her bowl and chopsticks down and turned toward Amina. "We will need your logistical prowess."

"Of course," Amina replied. "I will bring all of my skills."

"You three figure out the details." Jack texted McNaughton back. Game on. "Vince and I will go see Bau—who's probably going to bring an army of Cherub to arrest me."

"Which is why you are going with Vince," Eliška retorted. "Bau likes him."

"You know, we are the champions of the—" Vince began.

"Bashers, Bowlers, and Boundaries," all of them said in unison.

Jack helped clear the table and wash dishes, and he even grabbed a shower before he slumped onto an empty cot. His muscles were sore, and a heaviness pressed on his chest. For a while he stared up at tin slats hanging over one side of the rooftop. Vince, Eliška, Emma, and Amina were on their own cots as silence lingered. No one budged, even when Cherub lightforcers and benders returned shortly before daybreak.

Early morning shifted to shades of gray until sunrise broke through. Curled up on the cot, Jack opened his eyes and stared across from him. Emma was awake, seated on the edge of her bed. Her hands were clasped, and her head was lowered. He watched her for a moment, then rolled off his cot and stretched his muscles.

"Good morning." He exhaled. "Nothing like chow mein in my dreams."

Emma smiled slightly. "I wonder what Vince will cook for a victory dinner."

"Definitely not catfish and rice." Jack couldn't shake the heaviness that continued to press down on his chest. He blinked several times to clear his slightly blurred vision, but the rooftop remained fuzzy. "Cherub are not ready for the legion or the queen—and neither are we."

"Eliška, Vince, and Amina are downstairs with Professor Burwick," Emma replied, ignoring his bleak outlook. "No matter the odds, we must stick together. After everything we have done—and everyone we have lost—the hours ahead will determine our destiny."

"Honestly, there's no place I'd rather be."

66

HAPPY VALLEY CEMETERY

Headstones rose along the tiered hillside beneath overgrown golden shower trees and moss-covered paths. Weeds and dead grass sprawled wildly between and over the graves. A draining humidity was thick by midmorning, and sweat seeped down Jack's spine. Beyond the cemetery was Happy Valley Racecourse, a modern-day Roman amphitheater—once an oasis of thoroughbreds and riches, now an unkempt, abandoned field.

"What else did Xui Li tell you?" Jack asked.

"She spoke to Eliška when she met with her and Amina, along with Salomeh." Vince pointed ahead. "I was busy in Admiralty with the Cherub and faction squads, marking the buildings for tonight. All I heard was about the Happy Valley gateway, and . . ."

"I wonder what Bau wants to meet about." Jack didn't pay much attention to the names engraved on the headstones. "Natalie must've told him about Eden's Star."

"Before he arrives, there's something you should see." Vince motioned for Jack to follow as they climbed several tiers near a mausoleum. "Xui Li told Amina about it."

Jack's curiosity was piqued as Vince stopped in front of a simple grave. At first he wondered why they were standing there, but then he knelt in front of the headstone. No dates of birth or death. Only one line and a name which stopped him cold.

"Bella," he said, somberly. "'A most beautiful soul who lives forever.'"

"I'm not sure how Xui Li knew it was here." Vince's gaze shifted around the cemetery. "Thought you might want to see it for yourself."

"Thank you." Jack ran his fingers over the engraved stone. "Mom's spirit lives on."

An emptiness washed over him as he stared at the words, knowing all that was left beneath the dirt was decaying bones. He was surprised one of the Elders remained buried in Happy Valley, forgotten by the Cherub, instead of somewhere like Thalren or Karābu Island.

"Why didn't anyone tell me before?" Jack asked. "Especially Xui Li."

"Sometimes leaving the past buried is easier than dealing with the pain of loss in the present." Vince eyed their surroundings. "Bau is here, and he's alone."

Along the hillside, Bau walked between graves and climbed the ascending terraces. Vince offered a fist bump, but Bau was clearly in a mood. Jack stepped back from his mom's grave, noticing Bau was on edge.

"Where is Emma?" Bau asked, point-blank. "She is the one I need to speak to."

"You sent the text to my burner, the one Natalie gave me. You didn't say anything about Emma, so you'll have to settle for me and Vince."

"Why should I waste my time?" Bau asked, annoyed. "You lost Eden's Star."

"Listen, there's no time for finger-pointing," Vince interrupted. "Next play, Bau."

"Are you ready for the evacuations? If what Natalie said is true, we are out of time."

"We'll begin tonight in Admiralty." Vince pointed toward the mausoleum. "The gateway in Happy Valley is closer than Dragon's Back, so we'll use it for as long as possible. For those in Kowloon, the best gateway is still the House of Luminescence at Beacon Hill."

"Once Cherub realize we are not fighting back, there will be chaos." Bau folded his arms and turned his attention toward Jack. "You have at least three of the artifacts?"

"More or less," Jack replied, evasive. "I'm not giving them to you, Bau."

"Jack is keeping them separated from one another," Vince explained. "A safety net."

"We have the Rhoxen Stone, but only someone who is holding or touching the stone is able to move when time stops. So it's not much use when trying to evacuate a mass amount of people."

"You are saying the Rhoxen Stone stops time?" Bau asked skeptically.

Jack nodded. "I saw it with my own eyes during the Battle of Everest."

"I've seen it too—well, I was frozen, but Eliška and Amina confirmed." Vince stared at Jack, dumbstruck. "Hold on—*the* Battle of Everest?"

"It's a long, mostly unbelievable story."

"You cannot use the Rhoxen Stone until those in Kowloon are evacuated," Bau insisted.

"That could take weeks," Vince argued. "What about those on Hong Kong Island?"

"Exactly why I wanted Emma." Bau pointed his finger at Jack. "She solves puzzles."

"Evacuations need to happen in Kowloon and Hong Kong Island at the same time." Jack paced back and forth, struggling to make a deeper promise to Bau. "Listen, we won't use the Rhoxen Stone unless it's absolutely necessary."

"Best you're going to get," Vince chimed in. "Bau, listen to me."

"So if the Queen of Sakkhela arrives, then you will freeze the world to save yourselves?"

"We don't know when she will attack the city," Jack answered. "What else were you expecting to hear if you spoke with Emma? Evacuations are the priority until there is an attack."

"She is the only chosen left, other than me." Bau paused. "I trust her with my life."

"What's going on with you?" Vince asked. "We're on the same team."

"Fang Xue and the Council will not stand against legion or Florence Upsdell." Bau hesitated. "I am doing all I can to keep them from surrendering to the PRC and Merikh."

"You're the Cherub leader," Jack volleyed. "Or is that a smoke screen too?"

"Fang Xue anointed me." Bau shook his head. "But she will not stand aside."

No one wanted to distrust Bau more than Jack, especially with their history. But Vince was right—they were on the same team whether they liked it or not. As he stood in the cemetery, he finally admitted what Emma had long known. It didn't matter whether they were friends—they needed each other.

"What do you need from us?" Jack asked. "Name it."

"A renewed hope," Bau conceded. "Belief and courage will not survive without it."

Jack paced back and forth, searching for an answer. He stopped in front of his mom's headstone, remembering her in angelic armor battling the Nephilim king. He had sworn to honor Rachel's promise, but ever since then it seemed the highest Cherub were more concerned about protecting their gifts and burying the past. Elyon's voice broke through, clear and concise.

Uprisings begin when warrior souls dare to step into the hottest fire.

Jack turned toward Bau and Vince. "Signs and wonders."

67

Jack and Bau traveled through the Kai Tak gateway, then passed the Sky Garden on their way to Kai Tak Bridge Road. As soon as he said, "Signs and wonders," all three knew what to do. Vince headed straight to Quarry Bay to prepare for a night to be written about one day in the Eternal, maybe by Amina herself. Jack walked alongside the Cherub leader on the eastern end of the peninsula, surprised Bau hadn't objected to the idea.

Kwun Tong was a well-known district remembered in the historical archives for salt yards dating back to the Song Dynasty. McDougall taught on the districts in Kowloon and highlighted civil riots of the villagers and salt farmers in Kwun Tong, which had occurred right where they were walking.

We're not planning to start a riot, but we are going to spark a revolution.

Jack hated to admit it, but he was impressed by the way Bau carried himself—confident, with an air of arrogance that seemed to open the right doors. Jack had been on the run for months, fighting, chasing, nearly dying, and losing everything—so walking alongside Bau, a piece of him didn't feel like he belonged in the same league.

I guess that's how you roll when you're the Cherub leader—a step above.

"So the highest Cherub have been living in luxury at the Rosewood?"

"After the breakout and the citywide lockdown, many escaped to the hotel at Fang Xue's orders." Bau kept his sights straight ahead. "It was never supposed to be permanent."

"Doesn't seem right when everyone at Beacon Hill and the faction are struggling." Jack waited for a smart remark from Bau, but instead there was an awkward silence. "If we're going to have a chance, it'll take every last one of us—including the highest Cherub."

"When this is over, we will see whether you are right."

Jack took in the haunting familiarity around him, which raised the hair on his scarred arms. He was reminded of Sham Shui Po with its run-down apartments, barred windows, and trash piled in alleyways and strewn across sidewalks. He kept on Bau's shoulder, noticing Bau hadn't acknowledged anyone as they walked past. His mind flashed to Kati Pahari, when Emma stood among the Cherub as if she were reuniting with old friends.

Bau might be the Cherub leader, but he's not as openhearted as Emma.

Five minutes later, they reached an industrial warehouse, which was boarded up and chained. A young boy stepped out from behind a trash container and waved them around the rear of the building. Metal steps descended beneath street level to an iron door. The child unlocked the dead bolts, then waited until they disappeared inside. Jack heard the dead bolts reengage as he stood beneath dim light bulbs casting a dull glow across a storage room.

Bau stepped up to a walk-in freezer door, then hesitated. "Ready?"

"Emma's been right so far. I'm trusting you, Bau."

"And I am choosing to trust you."

Bau opened the freezer door wide enough for them to enter. Inside, the freezer was steaming hot and the shelves were bare. Bau shifted one of the shelves aside, revealing a hidden ladder which descended even deeper. Jack was curious to see what was next, but he waited for Bau to go first. At the bottom of the ladder, he stopped cold and witnessed an unexpected world.

Two stories below street level, the basement stretched the length of the industrial building. On both sides were adjoining tunnels where people were entering and exiting. A putrid stench filled his nostrils as he swallowed puke in his throat. Thousands were holed up and living underground in Kwun Tong. People slept on the ground while others cooked with dirty pots on single gas burners. Children's cries bounced off the walls, sending a twinge down Jack's spine.

"Definitely worse than Beacon Hill," he whispered. "Faction too."

"And the Rosewood," Bau admitted. "I found out about this place from Salomeh."

"Fang Xue never told you?" Jack already knew the answer by

the blank expression on Bau's face. "How many more places are there like this?"

"Impossible to know the number of those who have gone underground."

"How are we going to get all of these people through any of the gateways?" Jack was speechless at the crowds who continued to travel through the tunnel entrances. "Beacon Hill, Dragon's Back, and Happy Valley aren't going to cut it for those in Kowloon."

"Many who are here have never seen the gifts of a Cherub. Blind faith is all they have experienced, and I admire them for their steadfast belief."

"I've been in the City of Gods, Sakkhela, Charis, and fought in the Battle of Everest."

Bau's brows raised. "You have seen more than most, including me."

"I'm not anyone special, Bau." He hoped he was building a bridge with Beacon Hill's Head Boy turned Cherub leader. Elyon's voice echoed in his ears as he pushed away his feelings about Emma being passed over because she chose to stand by his side. *Uprisings begin when warrior souls dare to step into the hottest fire. You're the one chosen to light the match.*

One by one those milling about in the underground city turned their attention toward Bau. Everyone stopped what they were doing as he walked between men, women, and children barely surviving in squalor. *I don't know what their lives were like a few months ago, but today is a new beginning.* Bau was awkward when several reached out to touch him. He stopped in the middle of the growing crowd that surrounded him.

Jack grabbed a crate and pushed his way through, then set the crate down at Bau's feet. Whispers among the people grew louder as Bau stepped onto the crate and raised his hand, glowing with orangish auburn. His lightforce caused gasps when the force spread over the underground city, leaving everyone speechless and awestruck.

"Faith in Elyon keeps you alive," Bau called out. "A faith rooted in the core of your souls, and one that challenges your belief. You may not know who I am, but I am one of you."

The glow from Bau's lightforce shone brighter, radiating across countless faces. Soulweaver slipped into Jack's grasp. He handed it over to Bau, and in that moment it became the Rod of Elyon— the heartwood fading beneath a bright white illumination. Bau's lightforce merged with the powerful force humming from the rod, and his shoulders straightened slightly.

"In the hours ahead, our city will be shaken. Darkness threatens to kill, steal, and destroy our souls." Bau raised the rod above his head, and the crowd gasped as a streak of stark-white light exploded toward the ceiling and spread over them like an umbrella. "When the battle begins, you will not be forgotten—you will not be left behind."

Goose bumps bubbled on Jack's arms and neck. *Bring it home, Bau.*

"Today, your prayers are answered," Bau said with authority. "Leave Kwun Tong and travel the tunnels to Beacon Hill. Spread the word to all with ears to hear. This day, you begin your march to freedom."

Bau stepped off the crate as the crowd dispersed, rushing to gather what was left of their belongings while others headed straight for the tunnels.

"Headmaster Fargher better be ready," Jack said. "He's about to get swarmed."

"Never imagined I would one day hold the Rod of Elyon." Bau hesitated, captured by the heartwood in his grasp. "I cannot imagine the extent of its power."

Jack's muscles tensed as he questioned whether Bau was going to hand Soulweaver back willingly. He understood the feeling— he'd grown used to the power of the rod. He held out his hand and eyed Bau closely as the illumination faded and revealed the heartwood once again. Reluctantly, Bau handed the rod over.

"One speech down," Jack said. "Let's hit the next district."

68

Eliška glanced at the clock and paced the room where a map of Hong Kong Island spread across one wall, showing color-coded locations across Admiralty. Most of the afternoon the room had been packed with a few dozen lightforcers and benders, plus hand-picked faction with the skills to lead the extractions. Emma and Amina organized the gifted Cherub, while Eliška worked through logistics with her team and Vince.

Minutes earlier, the room had emptied.

"We cannot wait any longer." Eliška gripped the velvet pouch, knowing the original plan to use the Rhoxen Stone had been challenged hours earlier. "Are you certain?"

"He told Bau we wouldn't use the stone unless it was absolutely necessary." Vince adjusted his Kevlar vest. "If we can't stop time, then this will get squirrelly."

Eliška slipped the velvet pouch into her pocket. "Unless it is necessary."

Downstairs the vans and trucks idled, loaded with faction, light-forcers, and benders. Eliška climbed into the driver's seat of the first vehicle, where Emma and Amina were already in the cab waiting. She checked the side mirror as Vince slipped behind the wheel of the next vehicle in line. Shortly after midnight, the caravan left the parking garage of Quarry Bay—hours later than they'd anticipated.

King's Road was wide open as the caravan headed toward Central. For a few miles, the streets remained empty until they reached Gloucester Road. The vehicles split up at the intersection, with Eliška turning right and Vince following on her bumper. She accelerated as Emma and Amina remained quiet in the cab. Another left and the two trucks continued through Wan Chai.

"There is a checkpoint at cross street Fleming Road," Amina pointed out.

Eliška pushed her boot to the floor, and the truck sped up. Vince stayed on her bumper, flashing his headlights. She caught his signal, and both vehicles' tires screeched with a sharp left onto Stewart, then a quick right onto Hennessy. Emma gripped the armrest and kept her sights straight ahead, while Amina glanced between them as if waiting for one of them to break the tension.

"You two are enjoying this," Amina noted. "I would rather be behind a keyboard."

"Good for you to expand your horizons," Emma mused. "Keep close to us."

"Right." Amina glanced at the tablet on her lap. "Turn onto Cotton Tree Drive, near the Bank of China Tower."

Eliška barreled through a red light, glancing down a side street to see one of the other trucks whip past. If they were lucky, they'd all return. She gripped the steering wheel tight and followed Amina's instructions, cutting down Cotton Tree. Adrenaline pumped when she recognized a fluorescent orange emblem tagged on the side of a building.

聯合. *Unity.*

The fluorescent orange spray-painted emblems were Vince's idea, and they could only be seen after dark. Hours earlier, Vince had gone out with a small team of faction and Cherub to canvass Central and Admiralty. He found the spots they'd seen that night at The Peak with the colored flares, and tagged as many as possible. While the emblem wasn't huge, it was enough for someone to take notice if they were looking for it.

Eliška parked the truck on the street and waited. Vince drove past and pulled an illegal turn onto Tramway Lane, then disappeared from sight. She knew he was headed to Queen's Road Central, where others were waiting near Trois Café. Everybody had been instructed to leave their apartments right at midnight and find their way to the extraction points. On a night like this, everyone needed to risk it all.

"Amina, wait here," Eliška instructed. "Keep the engine running."

"Right." Amina held up her tablet, showing blinking red dots moving across Central and Admiralty in clusters. "I'll keep watch and shout if something goes sideways."

Emma slipped out from the passenger side and rounded the truck at the same time that Eliška climbed out with a semi-automatic weapon in her grasp. Each vehicle in the caravan had two lightforcers, one bender, and four faction. But Eliška and Emma decided the two of them were all that was needed to give the others more support. Eliška was certain Emma was priceless by her side.

"We need to be as quiet as a mouse," Eliška whispered. "And as fast as a cheetah."

Emma smirked. "Vince's humor is rubbing off on you."

The Murray lobby was abandoned, and all lights were off. Weeks earlier, power had been shut off to many of the districts across Hong Kong Island, and remaining tourists held captive by the PRC were moved to the Harbourview between two of the major checkpoints. Emma offered a slight glow from her palms, enough to guide their steps. Eliška pressed the butt of her weapon against her shoulder and moved with purpose.

In the stairwell, both climbed several floors stealthily. Eliška had been part of several extractions in Vietnam before she was captured by the Merikh—none of which she spoke about to anyone. As she kept her weapon pointed ahead, she knew this was by far the most dangerous. She was now the leader of the faction, which meant she needed to command the fight. On the fourth floor she stopped in the stairwell, then opened the door cautiously and stepped into a darkened hallway.

On both sides, the doors were wide open. Eliška guessed the PRC and Merikh had cleared the entire hotel one room at a time and left the doors open to be certain no one else was hiding. Her heart pounded as she stepped through each doorway to find empty, musty rooms.

"We were told they would be here," Eliška whispered. "I do not understand."

Emma asked, "Could they be on another floor?"

"I suppose." Eliška checked her watch. "We will be here for hours if we go one floor at a time."

Emma's lightforce faded a bit. "The hotel was marked the other night?"

"Vince is very detailed, and he checked the exact location." Eliška stepped into the hallway again and glanced back and forth. "Flares were seen on the roof."

"Seven Tribes—maybe the seventh floor is a lucky number."

Eliška trusted Emma's instincts, surprised by how decisive she was in the moment. Eliška led the way back to the stairwell and climbed to the seventh floor. With Emma at her shoulder, she stepped into the hallway and followed the same routine.

Each door was wide open, and each room was empty. Eliška neared the halfway point when, out of the corner of her eye, she noticed movement. Emma must've seen the same. Both spun around, and Emma's lightforce cast a bright glow on a boy standing in front of them. Eliška aimed her weapon, noticing Emma's fearlessness. She kept her head on a swivel as Emma approached the boy and knelt.

"Are you by yourself?" Emma asked softly. "Where are your parents?"

The boy sheepishly pointed past them, over their shoulders. Eliška turned with her weapon aimed ahead. She didn't wait for Emma as she moved swiftly from one room to the next. Three doors down, she entered a room and found a dozen people huddled together. In the dim light, she recognized the fear in their eyes.

Emma appeared in the doorway with the boy beside her as Eliška moved to an adjoining room. Another group was there in the same crouched position. A quick head count totaled thirty who were hiding in The Murray. Eliška lowered her weapon and held up her hand to show she was friendly.

"Come with me," she whispered. "And you will be safe."

69

CHERUB GATHERED IN THE HALLWAY of the seventh floor as Eliška led the way into the stairwell. Emma nudged everyone to keep up. Even the children were hauntingly quiet as footsteps pattered in the stairwell. Everyone moved with purpose until they reached the lobby.

Stealthily, Eliška crossed the marble tiles and approached the glass doors, then peered up and down the street. She eyed the peacefulness outside, then nodded at Amina, who waited behind the steering wheel. Close to leaving, Eliška hesitated as the back of her neck prickled. While the breakout at Shek Pik Prison had been chaotic, this rescue mission seemed too smooth.

"We need to keep moving," Emma urged. "Eliška . . ."

Gunfire erupted somewhere outside, followed by a loud

explosion. Emma stepped through the glass doors of The Murray. Eliška was caught off guard for a few seconds. Once she snapped out of a moment of bone-chilling terror, Eliška pushed herself to move in unison with Emma. With the back of the truck opened, Cherub climbed inside in a matter of seconds. Eliška kept her weapon readied as she guarded the rear door until it was closed. Another barrage of gunfire kept her on edge, questioning which team of faction and Cherub was engaging with the HKPF, PRC, and Merikh.

On the sidewalk, she reached into her pocket and grabbed the velvet pouch, tempted to use the Rhoxen Stone to prevent further attacks. *But then what happens? How can I save everyone on my own?* Not knowing where Vince might be left her more uncertain than she expected. Her mind riffled through a hundred scenarios in a millisecond—and all ended the same, with far too many dead.

Flashing lights appeared at the end of the block, a fleet of HKPF tactical response vehicles heading straight for them. Eliška hopped on to the running board and banged on the window. Wide-eyed, Amina rolled the window down as Emma slid into the passenger seat with her palms glowing.

"Drive," Eliška ordered. "Fast."

Amina shifted into gear and punched the accelerator, forcing everyone to hold on tight as the truck lurched ahead. Bullets ricocheted as Eliška gripped the truck with one hand and pulled the trigger with the other. HKPF vehicles charged forward while Amina shifted gears, leaving the engine sputtering.

"More gas," Eliška shouted. "Less clutch."

"I forgot to mention," she yelled back, "I have never driven a stick shift before."

"Do not slow down, Amina. No matter what is in front of you."

Eliška caught sight of Emma rolling down the passenger window and climbing out onto the running board on the opposite side. Minutes earlier Eliška had questioned the peacefulness, and then in a blink she was fighting alongside Emma amid the chaos. She fired more rounds, striking tires that exploded, leaving clouds of smoke billowing across the street.

Amina accelerated down Cotton Tree Drive, directly toward the HKPF tactical vehicles. Eliška held on tight, glancing at Amina, who white-knuckled the steering wheel. Eliška fired more rounds, piercing the bulletproof glass of the tactical vehicles.

Out of the corner of her eye, Eliška caught sight of Emma's lightforce glowing bright, but instead of unleashing her power she shifted her hands to one side. Eliška turned her sights to the HKPF vehicles as they careened to one side and the other. Amina clipped one of the vehicles as she barreled through the fleet, then skidded around a corner onto Garden Road.

For a moment, Eliška was airborne with only her fingers grasping the truck. She was about to fall off and skid across the concrete until an invisible force reeled her in. *Emma's powers are on fire.* Amina shifted gears and turned down Magazine Gap Road. Eliška kept looking back to see if they were being followed as the truck headed down a windy road covered by overhanging trees. She heard a splattering of gunfire and several more explosions, but they sounded further away.

Ten minutes later, the truck plowed through the open gates at Happy Valley Cemetery—a sign others had already arrived. Amina slammed on the brakes, and the truck skidded to a stop, smoke billowing from beneath the hood. Eliška hopped off the running board and glanced around for Vince. Emma darted around the back of the truck and opened the rear. Cherub stumbled out, clearly shaken by the roller-coaster ride.

Several of the faction headed in their direction, heavily armed. Lightforcers held their palms at the ready with a myriad of colorful lightforces. Eliška searched through the crowds, at a loss when Vince and his team were nowhere to be found.

"Emma!" Eliška waved her forward. "The gateway needs an offering."

While Amina remained frozen behind the wheel of the truck, Emma and Eliška darted up the hillside between headstones of the dead. Midway up the hill, they reached an open door to the mausoleum. Emma retrieved several coins and tossed them inside. A long line of Cherub, nearly one hundred, waited eagerly for their chance.

"With so few coins," Emma said, "I cannot say how long the gateway will remain open."

"We will worry about that when the time comes," Eliška replied.

Inside the mausoleum, a vibrant emerald glow flashed each time one of the Cherub left through the gateway. Faction were highly skilled in extraction, and they moved the group through the line quickly while lightforcers and benders stood guard. Eliška caught her breath as her adrenaline surged. She couldn't shake the dread of what she imagined was occurring in Admiralty and Central.

Emma held out the silver coins in her palm. "Only a handful left."

"Vince and his team are not here," Eliška said. "What should we do?"

"I will go with you to search for them."

Headlights beamed across the cemetery, capturing everyone's attention. Eliška and Emma darted down the hill as the truck barreled toward them. From the driver's side, Eliška heard Vince's voice, and her heart beat faster. She reached him as he hopped out of the driver's side and punched him in the arm.

"What's that for?" Vince asked, confused. "Back there was seriously insane."

"Get everyone to the mausoleum," Eliška ordered the faction team as she gathered her composure. "Vince, you were not supposed to attract any attention."

"HKPF and Merikh were waiting for us when we arrived," Vince answered. "Eliška, they knew we were coming. Without the lightforcers and benders, we would've been target practice."

70

Near a heliport at Kai Tak Runway Park, the sunrise reflected off the murky waters of Kowloon Bay. After an all-nighter way more intense than studying for McDougall's finals, Jack was exhausted yet satisfied from trekking through the tunnels. Across Kowloon, he'd stood by Bau's side from Hung Hom to Ho Man Tin.

In each of the squalid underground hideouts, Bau's message resounded with greater passion, and the symbol of the Rod of Elyon energized those who had lost hope. By early morning, Jack imagined word spreading beyond the tunnels to the districts— Liberation Day.

Impossible to believe Bau and I were enemies hours ago, and now we are allies.

"Headmaster Fargher will have his hands full, *and* McDougall will be barking in his ear for days." Jack's smile faded. "How will he get thousands of people from Nightingale's vault through the House of Luminescence gateway?"

"One wicket at a time—one dismissal to end each inning."

"You know, Tim loved the fact Vince gave him the game ball from the Bashers, Bowlers, and Boundaries." Countless memories flooded Jack's mind with Tim's addictive smile and sharp wit at center stage. A crazy dance with Amina at the Fabulous Friendly. A loyal friend who slept in the basement until Jack returned from Wan Chai. A fanatical birthday celebration in Kati Pahari culminating in kabaddi. "He named our band of misfits the Keepers."

"I always thought he was too much of a geek for Nightingale."

"He said once his first choice was Crozier, but he got stuck with us."

"Compassion brigade seems more his style than you lot." Bau paused. "He was a good bloke, and he never deserved what happened."

"Since all of this started, we've been on opposite sides. What you did last night will save many, Bau. You did what most are too afraid to do, especially Fang Xue and the Council. Respect."

"I am still learning what it means to be a leader," Bau admitted. "Far too many days have been spent locked away with Fang Xue and the selected council to find a way to settle with the PRC. Last night brought a renewed hope, not only to the people who heard the message but to me as well. I will not turn my back on the Cherub and the innocent who are questioning and searching for greater meaning—including the faction who have found purpose and answers in Elyon."

Of course there's no way he'll ever apologize for beaning Will on the cricket pitch, bullying me at the Sword and Fan, or sending Cherub to capture me for crimes I never committed. That's our history, but if he means what he's saying, then this is the future.

"Will was brought to Beacon Hill from the nether realm, and he's in rough shape." Jack hesitated, waiting for a snide remark from Bau. "Maybe you can hold off sending Cherub guards until we see how this ends."

"Perhaps I will do the same for you," Bau replied, matter-of-fact.

"Once the gateways settle." Jack checked his burner cell, noticing a dozen missed calls and texts from Emma. "She's freaking out, so I better respond."

"Some advice: you do not want Emma cross at you," Bau warned. "Take it from me."

"Noted." Jack fired off a text: Need a ride. "You know how to reach me."

Bau and Jack fist-bumped. "Do not read into this too deeply—a time will come."

"We both want to win, Bau. So we're on the same side—for today, at least."

"Not something we should spread far and wide, until this is over."

"If we survive what's coming, there will be a day to clear the air."

Soulweaver twitched on his forearm, and he spun around. Fang Xue and a half dozen Cherub marched toward them. He nudged Bau in the ribs, and his muscles tensed. The palms of the Cherub glowed in a myriad of colors as Jack balled his hands into fists, hoping his firing muscles would free Soulweaver to his grip.

"Arrest him immediately," Fang Xue ordered. "And take him to the Rosewood."

"Wait." Bau held up his hand, glowing an orangish auburn. "You will stand down."

Confused, Cherub lightforcers stood between Fang Xue and Bau Hu. A standoff Jack would rather not be part of, especially since Fang Xue intended on locking him away in some place like the Dungeon of Savages. *I'll bet the Cherub have more than one prison for the crazy beasts and evildoers throughout history.* He took a step back and eyed the Jetstream 41 on display, wondering whether he could run faster than a lightforce burst.

"Do you know what you have done?" Fang Xue chastised Bau.

"We offered them a message of freedom," Bau replied. "And I will not leave anyone."

"While you two were rats in the tunnels, the faction created chaos in Admiralty." Fang Xue crossed her arms. "PRC are demanding an explanation, Bau."

"We have delivered our answer," Bau replied pointedly. "Today is Liberation Day."

Fang Xue motioned the lightforcers to close in, but none of them took another step. Jack wanted to stomp around and point his finger at Fang Xue, taunting her for being so thirsty for authority that she was rapidly running out of a river of support. But he stood still as a statue.

"I am the leader of the Cherub," Bau stated. "And my decisions are final."

"You will allow an outlier who murdered our Elder and highest Cherub on Mount Hareh to go free?"

Bau leaned over to Jack. "You should exit stage left."

"Don't have to tell me twice."

Without a word to Fang Xue, he turned around and darted toward the Jetstream. On the way, he couldn't help glancing over his shoulder. Bau and Fang Xue were still in a standoff, but the Cherub lightforcers were backing down. Jack reached the jet and opened the door, then slipped inside with only one silver coin left in his pocket. He dropped the coin in the center of the cabin, and in a blink he pushed open the mausoleum door in Happy Valley Cemetery wide enough to slip through.

Jack breathed in the morning air and walked toward his mom's headstone. He wanted to take one more look, in case this was his last. *Bella. A most beautiful soul who lives forever.* A lump lodged in his throat as he fought against the tears welling up. He'd been taught from an early age that tears were a sign of weakness. But as he stared at his mom's name, he wondered if the opposite was true.

A motorcycle revved as it whipped through the cemetery in his direction. He started down the tiered hillside and met the rider halfway. Emma flipped her visor up and handed over another helmet. On instinct, he leaned forward and kissed her gently.

His cheeks flushed as he exhaled. "You won't believe the night I had."

"Well . . ." Emma smiled warmly. "That makes two of us."

71

Hours from the nearest city, tucked within a twisting and winding mountainous route, a serene lake with deep-blue waters kept a secret hidden beneath the surface. Dark clouds rolled in swiftly, smothering clear skies. Lightning pierced the water, ripping open the atmosphere as worlds collided. Legion swarmed, silhouettes whipping and streaking over the lake and mountains. Near shore, Florence Upsdell appeared, draped in a silver robe.

Eden's Star glowed in her grasp as she eyed the middle of the lake. From the scabbard strapped around her waist, she removed Scarlet Widow and stabbed the blade into the mud. Instantly the waters parted and revealed a granite stone on the rocky bottom. While the legion circled overhead, she walked toward the flat stone and stopped with an icy stare at the etching of a fire-breathing dragon—Slybourne's crest.

From the other scabbard over her shoulder she retrieved Dragon Soul and plunged the sword into a gap in the stone, one she had chiseled with her own hands in an age long ago. She turned the sword counterclockwise, and with a low rumbling, the granite rolled away and revealed an entrance to the Exodus Mines. Stone steps descended deep into the earth, leading Florence into an enormous cavern as if she were returning to Slybourne Castle in Sakkhela. A mountain of gold, silver, sapphires, rubies, necklaces, bracelets, brooches, statues, and crowns radiated magnificently. A smirk pursed her lips as she gazed upon her extravagant wealth— the spoils of war from when she stood alongside Ryder Slybourne.

Eden's Star continued to glow bright and pointed the way to what had remained hidden for centuries. Florence walked among her riches and slipped off her scabbards, then set the Windstrikers aside as the compass glimmered.

Medieval weapons were mounted on a stone wall.

From her pocket, she retrieved the ivory figurine depicting her reign and the power of Scarlet Widow. She set it down and allowed her silver robe to drop to the ground as she admired her craftsman-ship hanging on the walls before grabbing onyx armor from among the weapons. She slipped into the armor, and the dretium fit per-fectly. Her wavy hair draped over her shoulders as she grabbed the Windstrikers and tucked each one into the holsters that appeared in the shape-shifting armor. She tucked the ivory figurine beneath her armor and moved effortlessly across the cavern, slipping two scabbard sleeves over her shoulders. Sir Ryder Slybourne was the greatest Cherub warrior, but Queen Florence Upsdell was by far the most treacherous.

Within the Exodus Mines, the Queen of Sakkhela sauntered among relics of the past as Eden's Star drew her close to what she desired most. Her gaze locked on a funerary mask tossed aside into a pile of jewels. The magnificent gold and precious stones embedded into the mask depicted the ones she loved. On one side, a child's hand was imprinted. With her eyes ablaze, Florence crushed the mask into fragments and screamed bitterly.

She glanced down at the compass and stepped deeper into the cavern. Eden's Star raged in her palm, leaving her intense glare focused on a golden spin top. She retrieved the ivory figurine and inserted it into a small hole on the spin top. Surrounded by riches from this world and beyond, she knelt and twisted a child's toy. She watched as the top spun at an angle, causing the figurine to dance as ivory snakes slithered in memory of an unforgivable loss.

Florence left the cavern with the ivory figurine and spin top secured beneath her dretium armor. She climbed the steps and stood on the lake bottom, then snatched Dragon Soul and climbed to shore as the Exodus Mines sealed. On the banks, she grabbed Scarlet Widow and slipped both swords into the scabbards strapped onto her back. Legion thrashed frantically around their queen as she gripped Eden's Star—the hunt had only just begun.

72

Natalie walked through a crowded Rowell Library and nudged her way down the spiral staircase while a steady stream of people headed upstairs. Since access to Nightingale's vault was wide open, Headmaster Fargher had removed the oil painting of Beacon Hill from the early days. She never asked where he stored the uniquely designed canvas but was certain he kept it somewhere safe on the grounds.

Oliver and Winnie Bennett met her in the vault as she watched even more people arrive from the tunnels. Since early morning, Cherub from all districts across Kowloon poured into the vault. She'd grown used to responding to potential breaches on the grounds, and so far only those who were escaping the Merikh and

PRC had made it through. She eased off the edge a bit, knowing what was occurring before her eyes wasn't death, but a quest for life.

"We brought a few guests from Tai Kok Tsui." Oliver waved his arms around with a wide grin at the constant flow through the vault. "Everyone is moving to a new landlord."

"Salomeh warned us about Cherub arriving to travel straight through the House of Luminescence," Natalie replied. "Once they are through, Cherub will meet them on the other side at Mount Hareh and take them to a new home."

"Hundreds are traveling in the tunnels," Winnie added. "Thousands, possibly."

"I am guessing since the evacuations are happening now, there is a reason." Natalie got sidetracked for a second, struck by the sheer number. "Not sure where we will house those who are waiting to go through, though."

"Whatever we can do to help," Oliver replied, "we are here to serve."

"Natalie, any word from Emma?" Winnie asked, clearly worried.

"As far as I know, she is on Hong Kong Island with the faction." Natalie was cautious with her words so she wouldn't alarm either of them, but she'd heard rumors earlier about the night in Admiralty and Central. "I am certain all is well, or we would have heard differently."

Natalie excused herself and climbed the steps back to the library. She slipped through the crowds as Cherub organized a long line stretching through the library, the Main Hall, and down to the House of Luminescence. She'd spent most of the night tossing and turning, wondering whether Jack was okay. He was her family now, and the risks he faced, scars he carried, and impossible choices he made left her wide awake as she shouldered them too.

"Jack, what are you thinking?" She checked her cell, convinced he was behind the decision to escalate evacuations. "At least respond to my texts to tell me what's next."

Elevator doors opened and Headmaster Fargher stepped out. She hadn't seen Fargher go up in the elevator to the Zakhar in weeks. Shortly after the Shek Pik Prison breakout, the government had attempted to shut off all power to Beacon Hill—only to discover the school was somewhat self-sufficient with its own power source that was connected to the Zakhar. She didn't know how it worked, but it was enough to keep the lights on.

"Headmaster," Natalie called out, knowing he'd been secluded in Crozier Hospital since Will returned. She couldn't imagine nearly losing your son twice, and the aftermath had yet to be revealed fully. "Cherub are arriving through the tunnels, and so far the process is working." She looked past him toward the elevator. "Were you searching for something with the Zakhar?"

"Quite the contrary," Fargher replied. "For the foreseeable future, the Zakhar is nothing more than a transformer."

Natalie sensed the headmaster wanted the past buried. "How is William?"

"His health is improving slowly." Fargher's gaze softened. "But his wounds are severe."

"Any word from Fang Xue?" Natalie weighed her words. "Will she come for him?"

Fargher shook his head. "Honestly, I do not know what they will do."

"We should be prepared if she shows up unannounced."

Professor McDougall approached in a huff. "Look what they have done, Freddie."

"Who are you talking about?" Fargher asked.

"You know this was Jack Reynolds and the others who have created this crisis."

"We have been in a crisis for months," Natalie replied. "It was inevitable."

"What are we supposed to do with such a rush? There's barely enough space for those who are settled in the houses." McDougall groaned. "One more issue to fix."

"Salomeh and Xui Li guaranteed the gateway in the House of Luminescence would remain open for as long as needed." Fargher's gaze shifted between them. "We will do what we have done since the beginning—care for everyone no matter where they are arriving from and prioritize those who wish to continue on. We will follow Salomeh's lead and work around the clock to move everyone along."

"Freddie, once word spreads beyond the Cherub, the grounds will overflow."

"I think word has already spread, Professor," Natalie replied.

"We have survived this long," Fargher said calmly. "We will find our way."

Natalie left Fargher and McDougall to debate the inevitable. She remembered standing with Jack that day at the Tasty Lion snack shop. *Before this is over, others will find refuge here. When that day comes, Headmaster Fargher will be the one to lead them, but he will need someone by his side.* She kept her promise, and she was grateful McDougall, Windsor, Salomeh, Faizan, and now Xui Li were by the headmaster's side too.

Down another flight of stairs, Natalie stopped outside the

House of Luminescence as a long line of refugees entered one by one. A myriad of colors glowed inside the sacred room, which indicated the exodus was at full steam. She stepped aside while Faizan and Salomeh ushered the line forward, praying over each refugee. Xui Li moved through the crowd and stood beside Natalie, but remained quiet.

"Jack knew this day was coming," Natalie said in a lowered voice. "Now the time is here, and I cannot help but feel as if we are powerless."

"In our weakness there is strength when we confront our trials," Xui Li replied. "Jack's heart is one of a warrior whose fear of losing those he loves strengthens his courage."

"There are days I am afraid he will not survive—and he will be taken from us."

"When the Merikh captured and imprisoned me"—Xui Li paused—"my concern was not whether to live or die, but to protect him for as long as breath was in me."

73

QUARRY BAY, HONG KONG ISLAND

On the rooftop, Jack found a plank laid flat beside the wall. He searched the fencing until he discovered an opening. After an all-nighter and riding on the motorcycle with Emma, he found himself alone on the roof while the others were downstairs with faction and Cherub. He pushed the plank out until the far end reached another building.

He climbed onto the ledge and stared across, memories flashing of other rooftops and Areum's emerald-green eyes and tatted sleeves on both arms. *"At this rate, the sun will rise before you make it across."* He nudged his boot forward, legs shaking slightly. *I have to control my fear or else it will control me.* His heartbeat quickened even as he tried breathing slowly. With his arms out on both sides, he took one small step. The plank bounced beneath his boot, leaving him frozen for a few seconds.

C'mon, Jack, you can do this—why are you doing this again?

With one foot in front of the next, fear surged through his veins as he steadied his balance. *The only way to overcome fear is to stare it straight in the eyes and dare it to blink. But whatever you do, don't look down. Jack, you looked down—again.* He stopped halfway across the plank, paralyzed until his gaze hardened. With his eyes fixed dead ahead, he ignored the bouncing plank and walked directly across to the other side. Beads of sweat dripped down his cheeks as he stepped onto the opposite rooftop and exhaled long.

A voice called out. "Jack!"

He spun around to see Professor Burwick on the roof along with her sister, Eleanore. Sure, he'd made it across, but the bigger challenge was making it back. With both of them watching, he stepped onto the plank and walked across faster than before. He hopped onto the rooftop and wiped his sweaty palms on his jeans.

"Good morning, Jack."

"Surprised to see you," he said to Eleanore. "Figured you'd be in Puerto Natales."

"I will leave the two of you to chin-wag," Burwick interrupted soberly.

Eleanore remained silent until Burwick left the rooftop. Jack dug his hands into his pockets and waited for Eleanore to speak. Another awkward minute passed. Her eyes were bloodshot, as if she'd traveled all night. *She's a gateway creator, so she must know where gateways are around this planet. And she's a vision seeker, capable of controlling my imagination to make me see what she wants me to see. Hold steady, Jack.* He nearly spoke up but hesitated long enough for her to beat him to it.

"Harley says you and Emma made it through—" Eleanore began.

"Why didn't you tell us about the ivory figurine being a key?"

"Honestly, I hoped you would not figure it out." Eleanore was clearly struggling. "Your mum asked me to keep it a secret, but then the key disappeared. I do not know whether she meant for it to end up in Rachel's hands."

"You are a vision seeker. Have you seen any visions with the key?"

"I have never seen one which revealed anything about the key or the nether realm. When I saw you last, you mentioned your visions. Your father was a vision seeker, too, and if he is still alive, then the visions you are having might be somewhat altered."

"The one from the night in Sitio Veterans when Rachel was murdered keeps shifting. I'm certain it was Michael Chung who pulled the trigger, but I don't think he was the one who murdered her. I've suspected for a while that Addison was messing with my visions, so I'm not sure what to believe. While Chung is in each of them, chasing Rachel between the shanties, I've seen more than one person who might've been there that night delivering the final blow."

"Who else was there?" Eleanore asked inquisitively.

"Emma, as you know . . ." Jack paused. "Then my mom."

"Fascinating." Eleanore's brows furrowed. "You are not convinced of either."

"Deep down, I'm certain it was neither of them—but someone else *was* there."

"More needs to be revealed." Eleanore cleared her throat. "You and Emma found the gateway with the key, so you were destined to enter the nether realm. Keep the key close, Jack. I fear it will be needed before the war is won."

"I don't have the figurine any longer." Jack paused. "Did the professor tell you what we found? Florence Upsdell?"

"She mentioned the Queen of Sakkhela, legion, and William Fargher."

"But that's not why you're here," Jack surmised. "There's something else."

Eleanore stepped away and walked to the opposite side of the rooftop, away from the plank suspended between the buildings. Unsure of whether he was supposed to follow, Jack waited a few seconds, then sauntered over and stood beside Burwick's sister. He peered through the chain-link fencing at a city covered in a thick reddish-brown haze. Stillness was an invisible wall between them, to the point where he shifted his weight uncomfortably. Eleanore wiped a tear from her eye and turned toward him.

"I have deep regret for creating the gateway in Thalren," she admitted. "Harley and Salomeh protected me from the judgment of the Cherub and the dangers of the Merikh. However, there are other occurrences during those days I have never shared with anyone."

"Secrets not even the Elders would've known." Jack's heart pounded. Whatever haunted her was worse than he'd expected. "Eleanore, whatever you've done was to protect yourself and others. But I need to know the truth so I can stop this from spiraling."

"Your mum and dad never spoke about the artifact that was left behind." Eleanore wiped her nose with the back of her hand. "However, I witnessed the artifact from the nether realm that they brought into this world."

"Whoa . . ." Jack's legs nearly buckled. "Tell me what they found, please."

"A child," she confessed. "No older than three."

"Who is the child?" Jack's heart jackhammered as his fingers ran through his mop of hair. His mind flashed to the child he'd seen in the nether realm alongside Florence, before the child vanished. When Eleanore didn't reply, he continued. "In the Dungeon of Savages, Addison told me he'd kept one of the artifacts for himself, and there would come a time when he would use it to set him free. What did he mean?"

Tears welled up in Eleanore's eyes, spilling onto her cheeks, leaving Jack stupefied. He caught his breath and exhaled slowly, reeling from an answer he'd feared all along. As Eleanore sobbed, he clumsily reached over and wrapped his arm around her shoulder. He hugged her as she wept uncontrollably. The rooftop door opened and Professor Burwick appeared, then hobbled over as a deep sadness pursed her lips.

74

"YOU'RE LEAVING AGAIN?"

Jack expected the question, and he knew any answer wouldn't make sense. He was still shocked by Eleanore's story—one he'd yet to share with anyone. After Professor Burwick ushered her sister from the rooftop, he stared across the city skyline, playing out scenarios in his mind until Vince was the first one to return from breakfast.

Mom and Addison brought back a child. If I saw the child in the nether realm, then it must be Ryder Slybourne and Florence Upsdell's own blood. How is that possible? If time is suspended in the nether realm, then once the child was brought into this world, it's possible the child aged naturally. Out of all the supernatural surprises, I can't even begin to wrap my head around this one.

His cell phone buzzed. Evac. Green.

He replied. Ditto.

"Natalie's confirmed the evacuation at Beacon Hill is happening." Jack turned and faced Vince, who leaned against the round table with his arms crossed. "I know the timing is terrible, considering the legion and the queen might appear at any second, but I need to go to Karābu."

"Well, you shouldn't go alone." Vince's brows furrowed. "Give me your cell."

Jack handed over the burner and waited while Vince dialed a number, then switched to speakerphone. After a few rings, Joseph Tobias answered cautiously. His gruff voice blurted, "Who is this?"

"Dad," Vince replied, "it's me."

"Sorry, Son." Joseph's voice softened. "I didn't recognize the number."

"It's a burner." Vince glanced at Jack for a second. "Dad, we need your help."

"Supplies or cash? I'm assuming it's urgent."

"Neither, actually. We need a ride, tonight."

"Hello, Mr. Tobias," Jack interrupted. "Sorry to bother you."

"No bother at all," Joseph replied, surprised. "Tonight. Same place, Vince."

"Got it," Vince answered. "Thanks, Dad."

"Be safe. And don't be late."

"Thank you," Jack replied. "For everything, Mr. Tobias."

"Our pleasure, Jack. You two watch your backs."

"See you tonight." Vince hung up and handed the burner over. "Now what's going on, Jack?"

Emma, Eliška, and Amina stepped out onto the rooftop, and Jack grew quiet. *I don't want everyone knowing, or else they'll all want to go.* His ears perked up at a steady buzzing, and he looked toward the sky. Vince and the others did the same as a drone hovered overhead. Jack ducked underneath the metal roof near the cots, and the others joined him.

"Is someone spying on us?" Vince asked. "I can shoot it out of the sky."

Amina answered, "No one knows where we are—right, Eliška?"

"Hold on a second," Jack interrupted. "It's carrying a box."

"Could be a bomb," Vince suggested. "Boom."

The drone lowered and dropped the box on the rooftop. Jack held his breath, hoping Vince wasn't prophetic. A few seconds passed, and nothing exploded. Jack walked out in the open, picked up the box, and carried it over to the same table where he'd been talking with Vince.

Everyone gathered around as he used a pocketknife to cut the sides. He opened the box and peered inside, then looked up at the others with a grin. On top of a stack of hoodies was a handwritten note.

"After last night," Jack read the note aloud, "Khala Salomeh thought you might appreciate a gift to remember. We stand united. Your friend, Faizan."

Jack retrieved the hoodies from inside the box. Clearly the largest one belonged to Vince, and the second largest was his own. He handed the others to Amina, knowing it was better not to guess any of the girls' sizes. His fingers touched the dretium woven into the dark shades of violet—his second hoodie of the material so far. He noticed that stitched on the right shoulder in the same color were the characters 聯合.

"Hoodie is made of dretium, Elyon's handwoven armor strong

enough to withstand Dragon Soul. Of course, my last one took a shredding at the hands of Florence Upsdell."

"The Chinese characters on the shoulder mean *unity*," Emma added.

"No houses anymore," Vince chimed in. "Only one way—together."

"Unity." Eliška slipped hers on, admiring every stitch. "I have never been given such a gift."

"How did Salomeh get our sizes perfectly?" Amina asked. "We were never fitted."

"No clue." Vince stretched his arms and smiled. "Gotta admit—feels really good."

"We saw Professor Burwick with Eleanore downstairs. Both looked a bit distraught." Emma turned her attention toward Jack. "What was that all about?"

Jack fired off another text to McNaughton. Thanks to Salomeh. A thumbs-up emoji replied within seconds.

"You know my parents brought back an artifact from the nether realm," Jack explained. "And if Addison survived the Dungeon of Savages, then I know now where he's going next."

"We're hitching a ride with my parents tonight for Karābu," Vince interrupted.

"Why Karābu?" Amina asked. "What have they hidden there?"

"It's not what they've hidden . . ." Jack struggled to keep it vague. "Listen, I'll be gone a few days and then I'll be back, no worries. Each of you needs to stick to the plan."

"We know you don't want any of us to go with you." Vince tapped his finger against the Chinese characters on his shoulder. "Jack, we're in this fight together. You're not alone."

"Put it to a vote," Amina suggested. "Jack goes alone, or one of us goes with him."

"No need for a vote," Emma replied. "I will go with Jack."

"Then the rest of us will keep the evacuations going," Eliška agreed as she turned her gaze toward Jack. "Two days, or else we will come searching for you."

"Two days," Jack confirmed. "If there were another way, I wouldn't go."

"We understand, Jack." Amina smiled. "And we trust you to do what is right."

"Thank you." Jack's checks flushed. "I trust each of you too."

"It's settled then," Vince said. "But I'll ride with you both to Karābu."

Emma pulled Jack aside and gazed into his eyes. "What did they bring back?"

"A child." He kept a deadpan stare. "Slybourne and Upsdell's child."

MISCHIEVOUS ESCAPE OF THE NINE DRAGONS

Time passed, and the attack by Criberus on the Rhoxen village was lost to legend. Florence Upsdell and Ryder Slybourne embarked on the greatest of adventures across lands and seas, searching for the nine dragons and the ancient artifact. Both fought alongside courageous warriors and gifted Cherub during the First Great War, until victory was proclaimed against the Merikh. In the beginning of a century of peace, spoils of war were brought to a realm granted to Ryder and Florence by the Elders of old.

Sakkhela was a realm of abundance where warriors escaped the nightmares haunting them. Ryder and Florence, though battle tested, were wearied by the death from their blades and the survival of unexplainable darkness lurking in other realms. Slybourne Castle was built overlooking the peaceful land, a place of refuge and memories as time passed slower than in the world of man.

If you have read these pages before, then you already know the mystery of the mischievous escape of the nine dragons and the thief was solved by Ryder and Florence, yet the artifact remained lost to Cherub and Rhoxen folklore.

Nearing the end of a hundred years, Ryder and Florence gathered with the Elders of old in the Chamber of Shadowlight, on the verge of war once again. The greatest warriors known to the Elders were to lead a vast army of the Seven Tribes against the Merikh, while the enemy's alliances remained veiled in secrecy. In the depths of Slybourne Castle, the master bladesmith forged a mighty sword touched by Elyon's hand. Florence infused the blade with her lightforce as she had done with Dragon Soul, connecting the two swords as one—dragons and titanoboas.

Across the battlefields of the world, Ryder and Florence fought valiantly. Victory deepened their true love, and they relished moments of peace while embracing a bloody war shoulder to shoulder. The love between them only grew stronger beneath the Himalayas and the peak of Everest alongside tens of thousands from the Seven Tribes of Cherub.

Unknown to Ryder, his bride was with child.

Beyond the great stone wall loomed a snowcapped mountain with steep inclines, deep valleys, glacial crevasses, and an enemy unmatched by the strongest of Cherub. When a great cavalry of the Seven Tribes charged through the gates, Ryder was shattered and slain, fracturing Florence's iron will to defend the light. Death and defeat left the Battle of Everest shrouded in myths and tavern tales.

Rampage and insanity sparked the Age of Trepidation as the Queen of Sakkhela's soul hollowed into an abyss from an unbearable loss of the legendary knight she adored beyond the sword. Enraged, she hunted allies and enemies in this world and other realms. A Siege of Plagues crossed the earth, turning vast oceans to blood, raining down hailstorms mightier than the heaviest thunderstorms, massacring animals to extinction, swarming lands with deadly locusts, and condemning to death the firstborns of all Cherub and Merikh—until total darkness blocked the sun. Betrayal sparked an unwritten war lost to the pages of the Eternal, trapping a master bladesmith, fierce warrior, and scorned lover who possessed magnificently deadly powers at the edge of the Highlands.

Elders of old gathered the mightiest Cherub among them in an epic battle, leaving Florence and her demon legion lost for eternity in the nether realm—a land of torment beyond any realm known to Cherub—where beasts were banned from the world of man, as long as light never entered beyond the Highlands.

75

THE ROSEWOOD

A fleet of HKPF tactical vehicles was parked outside the hotel behind barricades on Salisbury Road, blocking access from Nathan Road and Chatham Road South. Silver Mercedes SUVs were allowed through the blockade of armed officers and Merikh, distinguished by all-black fatigues.

Fang Xue greeted Max Tsang as he climbed out of the middle vehicle. The chief executive officer of Hong Kong stood tall in a tailored suit and a five-hundred-dollar haircut. Bodyguards shadowed as they entered a packed lobby. Fang Xue ignored the curious stares from Cherub as she ushered Tsang into the BluHouse, one of the restaurants that was permanently closed.

"You should have notified me of the barricades," Fang Xue

said. "The presence of the HKPF and Merikh right outside has many of the Cherub afraid."

"My calls were unanswered," Tsang replied, matter-of-fact. "A decision is needed to keep peace, or else there will be more than the barricades to worry about."

"The council of the highest Cherub are close to a decision. Bau remains uncooperative."

"Move him aside," Tsang pressed. "He is a child—you are the one in charge."

"I must persuade him. I cannot force him."

"Why did you appoint him as your leader? Your judgment was mistaken."

"A necessary step to protect everyone involved, and to encourage the Cherub."

"PRC demands the four be handed over—and the standoff at Beacon Hill must end."

Fang stopped pacing across the white tiled floor. "I will need more time."

"You approached me with an offer, and now the words of a boy have created chaos." Tsang put his hands on his hips. "Bau's offer is being considered; however, we will not allow all Cherub to retain their gifts. It poses too great a risk to the PRC. Only a select group will be permitted, and the rest will be given the transfusion."

"One more week," Fang Xue suggested. "If I am not able to convince Bau, then the highest Cherub will take matters into their own hands. You have my word."

Fang Xue and Tsang spun around as footsteps echoed off the tiles. Bau Hu's gaze narrowed as he eyed them suspiciously.

"I was unaware of a meeting," Bau said pointedly. "And the guards outside."

"Both unplanned." Tsang smirked. "You brought this on yourself, Bau."

"Mr. Tsang communicated the PRC's willingness to negotiate," Fang Xue added.

"Perhaps my words have fallen on deaf ears," Bau retorted. "I have seen firsthand the devastation and pain inflicted by the PRC and Merikh on innocent Hong Kongers, as well as Cherub. We will not negotiate with the PRC. You will not steal our gifts from us. And we will not turn over the four you seek."

"I suggest you reconsider." Tsang's glaring disapproval was marked by his index finger pointed at Bau. "You are forcing the PRC, Merikh, and HKPF to consider the Cherub enemies instead of allies."

"Let us speak in private," Fang Xue interrupted. "No decisions are final."

Bau refused to stand down as he eyed Tsang with contempt. He waited until the chief executive officer left the restaurant, then turned his attention toward Fang Xue. She kept her back to him and stared across the balcony outside.

"Your ego will be our downfall." Fang Xue sighed. "And will lead to great division."

"I have been anointed the Cherub leader, and I am trusted to protect us all."

"You are refusing to take counsel from any of us, and you are making a grave mistake."

"Why are you so quick to surrender us and our gifts to the PRC?"

"A truce for peace is better than a call to war." Fang Xue turned around and faced him. "Have you forgotten how Jack murdered the great Elder and killed the highest Cherub? Why are you trusting him more than any of us? You are giving those within the city false hope that they will somehow escape the bloodshed."

"Many questions remain about the massacre on Mount Hareh, but there is no time in the present to concern ourselves with the past or with political games. I will do what is necessary to save as many as possible—so you are either on my side or you will need to step aside."

"I am the only one standing between you and the Council," Fang Xue retorted. "I am your mentor; I am not one of your peers from the houses of Beacon Hill."

"We cannot negotiate, and we cannot surrender." Bau stood his ground, unwilling to be manipulated by her words. "Highest Cherub have lived in luxury far too long. We will do what is necessary to help those in need, and we will sacrifice ourselves to ensure all Cherub are protected—not only those with deep pockets and influence."

"A naive and childish decision," Fang Xue argued. "For what purpose?"

"The deadliest of dangers is coming, and we will not survive unless we choose to unite and fight." Bau eyed her closely as she kept a dead stare. "The Queen of Sakkhela has escaped the nether realm and is hunting the artifacts."

Fang Xue paused. "Has Jack told you where he has hidden the ones he has found?"

"No," Bau replied. "And I did not ask him."

"Then you are the weaker one." Fang Xue's gaze hardened. "You do not understand the destruction caused by the Reynolds family. Our Elder, who mentored us both, warned me of the threat they posed to our future. For many years they dipped their souls in both Cherub and Merikh. Each one has disobeyed the Eternal to hunt for the artifacts."

"Jack is trying to stop what is coming," Bau replied, "and he will use the artifacts to do that."

"Many believed the same about Rachel—and yet she kept secrets of her own."

"We need the faction and Beacon Hill, and right now we need Jack and Emma."

Fang Xue stepped past him and said, "Choose a side, Bau."

76

REPULSE BAY, HONG KONG ISLAND

A ParkNShop delivery van swerved around large chunks of debris spread across the district, left untouched since the night an inferno surged over the apartments and houses. Jack still couldn't believe one of the most prized areas in the world remained deserted. Vince was behind the wheel. He pulled over along Seaview Promenade and switched the headlights off.

"We're a few minutes early," Vince said in a lowered voice.

Jack stared out the window at total darkness, imagining the innocent who had died. Emma reached over and squeezed his hand, as if sensing the battle raging within. A light blinked out on the bay. Vince turned off the engine and climbed out as Jack and Emma did the same.

A speedboat was a shifting shadow in the darkness until it

slowed near the rocky shore. Joseph Tobias hopped out of the boat and landed on a low boulder jutting out from shore. Imani quickly followed and then passed him as she hurried straight for Vince. Mother and son hugged for what seemed like an eternity.

Jack watched quietly as the weight of the moment hung heavy. Vince's Kevlar vest showed his parents that their son was a warrior. *How many our age have fought in battles over the centuries for the greater good? Countless.* Joseph approached his son and shook his hand firmly, then pulled him in close. Both were wide-shouldered and built with natural athletic ability.

"We are proud of you, Son." Joseph turned toward Jack and Emma. "And we are proud of you two as well. Your bravery is keeping the fight alive."

"How are your parents, Emma?" Imani asked.

"Doing as well as can be expected, thanks. Both are helping in Kowloon."

"Last time we saw you was quite a shock." Imani stepped toward Jack. "Vince told us everything—some of it we would never believe unless we heard it from his lips."

"Mr. and Mrs. Tobias, I am sorry for everything." Jack swallowed hard. "I never wanted any of this to hurt anyone, especially your son."

"Vince tells us this fight is about making things right," Joseph replied. "You are his friend, which means you are family to us. Whatever we can do to help, we will do."

"From what I've heard, you've both done a lot already to help the faction."

"We need to go to Karābu Island," Emma said. "Sai Kung Peninsula."

"And we'll need you to anchor there for a few days," Jack added, "until we return."

"Vince will not be going with you," Imani surmised. "Eliška has stolen his heart."

"Mom!" Vince blurted. "She's just a friend."

Jack chuckled. "Understatement of the millennium."

"The faction need me to keep doing what I'm doing," Vince bantered. "That's all."

"You've always put the team first." Joseph eyed their surroundings. "We better be going before someone notices the fugitives in Repulse Bay."

"Joseph," Imani chastised. "That is not funny."

"It's kinda funny," Vince laughed. "Mom, you're hanging out with the most wanted."

A moment of humor was much needed, and it broke the tension for a few seconds. Jack and Emma stepped back as Vince and his parents embraced again. To think, when this all started none of the Tobiases believed in the Cherub or Elyon.

I don't know whether Vince's parents are total believers, but they are on the right path. Elyon, protect Vince, Eliška, Amina, and all the others while we're gone. And keep those we love guarded in your arms.

Jack fist-bumped Vince, and Emma did the same. No words needed to be exchanged. Vince waited on the shore as they climbed down to the boulder, then jumped onto the speedboat. Joseph wasted no time, revving the engine and heading into the dark. Jack watched the shoreline until Vince disappeared in blackness. He could barely see ahead until he noticed flashlights aboard the *Pathfinder*. The crew waited as the speedboat approached, then helped them on board the mega yacht.

"You are welcome to come in," Imani said cordially. "Plenty of room."

"If you don't mind," Jack replied, "I'll stay out here and get some fresh air."

"Very well." Joseph squeezed Jack's shoulder. "Our home is your home."

"Thank you."

Joseph and Imani Tobias slipped inside the galley as the mega yacht headed toward West Lamma Channel. Jack noted Emma stayed outside with him. A stabbing pain rippled down his spine as his muscles knotted. Since the nether realm, the pain had lingered even though Eden's Star was gone. He'd hoped his body would recover, but there was a piece of him that knew the damage was done. If he showed any sign to the others, then he'd be left behind in a dark room. At times he noticed a shortness of breath, so as he inhaled the ocean breeze his lungs welcomed the air.

"Pretty sweet pirate ship," he mused. "Way nicer than the rooftop cots."

"My back is still hurting." Emma's smile faded. "Jack, are you okay?"

"I'm afraid of what we're going to find," he admitted. "I've been wrong all along."

"We will take it one step at a time and stand by one another."

"Everyone thought I was going to die when we entered the nether realm, but I survived while Will nearly died." Jack clenched his jaw as tears welled up. "I've failed as the Protector of Eden's Star, and I've unlocked the nether realm. Because of me, many have died, and there's no way to make it right."

"We cannot change the past—but we can fight for today."

"I've known for a long time . . ." Jack paused. "Not much time is left."

Emma's stare grew teary eyed. "There is still hope."

77

KARĀBU ISLAND

A quick jaunt from Repulse Bay and the *Pathfinder* anchored near Karābu Island. While Joseph and Imani Tobias watched from the back deck of the yacht, the captain steered the speedboat toward the dilapidated pier of the abandoned seaside village. Jack and Emma hopped from the speedboat to the pier and trudged up the sandy beach toward the overgrown forest.

Though the forest was pitch-black, they both knew the way. Jack took the lead through the thick bamboo palms. They hiked up a winding path until they reached the pillars with characters etched into the stone. Jack stopped at the rock Areum had carved on months earlier in memory of Rachel, and he stared at the dates and scripted characters. Pathfinder, *and* hunter. He swallowed hard, struggling to hold himself together as Areum's words echoed in his mind.

"Many were lost protecting the prophecy, and now we are few."

Emma headed for the rugged chapel and entered. Jack stepped back from Rachel's memorial with his head lowered. A moment passed before he followed Emma into the forgotten sanctuary. Wooden pews were still stacked against a wall. A violet-and-gold altar remained in the center of the room. Emma used her powers to shift the podium aside and reveal the trapdoor beneath.

"How did you know?" Jack asked.

"As soon as you said you knew where your father was going." Emma pulled the trapdoor open and peered down. "When Peter trained us on the island, we were forbidden from entering the Cave of Prophets."

Jack glanced around and noticed the once-brilliant reds, purples, blues, greens, and yellows lost their shine. *"Elyon's voice replaced with humanity's vices. . . . A great and terrible day is coming because of the sins of our ancestors."* Again, Areum's voice spoke truth—demanding a renewed determination to right the wrongs of the past.

"Rachel used the Cave of Prophets when she began her quest," Jack explained. "I'll go first if you want—it's quite a drop if you've never done it before."

Emma stepped aside as he approached and knelt. On the floor, he swung his legs over, lowered them into the hole, and let go. His free fall lasted for a few seconds before he hit a smooth surface, bracing himself as he slid into the darkness. As soon as the opening appeared, he stopped himself and popped straight up without face-planting on the damp floor.

In the quietness of the cave, he heard Emma approaching

and caught her as she appeared. With his arms wrapped around her waist, he pulled her in close and kissed her gently. When he opened his eyes, he noticed a sadness in her gaze. He let go and stepped back, glancing around at the cave he remembered.

"Follow me," he said. "You'll definitely want to see what's next."

Jack kept ahead of Emma to avoid talking about what was really happening. Deeper into the cave, a turquoise glow revealed a cavernous space where a sapphire waterfall gushed against the rocks and splashed into a serene pool. Even though it was his second time in this cave, and he'd been to Charis since, the magnificent beauty of the waterfall and pool left him awestruck.

"Stunning," Emma said in a lowered voice. "Elyon's presence is in this place."

"Okay, here's where it gets a little weird."

"That does not sound comforting. Like, how weird?"

Jack held out his hand. "Trust me."

With their fingers intertwined, Jack led Emma into the pool until they were waist-deep. He remembered the frigid water as his teeth chattered. *Strange, the last time I was in here I was terrified, but I'm not afraid anymore.* His grip on Emma's hand tightened as he stared into her disarming amber eyes. Peace washed over him, unlike anything he'd felt before. He knew in that moment, perhaps more than any other, they belonged together.

"What is your fondest memory of Rachel?"

"She took me and Areum to Yuen Po Bird Garden." Emma shivered. "The night we were chosen by Peter to train in our gifts and hunt for Eden's Star. We watched Hong Kongers walk birds in their bamboo cages. I don't know why, but we laughed until midnight. Rachel knew how to keep us together—to unite us."

"Keep that memory centered in your mind." Jack knew he was repeating what Areum had said to him. "When you are ready, go all the way under."

His mind flashed to the City of Gods when he'd fought alongside Rachel for only a moment. *Until we see each other again. Believe, Jack.* Emma lowered herself beneath the surface, and Jack felt her pull him down. He kept his eyes closed, then pushed himself to the surface again. With his fingers interlaced with Emma's, they appeared in the center of an empty riverbed and trudged across until they reached the other side.

"Last time this river was raging," Jack said. "Tons of trash plowed into us."

"Sitio Veterans." Emma exhaled. "Where Rachel's search began."

"She was murdered right there." Jack pointed toward a spot twenty feet away. "We need to find her grave, Emma."

Jack led the way as they walked between the tin shanties. A concrete basketball court was alive with teens shooting hoops. Techno music played from staticky speakers outside a makeshift grocery store and nighttime bar. Along the muddy roads, fires burned beneath local street food. He searched for a landmark to guide them to the graveyard, then shuddered once he realized which road they were on.

"Wilson is a Cherub with crazy strong gifts," Jack said. "On this road he created a lightforce a hundred feet tall against Chung and the Merikh. Oh, and he's the one who rescued us from the river of trash—and his granddaughter Mahalia saved us a second time when a jeepney crashed and exploded. We thought Wilson died after we followed Mahalia to the mountains. But then he found us and took us to Vigan. All of it was a whirlwind."

"Areum was always first to challenge the rules of the highest

Cherub and the great Elder," Emma recounted. "Rachel was not far behind, while I was a bit more hesitant."

"And look at you now," Jack mused. "You're breaking all the rules."

Emma replied with a slight smile. "For the greater good."

Locals passed and eyed them curiously since they were the only ones who looked out of place. As they walked down the muddied road, Jack stopped at another shanty grocery store and entered. An elderly woman with deep wrinkles on her face looked up from watching an American talent show on a small flat-screen television.

At first the woman ignored him, but then she stared intently and her eyes flared. She slipped from behind the counter and nudged him out of the store. Without a word, she waved them on as she shuffled across the dirt. Jack and Emma followed down one alley to the next until they reached the graveyard. An uneasiness lingered as the woman pointed toward shadowy shapes of tombstones in the darkness. Before he could thank her, she disappeared down another alleyway and was gone.

"Seems like everyone knew Rachel," Emma surmised. "And she recognized you."

Jack eyed the graveyard and stopped cold. "Emma . . ."

78

A SHADOW MOVED BETWEEN aboveground columbaria within a section surrounded by tin shanties. Jack remembered the area on the opposite side near Rachel's dirt-mound grave and a road which offered access in and out of the barrio. It was a dark day when he stood over her remains one final time, and now he'd returned—right back where he'd started.

When the shadow stopped, Jack froze only a few graves behind. He'd followed the shadow stealthily and approached with caution, while Emma moved swiftly along the other side of the cemetery. *Force and flow.* In the dim light, fresh flowers on the grave left him wondering who continued to pay their respects. *Probably all of Sitio Veterans remembers what Rachel did for them.* Soulweaver slipped from his forearm into his hand as his eyes darted around. Another step forward and the shadow shifted, keeping its back to him.

"I hoped you'd come," a gravelly voice murmured. "You're predictable, Jack."

"And so are you," he bantered. "How did you escape the dungeon?"

"A dark miracle, I'm guessing." Addison coughed. "Rachel was never supposed to die."

"You didn't love her anyway," Jack pressed harder. "What do you care?"

"Michael betrayed me," Addison barked. "And woke a beast in the nether realm."

"I was the one who killed him in Charis," Jack replied, vengeance dripping from each word. "I've been to the nether realm and seen the Queen of Sakkhela."

"And you made it back alive." Addison's gaze hardened. "Where is Eden's Star?"

"She took it from me." Jack gripped Soulweaver tight. "And now she's coming to this world to find the artifacts."

Addison's shoulders slouched as he coughed hard. "Rachel was the stronger one."

"You've been given a second chance."

"A second chance to take what was stolen from me," Addison rebuked. "Don't you want revenge against the ones who took Rachel from us, Son?"

"You never cared about either of us," Jack seethed, knowing his father was testing him. "Even though you messed with my visions, I know it wasn't Emma or Mom who ended her life. But you know who murdered Rachel."

"For a while I was convinced the Merikh Council were

responsible. In fact, most probably assumed it to be true until I killed them all." Addison held out his blackened and disfigured fingers. "What remained of my gifts was stripped from me in the Dungeon of Savages, and only then did I realize who else gained from Rachel's death. I tried to tell you, Cherub and Merikh turned me into who I am."

Words from Rachel's notebook flashed before Jack's eyes, and he knew there was no denying what she'd assumed. *Peter held back the truth—which haunts me now that I know. If I live beyond this journey, I will ask the Elders why. There are those who have turned from the Cherub, yet their gifts have remained powerful.* "You're talking about Peter Leung and the highest Cherub."

"Rachel was a threat to more than the Merikh. Without his gifts, Peter was too weak to stop her from uncovering his sins, so he needed another with greater power to do his bidding—someone who was loyal to him beyond the Cherub."

Jack stopped cold. "Fang Xue."

"She is the only one strong enough." Addison's dark eyes shifted toward Soulweaver, and a sly grin pursed his lips. "The Rod of Elyon can bring Rachel back, Jack."

Jack held up the rod. "You also know it by another name."

"Soulweaver," Addison whispered. "Light and dark know the power of the rod."

"Eden's Star guided me to Charis to find the Rod of Elyon." Jack harnessed his anger, allowing himself a moment to muster up the courage to ask one final question. "Tell me who Rachel was. Was she my sister?"

"You know the answer," Addison replied, stone-cold. "She was an artifact, but she was so much more. She was taken from both of us."

Lightning struck the graveyard, shattering stone and concrete. Legion swept across Sitio Veterans, shrieking and squealing. Jack scrambled behind a columbarium while Addison hobbled in the opposite direction. Jack peered around the side of the concrete grave as Florence Upsdell descended from the moonlit sky.

He whispered, "Where is Emma?"

Legion swarmed the graveyard but never attacked. He shot a quick glance to his left where Emma was crouched low. *She must be holding them back.* A split second later, Florence landed in the graveyard as Addison stumbled onto his knees. Her eyes were ablaze as she held Dragon Soul and Scarlet Widow, one in each hand. Addison was raised off the ground, bellowing in excruciating pain, when she stepped closer.

Adrenaline and fear pumped through Jack's body, and Soulweaver hummed in his grasp. Legion's shrieks and squeals were deafening, leaving those in Sitio Veterans haunted and hiding. Jack imagined after the last time, no one was going to face off with these dark forces—Chung was minor-league compared to legion and the Queen of Sakkhela.

"A thief in the night," Florence's voice resounded, "who stole my bloodline."

Addison coughed and gagged as his body went limp in the air. Jack watched Florence throw his levitating father across the graveyard, sending him slamming into a headstone. Crumpled on the ground, Addison was motionless. Florence walked toward him, then stopped and glanced up at the legion—who were frantically attempting to break through the force field. She turned toward the fresh flowers spread across Rachel's grave as Dragon Soul and Scarlet Widow erupted with black fire and crimson flames.

She's going to kill him—what am I supposed to do?

Soulweaver hummed as a white light wrapped around the rod. Whether Jack was ready or not, the rod made the decision. He darted across the graveyard, and the Windstrikers flew from Florence's belt. Soulweaver spun between his fingers faster and faster as the Windstrikers attacked. Sonic percussive pulses burst from the rod, narrowly missing the dretium war fans. He slid on his knees as the Windstrikers savagely attacked the spinning rod. Without thinking, Jack let go of the rod and rolled off to the side while the rod kept the Windstrikers locked in battle.

No time to figure out how that worked—keep moving.

Addison groggily rolled onto his knees and stared up at Florence as she wielded the most powerful swords ever created: Dragon Soul, forged by her own hands, and Scarlet Widow— a blade crafted in the hottest fires with a touch from Elyon. Jack was defenseless as he raced toward them, with no clue what he was going to do next. With chaos swirling around him, he kept his wits while he looked for Eden's Star. Florence spun around and glared into his eyes. A chill shot down his spine as her stare intensified while Soulweaver kept the Windstrikers captured in its power.

"No other has escaped the nether realm," she seethed. "Which tribe is yours?"

"I don't belong to a tribe," Jack replied shakily. "I'm an outlier."

Florence pointed Dragon Soul at Addison. "You are part of his bloodline."

"He's my father." Jack pointed toward the mound of dirt. "And she is my sister."

Florence's eyes narrowed. "My only child."

His mind riffled through a thousand ways he could die, attempting to keep Florence sidetracked a few seconds longer. "Rachel is still my sister."

Florence held up her hand and attempted to retrieve the Windstrikers *and* Soulweaver. The glint in her eyes was a dead giveaway: she recognized the rod. To his surprise, Soulweaver didn't budge, not even in the face of the Windstrikers and the queen's force. Out of the corner of his eye, he caught sight of Emma moving swiftly between the graves. In that moment, he recognized the strength of her gifts as she continued to keep the legion beyond the force field.

Addison's cold voice was weak. "Don't let her take the rod, Jack."

"I will take Soulweaver *and* the boy," Florence said calmly. "He will be your sacrifice for the sins you committed against the house of Slybourne."

Before Jack could make a run for it, he was lifted off the ground, helpless within Florence's powers. Without warning, a barrage of white light punched through the night. He fell to the ground as Florence was ambushed by Emma, who attacked stronger than Jack had ever seen. Her eyes were stark white, her palms were glowing, and she wasn't backing down. Florence turned her attention to Emma, then charged as if she had returned to the Battle of Everest.

79

A FLICKER CAUGHT JACK'S ATTENTION, and instantly he recognized Eden's Star. He scrambled to his feet and darted toward the compass—shining from the hilt of Scarlet Widow—as Florence hunted Emma. Before he reached the queen, she spun around and launched him backward. He crashed across the top of a columbarium and landed facedown. Searing agony rippled through his spine. Soulweaver flew across the graveyard into his grasp, and a surging energy flowed through his fingers into every muscle and heartbeat. The Windstrikers were loose, streaking across the skies searching for mayhem.

Jack gripped Soulweaver like a sword and charged with the Windstrikers chasing him. The feverish phoenixes engraved on the war fans spit fire. Sparks flared as Emma dodged Florence's attack and forced the Windstrikers off their path, sending them spiraling through the graveyard. Florence stood between Emma and Jack, swinging Dragon Soul and Scarlet Widow with deadly force, unafraid.

Legion burst through Emma's force field, swarming and attacking relentlessly. Besieged on all sides, Jack flowed with the rod's power in every strike. Though outnumbered, he refused to surrender as long as Emma kept fighting. Black flames struck at the legion, sending them scattering. *Where'd that come from?*

Florence whipped around, unleashing Dragon Soul and Scarlet Widow, sending the two-headed dragon and titanoboas to devour their prey. Emma's lightforce surged against the dragon and serpents with a magnificent force as the ground rumbled violently.

In a flash, legion and the Queen of Sakkhela vanished.

Out of breath, Jack lowered Soulweaver. "What just happened?"

"Your father . . ." Emma rushed past him. "His lightforce kept the legion away."

"I thought he didn't have any lightforce left."

"Jack, I am telling you that he found it somewhere within."

Bloodied, Jack snapped out of a daze and hurried over. He knelt beside Addison, whose charcoaled and crooked fingers grabbed at a crimson stain spreading across his chest as he leaned against a headstone, struggling for every breath. Emma reached out and touched Addison's bloodied clothes. His vindictive eyes faded to a sorrowful fright. Blood trickled down his mouth and chin. With her head lowered, Emma prayed in another tongue.

Wide-eyed, Jack couldn't understand what he was supposed to do. He'd wanted vengeance against his father for so long, but instinctively he reached out and grabbed Addison's hand. With clenched teeth, he kept his eyes locked on his father. He shook as he squeezed harder, struggling with waves of anger, rage, sorrow, and pity.

In a blink, the Executioner was gone from this side.

Emma opened her eyes and glanced up at Jack as he gathered the nerve to close his father's eyes and let go. With his hands clasped, he tried to stop shaking as he exhaled long and hard. A lump lodged in his throat, leaving him battling against the past.

"After all he's done . . . he protected us. Why?"

"I am sorry, Jack." Emma shook her head slowly. "What did he say about Rachel?"

"Finally, we know the truth." Jack's heart pounded. "Rachel is the child."

"Now the queen knows she is dead." Emma paused. "She will unleash her vengeance against Cherub and Merikh—those who destroyed the family she loved."

Jack stood and turned his back on Addison. "Emma, we can't leave him like this."

"We will bury him," Emma replied, "and then we must leave."

A crowd of Filipinos appeared from the shanties and alleyways, cautiously peering around to be certain the chaos was over. They gathered in the graveyard, surrounding Jack and Emma. Commotion in the rear of the crowd caught everyone's attention, and they stepped aside, allowing an elderly man to make his way through. In the darkness, Jack didn't recognize the man until he was close.

In Tagalog, Wilson gave orders to several others, who hurried past the crowd toward the shanties. Jack was paralyzed as Wilson glanced at Addison's body, then squeezed Jack's arm. Wilson nodded once, which was all Jack needed to know it would be done.

Strange, he found himself struggling to move while all eyes were locked on him.

Still in disbelief, he squeezed Wilson's shoulder as a sign he understood. He glanced around for Mahalia but couldn't see her anywhere. An innocent young girl didn't need to witness the aftermath of another lost battle.

"Wilson," Jack said somberly. *"Salamat."*

Jack stepped away and marched directly between the headstones until he reached the Windstrikers, which were pierced into concrete. He pulled the dretium war fans free and handed them to Emma.

"I will keep these with me," she said quietly.

"Good idea." Jack breathed in the surreal moment. "Emma . . ."

"There will be time to grieve—and question—but not tonight."

"Right—the night is not over."

Jack and Emma raced through Sitio Veterans, cutting down one alleyway to the next while following the route the woman had led them through earlier. Within a matter of minutes, both reached the barren trash river where the gateway had brought them.

"I don't know how to get to Karābu," Jack confessed.

Emma retrieved two silver coins from her pocket. "These are all I have left."

"We don't even know if this gateway will take us back."

"Only one way to find out for certain."

Jack grabbed her hand as she dropped the coins into a puddle. One thought struck a split second before the night pulled a curtain on Sitio Veterans.

Addison died where Rachel chose to live.

80

BENEATH A FULL MOON, Jack and Emma fell from the sky and plunged into the ocean, then sank deep before swimming to the surface. Both treaded water as they got their bearings. Even though it was the middle of the night, they could see the abandoned village on Karābu. A speedboat left white water in its wake as it approached. The *Pathfinder* crew slowed the boat alongside and pulled them aboard. By the time they reached the mega yacht, large towels were ready and wrapped over their shoulders.

Jack whispered to Emma, "You okay?"

"We cannot fight legion and Florence alone." Emma unzipped her hoodie slightly, revealing the dretium war fans beneath. "The Windstrikers will be helpful, but we will need every last Cherub and faction to fight too—including the highest Cherub."

"Florence might already be in Hong Kong to hunt for the

Rhoxen Stone and Slybourne's shield—which means the war has started without us."

Joseph Tobias was on deck waiting when they climbed aboard. "Mr. Tobias, how long have we been gone?" Jack asked.

He checked his watch. "Nearly six hours."

"We need to go to Quarry Bay—the faster, the better."

Joseph relayed the orders to his captain, and the rest of the crew sprang into action, raising the anchor and setting sail at top speed. Jack slumped down on a chair exhausted, physically and emotionally. His mind replayed the magnitude of the fight and the unexplainable sacrifice Addison made in his final moments. Emma sat beside Jack with her eyes locked on the blackness around them, then slowly placed her hand on his leg and squeezed.

"Would you two like dry clothes?" Joseph asked.

"No thanks." Jack ran his fingers over the dretium hoodie. "It'll dry soon."

"I'm fine too," Emma added. "Thank you, Mr. Tobias—for everything."

Joseph nodded before heading inside the lounge while *Pathfinder* barreled across West Lamma Channel. Jack's head pounded, and Soulweaver squeezed his forearm. Tension was thick as he dug his elbows into his thighs.

"Rachel was the chosen one from the prophecy," he whispered. "She was supposed to find Eden's Star and lead the Cherub into this war."

"The prophecy was never meant to be about me or Eliška," Emma agreed.

"Eliška is a descendent of Slybourne, so the prophecy still applies to her."

"The writings were meant for Rachel—she is the child of Slybourne and Upsdell."

"We can't tell anyone, Emma." He groaned as he pulled himself up and paced across the deck. Unsettled about what was ahead, he was a bit disoriented by Addison's revelation. *When Rachel hid the figurine and map inside the wall in Sham Shui Po, did she know who she was? Did Mom tell her and trust her to keep the secret safe?* With the questions lingering, Jack realized that Rachel may never have known the truth before she died. *It doesn't matter if she wasn't blood, she's my only sister. No matter what happens, that will never change the love we had for one another. But the truth about Rachel will leave the Cherub and faction divided even more.* He ran his fingers through his wet hair as he turned and walked back. "Only you and I will ever know the truth. Agreed?"

"A secret buried in Sitio Veterans." Emma stood and followed him as he stepped over to the railing. "Peter Leung must have known who Rachel was before she died."

"When she started questioning his intentions, his lies fell apart. He lost his powers years earlier when he stole Eden's Star and the map. So he needed someone to stop Rachel from uncovering the truth about what he had done—and the fractured Elders." Jack weighed Addison's words, knowing he'd come to the same conclusion. "Rachel was killed by a power more dangerous than the gifts Michael Chung corrupted for the Merikh—someone loyal to Peter Leung above all others."

Emma leaned forward and whispered, "Fang Xue?"

Jack harnessed the rage boiling beneath his skin. "She's the only one strong enough."

With waves crashing against the hull, the stars glided by as the mega yacht sailed near Sunshine Island. Emma leaned into him with her head pressed against his shoulder. Jack wrapped his arm around her and pulled her close. For a while only the hum of the engine and splashing of the waves broke through the silence between them.

Jack's gaze hardened once *Pathfinder* passed Belcher Bay and neared Star Ferry. All the lights on the mega yacht shut off, and the vessel slowed. At a slower speed, *Pathfinder* drifted into Victoria Harbour in the dead of night. Along Kowloon and Hong Kong Island, The Peninsula, the Rosewood, skyscrapers, and high-rise apartments were completely dark. No iconic neon signs. No lights in the windows. No streetlights. No headlights. Just pitch-blackness.

Six hours is an eternity when Eden's Star whisks one away.

"I got a bad feeling about this," Jack said. "Doesn't look right, Emma."

"Faith of a mustard seed gives us strength in our moment of need," Emma replied. "Elyon, grant us courage to defeat the darkness around us."

"I'd like a double dose, please."

Joseph and Imani Tobias stepped from the lounge, where the lights remained off, onto the deck. One look at their eyes and Jack recognized fear beating beneath their skin. Not only were they afraid of what they were witnessing, but he guessed they were even more fearful of what it meant for Vince.

"Once you leave us in Quarry Bay, head for open waters." Jack noticed the reluctance spread across their faces. "I promise you, I will find Vince and keep him alive."

"We are not only concerned about our son," Joseph said.

"You have proven your willingness to risk your lives," Emma chimed in. "However, the hours ahead will be the most dangerous. Please, listen to Jack and wait for a signal to know when the battle is over."

"Battle . . ." Imani blurted. "How can this be?"

"I'm sure Vince will tell you everything," Jack answered. "Until then . . ."

"Head for open waters," Joseph finished. "We trust you, Jack."

Pathfinder drifted past Central, Admiralty, and Wan Chai. Jack pictured the spot where they'd taken the gateway to Thalren with Xui Li and realized it was in the direct line of sight on the day he and Emma entered the Clock Tower near Star Ferry. *I had a view of the gateway to Thalren that day—and had no idea.* No doubt each district marked a piece of his life in one way or another—whether good or bad. In spite of what he'd been warned, he'd survived the City of Gods, the Highlands, Charis, and the nether realm—barely.

His heartbeat quickened as flashing memories struck like lightning. He gripped the railing and mustered up another ounce of tenacity. When Eden's Star was ripped from his body, he'd hoped to feel stronger yet feared his soul and spirit might be left cold and empty. But the opposite was true. Though the scars on his chest remained, and his body was failing, he stared into the night struck by how Elyon granted him enough strength to keep going in his weakness. His soul wasn't left cold and empty because his spirit burned with determination.

Pathfinder slowed even more and pulled alongside a concrete barrier near Quarry Bay. In the distance, shrieks echoed and sent shivers across those on deck. Joseph and Imani Tobias were terrified, while Jack and Emma remained determined. *Pathfinder*'s crew kept buoys between the mega yacht and the concrete barrier. The crew hoisted Jack and Emma high enough until their fingertips grabbed hold of the top of the wall. While Emma pulled herself up with ease, Jack struggled a bit more until she grabbed his arm and helped him the rest of the way.

Jack glanced down at the harbor and watched *Pathfinder* drift away from the concrete wall like a ghost ship lost at sea. He'd made a promise to Joseph and Imani Tobias, one he intended to keep—no matter the cost.

81

JACK AND EMMA'S QUICK PACE through Quarry Bay left him breathing hard as they cut down one street to the next. An eerie silence spread across the district, where abandoned cars were ablaze. Shattered glass was scattered across the sidewalks from blown-out apartment windows. Bone-chilling shrieks sliced through the smoke and fire.

Legion are hunting.

With their heads on a swivel, Jack and Emma slowed as they reached a corner one block from the eighteen-story multicolored buildings which served as the faction's base.

"She's being drawn to the artifacts," Jack said, out of breath. "Eden's Star is guiding her to Soulweaver, the Rhoxen Stone, Slybourne's shield, and the Windstrikers—so we're both a living, breathing target." He retrieved his burner cell, then dialed. *Beep. Beep. Beep.* "No connection or signal."

"Salomeh hid Slybourne's shield at Patel Custom Tailors," Emma replied. "If legion are searching on Hong Kong Island, then she is being drawn to the Rhoxen Stone."

"We don't know whether Salomeh has moved the shield," Jack suggested. "Do you really think she would be keeping it somewhere out of her sight?"

A familiar chill raised the hair on his arms, sending him ducking behind a burning vehicle with Emma alongside. Legion soared overhead and circled the buildings in a frantic frenzy. *Are those the same legion who shadowed Florence in the nether realm and Sitio Veterans—or are there thousands of others?* Another swarm appeared from Central. Skeletal onyx beasts armed with deadly spears neared Quarry Bay, leaving Jack and Emma crouched low.

"Definitely a lot more than before," Jack whispered. "Because of Eden's Star?"

"Impossible to know how many legion have followed their queen."

Jack's forearm twitched, but Soulweaver remained wrapped snugly. He noticed a few dead bodies near a flight of steps leading to the courtyard. He was even more on edge when figures moved across the square in formation. Emma must have noticed the same, as her palms glowed softly. Legion landed on the streets with lava dripping from their fangs, burning the concrete.

These ones look way stronger than Asiklua when we faced him in Nanimi.

Within the smoke billowing from charred vehicles, rapid gunfire erupted as shadows moved onto the streets. *Faction.* Jack glanced at Emma, waiting for her cue. She turned her attention toward him until her eyes stared into the core of his soul. Soulweaver slipped into his grasp as her palms glowed bright. Bullets pinged off metal and ricocheted off concrete. As the rod hummed with pure energy, Jack moved first and ducked around a vehicle.

Shadows dropped to the ground, while legion crashed into buildings, scattering shards of glass and debris in all directions. He stabbed one of the skeletal beasts as he darted toward the center of the battle. Emma moved alongside, unleashing bursts of lightforce striking down the deadly demons. Gunfire rattled relentlessly. Soulweaver spun between Jack's fingers, and he surrendered to the power of the rod. He forced the legion back with a tornadic thrust. He and Emma fought shoulder to shoulder as faction moved in swiftly behind, firing semiautomatic rounds.

Shrieks, shrills, and squeals were bone-chilling and deafening.

Legion surrounded as Jack stepped forward, grasping for one more ounce of bravery against the ravenous appetite of demons desperate to devour their prey. Fearless, Emma moved ahead with frosted eyes glowing white and arms spread wide. Streets rumbled and foundations cracked as her blinding lightforce summoned a myriad of colors streaking across the skies from the direction of Happy Valley. Energy from Soulweaver shot like a lightning rod and wrapped around Emma's lightforce, radiating with multi-colored beams before exploding in a glorious light.

Emma's gifts are strong enough to summon the power of Soulweaver. I'll bet even lightforcers evacuating through the mausoleum too. Elyon, she is definitely the strongest among us.

Awestruck, Jack lowered Soulweaver as the streets returned to remnants of a war zone, where dead skeletal beasts and faction were left in the aftermath. Even though the attack was over, the adrenaline surged through his veins. *It's only the beginning.* He spun around when a hand grabbed his shoulder.

"Vince . . ." Jack blurted.

"You two arrived in the nick of time," he replied. "We'd said our last prayers, bro."

"When did the attacks begin? How many—?"

"A few hours ago the power cut off, and the fight was on." Vince kept the semiautomatic in his grip. "Not long after those beasts attacked, Eliška used the Rhoxen Stone as a Hail Mary, but it left the rest of us sitting ducks while the beasts spread like wildfire. She hid the stone, and we grabbed what weapons we could to defend ourselves, leaving enough time for her, Amina, Professor Burwick, Faizan, and others to escape the district."

Emma stepped over. "What about Happy Valley?"

"As soon as time started again, we split up into three teams. Faizan led one to Happy Valley, and another was commanded by Eliška." Vince nodded at the tactical team who guarded their surroundings. "We stayed behind to give them a head start. Definitely had our hands full."

"The Queen of Sakkhela and legion are hunting the artifacts," Jack explained.

"We figured the hornet's nest was poked . . ." Vince paused. "What about my parents?"

"Both are safe," he reassured. "We told them to hightail it to open waters."

"Mom must be freaking out—Dad's always kept his emotions in check." Vince swapped an ammo clip on his weapon. "Eastern District is the nearest gateway." He waved the faction unit over and waited until they gathered around. "We're headed to Beacon Hill. Rendezvous with Faizan and his unit at Happy Valley. Protect the gateway."

82

THE ROSEWOOD

Bau woke in his bed and sat straight up. He slipped out from under the covers and groggily shuffled over to the window. Wide-eyed, he was caught off guard by flames erupting near Central across Victoria Harbour as another explosion boomed. Without hesitation, he put on his jeans and sneakers and grabbed a T-shirt on the way out the door.

In the hallway, several others poked their heads out from their rooms with a concerned look. Bau walked briskly toward an exit, and once he was in the stairwell, he bounded down the stairs in a hurry. He knew whatever was happening on Hong Kong Island was serious—and he couldn't shake the sense it had to do with Jack and Emma. He reached the lobby where several of the highest

Cherub council were gathered, as well as his parents, who were still in their pajamas.

"Lightforcers on every floor," Bau ordered. "Benders at every entrance and exit. And shut off the power to keep all lights off."

"Son, perhaps the disturbance is the HKPF and Merikh clashing with the faction," Winston Hu suggested. "We must keep everyone calm, or else there will be turmoil."

"Whatever is happening in Central will make its way to Kowloon." Bau glanced at the highest Cherub, who stood stunned. "Listen to me—we need to be ready." He waited until those who had gathered left before he pulled his parents aside. "Lightforcers and benders who are not stationed on the floors or by the doors need to prepare to leave."

"What do you mean, *leave*?" Betty Hu asked. "Bau, you are scaring us."

"Everyone should be terrified," he replied pointedly. "The battle has begun."

"Battle?" Betty's brows raised. "What are you talking about?"

"Please, do as I am asking because there is no time to explain."

"I will round up as many as possible," Winston said. "We will meet back in the lobby."

Bau hastily checked the empty restaurants and conference rooms, then took the stairs to the second floor. Cherub stepped out from their rooms, even more concerned than the ones on his floor, but he ignored them. He stopped outside one of the rooms, banged on the door, and waited. No answer.

"Where can she be at this hour?" Bau muttered.

Thirty minutes passed as he checked the lobby, restaurants, and conference rooms again. Fang Xue was nowhere to be found. Bau paced the lobby, attempting to make sense of what he was supposed to do next. He knew about the Queen of Sakkhela, but as far as he was aware there were no artifacts in the hotel.

"Bau," Winston called out, "we have spread the word. Now we wait."

"Why do you need the lightforcers and benders?" Betty asked.

"We are going to Beacon Hill," Bau replied. "Before daybreak they will need us."

While his parents waited in the lobby, Bau entered The Legacy House and headed straight for the floor-to-ceiling sliding doors overlooking Victoria Harbour. A moment passed as he stared across the water at a darkened skyline. Flames glowed from Central through Wan Chai, nearing Causeway Bay and spreading toward Quarry Bay.

For the next hour, Bau never left the window as his father entered several times with updates on the number of lightforcers and benders who waited in the lobby.

"Did the highest Cherub listen to my orders?" Bau asked.

"Lightforcers on every floor," Winston answered. "Benders at every door and exit."

Bau kept his gaze fixed ahead. "Dad, we need a force field around the Rosewood."

"Your mum has always been better than me at that one— however, we will use some of the lightforcers and benders who are already in the lobby."

"We need it right away," Bau pressed. "I should have left you both in Tai Tam."

"Nonsense," Winston protested. "Where else would we rather be than with you?"

"Thanks." Bau sensed his lightforce being disturbed. "I'll be there shortly."

Bau's attention faded for a second, boomeranged by dark silhouettes flying across the harbor. He raced past his father out of the restaurant and reached a packed lobby.

"Silence!" Bau shouted. "Not a word. Not a glimmer of light."

Bau stepped close to the hotel entrance and eyed the HKPF and Merikh stationed at the barricades. He flinched when legion appeared, sweeping the officers away. He heard gasps behind him and held up his hand, hoping they could see him in the dark. Steadfast, he remained close to the window and watched intently.

Legends of the Battle of Everest had seemed like campfire folklore on Karābu when Peter Leung regaled them with his endless tales. But the fallen angels who battled against Cherub on Everest were no longer in the nether realm. He couldn't believe his eyes as countless legion passed in front of the Rosewood, leaving everyone inside the lobby frozen like statues.

Bau's gaze narrowed as an army of legion stopped on the street directly outside of the hotel entrance—eight- to nine-foot-tall skeletal demons wielding spears with powers he couldn't begin to imagine. A half-living destrier horse with long mangy silver hair trotted into view, a woman riding on its back. In the moonlight shining down on the street, the woman was mesmerizing, with glowing locks of flaming-red hair draping over her shoulders. Bau dared not speak her name aloud, as she might hear his whispers.

Florence Upsdell.

The Queen of Sakkhela pulled on the reins, and the mangy destrier obeyed. She glanced around, then turned her sights on the lobby of the Rosewood. Bau was tempted to allow his lightforce to glow, but instead he clenched his fists. He could sense the tension and fear of those who were crouched and hiding throughout the lobby. Flames spewed from the horse's nostrils but didn't burst into an inferno.

Elyon, spare us from her wrath.

Florence Upsdell kicked the horse in the sides and whipped the reins. Legion continued on as she rode down Salisbury Road. Bau craned his neck and pressed his cheek against the glass until he was certain the legion and the queen were gone.

"If we travel through the tunnels," Bau whispered, "we will be too late."

83

KOWLOON, HONG KONG

Daybreak fought against gunmetal clouds as the Jetstream 41 door cracked open. Emma climbed out first, followed by Jack and Vince—whose broad shoulders barely fit through the door. Moments earlier they'd entered an abandoned Sai Wan Ho Market in the Eastern District and traveled through the gateway with the last few silver coins Professor Burwick left with Vince. All three headed down the old runway strip overbuilt with restaurants, retail shops, and warehouses.

How do we know whether Faizan and the other faction units survived?

"About five miles to the Rosewood," Vince said. "A real-life Lion's Den."

At the end of the runway path, a quick walk turned into a fast jog as all three kept a steady speed. Once they passed the sports park, they turned on to Shing Kai Road and picked up a few more paces. Jack was winded after the second mile and started to lag behind. He remembered barely being able to sit on the minibus bumper in Kati Pahari while Vince and Emma were equal competitors in kabaddi. So, the mere fact that he kept them in his sights was a victory. He glanced ahead as their rhythm remained synced.

"Hey!" Jack blurted as a piercing cramp caused him to halt. "Hold on."

Vince and Emma stopped at the same time and turned around. The clock was ticking, and he was the one slowing them down. One look and he knew they were amping to go even faster. He groaned loudly, then ran toward them and passed in a hurry.

He called over his shoulder, "Well, what are you waiting for?"

Within seconds Emma and Vince were alongside him before sprinting ahead again. He pushed himself harder, gasping for every breath while his muscles burned as the road wrapped around and turned into To Kwa Wan Road.

Too bad Soulweaver can't transport me like Eden's Star.

Beneath Fat Kwong Street Flyover, homeless people were asleep on the streets. Poverty in Hong Kong had been widely known for years yet kept from the tourist hot spots. Since the lockdowns, most of the city had been turned upside down, and living on the streets became normalized. Jack slowed as he passed a Kowloon Motor Bus depot, then whistled. For a second time, Emma and Vince spun around. They shrugged, then jogged back.

"I've got a better idea than a third heart attack," Jack said, breathing hard. "We'll need wheels anyway, right?"

"Do you even know how to drive?" Vince asked. "A double-decker?"

"I'm a natural." Jack smirked. "Ask Emma."

"He has been behind the wheel before," Emma replied, "but he doesn't drive as well when the double-decker is upside down."

"Everyone's got jokes," he mused. "C'mon."

In the early morning, the KMB depot was unlocked, and the entrance to the parking lot was open. Jack, Emma, and Vince snuck between the double-deckers parked in the lot. Jack pried a bus door open, and all three slipped inside. He checked around the driver's seat, searching until he found a key underneath, on the floor.

"We're in business," he said, semi-confidently. "Better buckle up."

Jack turned the key in the ignition and the engine rumbled. He shifted into gear and eased off the brakes, wondering whether he'd make it out of the parking lot without sideswiping the other buses. Everyone breathed a sigh of relief as the double-decker turned slowly onto Hung Lok Road. With both hands gripping the wheel, Jack pressed the accelerator a bit harder as the double-decker swerved onto the Hung Hom Bypass.

"Watch out!" Vince shouted.

Ahead were the shattered remains of a barricade across Salisbury Road. *Brake or accelerate.* Jack punched the pedal and the double-decker barreled down the street. Emma and Vince grabbed hold of the railings with both hands. The front of the double-decker burst through what was left of the barricade, then swerved onto Salisbury Road.

"Are we having fun yet?" Jack yelled. "I think I'm getting the hang of it."

"Keep it on four wheels," Vince said. "And watch your turns."

While he itched to go faster, Jack slowed the bus just enough as they approached another barricade that had been destroyed. He glanced out the windows to see bodies strewn on both sides of the street, leaving his hands shaking as he gripped the steering wheel tight.

"We are too late," Emma said. "Legion passed through already."

"We'll see them soon enough if Eden's Star leads Florence Upsdell to Soulweaver and the Windstrikers. Hopefully, the compass keeps the legion and the queen focused on the other artifacts so they don't see us coming."

A few blocks further down Salisbury, Jack pulled the double-decker over outside the Rosewood. He turned off the headlights but kept the engine idling. From behind the wheel he could see the entrance to the hotel.

"All the lights are off," Vince noted. "Power outage?"

"Hiding," Emma replied. "If there are enough Cherub remaining with gifts, then it is possible there is a force field around the Rosewood."

"Would've been nice for the faction to have a force field," Vince said.

Jack slid out from behind the wheel. "Let's go find out if anyone's left."

A banging on the bus door startled them, making Jack jump backward. He had to search before he found the right lever. All three braced themselves as the door hissed open.

"Nightingale and Rowell." Bau stood alone on the sidewalk. "Always tardy to the party."

84

THE DOUBLE-DECKER WAS packed with highest Cherub rounded up by Winston and Betty Hu, seated and standing shoulder to shoulder in the center aisle. Jack shifted into gear and the bus lurched forward before jerking to a sudden stop.

"Stay clear of Nathan Road," Bau said. "Take Hong Chong Road instead."

Jack glanced at a screen beside the steering wheel, which displayed a camera view directly behind the bus. He cranked the steering wheel and inched forward until he revved the engine enough to hop the curb. His cheeks flushed as he heard grumbling and muttering echo throughout the bus.

"You've got this, *Fast and Furious*," Vince mused sarcastically. "Might be safer to walk."

"Game on," Jack retorted. "Hang on for your life."

He shifted into reverse and punched the accelerator a bit more aggressively than he wanted, sending the double-decker slamming into a parked HKPF tactical vehicle. He ignored the outbursts, shifted into drive, and hit the gas harder. The front bumper scraped across several other vehicles, but he kept going until the gears shifted automatically.

Headed down Salisbury Road toward Chatham Road South, Jack listened to Bau recount what occurred at the Rosewood. In return, Vince filled them in on the attacks on Hong Kong Island. All the while, Jack and Emma remained tight-lipped about Sitio Veterans.

Tires screeched around corners as the double-decker leaned from one side to another before exiting off Princess Margaret Road toward Kwun Tong. Passengers hung on tight as the bus barreled deeper into Kowloon City. Jack gripped the steering wheel, crashing through every barricade and checkpoint. HKPF and Merikh were surprised, but they moved swiftly to chase after the bus. Jack glanced in the rearview monitor as flashing lights stretched far behind.

"How will Beacon Hill know we're on their side?" Vince asked.

"We will make it known." Emma nodded at Bau, who smiled slightly. "Right?"

Emma and Bau pushed their way through the aisle while Jack kept his attention fixed straight ahead. *If we can make it to Tin Kwong Road, then we have a chance. My second driving lesson in a double-decker, and it's going better than expected.* He never saw the tactical vehicle charging from the cross street before it slammed into the side of the bus. The double-decker veered violently, two wheels lifting off the pavement. Jack struggled to regain control until Vince reached over and grabbed the wheel, steering in the opposite direction.

Highest Cherub screamed and shouted as the two wheels bounced hard against the pavement. *Too many months in luxury while everyone else struggled. Maybe this'll be a little wake-up call.* He knew it was a dark thought amid the chaos, but it was true. He glanced at the monitor and eyed another camera angle from the top of the double-decker.

"Emma and Bau are on the roof," Jack relayed to Vince. "Mental Disruptor 2.0."

Vince gripped the handrail and peered over his shoulder. "Beaut bonza, bro."

"Tin Kwong Road," Jack called out as he swerved onto the street. "Nearly there."

On the monitor, Jack could see Emma and Bau kneeling with their lightforces glowing in their palms. Jack pressed the accelerator to the floor, punching the horn when muzzle flashes appeared. The double-decker barreled toward the gates while HKPF and Merikh, who surrounded the entrance to Beacon Hill, reacted with bullets ricocheting off metal before cracking the windshield. Emma and Bau released their lightforces from above, pulverizing the front gates of Beacon Hill.

Amid the pandemonium, lightforcers and benders guarding the grounds allowed the double-decker to pass but prevented HKPF and Merikh from breaching the entrance. Jack slammed on the brakes, sending the double-decker skidding to a stop with tires screeching and tread marks streaking behind. Smoke billowed from the rear of the battered bus as he pulled the lever. Highest Cherub hurried out the exits and gathered near the Main Hall.

"Well done, *Gran Turismo*." Vince slapped Jack on the back. "Let's not do *that* again."

Jack and Vince were the last ones off the bus and moved to stand beside Bau and Emma. Headmaster Fargher and McNaughton rushed out the door of the Main Hall. Jack glanced up at the clock tower as they bounded down the concrete steps.

Countdown stopped—so this is it.

"We need to take positions and establish a stronger force field," Bau ordered.

Jack couldn't deny that Bau commanded the highest Cherub with authority, moving them into action regardless of their age or status. Groups were quickly divided up and joined the lightforcers and benders already on the grounds of Beacon Hill.

"Queen of Sakkhela is coming," Jack said. "And she's bringing the legion."

Fargher's dumbfounded stare was evident. "You are speaking of Florence Upsdell?"

"The one and only," Vince chimed in. "She's not playing around either."

"Didn't Eliška, Amina, or Professor Burwick warn you?" Emma asked.

"They are not here," McNaughton replied. "At least we have not seen them."

"Go find Eliška and Amina," Jack said to Vince. "Bring them to the quad."

"Where is Salomeh?" Emma cut in. "And Xui Li?"

"I'll go fetch them," McNaughton answered. "Wait here."

Vince raced up the steps two at a time with McNaughton on his heels, both disappearing inside the Main Hall. Through the entryway, Jack caught sight of a hallway packed with people.

Headmaster Fargher's eyes widened as lightforcers and benders from every generation and ethnicity rushed toward the wrenched gates while others darted across the cricket pitch.

> *In the days when skies are filled with smoke and fire,*
> *The end will draw near; our nights will be dire.*
> *Amidst the darkness unchained through flames and strife*
> *Lies a hope our souls may be reborn from death to life.*
> *Along a silk road this secret will one day return*
> *To a story of mercy and love evil attempted to burn.*
> *Dreams. Visions. Prophecy. All have come to this last day. And I*
> *will pour out my spirit and my power on all with courage*
> *to believe.*

Jack listened to Elyon's voice speak with absolute clarity in his spirit. Emma grabbed his hand, and he knew she sensed a righteous fire raging in his soul. She squeezed and nodded slightly. Salomeh and Xui Li appeared at the top of the stairs with McNaughton leading the way. Both glanced around, then stepped casually down to the road.

"What's Salomeh carrying?" Fargher asked, bewildered.

"Slybourne's shield," Jack answered. "One of the artifacts, Headmaster."

"I suppose you will be wanting this." Salomeh held the shield up. "What else, Jack?"

"We need time to make it to Lion Rock—that's where the Testimony is buried."

85

VINCE PUSHED HIS WAY UP the stairs of the Main Hall, bursting into Rowell Library. A mass migration of people stretched from the stairwell to Nightingale's vault through the library and down the Main Hall stairs to the House of Luminescence. With his semiautomatic strapped over his shoulder, he reached the spiral staircase and pushed his way down until he was inside the vault. Among the thousands of people gathered—and hundreds more entering through the tunnels—Oliver and Winnie Bennett brought order to the chaos.

"Have you seen Professor Burwick?" Vince asked urgently.

"I am afraid not." Oliver recognized his concern. "What has happened, Vince?"

"We're about to be attacked by legion and the Queen of Sakkhela."

"Where is Emma?" Winnie asked, remaining controlled.

"She's upstairs with Jack and the headmaster, but I don't know for how long."

Oliver's brows raised. "Winnie, we should go and see if we can help."

"Good idea," Vince agreed as he stepped away. "Sorry, I've got to find the professor."

He left them in Nightingale's vault and headed straight to the tunnels. His eyes darted between the people he passed, knowing Eliška would never leave Burwick behind. Within the tunnel, children cried and the elderly shuffled slowly. This was a mass exodus of those who wished to be free, but for those this deep in the tunnel their chance of survival was dwindling. Vince's jaw clenched as he followed the same route he'd taken before toward Tsim Sha Tsui.

"Elyon, help me find them in this maze," he whispered.

A few minutes later he reached a crossroads in the underground tunnels, which left him with choices. He spun around, struggling to decide which tunnel to take because if he was wrong . . .

"Vince!" Eliška's voice called out. "Over here."

With a quick glance he watched Eliška and Amina shouldering Professor Burwick's weight as she moved slowly with armed faction surrounding them. Burwick didn't need the cane any longer, but he'd noticed in recent weeks she was more rigid and moved slower. He hurried over where all were drenched in sweat. Eliška reached out and hugged him tight with one arm, then kissed him on the lips.

"Not sure how that will help get us there any quicker," Burwick mused.

"Whoa . . . our first kiss. I needed that." Vince held out his arms. "Professor . . ."

"I am not too young to refuse a free ride." Burwick shuffled forward. "So, this is real."

"As real as it's gonna get." Vince's gaze shifted between Eliška and Amina. "Double time or we're gonna be too late." Vince shot a quick glance at the faction who were gathered. "Go straight to the Main Hall and ask Bau where he needs you most."

"Lead the way," Amina said as the faction team darted forward. "And we will follow."

Vince scooped up Professor Burwick in his arms and hurried through the maze toward Nightingale's vault. Eliška and Amina stayed on his heels as he pushed himself to run faster. His grip on Burwick tightened as he pulled her in close to his chest. Those inside the tunnels moved aside, allowing a clear path. In record time, he reached the vault and shouted for everyone to get out of his way. Eliška and Amina raced forward to clear the stairwell, but there were too many people.

"You have brought me far enough," Burwick said. "I will be fine."

Vince didn't argue and gently set her down on her own feet. "Professor—"

"Do not worry about me." Burwick turned to Eliška. "It is your time."

Eliška's stare hardened as she reached out and hugged Burwick. Vince was caught off guard by the outpouring of emotion. He hadn't seen Eliška react that way before—he expected her to always be fearless. In that moment he realized Eliška was as afraid of losing someone as the rest of them. Amina exchanged a curious smile with him, then all three headed for the stairwell and forced themselves through the crowds.

In Rowell Library, Professor McDougall barked orders intensely while Professor Windsor helped keep the endless stream of humanity moving. Vince nodded at McDougall and Windsor, and both nodded back. Eliška and Amina stayed on his heels and bounded down the stairs only a few steps behind. The chase left them racing through the corridors of the Main Hall out onto the quad. Lightforcers and benders moved quickly without fear and in control of their gifts. Along the outskirts of the quad, healers huddled together, preparing to respond when needed.

In the center of a dead grassy lawn, Jack stood with Emma, as well as Salomeh, Xui Li, Oliver and Winnie Bennett, Maduka and Oni Okonkwo, McNaughton, Bau, and Headmaster Fargher. Vince slowed to a quick walk as he approached the circle. Eliška stepped between Jack and Vince, while Amina headed straight for her parents and hugged them hard.

Salomeh peered toward graying skies, which seemed darker than hours earlier. Vince guessed she'd heard about Faizan being left behind on Hong Kong Island, but outwardly she seemed unwavering. She let out a high-pitched whistle, and an energy buzzed around the circle. Vince followed her gaze and looked up as a colossal bone-white eagle soared over Beacon Hill. *Sahil.* The pentaloon nose-dived straight toward the ground with wings spread wide and landed gently on razored claws.

Jack stepped forward confidently as the majestic creature's golden eyes peered steadfastly at each one within the circle. His fingers touched the pentaloon's velvety feathers and muscular body. Sahil responded by mirroring the same high-pitched whistle that Salomeh had used. Vince couldn't hold his tongue any longer—he was amping to get on with it.

"Looks like we just got our ride to Lion Rock."

86

ALL EYES WERE ON JACK AS HE STOOD in the center of the circle, and then to everyone's surprise Harley Burwick appeared from the Main Hall and limped across the dead grass. *Even in her pain, she remains determined.* Jack swallowed hard, knowing the stakes were higher, greater, sharper, and more lethal than ever. No time to bow to fear; a mustard seed was all that was needed.

"There are those who believe if the artifacts are found and returned to the Testimony, then Cherub who have lost their gifts will have them restored." Jack glanced around at everyone in the circle. "But for those of us who are not lightforcers, benders, or healers, the gifts granted to us by Elyon are equally needed to fight on this day."

"So what have you got up your sleeve this time?" Bau asked. "Better be a zinger."

"We don't have all the artifacts," Jack said to the group. "But maybe we have enough."

"If we take the artifacts to the Testimony," Emma chimed in, "legion and Florence Upsdell will hunt us."

"Once we reach Lion Rock"—Jack glanced at Eliška—"we will use the Rhoxen Stone and bring the fight to them on equal ground."

"Everyone trying to go through the gateway will need to shelter in place until time starts again," Emma explained calmly. "Mum . . . Dad . . . that means you too."

"Yes dear," Winnie answered. "We understand."

"Oliver, Winnie, Maduka, Oni, Natalie, Xui Li, and Professor Burwick." Fargher pointed out each one as he said their name. "Best you hide in Nightingale's vault near the tunnels. Please take Professors McDougall and Windsor with you."

"What about you?" Burwick asked. "Where will you be, Headmaster?"

"I will not leave William." Fargher's eyes shifted between everyone as shame reflected in his gaze. "There is not enough time to move him—and he is my son."

"You will not be alone," Salomeh offered. "I will go with you."

"And I will be there too," Xui Li chimed in. "Until time stops, I will stand by you."

Fargher turned his gaze toward the ground. "Thank you."

"Lightforcers, benders, and healers are stationed across the grounds," Bau interrupted. "If legion or Merikh enter beyond the force field, we will rain down a righteous anger."

"Elyon is with us—no matter whether we are Cherub, faction, or outliers." Jack turned slowly and eyed each one. "He gives us power and courage to face darkness in this world and the other realms. Right now, we are fighting for one another—and we are fighting for the light."

"I just got chills," Vince blurted as he held out his muscular arms. "You two are finally on the same side—and it only took the end of the world to make it happen."

"Better now than after the bell rings in the final round," Jack quipped.

Xui Li stepped forward and placed her hands on his shoulders. She closed her eyes and bowed for a moment. He felt a surge of peace wash over him, and then Soulweaver slipped from his forearm and he gripped the rod.

What is Soulweaver telling me? Why now?

Xui Li recited the warrior's prayer: "In the fiery battles of this world, Elyon promises strength with a righteous hand and courage poured out upon our bravery."

She released his shoulders, then stepped back. Jack turned toward Emma and picked up where the last remaining Elder left off. "We will not fear—and we will not be dismayed—for we are chosen to glorify Elyon and defend the light, in this realm and beyond."

Emma unzipped her hoodie and retrieved the Windstrikers, then stepped over and handed one of the dretium war fans to Amina. She held up the second one and tapped it against the one she'd just given Amina. With eyes ablaze, Emma picked up where Jack left off. "For us to live is Elyon, and to die is a gateway to eternal glory."

Salomeh gave Slybourne's shield to Jack, who walked directly to Vince with the legendary artifact in his grip. He held up the shield in front of Vince, who accepted it without hesitating. "Amidst the darkness unchained through flames and strife, lies a hope our souls may be reborn from death to life." Jack waited as Emma, Amina, and Vince gathered together. Eliška joined the inner circle with the red velvet pouch protecting the Rhoxen Stone in her grasp. "Elyon, we stand before you as one—united. Amen."

One day an endless night will be filled with a glorious light.

"Hold on a second . . ." Jack's mind raced with a possibility. "The Rhoxen Stone only works for the one holding it, right? So we need to break it up into pieces."

"Is that possible?" Emma asked Xui Li. "Can the stone be broken?"

Xui Li's brows raised. "If someone touches any part of the stone, time will stop."

Jack grabbed the red velvet pouch from Eliška and dropped the Rhoxen Stone into the palm of his hand. Immediately everyone around him stood frozen. But he still heard shrieks and squeals echoing in the distance—a sign that legion and the queen were drawing closer.

He knelt and set the stone on the ground while keeping his index finger pressed against the smooth turquoise. A gentle tap from the point of Soulweaver and the Rhoxen Stone cracked into dozens of smaller pieces. Without a second to spare, he scooped up the fragments and dropped them into the pouch. As soon as the pieces were in the pouch, the world spun on its axis again.

"Cover your hand with your sleeve." Jack held out the pouch. "Then reach in and take one."

Emma, Amina, Eliška, Vince, Xui Li, and Jack reached inside and removed the pieces of the Rhoxen Stone, then slipped them into their pockets. A moment passed as each one eyed the others in reverence.

Bau hurried over, unaware of what had occurred and a bit

annoyed they were taking so long to leave. "What is holding you up?" he asked, on edge. "You lot need to get going."

"Pieces of the Rhoxen Stone for you and your best lightforcers and benders." Jack paused, tempted to unload what he believed about Fang Xue—but instead he held his tongue and handed over the pouch. "You need to touch the stone as soon as it glows turquoise. You'll only have a few seconds before the world around you stops."

Sahil lowered her pointed beak and lifted Jack onto her back with her velvety feathers. Emma was next, then Amina and Eliška. Without any help from the pentaloon, the final Keeper to mount the majestic creature was Vince Tobias.

"Hold on a second!" Bau called out as he looked up at Jack. "Bring Dragon Soul back where it belongs, mate."

"We'll do our best." Jack looked past Bau and realized Salomeh, Xui Li, the Bennetts, the Okonkwos, McNaughton, and Fargher were on their knees in a circle, praying. He glanced over his shoulder and said loud enough for the others to hear, "We're doing this in the name of Elyon—but we're also doing this for Tim, Rachel, Areum, Dabria, Darcy, Mrs. Fargher, and the nameless who have suffered. No more running. Are you ready?"

All of them responded in unison. "Ready!"

Emma whispered into his ear and hugged him tight. "I love you, Jack."

"I love you too." Jack gripped a handful of feathers. "Until the end."

Sahil lifted off the ground and flapped her powerful wings, ascending into the clouded skies. Jack sensed the power of the magnificent creature as they flew overhead. He glanced down, and dread punched him in the stomach. Merikh and legion broke through the force field, those with corrupted powers of Cherub and fallen angels of Elyon from ages past with souls as dark as the waters of Tombé falls and the Chasseuse River.

In the skies, a swarm of legion soared on both sides of the Queen of Sakkhela with her flaming-red hair flowing in a gusty wind. Jack's eyes widened at the sight of the beast Bau had described—a half-living destrier horse with a long silver mane. From the beast's nostrils, flames burst across the grounds of Beacon Hill. A quick glance from Florence Upsdell in his direction, and the legion in the skies shifted attack formation. Jack squeezed his legs against Sahil's body, and the pentaloon swooped low over Prince Edward Road at breakneck speed.

87

THUNDER RUMBLED AND LIGHTNING streaked across the skies, striking high-rise buildings and city streets. Fire raged beneath, but Sahil's flapping wings remained strong and rhythmic. She soared higher toward the clouds, then broke through—with legion and the queen riding her destrier closing in. Jack hugged the pentaloon's neck tight as the colossal eagle tucked her wings in and dove straight down. She picked up even greater speed as typhoon-force winds rushed against them, leaving Jack and the others holding on for their lives, on the verge of ripping apart from one another. The pentaloon burst through a grayish wall of ice particles and trillions of water droplets.

"Sahil," Jack whispered, "take us to the rock."

The pentaloon stopped her dive abruptly in midair and floated gently onto a rocky cliff. Boulders dislodged beneath her razored claws, tumbling down the mountainside. In a hurry, everyone hopped off, and Sahil lifted back into the air and flew straight toward legion and the queen.

Right away, Jack knew they were on top of Lion Rock. He'd hiked to the summit with Rachel once, complaining the whole way because it was a steep trek. Seconds passed as he stared out across Kowloon from the lion head–shaped boulder. His heart shattered into a million pieces when he saw the legion attack and ravage Sahil with a deadly vengeance—the pentaloon's lifeless body plummeted toward the ground.

"Jack, what are we doing?" Vince shouted, snapping him back. "Fight or flight?"

"We need to split up." Jack desperately kept his wits about him. "It's time."

The weight of Sahil's sacrifice was evident in everyone's eyes as they reached into their pockets and removed their piece of the Rhoxen Stone. Each fragment radiated a glorious turquoise. The squeals and shrieks above them were deafening. Jack's stare locked in on legion and the queen as they advanced swiftly.

How many lives in this world just stopped, hanging in the balance? Elyon, I pray Bau and the others have seen the light in time.

"How are we supposed to fight *and* hold the stone at the same time?" Vince asked.

Jack took his piece and slipped it under his hoodie sleeve. "Keep it touching your skin."

"Splendid." Amina was first to follow Jack's lead, then the others did the same. "Whatever you do, do not lose your piece of the stone."

"Emma, Amina, and Eliška, go to the Testimony," Jack said. "Vince, you're with me."

"Jack . . ." Emma protested. "We should stick together."

"If they catch you with me, then this is over. You're the strongest among us, Emma."

"No time to argue," Eliška interrupted urgently. "Emma, lead us to the Testimony."

Jack couldn't keep his eyes on Emma any longer, or else he'd change his mind. He shot a quick glance toward Amina. "Keep them alive."

"None of us are dying today," she replied, resolute. "Elyon is with us."

Emma, Eliška, and Amina disappeared into thick bushes and dense trees. Soulweaver hummed and vibrated in Jack's grasp as he inched back from the edge of Lion Rock. Vince gripped Slybourne's shield and tucked his forearm between the leather straps on the back. He stood a few steps in front of Jack—the first line of defense. Jack felt the piece of Rhoxen Stone beneath his hoodie sleeve, a reminder of the defeat in the Battle of Everest.

The Rhoxen Stone isn't slowing the queen and legion down, but hopefully it will stop the world around us and help Bau and the others against the Merikh at Beacon Hill.

Legion shifted direction toward the path Emma, Amina, and Eliška took toward Amah Rock—a landmark where Jack and Emma had buried the Testimony. The Queen of Sakkhela kept her sights on her prey and swooped down toward Jack and Vince.

"Any idea how the shield works?" Vince asked. "Besides being a battering ram."

"Honestly . . ." Jack braced himself with Soulweaver. "I've got no idea."

"Trial by fire then—exactly how I like it."

Jack slammed the point of Soulweaver into the mountain, sending cracks and shock waves through it. It was a warning to the queen as she landed on Lion Rock riding the half-skeletal destrier. Flames burst from the beast's nostrils, blocked by Vince as he held up Slybourne's shield. An inferno raged against the shield while Jack ducked low. He peered around the side and watched the queen climb off the destrier in full battle armor.

"Bow your knee to me, boy," she seethed, "and you will be shown mercy."

"You're not serious, lady," Vince called out. "You're gonna roast us like marshmallows."

Jack rolled out from behind the shield and pointed Soulweaver straight ahead. A white light punched the destrier, knocking the beast off balance. He didn't wait for retaliation as he stabbed Soulweaver's lightforce again and again. The destrier's hooves danced as the beast retreated sideways, and with one final punch the queen's steed tumbled off the ledge of Lion Rock.

Florence's stone-cold gaze narrowed. "Death awaits you from the blades."

Vince moved quickly to step in front of Jack as the queen retrieved Dragon Soul and Scarlet Widow from their scabbards and held one in each hand. Bright glints from the handcrafted swords reflected across the rock and dirt where Jack and Vince stood.

"Probably should've brought Bau with us," Vince mumbled. "He controls Dragon Soul."

"Just you and me, Vince, against a legendary warrior with supernatural swords."

"Yeah . . . doesn't seem fair, does it?" Vince paused. "She's got no chance."

Jack ducked behind Slybourne's shield as black and crimson flames poured over them. Vince dug his shoulder deeper into the shield and grunted as his boots scraped backward against the rock. Jack shoved Vince hard in the back to steady him while both forced the shield forward. *One step closer.* A golden glow emanated from the shield and wrapped around them.

"Keep going!" Jack shouted. "No retreat . . ."

"No surrender," Vince yelled back. "Hang on to the rod, Jack."

Vince growled as the two-headed dragon surging from Dragon Soul attacked. Jack punched Soulweaver from one side of the shield to the other, attempting to blindly hit the unrelenting dragon. He peered around again, then realized the dretium in the shield was splitting in half. Soulweaver rapid-fired white bursts of lightforce, but the fight remained a stalemate.

"On three, go left!" Jack called out. "One . . . two . . . three!"

Vince dodged to the left while Jack slid to the right on his knees. Soulweaver spun between his fingers as it had done before, only this time the pulses of power were stronger. They struck the two-headed beast protruding from Dragon Soul with an unrelenting barrage. Jack gripped the rod tight as the heartwood shook in his grasp.

At the same time, the Queen of Sakkhela stabbed Scarlet Widow into the ground, held up her hand toward Vince, and unleashed lightning from her fingertips. Slybourne's shield split in half, leaving Vince darting across the rocky ledge as boulders exploded at his heels. Out of the corner of his eye, Jack caught sight of Vince sprinting swiftly before being lifted off the ground and thrown over the ledge.

Fear paralyzed Jack as he cried out, "Vince!"

"Now it is only you and I," Florence raged. "Return what belongs to me."

"The Rod of Elyon protects the light." Defiant, Jack held up the rod as it continued to spin. "But I'm not afraid to unleash Soulweaver."

"Blood was shed in the name of Elyon, and my soul is blackened from the deaths of my loves." Florence's gaze narrowed. "Are you willing to die to save those you love?"

"No one is being buried today," Jack rebuked, "except for you and the legion."

Soulweaver slowed, and he gripped the rod with both hands. Florence snatched Scarlet Widow, and the titanoboas slithered on the blade with their venomous fangs spewing. Jack ducked as the venom seared his dretium hoodie. Images of the scars from his arms and chest flashed in his mind as the two-headed dragon breathed black fire and the snakes' fangs spit fiery crimson flames. He defended himself with Soulweaver as Florence swung the swords with lethal force against the rod, splintering the heartwood in half. Before he reacted, the dragon's inky inferno struck him with stinging accuracy.

On fire, Jack rolled across the rock and dirt, gasping for breath. He scrambled to his feet as blood flowed from his nose onto his chin. His skin burned as the dretium hoodie was seared to his flesh. He gripped both splintered pieces of Soulweaver—one in each hand—and glared at the queen, whose stare was unnerving and soul-crushing. A memory pierced his spirit: a stabbing pain inflicted by a silhouette in the Chamber of Gods—a darkness in the corner of his soul which helped him survive in the nether realm.

Loss seared his resolve to hold fast to another mustard seed.

Elyon, give me the strength to fight to the end.

A white light sparked fireworks as Jack lunged forward, swinging the shattered pieces of Soulweaver. Explosions landed against

Florence, and the fear of losing vanished from Jack's mind as his soul surrendered to ending the darkness. He struck Dragon Soul from the queen's grasp, sending the blade spinning across the mountain. Venom sprayed from Scarlet Widow, leaving him struggling to see clearly—yet he kept attacking. Fangs sank deep into his arm as one of the titanoboas wrestled him to the ground. With his insides ablaze and his skin burning from the toxins, he fought to free himself from the deathly bite before scrambling to his feet.

Florence stepped closer, and Jack snatched a piece of Slybourne's shield, throwing the sharpened edge at her. She grimaced in pain when the shield lodged in her shoulder, causing her to stumble slightly—a split second Jack desperately needed. He pounced like a wild animal and stabbed the heartwood's lightforce, refusing to give up as light pierced through the queen's armor. His eyes widened as venomous snakes wrapped around his body and crushed against his ribs.

Unbearable pain riffled through him as he gasped for every breath. Florence raised her hand, and he could feel his heart pulling from his chest. He grimaced as he pointed the edges of the heartwood over the queen's body, desperate to end her life—yet he hesitated.

I can't kill another, not even the queen.

With a cry to the heavens, Jack surrendered and let go of the heartwood. To his surprise, the pieces of Soulweaver didn't drop to the ground. Instead, they plunged into Florence's chest under their own power—just like the rod had done in Charis. Soulweaver did what he was unable to do, and he was grateful. A black flame rose from the queen and wrapped around the pieces of Soulweaver still piercing her body, then drifted away before swooping in a whirl downward beneath the dirt.

As quickly as the vicious onslaught began, it was over. Jack stumbled forward, unable to see how close he was to the edge, then fell facedown. He struggled to roll onto his back, a pain searing his insides as his breathing constricted. With tunnel vision closing in, he imagined Sahil raising him to the heavens beyond the cloudy skies. Barely conscious, he sensed the snake venom seeping through his skin into his bloodstream.

Hazy flashes of Rachel, Areum, and his mom struck in his mind—only this time, they were not wearing angelic armor inside the Temple of the Nephilim. All three stood side by side with their hands outstretched. Tears welled up in his eyes as he desperately wanted to grab hold, but they were out of reach. He blinked when he heard movement, powerless to defend himself.

Vince skidded across the rocks and knelt beside him, terrified. "Jack . . ."

"You're alive." Jack coughed as his windpipe constricted. "I thought—"

"She nearly knocked me out cold, but I vice-gripped a rock hanging over the edge." Vince touched Jack's arm, but he barely felt anything. "We need to get you to Amina and Emma."

"Help me up, one more time."

Vince pulled Jack to his feet. The world around him spun. His legs were shaky as he stumbled toward where Florence's soulless body remained. Vince grabbed him under his arm and carried him the rest of the way. Tears streamed down Jack's cheeks as he grimaced with clenched teeth. Vince lowered him to his knees, blood dripping from Jack's nostrils.

"Jack . . ." Vince squeezed his shoulder firmly. "You need Emma and Amina, bro."

"We can't leave without the artifacts and compass. Grab the swords too."

Jack crawled on his knees until he was right beside Florence's body, then searched her armor until he found what he was looking for. He slowly pulled the splintered heartwood from her chest and gripped what remained of Soulweaver.

Vince hurried to snatch Dragon Soul and Scarlet Widow, then gathered the pieces of Slybourne's shield—including the fragment lodged in the queen's shoulder.

"Is Eden's Star still in the hilt of Scarlet Widow?" Jack asked weakly.

Vince lowered the handle of the sword toward Jack. "Is this what you mean?"

"That's it." Jack touched the compass and squinted as his vision blurred. "You'll need to show me the way."

"Better make sure she doesn't come back from the dead." Vince picked up the queen's corpse, then carried her over to the ledge. He glanced over his shoulder for a split second, then tossed Florence Upsdell over the edge of Lion Rock. He turned and faced Jack, unable to camouflage the worry in his eyes. "Let's finish what you started."

88

AMAH ROCK WAS A HUNDRED YARDS AHEAD—but an eternity away unless the advancing legion were stopped. Emma's ears perked up at the sound of sweeping and rustling: demons were moving swiftly within the brush. With a flick of her wrist, her war fan opened and a reddish-orange phoenix engraved into the dretium burst alive. Amina stood alongside and flicked her wrist, too, opening an identical fan and syncing the Windstrikers. Emma glanced over her shoulder at Eliška, who scrambled toward the spot where Emma and Jack buried the Testimony.

"Is the Rhoxen Stone still working?" Emma asked.

Amina slipped her piece of the stone from beneath her sleeve and frowned. "Nope."

"Eliška will need more time to dig up the Testimony." Emma

retrieved the stone from beneath her hoodie sleeve, then stared intently at its dullness and shook her head. "We were wrong about the Rhoxen Stone remaining powerful enough with only a small piece each. Prepare yourself, Amina."

"Sword and Fan—except this is not a performance."

"Force and flow," Emma reassured. "The Windstrikers will follow our lead."

Emma's pupils dissolved to bone white as her palms glowed. She steadied herself, fearless of the stampede rumbling the ground beneath her boots. *An army of legion are charging, and we are left to stop them.* A quick glance at Amina and she was certain Jack made the right decision, as hard as it was to accept the risk. She exhaled slowly and braced for an onslaught, surrendering her gifts and spirit to Elyon.

Legion burst through the bushes across the mountaintop. Spears flew through the air, narrowly missing Emma as she ducked and dodged. Amina was on her heels as each Windstriker phoenix spread its wings wide across the dretium fans. Dirt rose from the ground into the air as boulders and tree trunks ripped free before slamming into legion, who closed in fast.

Though they were outnumbered, Emma's lightforce and bender gifts flowed with precision. Amina threw her Windstriker off to one side, not to surrender but to allow the dretium war fan to attack from another angle. Emma launched her Windstriker in the opposite direction, and the phoenix flew mightily.

"Climb!" Emma grabbed Amina and yanked her alongside. "Now!"

Emma stopped and stood her ground while Amina scrambled onto a boulder and climbed. Legion snarled and growled with fangs desperate to devour. The Windstrikers boomeranged, their razored edges slicing through the skeletal beasts. Amina caught both Windstrikers, and without hesitation she hurled the war fans a second time, sending legion scattering.

Every demon struck down energized the lightforce erupting from the core of Emma's soul, glowing startlingly brighter as pulses burst from her palms across the mountaintops. She launched herself into the fray, sweeping legs and landing stunning blows as if she were an army of a thousand. The Windstrikers swarmed the legion, leaving demons' bones in ash. Amina jumped from the boulder a split second before legion spears shattered the rock. She was on the run again, catching the Windstrikers and tossing them for a third time.

Bloodied and muddied, Emma was fueled by Amina's bravery as both fought with every ounce of their strength. She snatched a sharp-pointed spear stuck into the ground, then stabbed and thrusted as she battled her way through the dwindling battalion. Adrenaline flowed with Elyon's power, surging through her as she threw the legion's spear. Amina ducked as the spear soared past her before pulverizing skeletal demons who were right behind her.

The shrieks and shrills were earsplitting.

From the overgrown trees, Vince emerged with a bellowing battle cry, pointing Dragon Soul straight ahead. Emma could see by the way he gripped the hilt of the sword that he was struggling to control the flaming two-headed dragon. *Vince is strong enough to hold the sword, but he cannot tame the dragon.* She flinched when Vince tossed a second sword in her direction. Its pointed blade stabbed the dirt, and her eyes grew wide. *Scarlet Widow.* Emma grabbed the sword and eyed Eden's Star placed perfectly in the Queen of Sakkhela's weapon of choice.

Venomous titanoboas slithered across the blade as she flanked

462

the legion opposite Vince, who charged like a battering ram. Amina chased, caught, and cast the Windstrikers, and the dretium fans remained unrelenting. All three fought valiantly as Dragon Soul, Scarlet Widow, and the Windstrikers struck down remaining legion until a haunting silence swept over Lion Rock.

Amina raced over with both Windstrikers in her grasp. "Are you two okay?"

"You were outstanding." Emma exhaled, catching her breath. "Amina, you controlled the Windstrikers as if they were made for you." She turned her attention toward Vince and recognized his sorrowful gaze. Tears welled up in her eyes. "Vince, where is—?"

Jack appeared from the bushes, staggering and struggling to stay on his feet. Emma locked eyes with him, and her momentary relief faded quickly. She darted toward him as he crumpled to the ground. Vince and Amina raced in the same direction, all three reaching him at the same time. In the near distance, Eliška left Amah Rock and scrambled toward them.

"Jack . . ." Vince shook him hard. "Wake up, bro."

"What is wrong?" Eliška called out as she approached. "Vince?"

"Amina, I need you," Emma said urgently as she knelt beside him. "Jack . . ."

A lump lodged in her throat as she touched his bloodied wounds beneath the torn and ravaged dretium hoodie. Amina pressed her palm against Jack's chest, and Emma did the same. For a moment, Vince and Eliška stood back while the healers prayed.

"Everything happened so fast." Vince's fingers balled into a fist. "He fought against Florence—but she used Dragon Soul and Scarlet Widow against him."

"Keep believing," Amina urged. "Elyon can heal him."

Eliška and Vince knelt alongside and held their hands over Jack. For a moment, whispers drifted in the air as each prayed earnestly. Jack's eyes opened, blood trickling down his chin from both nostrils.

"Amina . . ." he said weakly. "Tim loves you more than words."

Tears streamed down Amina's cheeks. Emma leaned in close and kissed Jack gently on the lips. She swallowed hard, desperate to save him yet fighting against total devastation.

"Light in your soul," Emma said softly, "conquers the darkest corners."

Jack gazed up at her as she peered deep into his soul. She'd walked with him—carrying the burden of his torment, fear, anguish, and guilt while embracing his love for her and the others. His eyes slowly closed as she kept her gaze fixed on him, sensing an overwhelming rush of peace amid an unrelenting storm raging within.

As tears poured down her face, Emma grabbed his hand and squeezed hard—feeling his heartbeat slowing one beat at a time. "Stay with me, Jack."

"No . . . no . . . no . . . this isn't happening," Vince protested. "It can't end this way."

"Emma, what else can we do?" Eliška asked urgently. "How do we keep him alive?"

A magnificent white light broke through grayish clouds and spread across Lion Rock. *There is not much time left, Emma.* Elyon's gentle voice nudged her to squeeze Jack's hand even harder, urging him to stay with her a bit longer. Her heart pounded through her chest when his eyes opened suddenly.

"From the start," Jack said, hardly above a whisper, "I've loved you, Emma."

"I love you too—more than anyone in this world."

A wistful smile pursed his lips as he stared toward the light. "Elyon, I surrender."

She kissed him on the cheek as he whispered so softly she barely heard what he said next. *You're the one.* Amina slowly removed her hand from Jack's chest. Vince grabbed Dragon Soul and tossed the sword across the mountaintop. Eliška buried her face into Vince's chest and sobbed.

All three stepped back from Jack, allowing Emma one final goodbye as the white light hovered overhead. On her knees in total shock, she reached out and closed the lifeless eyes of her true love. As she let go of his hand, she found herself gripping the ivory figurine and spin top.

Emma braced herself with the point of Scarlet Widow digging into the dirt, shattered by the indescribable loss. Stricken, she turned toward the others and shook her head. The brilliant white light surrounded Jack's body, and then in a blink the light shot skyward like a rocket and disappeared beyond the clouds. Emma wanted nothing more than to unleash her lightforce against the darkness in vengeance. But in the midst of her agony, she exhaled slowly and surrendered her will to Elyon's.

Jack has passed from this world to beyond.

Utterly devastated, she said somberly, "This is not over."

89

BEACON HILL—MOMENTS EARLIER

Lightforcers and benders fought valiantly as legion and Merikh breached the outer walls while HKPF remained beyond the grounds. Fighter jets flew overhead, back and forth amid the chaos before being knocked out of the skies by legion and crashing into nearby apartment buildings. At the gates, Bau led the charge and crossed the cricket pitch with lightforcers and benders on both sides. Suddenly, HKPF officers near the front gates froze like statues.

"You need to touch the stone as soon as it glows turquoise."

Bau shouted over his shoulder as he darted down the front lines. "Rhoxen Stone!"

Lightforcers and benders reached for a piece of the glowing

stone Bau had given them and gripped it firmly in their palms. Some were not quick enough, so they stood frozen mid-fight. Moments passed as Bau released his lightforce against a swarming legion who were unfazed by the Rhoxen Stone's powers. He dropped them one by one, then as quickly as the world had stopped spinning, the stone in Bau's palm stopped glowing. He realized the axis of time had shifted once more, especially when he caught sight of Merikh racing toward the Main Hall.

Bau sprinted across the grounds, fully aware that if Merikh or legion entered the Main Hall, then everyone inside would be dead. Lightforcers of all ages appeared in the entryway and fought against the attack, while others pulled back from the outer walls of the grounds to form a last line of defense.

Salomeh stood in front of the door, fighting with a miraculous strength. Legion were no longer swooping through the skies; rather, the fallen demons were marching toward them with spears at the ready.

"We're not going to be able to hold them off much longer," Salomeh said.

Bau swept his hands to both sides, clearing away the Merikh who charged. He cracked the door open and peered inside, hoping for more lightforcers. Instead he stared at Cherub refugees without gifts huddled together in utter fear. Oliver and Winnie Bennett grabbed a group of refugees and pulled them further down the corridor.

"We have to stand our ground, Salomeh." Bau's lightforce grew stronger and more lethal. Legion shattered while Merikh fell. "The Rhoxen Stone only slowed down the inevitable—we need to hold the line or else this will be over far too quick."

"Then we must hope there is still time left."

Salomeh stood beside Bau, generations alongside one another, and fought with unrelenting power. Her voice rang out in a language foreign to all except Elyon. More lightforcers and benders—those willing to sacrifice their lives for a greater purpose—pulled back and gathered along the front of the Main Hall. Legion stopped along the road, and in unison pointed spears in their direction. Merikh stood behind the legion with lightforces visible in their palms. One woman stepped to the front: a Cherub who shocked them all.

Fang Xue.

Bau exchanged a stunned look with Salomeh, then spun around when the Main Hall door cracked open. Will hopped over, leaning on crutches. Bau's brows raised as the headmaster's son waited quietly. No words were exchanged, but it was clear Will had made a choice. In unison, legion stepped forward with lava spilling from their jaws.

"Seems Fang Xue is not the only one who has switched sides," Salomeh noted.

"Let's get on with it," Will said under his breath. "And end this once and for all."

Without warning, Will raised his hands and a purple lightforce shot like a cannon, pulverizing the front row of legion. Bau took the cue and released his lightforce, along with Salomeh and every last lightforcer standing. Benders reacted by sweeping aside the bones of the skeletal beasts.

Near the quad, Faizan and his team appeared as legion and Merikh charged across the grounds of Beacon Hill. Along with hundreds of lightforcers and benders, Faizan stormed alongside Cherub and faction as Bau, Will, Salomeh, and the others stood their ground. Legion's chilling shrieks, high-pitched squeals, and growls grew louder and more intense—agitated and tormented.

Light and dark clashed on the steps of the Main Hall, the explosion of a battle that had been dormant for ages. Will's powers were stronger than Bau expected, in spite of the darkness that remained in his soul. Legion crumbled into ash and Merikh fell lifeless to the ground. Within minutes Cherub and faction had the upper hand as benders on the rooftop darted back and forth, keeping the remaining legion from gaining further ground while stopping them from taking flight. Bau locked eyes with Fang Xue just before she darted across the front lines of the legion.

"She's getting away," Bau yelled.

Salomeh kept battling with her lightforce. "You are faster than me."

"We got this," Will blurted. "Chase her down, Bau."

Bau peeled away from the line and sprinted along the outside corridor as explosions shattered windows and blasted concrete walls near him. He reached the other end of the Main Hall and rounded the corner. Fang Xue was barely visible as she darted in the direction of Nightingale Pavilion. With the battle fading in his ears, Bau stepped down rows of concrete bench seats covering a hillside. Fang Xue stood near the Wishing Tree, a four-hundred-year-old banyan tree given to Beacon Hill by the Cherub. Bau approached, anticipating she would not surrender willingly.

"You betrayed us all," Bau said pointedly. "Highest Cherub and followers of Elyon."

"I tried to protect us from this war." Fang Xue's gaze hardened. "You refused to listen."

"Your counsel was to surrender our gifts to our enemies." Bau took another few steps closer. "And today you stand with legion and Merikh."

"The Queen of Sakkhela will restore order," Fang Xue disputed. "Cherub will lose this war, Bau. Allies among our enemies are necessary. Your mentor, the great Elder, believed the same."

"What do you mean, Fang?"

"Peter wished to find the artifacts to protect the Cherub, a secret kept from the highest among us and those who believe—including me." Fang Xue remained stone-cold. "Rachel was the first one chosen, and she willingly broke the commands in the Eternal when she searched for Eden's Star in the Philippines. Peter confided in me that Rachel had become unreliable and reckless, and he believed she was keeping far too many secrets. So he met with the leader of the Merikh—Charlotte Taylor—and struck a deal to ensure a future for the Cherub."

Bau kept his lightforce ready. "What kind of deal?"

"Balance between Cherub and Merikh if the artifacts were found." Fang Xue paused. "Addison Reynolds and his children were pawns. I warned you, but you are too blind and too arrogant to see how the Reynolds family has brought pain, suffering, and chaos to this world and the other realms. So I did what was necessary to protect the Cherub from Peter's transgressions, sins of the Elders, and the strongest one chosen among you. I followed my calling to prevent anyone from breaking the commands in the Eternal."

Bau stepped closer until he stood face-to-face with Fang Xue, both of their lightforces glowing in their palms. "What sins did you commit in the name of Elyon?"

"Rachel had to be stopped," she replied, "when Chung and the Merikh failed."

"You are the one who killed Rachel in Sitio." Bau clenched his jaw, shocked by her words. "And that is why you have pressed me to bring justice to Jack."

"We are in a battle, but there is one final chance to bring peace."

Bau looked past Fang Xue, noticing Salomeh appear behind her. Fang Xue lifted her hands as he struggled with whether to strike her down. Her palms glowed stronger as she lunged forward, but she stopped midway. While her lightforce remained, she was unable to move any closer. Salomeh approached with her arms wide. Then she released a bright-orange lightforce that struck Fang Xue to the ground and knocked her out cold.

"I have heard enough." Salomeh said. "Fang has always been self-righteous."

Bau's brows raised. "Did you know she was the one?"

"Professor Burwick was the first to suggest it, but there were signs." Salomeh's lips pursed. "She will wake soon, and I would suggest we have her secured before that occurs."

Bau pointed over his shoulder. "What about the legion and Merikh?"

"We fought valiantly this day, and we are victorious." She smirked. "Legion and Merikh are defeated, but I suppose the HKPF beyond the gates are wondering what in the name of Elyon has happened to their city. I have ordered lightforcers and benders to remain on guard until we know the fate of the others against the Queen of Sakkhela."

90

LION ROCK

Emma wanted to say something, but she couldn't speak a single syllable. One word and she would fall into the despair of loss beyond the sorrow she had experienced in the nether realm. She swallowed hard and turned toward Amah Rock. Vince, Amina, and Eliška walked silently alongside. A hundred yards ahead they reached a hole near Amah Rock where she imagined Eliška had dug frantically during the battle. Brows furrowed, Emma glanced over her shoulder with tears in her eyes on the verge of spilling over. She noticed Vince's arms wrapped around Eliška and Amina as if he were holding them up.

"You weren't chosen because of your gifts, but because of your strength."

In the stillness, Emma heard Jack's voice clearly as she reached out her hand. Dirt shifted, deepening the hole until the earth revealed the Testimony. She reached down and picked up the gold-covered acacia chest carved with intricate figures, then set it down on the ground. Deep within, she struggled to keep going, wanting nothing more than to curl up and cry forever. In her weakness, Elyon granted her enough strength to do what needed to be done.

Vince was first to step forward as he set the artifacts down. Amina and Eliška followed and knelt in a circle while Emma opened the chest. Each sobbed quietly as Emma picked up the broken heartwood pieces of the Rod of Elyon and set them both inside. Branches of a tree engraved into the gold acacia of the box waved with an emerald glow. Vince grabbed the shattered pieces of Slybourne's shield, and as he set them inside, the pieces shape-shifted to fit into a smaller space. On the side of the chest, an etched lion shimmered in metallic bronze. Amina went next and placed the Windstrikers inside—miraculously, the war fans fit as well. Violet gleamed from a temple etched on the box along-side the others. Eliška held dulled pieces of the Rhoxen Stone in the palm of her hand, including the piece from beneath Jack's hoodie sleeve. She wiped her cheeks, then placed the stones into the Testimony. A turquoise etching of a ship glimmered.

"We will need the pieces of the Rhoxen Stone from Bau," Eliška said somberly.

Emma nodded. "Jack captured light and left a piece with each one of us."

"What about Scarlet Widow?" Vince asked, subdued.

"The prophecy has been fulfilled, and the Mercy Covenant is no longer in place. Perhaps an artifact is needed in this world to restore peace." Emma stared hard at the inside of the acacia chest, struggling to control her emotions, then glanced toward Eliška, knowing the truth about Rachel. "Eliška should be the keeper of Scarlet Widow."

"And we should return Dragon Soul to Bau," Amina added. "Balance."

"The only way to ensure balance"—Emma removed Eden's Star from the hilt of Scarlet Widow—"is for me to be the Protector."

Emma tucked the compass into an inner pocket of her dretium hoodie. She looked toward the grayish clouds, hoping the light might return. No legion remained in the skies or on the mountain. When she closed her eyes, flashes of Jack struck rapidly—a whirl-wind adventure and a romance she would hold close to her soul forever. A moment of silence lingered. No one moved until Emma gently closed the top of the acacia chest.

"Now that artifacts are inside, can the chest be touched?" Amina asked.

"A promise was made to return the Testimony to where it belongs," Emma replied, resolute. "Even though the Testimony is not meant to be touched by anyone from this world, there is no other choice. By faith I am strong enough to contain the power of the artifacts."

Vince shifted awkwardly. "We need to bring Jack back to Beacon Hill."

All four left the empty hole near Amah Rock as Emma carried the Testimony. Devastated and staggering, she felt the magnitude of the power within the acacia chest. Vince removed his hoodie and wrapped it around Jack, then gently scooped up his body. Eliška and Amina respectfully kept their distance, but Emma remained by his side.

"He fought until the end," Vince said shakily. "Doesn't matter who doubted him."

Emma gripped Jack's hand for a moment, as if deciding whether to let go. "He saved us from more than just this day, Vince."

"Be sure to convince Bau, the highest Cherub, and all who believe."

Emma bit her lip, struggling to hold herself together. "I promise."

For the next forty minutes, Vince carried Jack as they descended the steep mountain trails normally traveled by Hong Kongers and tourists. With protests, lockdowns, and turmoil lasting for months, the mountain had been abandoned. Emma's lightforce glowed as she harnessed the powers within the Testimony. She knew that Vince's muscles ached and burned, but he wasn't going to set his friend down until they reached Beacon Hill—and she wouldn't let go of the Testimony until she knew everyone was safe.

Eliška eyed the skies as they reached the end of the trail. "No more legion."

"We must pray those at Beacon Hill survived," Amina said. "Emma . . ."

"It is a long walk." Emma pushed her shock aside. "Vince?"

He nodded and led the way along the sidewalk, beginning the four-mile trek down Waterloo Road. The sidewalks were empty; no others were on the streets. In these moments when the world around her made no sense, Emma found refuge in singing ancient Cherub canticles. Amina harmonized with her melody.

One by one, Hong Kongers emerged from apartment buildings while those living on the streets in fear of the Merikh cautiously showed themselves. The growing procession approached a flyover where Prince Edward Road crossed beneath. An eeriness lingered as flames died down and rubble smoldered. Dozens turned into a thousand, drawn by the Testimony and the haunting harmonies of the deep-rooted Cherub canticles.

Emma knew if she allowed the lyrics to pierce her soul, she'd be left broken. She kept herself distant by shutting down her mind and heart to get through the miles ahead. As the mass of humanity approached Argyle Street, she remembered the march from Shek Pik Prison across Hong Kong Island—a march to freedom that reverberated across the city and beyond. They turned left onto Argyle Street, and her voice remained steady while the canticle stayed subdued.

HKPF and PRC military tanks were lined up beside tactical vehicles, blocking Argyle near the corner of Tin Kwong Road. Sweat seeped down Emma's spine as she gripped the Testimony a bit tighter. She picked up the pace ahead of the others to clear the way, a dull glow emanating around the acacia chest. To her surprise, HKPF officers and PRC soldiers stood down and pulled the barricades aside. She guessed whatever they'd witnessed before and after the effects of the Rhoxen Stone had left them mystified, dumbfounded, and terrified.

"Along a silk road this secret will one day return, to a story of mercy and love evil attempted to burn." Emma slowed, and Vince, Amina, and Eliška matched her pace. "The earth is spinning—so why does it feel like the world has stopped?"

The four of them led thousands up Tin Kwong Road in Ho Man Tin along the stone walls of Beacon Hill. HKPF and PRC stood in a long line, allowing them a clear path. Butterflies swarmed in Emma's stomach as they neared what was left of the gates.

Lightforcers and benders stepped out from the grounds, prepared to defend against whoever was approaching. All of them relaxed when they recognized who it was. Emma kept walking as lightforcers and benders fell in with thousands who walked across

Kowloon Tong. She was first to see the aftermath of the war zone within the grounds as healers moved between the injured.

Bones of legion were scattered amid shattered glass and chunks of concrete dislodged from the Main Hall. On the steps stood Headmaster Fargher and Natalie McNaughton, while Faizan and Professor Windsor were among the healers. Although the fighting was over, destruction and devastation unfolded before Emma's eyes. Bau approached from the carnage, and Will hobbled on crutches near the Main Hall steps.

Vince stopped at the bottom of the steps with Jack still in his arms. Bau, McDougall, and Windsor peeled away to follow him. Emma noticed a sharp glare from Vince toward Will before they climbed the stairs. Out of the corner of her eye, she caught a glimpse of Fargher and McNaughton, who were clearly distraught. She didn't need to glance over her shoulder to know that Amina, Eliška, and Faizan were right behind her.

While the thousands who'd followed across Kowloon Tong waited outside the Main Hall, long lines of refugees were still inside, desperate to leave through the House of Luminescence. Emma carried the Testimony into the auditorium, where the flags of Nightingale, Upsdell, Crozier, and Rowell Houses hung overhead. Vince dropped to his knees and gently laid Jack down.

"Jack," he said, loud enough for Emma and the others to hear, "you're home now."

91

Professor McDougall removed his hand-stitched coat, woven by the children of Kati Pahari, and laid it over Jack's body. He squeezed Vince's shoulder as the others entered the auditorium. Chairs were stacked against the walls, leaving a large open space in the room. Emma kept her gaze fixed on the floor until Oliver and Winnie Bennett arrived. Her parents embraced her as she cried softly. Maduka and Oni Okonkwo were close behind and wrapped their arms around Amina. Headmaster Fargher waited in the back of the auditorium alongside Will, while Bau remained between his parents.

Emma watched Faizan, Salomeh, and other healers attempt to bring Jack back to this world one final time. She had witnessed pentaloons and Rhoxen soldiers healed from the legion attack near

Mount Everest in another age and realm, yet others had passed into eternity. Still, she hoped desperately for a miracle to bring Jack back to them. But as the minutes passed, the only place she sensed his presence was in her soul.

I believe Elyon determines the path traveled on this side. Well done, Jack.

Her gaze shifted toward the windows where a thumping of rotors broke the silence seconds before a helicopter landed in the quad. At the same time, Professor Burwick—a mother who knew firsthand the pain of loss—appeared in the entryway and stopped cold. Xui Li knelt beside Vince, who hadn't budged since he brought Jack into the Main Hall.

Salomeh eyed Xui Li closely and shook her head. Only then did Xui Li wrap her arm over Vince's shoulder and whisper in his ear. Emma couldn't hear what the Elder said, but she knew the words would remain with Vince forever. Sorrow struck in the depths of her heart as Vince surrendered and joined the rest of the circle beside Eliška and McNaughton.

All who gathered stared blankly at one another as their shock reverberated from this world to the other realms. Emma's stare locked in on McDougall's colorful coat; then she glanced toward Will, whose blank gaze remained fixated on the floor. Finally, Burwick gathered the strength to shuffle into the auditorium and stood in the background beside Bau.

In the midst of their disbelief and grief, Max Tsang was next to appear in the doorway, shadowed by his bodyguards. A twinge of anger rippled down Emma's spine at the sight of the chief executive officer of Hong Kong. All eyes turned toward the man, who wore jeans and a polo shirt instead of the customary tailored suit he wore on television. Emma realized he was aboard the helicopter that had landed in the quad, but she was left questioning why he was at Beacon Hill.

Winston whispered loud enough for her to hear. "Perhaps now is not the time, Son."

Bau hesitated as he locked eyes with Emma. She nodded slightly. He ushered Tsang into the auditorium, and the tension grew thick. Emma scrutinized Bau and Tsang, wondering what Bau was doing while understanding peace still hung in the balance between Cherub, Merikh, and PRC. She glared at Tsang, refusing to blink, tempted to unleash her lightforce against him and scorch those who had pushed them beyond the brink.

"I know the moment we find ourselves in, but this must be done now," Bau said solemnly. "Cherub defended the light this day, and bloodshed brought victory against Merikh, legion, and the Queen of Sakkhela. We have fought battles to protect the innocent—and the losses are heartbreaking." He turned his attention toward Tsang. "The war is over, and it is time for peace. But in order to have peace, we must form a truce. Only then will we live free."

"We are on the verge of a full military invasion from the PRC," Tsang said. "The events of the last twenty-four hours have been monitored, and the chairman is prepared to end the chaos in Hong Kong Island and Kowloon with extreme force." He held up his hand. "What we have witnessed is unexplainable, and I fully understand we are on opposite sides this day. But those in power will only halt the invasion if a truce is agreed upon and calm is restored to Hong Kong. You have my word: the truce will be binding for all. Those who remain in Beacon Hill will be free, and as requested, Detective Ming will be released from confinement before nightfall. Cherub who reside in the city will be left to themselves, as long as their gifts remain hidden from Hong Kongers at large. In return, we ask the Cherub to protect Hong Kong and, if needed, the Mainland."

"You're a day late to ask for peace," Vince grumbled. "Too many have died."

"I will assure you," Tsang replied calmly, "our desire is to be an ally, not an enemy."

Emma wanted to shout at the top of her lungs. They had been targets of the Merikh and PRC for months, and now the chief executive officer waltzed in to shake hands for a peace plan. Of course, witnessing legion, the queen, Merikh, and Cherub battle across the city left everyone shaken to the core.

"We do not live in a perfect world." Bau eyed Emma closely. "But we are called to protect the innocent against the forces of darkness that threaten all of us. We will accept this truce with a promise to continue offering our gifts toward the light."

Tsang reached out and shook Bau's hand. "I am gravely saddened by your loss."

The auditorium remained quiet, everyone wrapping their heads around what was unfolding while Jack's lifeless body remained in the center of the room. Emma knew Tsang was far from sincere, since Merikh remained loose across the city and in Asia. But a truce was better than being confined to Beacon Hill or giving in to the PRC's eagerness to remove all gifts through transfusions. *Maybe the Cherub whose gifts were taken will find them restored again one day.* Her soul shifted between a desire to fight and a broken heart. Jack had seen who she really was, not who everyone expected her to be, and she loved him because of who she was when she was with him.

You fought for peace and died for love. I must honor you, Jack.

Without a moment more to grieve, she acknowledged Bau's ability to ensure Cherub were protected from the PRC's bloodshed. He was steadfast in the face of the crisis, and she admired him for it. Battles and wars were more significant than the loss of one person—even though she was convinced that Jack was the most courageous among them. She thought about the first night she'd seen him from the stage at the Fabulous Friendly. One look into his eyes and she was willing to sacrifice herself to protect him, but in the end he was the one who protected them all.

Everyone watched Tsang leave the auditorium.

"Please understand the truce with the PRC needed to be made." Bau paused. "If we had not spoken with the chief executive officer, he would have brought another war to us that we are unprepared to fight—especially after this day."

"A time will come for each of us to grieve, and to celebrate the lives lost." Emma swallowed hard. "Bau, you have fulfilled your promise as our leader."

"Fang Xue and the Council betrayed what we believe, threatening to strip our gifts from us and enslave us to the PRC." Bau glanced down at the colorful coat over Jack's body, and his voice shook as he continued. "I have made many mistakes and allowed my ambition to cloud my judgment. Please forgive me."

Now you see Bau's humility, Jack, and you understand why you both were needed. Your body is broken and your soul is lifted into the heavens, but I feel your presence here with us. I will forever love you.

"In honor of all who have sacrificed"—Bau cleared his throat and gathered himself—"I am anointing a new council: Jin Qiaolian, Aki Katsuo, Salomeh Gashkori, Professor Burwick, and Faizan Khalid." He motioned for each one to stand beside him. "I am humbled by your wisdom and the unique hearts with which you serve." Bau glanced around at those gathered in the auditorium. "Jack was right: I am not the one to lead the Cherub—alone."

Emma realized what he meant before anyone else, and she set the Testimony down on the floor. She stepped back from the circle, then retrieved Dragon Soul and Scarlet Widow, which were leaned against a wall in the auditorium. She ignored the stares, knowing some of those present realized she was strong enough to wield both swords. She walked between those in the circle and nodded toward Eliška, who joined them in the center.

"Amidst the ashes, the prophecy is fulfilled," Emma said soberly. "And we are one."

She handed Dragon Soul over to Bau, then released Scarlet Widow to Eliška.

Benders who were gathered outside of the circle stepped forward with hands extended. Jack's body rose off the tiled floor and hovered in midair. Emma struggled to hold in her agony. Benders walked alongside as his body floated across the auditorium to where Professor Windsor waited near the doors. She motioned them into the hallway and followed the procession out of the auditorium.

Emma wept inconsolably as Amina and Eliška wrapped their arms around her and sobbed too. No one in the auditorium held back their tears or grief. Vince split from the circle, glared at Will, and stormed out.

92

DEAD FLOWERS AND PATCHY GRASS revived to their usual beauty only days after the Battle of Lion Rock. Chinese elm hedges grew thicker, guarding a garden at the end of a stone path at Beacon Hill. Wisteria dangled from overhanging branches in faint royal purple and powder blue. Beautiful plum blossoms, roses, lilies, daisies, and hydrangeas were restored, honoring those who were gone.

Within a matter of days, the mass exodus which flowed from the tunnels beneath the city through the House of Luminescence dwindled. Those who sought refuge at Beacon Hill either continued through the gateway to a new life or returned to the lives they'd fled from during the darkest of days. Word of the message Bau gave in the underground tunnels of Hong Kong shortly before the battle began continued to resonate with Cherub, faction, and followers of Elyon—and would forever be remembered as part of Liberation Day.

Earlier in the morning, Headmaster Fargher gave a melancholy speech to those at Beacon Hill, announcing that classes would return to a new normal. Students from across Hong Kong and beyond returned, and those refugees who remained settled in on the lower grounds, where benders were busy building an off-the-grid community. Fargher announced new mentors, including Salomeh Gashkori, Oliver and Winnie Bennett, and Winston and Betty Hu. Along with Professors McDougall and Windsor, each would have their fingerprint on the future of all who studied at Beacon Hill in the Cherub way.

In the garden, Vince, Amina, and Eliška stood over a simple grave and headstone. The decision to bury Jack in the Oasis of Remembrance had been left up to Natalie McNaughton. She'd asked them what they thought he'd want on the headstone. Vince remembered the night they broke into Nightingale's mausoleum to find the original drawings—and the words they'd read carved into the stone wall.

"'A thousand memories open a doorway to eternity,'" Vince recited. "Still hard to imagine any of this has happened, but it did. I believe in Elyon because of Jack. I'm forever grateful."

"What happens to us now?" Amina asked. "I am staying at school for my final year."

"I'm leaving with my parents tonight," Vince answered. "I promised I would spend time with them since I was MIA over this last year. A quick trip to Tokyo aboard *Pathfinder*, then I'll be back to finish out my last year too." He smiled at Eliška, whose gaze remained on the headstone. "I'll keep serving the faction, Cherub, and Elyon in whatever way is required."

"Bau asked me to meet with him and the Council before gathering Cherub on Dragon's Back," Eliška added. "There are plans to build a new sanctuary on the mountain."

"We are the last of the Keepers, so it is good we will stay together and grow in our gifts." Amina grew teary eyed, but she didn't break down. "Do you think Tim and Jack are watching over us?"

"Always," Eliška replied, barely above a whisper. "And forever."

Vince hugged them both as they took another moment to remember. "Ready?"

They headed to Nightingale Pavilion as new and old students milled about the quad and the Main Hall. Headmaster Fargher had asked about the time capsule—Amina's idea since the Fabulous Friendly—and suggested that instead of a grand ceremony, they might want to bury it privately. A shovel was propped up against the Wishing Tree.

Amina and Eliška sat on the front concrete benches of the pavilion while Vince dug the shovel into the grass until the hole was deep enough for the square box. Amina carried the time capsule over and set it down on the grass. She opened the lid so they could peer inside.

"Heavenly Fuel." Vince smiled at the power bars and the can. "And a Spitfire Jolt."

Amina picked up a stack of photos and spread them out like a deck of cards. Snapshots from Karachi, including the night they'd celebrated Tim's birthday in the hostel. Another photo caught Vince in full stride with Emma chasing him as they competed in a game of kabaddi in Kati Pahari. A third captured a profile shot of Jack and Emma standing together on the balcony overlooking the river in Ine Town. And a fourth showed all of them on the night they rescued Cherub from Shelter Island.

Amina set the photos back inside the box beside house patches of Nightingale, Crozier, Upsdell, Rowell, and an original copy of *Mischievous Escape of the Nine Dragons* taken from the faculty clubhouse—as well as Jack's bloodstained dretium hoodie and a copy of the video that honored Rachel's memory shown at the Fabulous Friendly. Amina closed the lid, then placed the box into the hole and stepped back.

"I feel like we should say something," she said. "But I do not know what."

"Yesterdays are precious," Eliška replied, "so our todays are priceless."

93

Blue skies were painted across a lazy afternoon as a sampan drifted away from the boathouse. Emma steered the sampan downriver. She'd traveled through a gateway to Kyoto a day earlier and had rested at the boathouse alone. Since the Battle of Lion Rock, she'd kept to herself and spent time only with her parents. She knew Amina, Eliška, and Vince were worried, but she needed space to accept that her greatest fear was now her reality.

"I have seen a beast swallowed by darkness, slumbering amidst wild waves of the sea and wandering stars in the skies. Light must never be brought into this realm." We brought light into the nether realm and defeated the Queen of Sakkhela, legion, and Merikh—yet my soul remains troubled.

Hours passed as the sampan headed deeper into the Highlands before reaching Nanimi and continuing on. Emma noticed how the river village was rebuilding from the destruction left by Chung and the Merikh. Her mind pictured the safe house where she taught Jack about force and flow. A smile curved her lips as she remembered several snap kicks that got his attention. Deeper into the Valley of Grace, she reached the shoreline near Arishiyama.

With the Testimony tucked inside the duffel over her shoulder, she left the sampan at the water's edge and trekked to the highest peak of a steep mountain. The panoramic landscape of the Valley of Grace unfolded below her in all its splendor. Emma followed the path she remembered and reached the other side of the mountain, hiking down through a rainbow of gold and emerald rice paddies, which amplified the breathtaking view.

Another few miles and she approached the stone pillars camouflaged within the overgrown jungle. She climbed over massive roots, a reminder of the roots in the House of Luminescence. Burnt-orange and red leaves hung from branches overhead as she approached Arishiyama. The bamboo forest remained an enchanted world lost to civilization. Awestruck, she stopped at the naturally formed entrance between the stone pillars carved with ancient figures.

"Elyon, I sense your presence with me," she whispered, "once again."

She retrieved Eden's Star from her pocket and held it in the palm of her hand. The compass glowed magnificently as she stepped through the force field and walked toward Charis. Amid the thick bamboo swallowing a narrow trail, Asiklua appeared. Milky skin, toned muscles, and mighty wings of bone-white feathers. His angelic eyes welcomed her into the sacred grounds.

For an hour she walked alongside Asiklua, comforted by his presence. While his wings could have flown them to the top of the last mountain, she was grateful to be within the wondrous beauty of Charis once more. They reached the waterfalls cascading over the rocks into a tranquil turquoise pool. She slipped the duffel off her shoulder and retrieved the Testimony, then held out the gold-covered acacia chest.

Before Emma left Beacon Hill, Bau had returned the last pieces of the Rhoxen Stone, which she'd placed inside along with the heartwood of the Rod of Elyon, the Windstrikers, and Slybourne's shield. She had also found in Jack's backpack a folded piece of paper with Rachel's poem scribbled on it, and she knew it was the perfect symbol to be included in the Testimony. She heard Rachel's voice echo the final two lines: *"Along a silk road this secret will one day return, to a story of mercy and love evil attempted to burn."*

"I am afraid one of the artifacts has not been found, and not all have been returned. Some are in pieces, so I do not know whether their powers remain—but I am certain each belongs in Charis." Emma held up the compass, aware she never mentioned Scarlet Widow. "I will be the Protector of Eden's Star."

"As Elyon has designed." Asiklua's gaze softened. "Come with me."

She followed Asiklua as he climbed the stone steps behind a waterfall and approached Elyon's Vine in all of its splendor. The king cypress flourished with pure-white bell-shaped flowers, casting a massive crown over vibrant crimson plants amid lush emerald grass.

Asiklua set the Testimony on the ground in front of Elyon's Vine, and immediately flames erupted from the earth and scorched burning emblems into the perfect blades of grass around the king cypress: a lion, a tree, a deer, a ship, and a temple. Emma stared at the Cherub tribes for a moment until she realized the one emblem missing besides Scarlet Widow's serpent was a wolf. A twinge shot down her spine, as Gabriella's words haunted her mind—again.

"I have seen a beast swallowed by darkness, slumbering amidst wild waves of the sea and wandering stars in the skies. Light must never be brought into this realm."

At first, she had thought the beast was the Queen of Sakkhela—or the creature she killed in the Mourning Labyrinth—but as the days passed she grew more convinced that while the gateway to the nether realm was opened when she entered through with Jack, there was another who escaped—one who knew about the seventh artifact.

"You are a great warrior," Asiklua said reverently. "And you are not alone."

She spun around and saw someone standing in the near distance. Tears welled up, and her hands shook by her sides. Barefoot, Jack walked across the pristine grass as if he were out on a stroll of the Beacon Hill grounds. She watched him for a moment, realizing he didn't know she was there. From deep within, a desperate cry longed to call out to him. Instead, she stood in silence and imagined the life they might've lived.

"A day is coming when you will be together again," Asiklua said. "Until then, there is more you are called to do to protect the light."

Tears rolled down her cheeks. "You are finally healed, Jack."

Emma breathed deep as Jack simply faded away. Then she squeezed Eden's Star. A bright light emanated from the compass, blinding her view of Asiklua. She closed her eyes in full surrender, and in a blink she was gone.

94

A stack of luggage was piled near the door of the Main Hall. Headmaster Fargher and Professor McDougall grabbed two bags at a time and loaded them into a minibus parked at the curb. Above, Beacon Hill's lion-crested flag swayed in a gentle breeze as the clock tower marked ten past nine in the evening—time moved on since the clock started again days earlier.

Will walked awkwardly in front of names etched into the walls near the polished glass case featuring the House Champions trophy, as well as the Bashers, Bowlers, and Boundaries trophy. He was still getting used to the artificial breilium limb which Professor Windsor had customized for him. He hobbled toward the display of photos dating back a century. New photos had been added showing those who lost their lives since the nightmare began—including Rachel, Tim, and Jack.

He stopped in front of a bronze plaque engraved with the names of students who were killed during the first attack on Beacon Hill. Guilt lingered beneath the surface, despite his commitment to a new beginning. One way or another he was determined to right his wrongs, but sometimes he questioned if it was even possible.

How can Elyon forgive me for what I've done? How can anyone forgive me?

Dabria's voice echoed in his memory. *"Elyon forgives all who ask. It is never too late."* He prayed her words were true—and that one day he would accept them.

Will leaned down to grab a cordless screwdriver from a toolbox and nearly fell over. He braced himself against the wall and stood up straight. With great care, he added two bronze strips beneath the plaque and tightened the screws carefully. He hobbled backward and stared at the names—among them now were Timothy Lloyd and Jack Reynolds. The weight he carried grew heavier as he eyed his surroundings and the walls of heroes.

"We are all loaded up," Fargher announced. "William, are you ready?"

"Yeah." Will nudged the lid of the toolbox closed with his foot. "Ready."

Salomeh and Professor Burwick rounded the corner mid-conversation. He heard them talking about Cherub benders who planned to help the PRC rebuild the underwater tunnels between Kowloon and Hong Kong Island. Another rush of shame silenced him from engaging in any trivial conversation. His quick wit was buried beneath the destruction he'd caused to so many. His mind flashed to the night on the roof of Shek Pik Prison and the darkness that had consumed him. Out of the corner of his eye, he caught Salomeh watching him closely. He knew it was because he still had the gifts of a Cherub even though he'd betrayed them all. There was no excuse for his actions, but he hoped for undeserved mercy one day. He'd prayed to Elyon for forgiveness a thousand times, but he still didn't feel forgiven.

"Come along, Salomeh," Burwick mused. "Our chariot awaits."

"Imagine what we will be able to accomplish," Salomeh replied excitedly.

"It is a shame that Bau and Eliška chose not to travel with us." Burwick chuckled. "Remember in our younger years when we had energy and passion for every second of the day?"

"At least they seem to be getting along better."

Will picked up the toolbox and walked with a jerky gait toward an open door beside the trophy case. He set the toolbox on a shelf inside, and when he turned around Salomeh and Burwick were already outside. A labored stride carried him across the Main Hall to the front steps, where he gingerly took one at a time down to the waiting minibus. Salomeh and Burwick were seated in the middle, and McDougall was behind the wheel with the engine idling.

Will's mind flashed to the last time he was in the vault at Kreidler—and the vast treasures that were left behind. In a matter of hours those treasures would be returned to the Cherub, and maybe he would be one step closer to being free from the chains around his neck.

"You will get used to it, Son." Fargher held out his hand. "Give it time."

Without his father's help, Will fell into the bench seat behind McDougall and Salomeh, then adjusted his artificial limb. Fargher closed the sliding door and climbed into the front passenger seat.

McDougall pulled a U-turn in front of the Main Hall before heading through the newly installed gates of Beacon Hill. Will kept his gaze out the window as the minibus drove through the streets of Kowloon. He'd loved the city since he was young, but without his mum it wasn't the same. He couldn't help but wonder whether one day the Cherub would demand retribution for his sins.

"I have never flown on a private jet before," Burwick said. "Only economy."

"Unfortunately, there are no gateways near our destination," Salomeh noted. "We have Natalie to thank for the ride, as she has made all the arrangements."

Fargher glanced over his shoulder and offered a father's smile to his son. Will's lips pursed slightly, but that was the best he could do.

"Zurich," McDougall announced, "here we come."

95

SITIO VETERANS, PHILIPPINES

By late afternoon, humidity hung thick as Emma's shirt stuck to her body in the sweltering heat. She'd arrived in the barrio near the graveyard without fanfare and headed toward the mountains. In a twenty-four-hour period, she'd climbed one mountain after another to reach Charis—and refused to stop as Eden's Star guided her until she was done. Now she hiked deeper into the dense forest. Purple-and-red hornbills chirped as they flew from one massive rosewood to the next.

Emma reached a dirt trail between fiery-orange orchids and hoped she was on the right path. Along the trail, she slowed and eyed each one of the tree trunks, attempting to decipher which was the right one. A hornbill chirped, then a response echoed within a split second. She stopped on the trail and glanced around. Again, another chirp followed by one a second later. Her palms glowed as she braced herself for an ambush.

A rope ladder with carved bamboo steps dropped from a rosewood twenty feet ahead, and her lightforce faded. She hurried over to the ladder and climbed. A sweet smell permeated her nostrils from the rosewood as she climbed even higher until she reached the top. The man from the graveyard she had met the night Addison died and a young girl waited with warm smiles. *Wilson and Mahalia.* Mahalia hugged Emma tight, then grabbed her hand and pressed it against her forehead.

"Your friends here," Wilson said. "Come."

Emma stood on the edge of a suspended bamboo bridge, taking in Vigan for the first time. She followed Wilson across the rope bridge, which connected gigantic rosewoods. Dozens of tree houses were scattered throughout the jungle; some clustered together while others were spread out and bigger. She eyed the largest tree house in the distance and couldn't help but wonder what could have been with Jack by her side.

"Emma!" McNaughton called out. "You made it."

She offered a warm smile. "Already at home?"

"We arrived late last night, and I got the best sleep I have had in months." McNaughton approached as Emma stepped off the bridge. "Vigan is an amazing place. Xui Li knows everyone, and she's already settled me in." McNaughton pointed toward Dabria's tree house and chuckled. "Strange, she chose the largest one for herself."

"Jack described it to me as Dabria's home," Emma said. "I suppose it is for the Elders."

"Now that makes sense." McNaughton shrugged. "She will be glad to see you."

"Were you able to bring everything in one trip?"

McNaughton laughed. "Downsizing to one backpack is no joke."

"Feels good, right?" Emma chuckled. "A simpler way of life."

"Definitely a more beautiful one than living in a concrete jungle."

Wilson and Mahalia crossed another bridge ahead of them. Emma and McNaughton walked behind and followed at a distance. She noticed those near the other tree houses watched them with curiosity and smiled as they passed.

"Everything go as planned in Charis?" McNaughton asked in a lowered voice.

"Package delivered, as they say," Emma replied. "Asiklua will guard the Testimony."

"I heard earlier from Xui Li that Fang Xue has been transported to an undisclosed location—sounded a lot like the Dungeon of Savages redux. I guess it is the only way to prevent her from using her powers. And I spoke to Detective Ming before my flight, and she is grateful."

Emma nearly blurted out the truth about Fang Xue murdering Rachel, but she held back, knowing the secrets she kept with Jack went beyond the grave. Instead, she pulled up her sleeve to show McNaughton the latest inked art.

"Before leaving Hong Kong, I wanted to add to my story, so I thought of what would help me remember Jack the most." She pointed at the Rod of Elyon, depicted with Chinese characters scripted along the heartwood. "In Chinese, these represent courage, truth, and unity." McNaughton stared at the intricate inkwork, and Emma knew the message resonated with her too. "He wanted to know the stories of my tattoos, and now he is part of them."

"It is beautiful." McNaughton paused. "What are you wearing around your wrist?"

"A bangle given to me by Salomeh in Kati Pahari." Emma ran her fingers over the inscription. "'In raging seas and surging tides, Elyon draws close to all who call upon eternity's glory.' I gave it to Jack, and now I wear it to keep him close."

"I had a vivid dream about him last night." McNaughton's gaze softened. "He was walking near the most incredible waterfall I've ever seen."

Emma's brows raised, but she kept what she'd witnessed in Charis to herself. "Really?"

"He seemed to be at peace." McNaughton got choked up. "Sorry . . ."

"Natalie, it is good for us to remember him." Emma swallowed a lump in her own throat. "We must dream about those we love so we can keep them in our hearts."

"I've lost people I cared about before," McNaughton confessed. "But with Jack it is different—he's as close to family as I've ever experienced."

"You are a big sister," Emma teased, "who carries a gun."

McNaughton laughed. "Rachel was the one with powers, not me."

"He said once that you were the first to tell him the truth about Rachel. I believe from that moment, he decided you were family—and you are family to me too."

"I always needed a younger sister who is a lightforcer, bender, *and* healer. And do not think I missed the fact that you wielded Dragon Soul *and* Scarlet Widow." McNaughton winked with a slight smile. "More than a trifecta if there ever was one."

Wilson and Mahalia stopped at the bamboo steps leading to

a cluster of tree houses that wrapped around a massive rosewood trunk.

"Rachel home." Wilson pointed. "Now it is you."

Emma inhaled deep as she stared up at the tree house, awe-struck. Mahalia hugged Emma and McNaughton, then followed Wilson across bamboo bridges deeper into Vigan.

"Rachel was more than a chosen Cherub," Emma said solemnly.

McNaughton remained quiet for a moment. "Why are we here, Emma?"

"Every ending creates a new beginning . . ." Emma stared straight ahead at rays of light casting shadows over the vast jungle. From her pocket she retrieved the ivory figurine with the golden spin top, then held the key in her palm for McNaughton to get a better look. "Something or someone other than Florence Upsdell and the legion escaped when we brought light into the nether realm." With Eden's Star hidden on a chain beneath her shirt, she gazed toward the fiery crimson and amber skies aglow with the promises of Elyon. "So there is still one artifact left to find—until the end."

Acknowledgments

A SPECIAL THANKS TO readers who have journeyed along on this epic adventure to capture the world of Beacon Hill within the pages of these books. I never imagined the unexpected twists and turns. Along with all who have enjoyed the series, I've fallen deeper in love with the characters with each passing chapter. My hope is all who read these books will see themselves reflected in Jack and his band of misfits. Every page written is for each reader, and every book finished is because of the support and sacrifice of those close to me. You know who you are, so no names need to be mentioned.

To Don Pape, your friendship is more valuable than any publishing opportunity. You have chosen to stand with me in the trenches, and for that I am grateful. You believed in the series when it was a spark of an idea, and you have walked with me through the peaks and valleys, offering your wisdom as only you can. As the pages turn, know that you are one of a kind, Mr. Pape.

To the Wander team, those who have fought alongside me, your creativity and behind-the-scenes effort have allowed me the freedom to unlock the world swirling in my imagination. You have sacrificed more than anyone will realize, fighting through challenges and roadblocks to bring this series to the final page. Your willingness to collaborate with humility is evidence of your unique character within our Beacon Hill circle. One day we'll sit around a bonfire and share stories that only we will know. We have traveled a narrow path together, courageously to the very edge, and we survived. You are fighters—and that is what I am most grateful for above all else.

Until the end.

About the Author

With the DNA of a world traveler, D. J. WILLIAMS was born and raised in Hong Kong, igniting an adventurous spirit as he ventured into the jungles of the Amazon, the bush of Africa, and the ancient cities of the Far East. His global travels have submerged him in a myriad of cultures, giving him a unique perspective that fuels his creativity.

Providing a fresh voice in mystery, suspense, and YA fantasy, Williams's novels have climbed the charts, ranking as high as #1 on Amazon Hot New Releases. His books *The Auctioneer* and *Hunt for Eden's Star* have received stellar reviews from *Kirkus Reviews*, the most trusted voice in book discovery.

The trailers and documentary of his latest YA series, Beacon Hill, have reached over 1.8 million views. *Battle of Lion Rock* is book three in the Beacon Hill series. Williams has also been an executive producer and director on over five hundred episodes of broadcast television.

To learn more, visit djwilliamsbooks.com.

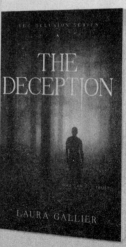